F. P. DORCHAK

ERO

A NOVEL

"Witty and fast-paced—blending a thorough understanding of space technology, satellite operations, and UFO history—Frank Dorchak's latest novel is pure genius. Having worked with Frank in real-time satellite ops, I know that his unique perspective will grab you and take you where you've never ventured before."

Dan Brune, former Major (USAF), and Satellite Mission Director

Copyright 2013 by F. P. Dorchak
Published by Wailing Loon, 2013
Cover design by **Kirschner • Caroff Design Inc**.
Print formatting by **A Thirsty Mind Book Design**

ISBN-13: 978-0615859620
ISBN-10: 0615859623

**WAILING
LOON**

I thank the following for all their help and inspiration: Rob Butts, Dan Brune, Madelon Rose Logue, Dave Lirette, Jan (C.J.) Jones, Bob Garner, Karen Lin, Andy Krajnak, Whitley Strieber's *Communion* books, Dan Sherman and his book *Above Black—Insider Account of Alien Contact and Government Cover-up* (and his gracious allowance of my incorporation of his actual Intuitive Controller experience into my novel), the International UFO Museum, at Roswell, NM, Barry McMillan, Jerry Johnston, Nathan Kettner, Sherry Fields (for keeping me on the straight and narrow!); my dad (ex-U.S. Navy submariner RM1SS), journalist mom, and the rest of my family; Tom Heaton, Matt Bille, Liz Scheier, Steve Saffel, Cherry Weiner, Don McCall; my incredible cover artist, Lon Kirschner, my incredible formatter, Pam Headrick…and of course the *X-Files*. A very special thanks to astronaut and ex-coworker Colonel (USAF, ret.) Rex Walheim, STS missions 110 and 122.

Above all, I am ever grateful to my wife, Laura, for her constant *unwavering* support and faith.

Of course I took liberties; this *is* fiction…

…or is it?

FPD

For Laura

It has been said within the intelligence community
that the more unbelievable, far-fetched, or improbable their actions…
the less likely the public will believe.

Chapter One

1

100-Mile Low Earth Orbit
4 November 2021
0903 Hours Zulu

The missile, a brilliant fuzzy puff of light set against the stark blackness of space, arced from around the backside of the globe and above the thin, fragile blue film of the Earth's atmosphere, its Multiple Independently Targeted Reentry vehicle packed with nearly a dozen five-hundred kiloton warheads. The MIRV hurtled unerringly toward destinations on North American soil. Behind it, like a bizarre thermonuclear biker gang, followed a chorus of additional fuzzy puffs, also targeted for twenty-nine-to-forty-nine-degree northern-latitude impact locations. Missile warning's Space-based Infrared System tracked the MIRV, but its link to midcourse shoot-down capability resources were already elsewhere employed.

Above and below the 100-mile Earth orbit, flashes spiked against the Earth's backdrop as satellites were attacked by kinetic-energy anti-satellite weaponry. ASATs that plowed directly into orbiting hardware, burrowing through telemetry, tracking, and control modules, pulse-code-modulation boards, and nickel-cadmium batteries like cosmic buckshot, smashing them into useless space junk.

Other targets found their defensive countermeasures useless as they experienced a barrage of intense particle-beam attacks. Still others fell victim to the more subtle, unseen electromagnetic pulses that fried internal components.

Yet, within minutes those satellites that had survived had activated dormant payloads and unleashed massive electromagnetic pulse bursts directed toward Earth itself, which seared through the circuitry of airborne and ground-based equipment. Other orbiting platforms launched miniature warheads toward preselected objectives. Terrestrial and airborne defenses answered back with additional kinetic ASAT launches and directed-energy blasts.

* * *

BE-4701, also known by its more industry-common name ERO 28, orbited in the midst of the space war. Despite the carnage, ERO 28 continued spying Earthward with its advanced electro-optical telescopic eye. It deployed its own defensive countermeasures and sent occasional bursts of directed energy particle beams toward objects it considered threats. As ERO 28 maintained its decaying orbit, it passed through a field of satellite debris, which took out two of its four solar panels on one side, one on the opposite, two of three hardened batteries, and further crippled its already damaged superstructure and subsystems. The debris also largely disabled most of its remaining defensive countermeasure capability.

ERO 28 could, however, continue to attack.

As the spy platform came within striking range of CHINASAT-102, it swiveled its laser toward the intruder and fired off a burst. CHINASAT-102 fell silent.

ERO 28 continued its orbit over the Asian continent, collecting intel and sending bursts of laser fire aimed at both terrestrial and on-orbit objectives.

Another object, an advanced unmanned space vehicle, its light-absorbing hull dark against the background of interplanetary space, vectored toward ERO 28. The platform sensed its approach and fired at the object, which it identified via an updated data load, as USV-A-7. But USV-A-7 deflected the attack by shedding its radar-and-laser absorbing skin, continuing undeterred. Although the intruder did not behave as ERO 28's upload predicted, ERO 28 continued its attack, blasting away more of USV-A-7's onion-like outer hull to expose the titanium battering ram core that had been housed within the composite skins.

ERO 28 updated its data, immediately downloading this critical turn of events through classified satellite relays, and initiated evasive maneuvers by attempting to autonomously fire its thrusters to change its orbit.

Those thrusters that still operated.

The titanium battering ram remained undeterred.

ERO 28 fired lasers until it had exhausted its remaining power supply.

The hurtling ASAT impacted ERO 28 with a soundless flash, a collision that was not as full an impact as had been intended, given ERO 28's partially executed evasive maneuvers. But it had been enough to put any remaining satellite system capabilities out of commission, as subsystem after subsystem sputtered and began to shut down…

Mission Specialist James Cherko's head slammed back into the bulkhead behind him, the sounds of his own screams, as well as those of warning klaxons and sparking and exploding equipment panels ripping into his head. Acrid smolder tickled his nostrils and filled the enclosure.

Images flashed.

Playing with siblings in the woods.

Star patterns.

Earth.

A woman laughing.

Astronaut training.

Deer.

Earth, Earth, *Earth…*

A jarring volley of rifle fire?

Hiking through a wintry and wooded back forty…

Straining, he tried to move.

Pinned.

He was *pinned?*

Lightheaded—dizzy—and confused, he opened his eyes. Sparks and smoke filled the module. Flashing lights, lots of flashing and steady-state lights. Red and orange. Indicator "idiot" lights on control panels. And those damned klaxons….

Time. He was running out of time.

Why hadn't the fire suppression system kicked in? He was gonna choke to death if he didn't—

He glanced at a time display unit.

0905 hours. Zulu. 0405 hours Eastern.

Why was he running out of time?

What was his timeline? Time for what?

There was something…*something* he needed to be doing….

Cherko tried to get to the control panel, free his arms, his legs, but

What the hell?

Pinned. All were firmly pinned.

In his head he'd already begun running emergency procedure and malfunction protocols. Mentally trying to project what had possibly gone wrong, what could be affected, and what to do next. Mentally searching out and disabling shorted panels, initiating CO_2 fire suppression, and verifying backup life support subsystems were green and operational. He was—

Pausing, he scanned the length his body.

What the hell, goddammit—what the hell was the matter with him?

The interior of the space station swam crazily before him.

How was this possible?

He was wrapped within an unreal, cocoon-like structure that encased his body like a form-fitting cage. From shins to collar bone he was held within an unyielding metal grip. Cold, unforgiving. A grip that proclaimed, *nothing personal, pal, it's just my job.* As if the station itself had, for some insane, ungodly reason, reached out and wrapped itself around him.

Cherko continued struggling—he had to act *now*—but was firmly anchored within this absurd confinement. Sturdy strips of metal crisscrossed his body like wide X's, pinning his arms to his sides and his legs against each other. On this structure were also blinking and steady state lights and switches. Entire panels of them.

"God*damn* it."

Cherko stopped; intense dizziness again sweeping over him. Images of His wife's face.

Standing before a wall?

Pouring over training manuals—

Writing them?

Something round, something high, something *red*...staring out across an expansive, open field...hacking at something with an *ax*....

He blinked; shook his head.

Get your head out of your ass!

Shut down those panels!

Idiot lights...have to deal with...klaxons...safe the vehicle and payload!

Idiot lights...*what was it about frigging idiot lights?*

Focus.

Cherko stared at the panels.

Think, goddammit, *th*—

Where was he?

He scanned the module.

Where was he? What were the lights trying to tell him?

Life support panels.

Communications and control panels.

Encryption modules.

Command module. He was in the command module of—

They'd been attacked...*there'd been a* collision?

ELINT.

SIGINT.

He was...

He was on an electronic and signals intelligence space station. A...manned...*orbiting*...laboratory? Yes, that was it. *MOL.*

He grunted.

A spy platform? There was nothing experimental nor scientific about any of this.

Okay...he was onboard an orbiting platform collecting intel. Fine. But, good Lord, things had finally gotten so seriously out of hand, and someone...someone had goddamned *launched.* Pressed the button and goddamned started world war fucking three.

Wife kissing him.

Making love.

Maneuvering through a mountain pass.

She's laughing…about what?

World War III.

Where did that leave Humanity? Where'd it leave *him?*

In an empty command module on an orbiting spy platform on the receiving end of thermonuclear disaster.

Armageddon.

That damned noise! Could someone *please* turn off that frigging racket!

Was he the only one onboard? Where were the others? He remembered…

Launch.

Aboard the Orion…a booster…three of them. There had been three of them.

Roscoe Pullman. NSA.

Wayne Garcia. U.S. Navy.

And him. U.S. Air Force—

Good *God* that noise was deafening!

Again Cherko struggled against his restraints, wrinkling his nose against the growing, module-filling smoke.

What the hell was happening? Why the hell am I pinned onboard a dying space station?

Flashing lights everywhere. Frigging idiot lights.

Another memory.

Close…he…

Had to hurry. Checklists. Running out of time. No time. The *coup d'grace* would come. Would it be another kinetic energy projectile? An EMP blast? He was about to quickly become an unknown and unremembered casualty of war, floating (the proper term was "falling," actually) overhead a population in which some 90% would be annihilated or driven to extinction from collateral damage anyway. No tears would be spilled over him. He was just a spy, and all spies went unremembered and unacknowledged.

Making love in Garden of the Gods with—

He again looked to the time display unit.

And what was it about the time?

Besides his immediate situation, why was he so certain he was quickly falling behind some timeline?

God, he felt like such an *idiot!*

How could he have gotten himself stuck like this, a hundred miles above any help?

Idiot.

Idiot lights!

That's what they'd called them, back then, back in…in *flight* training.…

2

Mather Air Force Base, California
21 September 1983
0700 Hours Pacific Time

Second Lieutenant James Francis Cherko sat in the cockpit of the T-37B "Tweet," twin-engine jet trainer, scanning its console. He couldn't believe he was actually, *finally*, here.

Navigator training. Class 84-11, baby!

Mather Air Force Base, Sacramento, California. All the paperwork was signed, oaths taken, and medical examinations—which included in-depth physicals, max VO tests, and finger and footprints taken—*done*. He'd passed with flying colors, to pardon the expression, except his eyesight hadn't been grand enough to land him that coveted pilot slot.

But his vision had been good enough for the Backseater role, the Navigator, EWO, or Wizzo. As an Electronics Warfare Officer or Weapons Systems Officer he could still fly (jets or heavies), whatever his role finally ended up being upon graduation. In this day and age navigators rarely just *navigated* any more. These days they dropped bombs, pulled triggers, or worked complex electronic eavesdropping or jamming gear.

And it was so weird, he—and the rest of his class of the 452nd Flying Training Squadron—had even already gotten a chance to actually *wear* their wings. They'd worn them when they'd had their photos taken during in-processing. Hadn't even begun training, yet there he and the others were with those burnished navigator wings firmly planted upon their proud chests above their left-breast uniform pockets. A taste, a teaser, of their collective goal. Their pictures taken early so that upon graduation the governmental publicity machine, which had already kicked into action, would send Hometown News Releases and photos everywhere. And to him those wings had felt so heavy, so *important*. This was Real Life. Real Stuff, baby, no longer theory and textbooks, no sir, this was out there in the Real World, flying around in million-dollar aircraft trying to keep the Free World free by dropping bombs, pulling triggers, and fucking with enemy electronics.

And now he was seated in the side-by-side cockpit of the Tweet training simulator, preparing to be briefed on its controls and procedures. Instructed about idiot lights and Emergency Gang Loading of the oxygen regulator: *in the event of a loss-of-oxygen situation, slam all three switches into the "up" position for emergency maximum flow of oxygen.*

Idiot lights.

The Instructor Pilot had briefed that moments ago.

Idiot lights.

The IP went on to point out all the controls and indicators and brief them about proper cockpit entry and egress, and that when they heard two words, uttered three times by the pilot, there was to be no debate about it, no conversation—no *thinking*. Action and only action, and you couldn't do it fast enough. With these words came two simple actions. Raise the yellow handgrips on both sides of the seat, then squeeze the single or double triggers, depending upon which model within which they flew.

Bail out! Bail out! Bail Out!

The words.

Hand grips raise…trigger(s) squeeze!

The action.

Unthinking. Ingrained. Like covering your nose and mouth to sneeze.

He'd just memorized his first checklist.

But the idiot lights…that term just struck him funny. Funny, in a bizarro *Twilight Zone* sort of way. If he were to ever deal with idiot lights, he hoped it wouldn't be at 60,000 feet, in a ground-sky-ground-sky-screaming-toward-Earth fighter jet emergency…but he truly felt that sometime, perhaps way into his future, Idiot Lights were going to, indeed, play a major role in his life. Idiot Lights were going to wake him up in a manner of speaking he couldn't yet fathom. Idiot Lights, he felt deep down into his twenty-two-year-old soul, were going to play a huge life-changing role in some disturbing, indefinable way, and it was truly going to be a matter of life or death.

Idiot Lights.

Chapter Two

1

Colorado Springs, Colorado
1 November 2010
0537 Hours Mountain Time

Jimmy Cherko checked his e-mail one last time as he saved *Brilliant Eyes*, his newest fiction manuscript, to his hard drive. He was cutting it close. Not that he absolutely had to be at work at any specific time, but the later he got into work, the longer he had to stay to make his "eight," and he liked leaving relatively early in the day. It got him into the gym before the after-work rush-hour crowd, and got him home, again, at a relatively early hour. There was no real reason to this schedule, except that it was just what he'd always done, and was probably brought on from his time in the military. Twenty years ago, he'd done seven years, and part of that time had been out at Schriever AFB, on the plains east of town. Though he'd worked shift work for most of his sixteen years at Schriever, as both an Air Force officer and a defense contractor, he'd found that if he'd arrived to work an hour or two before the masses did, he beat most of the traffic—out and back—which could severely snarl one's commute.

Twenty years. Twenty years doing contractor work for the Air Force. He'd never envisioned himself where he now found himself. Had always felt he'd been destined for greater things, something…*important*.

Astronaut.

Legendary writer.

Failed at both.

Well, not entirely. He was, after all, getting paid to write "books"…technical orders, actually. *And* making quite a bit more than your average fiction writer. The average advance for traditionally published fiction writers was five-to-fifteen thousand, while he was pulling in—with seniority and all—nearly ninety grand. Not a bad gig after all.

And as happy as he tried to be around his wife, family and friends…well, he wasn't. He was just biding time, time for what, who knew. He had a great life, a great family (on both sides of their marriage), a great job that paid well and was secure for the next ten or so years, given they'd just won the follow-on contract...but he was, to himself, a failure.

And he'd come to accept that.

As long as he could *write*. His unsold novels and short stories. Hadn't sold one novel, ever, yet occasionally sold a short story. But it was the *writing* that was important, not the selling. As long as he could do what *seemed* to be in his soul.

At least, that's what he kept telling himself.

So, at forty-nine, Jimmy had come to terms with his dreams of grandeur being nothing more than smoke-and-mirrors. That he'd never really been destined for any kind of importance. He'd chalked it all up to having a healthy ego, of being told by his parents he could do and be anything he wanted if he just *worked* hard enough. Of having been brought up a big dreamer and voracious reader, raised on Aldiss, Blish, Clarke, Pohl, and Heinlein. Cordwainer Smith. He'd always written about material outside his work-a-day experiences, and, he thought, hmmm, maybe that was the problem. He had a wealth of experience in the techie world, the world of satellites and government bullshit, so, he finally realized, why the hell not break down, give in, and write a goddamned full-on science-fiction novel?

So, that's just what he did. What he'd saved this morning. A genuine science-fiction thriller set in the near future. And as much as he'd gone out of his way to avoid incorporating his work experience into his fiction, he was going to face it all head on, and totally incorporate *everything*. Everything, that is, that was unclassified and didn't compromise himself or national security. He might have no direct experience with UFOs and highly covert and compartmentalized classified government operations, but given his healthy imagination and time in the service and as a contractor working for the Air Force, he had a wealth of firsthand experience.

And if *Brilliant Eyes* didn't work...then he would *again* sit down in his home office, and *again* start at page one with a new manuscript, and would *again* continue...until death did us part.

Writing is what he *did*.

It was in his blood; his mother was a writer, and various family members dabbled in it, but life seemed to have had other plans for him. Just because something was in your blood didn't necessarily mean it was your life's purpose—or even good for you. Or that writing was meant to be an end-all.

Living was its own end-all. Breathing *air*.

Growing as a person and doing what you had to do to make your life—and the lives of others—better. That's what it was all about, was what Jimmy did with his own life, when he realized he wasn't to be famously, nor handsomely, published by thirty. He was gonna live life the best he could, tortured artiste or not.

Yes, he had a wonderful life, and he knew it.

So, *Brilliant Eyes* saved, he backed out of his laptop and closed up shop. It had been quite the productive morning.

It was dark and cold as he pulled out of the garage at 0610, spooking a small herd of deer nibbling on fallen crabapples beneath a bare Crabapple tree. He glanced at them as they loped away in their huge, graceful high arcs.

Fastening his seatbelt as he ensured that the garage door closed, he backed up into the street and paused, staring at the location of their bedroom. His wife would still be there, in bed, peacefully unaware of all the work he'd already performed this morning before even arriving at his paying job. She joked at how he had this entire life he lived in the early, wee hours of the morning, before anyone else got up. She loved his work, his writing, and constantly remarked how he created these worlds while most of the world in this hemisphere had been asleep. It impressed her. She was so proud of him, and Jimmy, in turn, loved her deeply. She was his rock. Someone who believed in him no matter what. He couldn't have done any better in marrying her. She was an absolutely incredible find, and he positively adored her.

Jimmy put the Honda into drive.

As much as Jimmy loved high summer and the month of July, he also loved the dead of winter—even though, technically, it was still fall. He could never understand it, but he loved the sense of desolation that came with the winter months. The grayness...the snow and cold. *The internal density of being.* Perhaps it was the way people tended to look inward during these months. During the summer, people (him included) were outdoors, doing outdoorsy things, but during the colder months people (skiing, snowboarding, and snowmobiling aside), tended to stay indoors more, and with that, came memories of warm, sunny days, and—he suspected in others, because he knew that people were people, and if *he* did it or thought about it, he was sure there were others out there who also did it or thought about it—going "internal." Pensive. He liked that. He loved recalling fond memories from his childhood. Of good times. He loved *thinking*, and he loved thinking about the length and breadth of his life.

Jimmy tapped the brakes as a fox darted out in front of him as he crossed the intersection of Uintah Street and Nevada Avenue.

He smiled, watching the fox dart off down an alley.

And he lived in a great part of town. The West Si-*iiide*, as they (the locals) called it. The older part of Colorado Springs. More established neighborhoods and trees, lots of wildlife.

Jimmy slowed and came to a stop as he hit the El Paso Street stop light. He watched as a car and a garbage truck pulled out onto Uintah in front of him. He liked how car exhaust curled and wafted ghost-like into the cold air.

There was just something about the winter months!

The light turned green and Jimmy drove forward, shortly coming up behind the garbage truck, its orange lights blinking.

Blinking.

He followed it up the inclined, narrower part of Uintah as they approached Union Boulevard. It used to be two lanes up and one down this hill, but had been changed to one lane each way, which was probably for the best. It definitely gave drivers more room. The bare, skeletal branches above overhung the road and were pitch-black silhouettes against the slowly brightening sky. He loved the cozy feel on this stretch of street.

The garbage truck braked, and Jimmy hit his, as they came upon another light at Hancock. As he sat there, still behind the garbage truck, he found himself staring at the blinking lights. Blinking. Orange lights. Rotating. Blinking.

Orange.

Yellow.

Red.

Blue.

Rotating.

Blinking...blinking...*blinking*....

Jimmy pressed down harder on the brake pedal. His palms sweated and his heart palpitated. Everything before him blurred. He blinked; shifted uneasily in his seat, under his seat belt. He opened the windows several inches.

His vision began to tunnel. Grayed out into that crazy narrowing cone. He shook his head and tensed his calves and legs. *Hard.*

The light changed to green.

Jimmy hit the accelerator...then promptly blacked out.

2

Jimmy awoke to the alternating flashing of red, clear, and blue lights and shadows busying about him. He blindly lashed out.

"Somebody grab his arms!" a voice called out.

"*No!*" he yelled, as one of the shadows leaned in to his face. Jimmy tried to break free, but was unable to.

"Hey—*hey!*" the same voice again called out. "*Hey!* Buddy! It's all right, calm down...calm *down*...."

Jimmy blinked and looked about him. He was lying in an ambulance, paramedics and police everywhere.

"What?"

"You're okay…can you see me? See my hand?" the paramedic asked.

Jimmy blinked, waving away the hand. "Yeah, yeah, I see it. What happened?" He tried getting up.

"Whoa, buddy, not so fast. You just rear ended a truck—and pretty hard, too."

"I what?"

"A garbage truck. You'd been at a light. Light turned green, you gunned it…right into—"

"Oh, *shit*. My car—"

"Yeah, your car. Your air bags went off, but you're okay. Your Honda'll need some front-end work."

Jimmy lay back, dizzy.

"What happened?"

"You remember anything?"

Jimmy took in the group clustered around him. Saw the police officer intently staring at him as she wrote stuff down on a notepad.

What was she writing down?

"No…not really. All I remember…was sitting at the light…watching the"

(*lights*)

"truck in front of me; saw the light change. Next I know…"

The cop wrote down everything, and, Jimmy'd noticed, nudged herself right up to him. He looked to her, still blinking, trying to regain some sense of dignity.

"That's, ah, that's all I honestly remember."

"Have a history of seizures?" the paramedic asked.

Jimmy stared at him like a deer in headlights.

Was he kidding?

Were they in a movie?

Things like this just didn't happen to him. But, apparently, they really did ask these kinds of questions.

"No…no, never had any seizures…"

"Your family?"

"No. Nothing."

"Were you drinking?"

Jimmy looked at the paramedic askew. "I assumed you already checked for that, but no. I don't drink and wasn't."

"Had to ask, buddy."

"Okay," the officer said, "take him on down to Memorial Emergency. Get him checked out." Then she addressed him directly, "We've already called your wife and told her to meet us down there."

All Jimmy could do was nod. And *that* hurt.

Whiplash?

He knew where this was going, and he didn't have a problem with that—a day off…at home. He doubted he was seeing the inside of his office today, but damn it, *what'd happened?* He'd had strange experiences before, but had never actually, well, *blacked out* before.

As they packaged him up into the ambulance, he glanced out the rear of the opened truck to his car…and groaned.

3

On 1 November 2010, 0517 PST, a Lockheed Martin Evolved Expendable Launch Vehicle, or EELV, lifted off from Vandenberg AFB, in Southern California. Its classified payload rocketed skyward, only to fatally malfunction on-orbit. It had made all the headlines.

Except that the payload actually *had* achieved orbit, after having deployed another classified payload to mislead observers into thinking a catastrophe had occurred. The actual payload achieved its 100-nautical-mile orbit and immediately proceeded in deploying its solar arrays, charging up it nickel-hydrogen batteries…and initializing its artificial-intelligence mission package.…

Chapter Three

1

Falcon Air Force Station, Colorado
31 October 1985
0530 Hours Mountain Time

First Lieutenant Jimmy Cherko pulled his '85 Toyota Celica up to the gate shack before Falcon Air Force Station. The guard, bringing his M-16 into the ready position, approached. It literally was a gate "shack," more of a temporary telephone-booth-like thing barely big enough for the hulking Air Force Security Police Master Sergeant who looked an easy six-foot-six, and barely fit into his utility jacket and uniform. His black beret was smartly canted on his head and his face looked as if freshly chiseled from very unsmiling granite.

"Morning, Lieutenant," was all he said, as Cherko displayed his orders through his rolled-down window. The SP took and read them, holding them against the stiff wind. He glanced around the open, empty, plains and road behind him, then back toward what existed of the brand-new site still ahead of Cherko. They were apparently the only two present, ten miles east of Colorado Springs, Colorado, and two miles south of Highway 94.

"Please park your vehicle over there, sir," the SP said, directing him off the road, but not inside the site, "and shut down your engine." The SP reentered the guard shack.

"Thanks," Cherko, said, nodding. He retrieved his orders and backed his Celica up a couple feet, pulling slightly off to the right as directed.

Cherko took in his new surroundings. Falcon Air Force Station was supposed to be the military's premier new space operations center, and it wasn't yet completed, yet here he sat, out in the middle of nowhere, a massive Air Force SP eyeing him, the main road into Falcon not even graded, its twisting dirt road winding up and over and around massive dirt mounds like an afterthought.

Man, just what kinda assignment was this?

He barely had time to answer that before he saw the approaching vehicle. Appropriately enough, a black Jeep CJ. Cherko looked back to the SP, who was just returning his "brick," or walkie-talkie, to his side. He again exited his tiny guard shack as the Jeep arrived. Cherko started up his vehicle, when the guard quickly shot one hand for his M-16, the other extended toward him in a "please don't make me shoot you" gesture.

"Sir! Turn *off* your vehicle!"

Cherko complied, grimacing and raising an apologetic hand. His red face nicely contrasted with his blue uniform.

Feeling eminently stupid, he watched the Jeep perform a U-turn around the guard shack. It pulled to a stop alongside the guard, who lowered and relaxed his hands, but kept an ever watchful eye on him. Slightly nervous, Cherko observed the two interact, both occasionally looking over to him.

What the hell had he gotten himself into?

Finally this new guy, a hat-less major sporting a sharp crew-cut and trim physique in the standard Air Force "blues," and wearing a partially open Poplin jacket like himself, got out of the Jeep. He carried a clipboard. Cherko rolled down his window and flinched from the sudden gusts and dust.

"Lieutenant Cherko?" the major asked, raising his voice above the wind. "James Cherko?" The major's voice was crisp, punctuated, and articulate. Made Cherko just wanna snap-to.

"Yes, sir," Cherko responded, saluting. He noted the Master Pilot wings over the major's left breast pocket.

"May I see some identification and orders?"

Cherko quickly and nervously reached into a back pocket and removed his wallet. Producing his green military ID, he handed it over with his orders. The major took them, compared them against whatever he had on the clipboard, and returned both.

"Major Bernie Turnbull."

Turnbull reached in and shook Cherko's hand.

"We'd like you to leave your vehicle here and accompany me in the Jeep," Turnbull said, simultaneously turning to the SP and nodding an "it's OK." Hulkster SP reentered his post and continued to scan the terrain, M-16 at hand.

"Sure," Cherko said.

Turnbull backed away from the Celica. Cherko grabbed his satchel, exited the car, and locked it.

"A little trouble in nav training, I see," Turnbull said as they both buckled up inside the vehicle. Turnbull started the engine and put the Jeep into gear.

Cherko smiled uncomfortably. "Ah, yeah, had problems doing mental calculations."

Turnbull nodded and pulled out.

"I could do them on paper, just didn't have the head for them in-flight. Mountains come up pretty fast."

"Sure do," Turnbull said, flatly.

Cherko looked down to the clipboard between the seats, and saw that it had official documentation on it concerning him, and his military photograph from nav training. The one with his wings anticipatorily planted on his chest. He caught some bits of information on there about himself, which did, indeed, list his failed attempt at nav training.

Great first impression.

Turnbull glanced over to him.

"How was North Dakota?"

"Windy."

"You oughta feel right at home, here, then."

Cherko smiled uncomfortably. He could envision this man's professional and sharp voice filling his ears within a cockpit, barking out headings, DRs, or ordnance releases. Now, something he would never experience, except in his imagination. So much for boyhood aspirations.

The short jaunt onto the site felt longer than it actually took, but they'd finally arrived to another dirt parking lot alongside a huge building that looked a lot like it was made out of rock. It had absolutely no windows nor any other building identifiers. It looked like your basic cube construction, several stories high, faced with a tan pebble material that made it look like a vertical insanely pebble-strewn beach. It fit in nicely with the surrounding barren landscape. But it also reminded him of his assignment up at the Perimeter Acquisition Radar Attack Characterization System, in North Dakota. Turnbull pulled to a stop and snapped on the parking brake.

"We're going to enter through those doors before us," Turnbull indicated to up ahead, "at which point you're going to be searched."

Cherko sat up a little straighter.

"Standard protocol. You'll go through this every day. Once inside, I'm going to take you to our module, where you will be in-processed, and we'll go from there. Questions?"

Of course Cherko had questions, lots of 'em. He may be "green," but he knew better, felt the total politeness being extended; it wasn't meant to be acted upon.

"No, sir."

Turnbull and Cherko entered the doors, and true to the major's word, both of them were searched. Both were "swiped" by a search wand, then only he was patted down. He was then asked to open his satchel, whereupon another SP poked around inside it with the butt end of a number two pencil. Satisfied, both were allowed to pass. Turnbull then clipped on his restricted area badge, which he pulled from a pocket. Cherko was issued his own and similarly clipped his to the lapel of his dark blue Poplin.

Turnbull then led him through the entryway, straight on toward another door, where Turnbull removed his badge and swiped it through a card reader alongside the door. A reflective metal sign declared the use of deadly force was authorized. The green light from the card reader allowed them passage, they entered, and Cherko heard it click behind him as it closed and locked. As if on cue, Turnbull did an abrupt about-face, which landed him squarely into his own personal breathing space.

"And one other thing before we proceed any further. Everything, absolutely *everything* that is said and done inside here—including how many times you take a shit—*stays* inside here. Do I make myself clear, Lieutenant?"

Swallowing hard, and beginning to sweat, Cherko nodded. "Yes, sir."

Turnbull nodded, then again about-faced and took him down the long corridor that seemed to go on forever.

Turnbull had taken him into another module, with another card reader behind another door that had another *Use of Deadly Force Authorized* sign affixed to it. Sat him in a waiting area. He then disappeared into the depths of this new enclosure. It was cooler in here, and he was glad to be rid of the major for a spell. Gave him a chance to assimilate his situation. He was on a site that was still under construction, had very little personnel, yet still managed to have some kind of a highly classified, apparently operational, unit. A unit no one talked about, and where mannerisms were measured and scrutinized.

Again, *what the* hell *had he gotten himself into?*

North Dakota.

He had North Dakota to thank. Or more specifically, one Lieutenant Colonel Willie Masterson, site commander...

Cavalier Air Force Station, North Dakota
8 May 1985

"What do you really want out of life—the military?" Colonel Masterson, known widely on site as "Willie" out of uniform, asked. They sat bullshitting in the on-site rec room. "Because once your desires and the Air Force's diverge," he said, making a "V" with his hands and shooting them off in diverging directions, "then it's time to punch."

"Well, sir, to be totally honest, I'd always wanted to be an astronaut. But things just haven't gone my way."

Masterson nodded. "I see. Well, you know, there's more than one way to skin a cat. Have you tried looking into becoming a payload specialist? Or a shuttle flight controller?"

"I'd applied to the Manned Space Flight Config Center, down in Houston, but was told that what Air Force personnel were already down there were being released. I also had a By-Name Request in for flight-control work in Sunnyvale, California, with a Colonel Logue, but that also fell through. I'd called to check on the status of things, and the colonel told me he had an office all ready…that all I had to do was report in…but when I called Personnel, some Valley Girl lieutenant told me flat out that Space Command wasn't releasing me No-Way, No-How. I was slated for some new base opening up in Colorado Springs, by way of the Mountain, as an Events Verification Officer. More missile warning."

"I see." Masterson paused. "You still interesting in staying in…if you can get some kind of space work?"

"Well, the goal—"

"The goal is to become an astronaut, I understand. But, you could get your foot in the door from one job, which could eventually lead you to your goal. How are you at flying?"

"Well, as much as I love it, I get airsick."

"Right, you had a hard time there."

"But did close out my in-flight checklists."

"Good…good. I do know some flyers who kept getting airsick through Fighter Lead-in training, but once they got operational were usually able to handle things. That's always an issue, I spose. Anyway, I mention this because—if you were interested—you could try to get into Flight Test School, out at Edwards."

"I'd thought of that. But I am a bit worried about the whole air sickness bit."

Again, Masterson nodded. "Well, then, I guess you got some decisions to make."

Cherko nodded.

"You're going on crew rest, aren't you?"

"Tonight's my last shift, then four days off. Heading to Iowa to visit my girlfriend's folks."

"Come see me when you get back. I might have something for you. Got anything to hide?"

"Sir?"

"Got any skeletons in your closet? If not—or you don't mind confiding them to Father Confessor U.S. Government—I might have a very interesting position for you."

"Nothing to hide, sir."

Masterson nodded. "Think things over, Jimmy, and stop by when you get back."

Masterson got up, slapped him on the back on the way out, and said, "Hate to lose a good officer."

Wearing his sharply pressed "crew blues," adorned with the silver Combat Crew badge over the right breast pocket, the basic space badge over the left, and a fresh haircut, Cherko knocked on Lieutenant Colonel Masterson's office door.

"C'mon in Lieutenant!" Masterson hailed from inside, "close the door."

Cherko entered and closed the door. He was about to come to attention, when Masterson put him At Ease.

"Have a seat, son. Have a good trip?"

Cherko nodded. "Yes, sir."

"Think through things? Get laid?"

Cherko cleared his throat, smiling, and turned a little red as he shifted in his seat. "Ah, yeah—yes, sir."

Masterson chuckled, waving an unconcerned hand between them.

"Okay, I got something for ya, and as I said last week, I think you're gonna like it. There's a unit, a highly classified one not talked about in the community, taking up residence at a new base east of Colorado Springs. I know a little about what they do, but not a lot, since I touched base with them in a previous life. Anyway, I contacted the commanding officer there, and he said they were actually short a man and would consider you. So I sent them your file—hope you don't mind—"

Cherko shook his head, smiling. "No, sir, not at all."

Masterson nodded. "Well, they took a look and are checking into your background. Don't know if you're familiar with how this world works—it's called the 'Black World'—but everything's hush-hush. When you go up for one of these jobs you don't know what it is unless you're already inside…and even that's not a given. When you go for one of these jobs you have to have focus and God and Country, because once you're in, you're in, there ain't no going back, at least not until your hitch is up. From what I've heard about this job, the work is fascinating, though they can't tell you what the job is until you're cleared and inside. Understand?"

"Yes, sir."

"Still interested?"

"Yes, sir."

"Good man. They'll get back to me soon, since I told them you're ready to PCS. I told them it's only a matter of months before you leave, but they said no problem. Once I get your foot in the door, it's all up to you, but I sense you're a good man looking to jump-start your career, and let me tell you, if you make it in there, you will have a career like no one else. Not even bland old astronauts."

"Really."

"I wish I could tell you just the little I know and have heard. These guys know about shit no one'll ever know."

"Wow."

"Wow is right. So," Masterson said, getting to his feet and extending his hand across his desk, "welcome back, Lieutenant, and keep your fingers crossed. You're about to embark on quite the career change, one that Valley Girl butter bar down in L.A. would kill to get into."

"Yes, sir!"

Falcon Air Force Station, Colorado
31 October 1985
0601 Hours Mountain Time

So, here he sat, in a tiny waiting room, inside some massive rock-like building, inside an empty module, awaiting further contact for in-processing into an organization that officially didn't exist, for a job about which he had no clue, on a base still under construction.

"Lieutenant Cherko?"

A buzz-haired captain popped his head into the room.

"Yes?"

"Ronnie Morrow. I'm your sponsor—and will also be your trainer."

Cherko stood and shook hands. "Good to finally meet you."

"Would you come with me, please?"

Cherko grabbed his satchel and followed Morrow down another, much narrower and smaller hallway, all the way to the end and another door. The place was empty and smelled new, their footsteps thumping down the corridor. There were many doors, all closed, with combination locks on each of them. Morrow stopped before the last one, quickly entered a combination, and popped it open. They entered a much smaller enclosure where Cherko saw elevator doors immediately before them. Morrow directed him into the elevator and followed in and hit a selection. Down they went.

"So, how was the drive down?" Morrow asked.

"Long."

"You find a place okay?"

"Yeah, thanks. Took your advice and am staying at that apartment complex you recommended."

Morrow nodded. "Good—hey, here we are!"

The elevator came to a stop. The doors opened and Morrow led the way out. They exited into yet another enclosure, at the short end of which was a security checkpoint and gate. Morrow went before him to the bulletproof-glass-and-wire mesh that enclosed the guard.

"We've got your paperwork in order. Just show your ID."

Cherko did as instructed. The guard checked his ID then shuffled some paperwork back to him, through a slot in the glass.

"Sign this. This is your temporary badge," the guard said, "you'll use this one just for down here. The captain'll show you how to use it. For now you're coded as a 'visitor,' so it won't work anywhere without an escort. We'll get your biometrics set up for that during in-processing."

"Biometrics?"

"Physical attributes associated with your entry into closed areas, like fingerprints."

"Oh."

"Welcome to the unit, Lieutenant," the guard said.

Cherko nodded.

"Okay, for now I'll be escorting," Morrow said, "so once I enter, swipe your badge and follow me in, okay?"

"Kay."

Morrow stepped upon a platform, swiped his badge, then bent over a device that he appeared to be looking into.

Cherko followed. "Just swipe the badge?" he asked Morrow.

"Just swipe the badge," Morrow said.

Cherko swiped the badge and moved on. The guard nodded as they went through the door on the other side of the gate.

They entered another hallway, similar in size to the module above, but in this one were people, both officers and enlisted, busily hustling about. Cherko and Morrow wove a short diagonal across the hallway into one of the open-door offices on the right. Here there were office signs, and this one said "Orderly Room." Morrow spoke with someone at a desk, then turned to Cherko.

"The colonel'll see you now," he said, showing him the office. "We'll be seeing more of each other later. Good luck, and welcome to the unit!"

"Thanks," Cherko said.

"Cherko?" came a hail from another office, in farther and off to his left. Cherko followed the voice and entered the colonel's office. An office nameplate "Lieutenant Colonel Galen Laasko, Commander," was on the wall. There was no organizational identifier.

Cherko snapped to attention before the colonel's desk.

"First Lieutenant Jimmy Cherko, reporting for duty, sir!"

"At ease, Lieutenant," the colonel said, coming out from around his desk to shake his hand. "Pleasure to have you aboard! Have a seat," he said, motioning to a chair.

Cherko sat, and the colonel returned to his seat.

"So, I take it—and you better not—have any idea about your job?"

Cherko chuckled, shaking his head, "No, sir, I do not. But I'm looking forward to new and important work."

"Oh, it's important, alright. Perhaps one of the most important jobs you'll ever do. As you may have guessed, you've been cleared for the position at a Top Secret/Codeword level, which you'll be briefed upon when you in-process. It was quite helpful getting your polygraph done up in North Dakota, really sped things along for in-processing, and will help us out in the long run. Anyway, I welcome all newbies as soon as they're brought in. You'll find us a tight knit bunch. A real family. We work hard, play hard. You come highly recommended from my old buddy, Willie, so we're looking forward to great things from you. All our OER ratings are tops. There are no slackers here, and no one ever gets below a 'one' on any evaluation. If they do…they're out. That simple. Every one of us, from me on down to the stripers are highly, highly motivated, top-notch professionals."

Colonel Laasko flipped through the papers on his desk before him. "So…I see you're twice highly qualified at PARCS. Never nailed with a Crit or even a Minor, is that right?" he asked looking up.

"Yes, sir. I knew my job and did my best. My trainer trained me to perform multiple inputs all the time, even when not necessary."

"Explain."

"Well," Cherko said, "on grave shifts, when no one was around, he'd purposely overload my training scenarios with no-win situations, and almost every input was paired with another critical or no-win situation, so I was constantly making judgment calls—many of which involved life-threatening situations. It forced me to make quick—though informed—decisions. To think on my feet. Sometimes a two-hour scenario was over in half an hour or less."

Colonel Laasko nodded, raising an eyebrow. "I see. So, how do you explain chewing out a major?"

Laasko set down the papers and regarded him squarely.

Cherko squirmed.

"I assure you," Laasko said, "Major Turnbull, *our* Director of Operations, will not be so easily handled."

"Sir, it's not what you—"

"I'm all ears."

"I was in a training evaluation on day shift. There were a lot of civilian contractors, and even government personnel, in the area. My trainer made the mistake of not placing himself between me and the phone to NORAD—the one we use to pass system assessments. So, while I'd been performing the training scenario, out of the corner of my eye I noticed my DD—my Deputy Space Systems Director—was dealing with an input, and as he went for the phone, his trainer, who stood directly between him and the phone, physically body-checked him back away from the phone as he leapt for it. I thought that funny at the time, but was busy with my own scenario. No sooner had I observed that than I experienced an input on my screen that appeared to be a real-world threat indication—not a training input. So, I'd implemented system reporting—for real. I was on the phone to NORAD. To make a long story short, my DO had entered the area while I was on the phone, wondering what the hell was going on. Both he and my trainer, who *still* sat on the other side of me, stared at me. My DO told me to give him that phone, that he didn't want some second lieutenant selling the site down the drain. I insisted to them both that I had what looked real—not a *training* input—but my DO was giving me a lot of…well, grief. We never got along all that well to begin with, and he told me to hang up. I held out the phone to him and told him that if he felt it was a false event, then *he* could tell NORAD. It was soon found out that training had made mistakes in setting up that scenario and that I had acted properly. Once all was taken care of, I politely asked the major to step outside the TOR—our Tactical Operations Room—and down the hall a minute. Once down there, as respectfully as I could…yes…I chewed him out."

"Chewed him out? How is that any kind of respectful?"

"I told him that in the TOR, *I* was in charge, and that no one—not even the site commander—could tell me what to do, if I felt I had a valid event…that technically *I* had the last word in there in things relating to missile launch detections—and that further, he had absolutely no right to chew me out in front of a room full of operators and contractors. And, finally, I demanded an apology."

"And you did all this as a First Lieu—"

"*Second* Lieutenant, sir. I hadn't yet been promoted."

"I see."

"Well, he just stood there and took it, his mouth open in utter surprise the entire time. When I was done, he said that was the first time a second lieutenant had ever chewed him out."

"I bet. Were you right?"

"Sir, I was. I didn't call him any names, and just stuck to the facts. There was nothing he could say. To his credit, however, I had to hand it to him—he never held that against me the rest of my time there. In fact I had to spend the rest of the day filing higher-headquarters reports for that incident, since it really was a training mistake and not a real launch. Doing all those reports had made me stay so late that I had no ride back to the barracks, because I'd ridden in with my DD in the government van and he'd already left. So, here I am, still kinda pissed at the DO, finishing up my report, and in he walks…asking me if I need a ride back. Then it hits me…I didn't have one—not that it was a long walk back, it wasn't—but the fact that he offered me a ride blew me away. He held absolutely no grudges that I ever detected, but I was extremely uncomfortable the entire ride back."

"Ever get that apology?"

"Yes, sir."

"Well, that's exactly the kind of officer we want in our ranks. Someone not afraid to take a stand."

Laasko glanced to his watch.

"Okay, I think I've taken up enough of your time." Laasko got to his feet, as did Cherko. "As I said," Laasko said, shaking his hand, "this will be quite the challenging job, and one of the most important

"most important

"most important

"most important

"jobs you'll ever perform, and you're just the kind of officer we're looking for."

Cherko eyed the colonel. He was about to ask if he was all right, when Laasko continued.

"Our last individual had an emergency permanent change of station and we really needed to fill that billet. It looks like we made a good choice."

"Thank you, sir," Cherko said, still eyeing the colonel.

"Oh, and one more thing. Everything that goes on in here—and Security will reemphasize this—everything from our conversation this morning to Sergeant Lefty's cold, to a display monitor's PMI—preventive maintenance inspection—is supremely classified. What goes on in here, stays in here, even from those in the mod above us. This is a highly compartmentalized world, Lieutenant, which means strict need-to-know."

"Yes, sir."

"Good to have you onboard!"

"Good to be here, sir."

Cherko turned to leave.

"And, Lieutenant—"

"Sir?"

This place doesn't exist. I don't exist—and neither do *you*."

2

Cherko exited his car in the Templeton Park Apartments parking lot in front of the building to his new home. Apartment 222. He stood there a moment, staring up into the overcast sky.

He'd come a long way from Lake Clear, New York, and that kid excited by *Star Trek*, spaceflight, and models of jets and spaceships. Staring up at the clouds reminded him of the time up behind the house, behind the chicken coop and by the pump house, where he'd stood on the top-most extrusion of curved granite, also during a gray October day. Standing there in the clearing as that teenager, he'd been having difficulty in dealing with some youthful angst he'd long forgotten on a particularly troubling day. But he did remember staring skyward at the fast moving gray and black clouds. Thinking how he swore he was gonna make it in this world, gonna attain his dreams, and nothing was gonna stop him. He was gonna show the world…some day…make it big. He was gonna show them, yes he was.

So, he'd applied to the Air Force and Naval Academies at Colorado Springs, Colorado, and Annapolis, Maryland. He really wanted the Air Force. But, as "most improved" as he might have been in high school (school had never been his strong suit, though he was always slightly above average), it wasn't enough to get him into the Air Force Academy. But for the Naval Academy he'd managed a nomination from Senator Moynihan, of New York.

He couldn't believe it!

All he now had to do was get the actual appointment. He could follow in his dad's footsteps in the service he had served as a submariner, but only he would be an *astronaut!* His dad below water—him above.

But, alas, those hopes were also soon dashed, and were the start of his life-long list of failures.

He hadn't been good enough to get in to yet another academy.

He'd found out years later in talking to his father that he'd missed that Annapolis appointment by *one point*.

One stinkin point!

His dad had told him that the Annapolis superintendent had actually called him and told him that he had just missed the entry criteria by a *single point*, and could he quickly retake the tests? There was still a chance.…

But his father had informed the officer that where they lived, in boondock upstate New York, those tests were only administered once a year.

Persistent teen he was, he figured, try another route on his quest for space. He'd applied to a couple colleges and found he'd been accepted to two in Arizona. He'd picked Northern Arizona University, at Flagstaff. He'd shoot for an astronomy degree, and try to enter pilot training. So, Cherko applied for the Reserve Officer's Training Corps through college and took the entry tests at Rensselaer Polytechnic Institute, at Rensselaer, NY. Though he failed to qualify for a pilot slot (how quickly the failures were piling up…), he did qualify for a navigator slot.

Flying high, he headed off to college, and graduated with a physics degree—with an emphasis in astronomy. NAU had not yet had an astronomy degree, though Lowell Observatory was up on a hill just west of Flagstaff, the same observatory where Percival Lowell had discovered Pluto in 1930. A fresh butter bar second lieutenant, he launched into navigator training, at Mather AFB, California. He did well in the academics (a ninety-eight average)…but couldn't perform cockpit in-his-head calculations, and choked during a nav procedures laboratory exercise, wherein which he plotted a course leg directly through a thunderstorm.…

What the hell was the matter with him?

Couldn't he do anything right?

How the hell did he expect to become an astronaut if he couldn't do any of these things correctly?

Then after three more attempts at getting an astronaut slot while in the Air Force, he again failed, failed, and failed. It was like he just wasn't destined for greatness, no matter how intensely he promised his teenage self on that little patch of granite up back behind the chicken coop. He'd always thought he'd been destined for something big, but was quickly beginning to doubt any of it.

Cherko turned away from the dark skies, and made for the apartment steps that led up to his second-floor apartment.

So…he found himself in missile warning, and now some cool job (he was told), about which he still had no idea.

But it wasn't flying, and it wasn't as an astronaut.

But it *was* about space.

And maybe that was all he could settle for. Second best. Never first, never last, but always—*always*—somewhere in between. A guy had to grab what he could, when he could. Second best was better than last.

After spending the day in-processing into a super-secret unit that didn't officially exist, on an Air Force installation that wasn't completely constructed, he would take what had been graciously handed him by a colonel who had seen something in him.

But, still, his little voices nagged, did he get the job based upon his *own* merits?

No.

He'd gotten it from his commander doing him a favor.

Couldn't he do anything right—or on his own? Couldn't anything go the way *he* wanted things to go?

Life was tough, but he had it good, so quit whining. Grow up and be a man, for Chrissakes. Things happened for a reason, and he may not understand it at the time, but everything that ever happened to him always seemed to bear itself out at some point. He had a college education, was gainfully (if covertly) employed, so call it a day and move the hell on.

Standing on the landing before his apartment door, Cherko reached into his pockets and fished out his keys. As he began to insert his key into the door, the apartment door next to him opened.

"Hi!" the longhaired redhead beauty greeted, closing and locking her door.

Cherko smiled, still trying to open his door. "Hi."

"You must be the new guy?"

"Yeah; just moved in this week. Jimmy Cherko," he said, turning to the woman and shaking her hand.

The woman smiled an absolutely stunning smile, eyes deep and dark, and shook his hand. "Pleased to meet you, Jimmy Cherko. I'm Erica. Erica Taylor."

"I seem to be having issues with this lock," Cherko said.

Erica eyed him as she made like she was looking for something in her purse. Cherko again tried the lock.

"Oh," Erica said, "sometimes these locks just need a jiggle or two."

Cherko jiggled it. Jiggled it again. It opened. He smiled back to Erica, who had returned to her faux pocketbook search.

"Well…," Cherko said, just about to enter his apartment.

"Where you from?" Erica quickly asked.

Cherko paused, and set down his satchel just inside the doorway.

"Originally upstate New York."

"Really? I'm from Vermont! Burlington."

"Well, isn't this a small world. I've been to Vermont—Burlington—a couple times. I love riding that ferry across Lake Champlain."

Erica smiled a big, open-faced smile; checked and smoothed out her ponytailed hair. "Wow, never met anyone out here who even knew about Burlington, let alone the ferries!"

Erica stopped searching in her purse, clasped it in both hands and set it down before her. Cherko now looked to her and totally took her in. She was absolutely stunning. Tall, extremely well built, and, he now also noticed, attired in work-out garb (Spandex and sweat shirts; she wore two sweat shirts, it looked like) that really made her physique stand out.

"So…heading to the gym? Know of any you could recommend?"

"Sure," Erica said, "there's a couple around town, Lynmar Racquet Club, a couple Bally's, but I really like this little one called the Holiday Health Club down on Academy and Galley—Academy's the main north-south drag through town. In fact…I even have a card. Here," she said, and turned around to reach down into her gym bag behind her. Cherko raised an amused eyebrow, smiling, as he caught an extremely good shot of her tight behind.

"Here you go," she said, standing back up and handing him the card. "What are you smiling about?"

Cherko took the card. "Uh, Holiday Health Club? Cool. Thanks, I appreciate that. You heading there, now?"

"It's just a couple minutes south on Academy, on the right, just before Galley. In fact, here," she said, suddenly taking back the card (and touching his hand in the process), "I'll write directions down on the back…and my number," she said, glancing up to him. "In case you have trouble finding it…or have any other questions." She handed back the card, smiling and shifting her weight to one foot. "Hope to see you there."

"Maybe you will."

As Erica bent over and gathered up her gear, Cherko again got another shot of her well-formed back end.

Erica made her way past him, lightly brushing against his hips, and Cherko found himself unable to look away. She gingerly stepped down the concrete-and-metal steps to ground level, where he found he continued to watch her as she got into her car. She again, casually (or so it seemed), looked up to him, smiling and waving goodbye as she pulled away.

Smiling—and embarrassed—he waved back and entered his apartment. As he closed the door behind him, still grinning ear-to-ear, he thought, okay, unknown job, second-rate career choice…but—*wow*—a *knockout* for a next-door neighbor.

Maybe things were finally looking up.

Chapter Four

1

Eastern Plains of Colorado
1 November 1985
0030 Hours Mountain Time

The window-blackened blue Air Force van that carried First Lieutenant Jimmy Cherko—in civilian clothes—rattled and shimmied over what felt like hard dirt road. He didn't know how long they'd been on it (he'd been directed to leave his watch at his apartment), but they went down on this road after having taken a right turn off smooth pavement.

Cherko had finished his orientation into his new ERO unit what-was-now-yesterday, had met his commander, Director of Operations, trainer, and other assorted personnel, and after filling out some paperwork had begun training. But, when he'd returned to his empty apartment later that afternoon (after having met that hot chick on the landing), he'd received a mysterious call from DO Turnbull. Turnbull had told him that at midnight *tonight* a dark blue Air Force van would arrive at his apartments. He would have three minutes to get into it. He was to ask no questions, say nothing to the driver, dress in civilian attire, and leave his watch and all questions behind. When the van arrived at its destination, he was to disembark and proceed into the building he was dropped off before. Pass through two sets of doors.

That was all the major had said before hanging up.

The van had shown up precisely at midnight. Hitching his glasses up on his nose (he couldn't wear his contacts 24 hours a day) and hurrying down the apartment stairs, he entered the vehicle. Once inside he saw all the windows had been blackened out and he was separated from his driver by another blackened window that stretched across the front.

Road trip.

But, now, the van was slowing down, though Cherko's pulse was picking up.

Where the heck was he and why all the drama?

Fleeting images flew through his head.

He saw himself sitting before a console. Something *peculiar* was going on...a display before him.

A display within a display?

Something about a desert, bright lights, lots of people....

The van came to a complete stop. Cherko sat motionless for a moment longer. He then unbuckled his seatbelt, slid across the seat, and exited. As soon as his feet hit ground (there wasn't a parking lot, sidewalk, or road around him—the bus just seemed to park out on open prairie), he looked up and paused; a waning gibbous moon was part way across the cold dark sky. He remembered star-and-moon gazing as a kid with his dad's huge ex-Navy binoculars....

The van honked.

Cherko glanced back to the shadowy vehicle. Looked to its headlights. Highbeams that shot out into dark nothingness like laser beams.

No trees, no buildings, no roads.

Out in the middle of nowhere.

Then he turned back around and looked to the odd structure before him. He couldn't quite make everything out in the darkness and shadows, or the building's exact scale and his proximity to it, but it was some kind of apparently small, box-like construction. He found it hard to define it a "building." It actually reminded him more of a hut, like an ice-fishing hut. Or storage shed. One lone light shone above its door, a plain metal door with a simple vertical pull-bar for a handle. There were no other markings on it. No signs, no "Welcome to Hell," no nothin. As Cherko approached the door, he startled several nearby pronghorn. He watched them dart off into the darkness.

Cherko approached the structure and grabbed the handle. It was heavy, solid. Cold. Belied its appearance. He glanced back to the idling van one more time before pulling open the door and disappearing behind it.

It was warmer in here, but not by much. And it was quite a small vestibule he found himself standing within, much like a closet. But there was another door before him.

Turnbull had mentioned two.

The door he just passed through closed with a smooth though heavy clunk, and he turned back to it. Gave it a push. Locked solid. Not an ounce of give. This was definitely like no ice hut he'd ever been in.

"Great."

Cherko gave the door two more good pushes for the hell of it before returning to the other door. He was "in," and there obviously wasn't any room for changing one's mind. He approached Door Number Two.

The door was smooth, no handles, and blended in nicely with the walls. Too nicely, actually. In fact, it reminded him of the doors on *Star Trek's* starship *Enterprise*, except that there was a metal plate on the wall to the left of the door in the shape of a left hand. No brain surgery here. He cautiously placed his left hand into the grooved-out area of the wall plate. No electric jolts, but the door did as expected, and swooshed open, just like the *Star Trek* doors. He recoiled a step, left hand still upraised, surprised at how quickly the door had zipped open. Remained open.

Cherko lowered his hand and peered inside.

An elevator.

"Doesn't anyone do anything above ground, anymore?"

He entered it.

As soon as he was inside, the doors swooshed closed and the elevator shot into action, throwing him momentarily off-balance as the floor seemingly dropped out from underneath him. But no sooner had he regained his composure, when the elevator stopped and its doors again opened—this time, into a small chamber approximately six by ten.

"Well, ain't *this* cozy."

Cherko cautiously entered the chamber. The elevator door quietly swished closed behind him. He also re-approached this door, but this one *did* open. He stared into the empty elevator a moment before backing away.

"*Please sit, Lieutenant,*" came the soft voice from behind. Cherko spun around. The voice was a mixture of electronics and what had to be human vocals, and came from the empty room. Cherko saw no speakers, but found a chair to his left, beside a computer workstation set into the wall. It was under a large, dark, plate glass-like window. The monitor for the computer workstation was also large, perhaps 30 diagonal inches. A keyboard sat beneath it. The monitor was blank. Cherko noticed that though the air he was breathing was cool, he was not uncomfortable. He removed his jacket.

"You are the first," the soft, attractive (he now noticed) female voice announced. "Prepare for training."

"Training?"

At this point the huge plate-glass "window" activated, displaying a beautifully three-dimensional starfield. Cherko took his seat.

"Cool...."

"In 1960 a project was initiated. You are a result of that project."

Result?

"What was this project's purpose?" Cherko asked.

"You are not authorized an answer to that question."

Cherko raised an eyebrow.

"But I am the first?"

"You are the first.

"You possess unique abilities that will be tested and advanced. You are never to discuss this training, this room, nor your travel to and from here.

Major Turnbull is your only contact on this project. You are not to discuss this training or anything else about this place with him."

Turnbull's three-dimensional image briefly appeared on the huge screen, as the voice instructed. It was a little too much Turnbull for his tastes.

"You will continue all unit training at your operating location, then you will be picked up by the van that delivered you here tonight."

The van's image briefly flashed up on the large screen.

"Here, you will perform project training. Training will last as long as it takes for you to master all skills. If you advance quickly, training will accelerate; if you require longer, training will adjust.

"Prepare for your initial lesson."

The computer screen before him fired up, and on it, in green phosphorescence, were displayed ten evenly spaced 3-D boxes, each containing the laying down, reverse "S" of a stationary sine wave. The sine waves took up the main center portion of each of the ten display boxes. Each box also contained twelve hash marks running down the left side ordinate axis of each individual sine wave's box. In the upper right-hand corner of the screen were the words "Total" and "Recent."

"You will now hear a tone, and on your screen see ten sine waves."

Cherko jumped, swatting at the air around his head.

He did hear a tone, but it sounded as if it was right up against—actually *inside*—his head, as if he'd wore a headset, or came from some buzzing bee. He again swiped at his ears, but of course that didn't affect anything. Working his head and shoulders, he settled in.

"You will now listen to the tone and mentally duplicate it. Mentally hum it without verbalizing it.

"Begin."

Cherko looked to the sine waves on his screen as he listened to the tone. It was actually a pleasant sound, one that reverberated within him in an oddly comfortable manner. Cherko mentally reproduced the sound.

"That was easy," he said.

"Now examine the sine wave in the first box on your screen. Look for movement."

Cherko studied the box.

"Movement?"

Though the sine wave was perfect, rock-stable, and non-fluctuating, he could swear he detected a hint—just a *hint*—of movement. He didn't know if it was just wishful thinking or something he was actually doing, but he continued to stare at the wave and mentally reproduce the tone that filled his head.

"As you gain proficiency, the sine wave will flatten toward the center axis-of-abscissa coordinate line. Each hash mark to the left defines thirty degrees of flattening from the 180 degrees of sine wave. You are to flatten each sine wave toward the abscissa axis, making a straight line."

Cherko chuckled.

"Oh, I will, will I? And I am to do this by just *thinking* about it?"

"Please focus," the attractive voice gently chided.

"You gotta be kidding—"

"As you do this, an indicator line will display atop the flattened sine wave indicating your degree of flattening by pointing to the hash marks. In the upper right-hand portion of each box you see 'Total' and 'Recent.' 'Total' represents the flattest you've ever attained for that sine wave, and 'Recent' is your most-recent degree of flattening for that sine wave."

Cherko continued mentally humming the tone and focused on the first sine-wave box....

For the next several hours Cherko performed in this manner, when he finally experienced a mental "click" inside his head. With this "click" he saw the positive portion of the sine wave above the abscissa x-axis in the first box suddenly flatten, or "squash" down *toward* the abscissa axis coordinate line, as if a hand had forced it down. As this happened, another horizontal line appeared on *top* of the squashed sine wave, reaching out across to the hash marks on the left.

"I did it!" Cherko shouted, jumping to his feet. "*Yeah!*"

But he'd only flattened the top part.

"How do I flatten the bottom?"

"Focus on each portion."

Cherko sat back down. As he focused on the bottom portion, the top portion began to return to its original sine form.

"Crap!"

He sent it back to where he'd had it.

"That's more like it."

Cherko focused on the bottom portion of the wave, while continuing to maintain the top portion's flattening. It took some effort, but eventually he was able to flatten both portions of the sine wave to within one hash mark on either side of the center line.

"Come *on*," Cherko said under his breath, "I can do this...."

Both halves of the wave flattened to a perfectly straight line, and "Total" and "Recent" both read "180."

"*Ha!*" Cherko exclaimed, again jumping out of his seat. "I can't believe this—I did this with my *mind?* This for real?"

"This concludes this session's training. You will return tomorrow at the same time to continue."

"That's it? No hug? No kiss?"

Silence.

Cherko's screens went blank, and the lighting in the chamber dimmed.

Cherko looked around him and got to his feet. As exhilarated as he was, he was also physically and mentally exhausted. He'd had a long day, with two full-on training sessions, and was going to have to start it all over again tomorrow (well *today*). Grabbing his jacket, he headed toward the elevator. It swooshed open to allow entry. He entered and turned back around to face the chamber. Just as the elevator doors began to close, the chamber's lighting faded to black.

Cherko exited the strange building into the early morning darkness to find his idling, dark blue chariot awaiting. He entered it, glancing back to the structure within which he'd just spent a handful of hours. As the door closed, he saw the light above the building's heavy metal door extinguish.

The hut just seemed to have *vanished*.

This job just kept getting weirder and weirder.

He thought he'd been assigned to one deep black program, only to find he seemed to be assigned to something far more…dark.

Had Colonel Masterson known about this?

Had he known when he pushed for his assignment to ERO what he was getting him into?

He supposed even if he had wanted to talk about it he couldn't, given the highly classified nature of, well, *everything*.…

And over and above any other mundane considerations…*what the hell had just happened in there?*

Okay, he wasn't any kind of engineer or computer geek, but he was also no idiot. He'd studied physics, rudimentary electronics. He knew that whatever had just happened, whatever he had just done (barring whether or not he was being manipulated and it was all *fake*)…he had (apparently) just effected a change to some computer program *with his mind*.

How was that possible—even given his limited knowledge of quantum physics?

Was his ability unique?

He was the first.

First of *what*?

And a reasonable follow-on question would be…were there to be others?

More?

Toward what end?

What was the purpose of this training program?

And what was *he* to be used for?

2

ERO Operations Center
1 November 1985
1253 Hours Mountain Time

Cherko exited the elevator onto the ERO level to find Capt Morrow awaiting.

Was Morrow part of the Project?

Cherko hadn't slept all that well, and had had the most unusual dreams—but nothing he any longer remembered.

"Afternoon," Morrow greeted, smiling and sipping coffee.

"Ditto," Cherko replied. "Smells good; wish I drank the stuff."

"Didn't catch up on your sleep all day? Well, no worries. We got your basic selection in the break room. Ready to begin training?"

"Aye. But, I think I will need some caffeine."

"Before we get started, Turnbull needs to see you. I'll escort you there."

"Haven't been here long enough to *do* anything," Cherko said, following the captain.

He had an image of himself high above the Earth....

Could this be what he thought it'd be about? Were things already set into motion? Was Turnbull going to discuss what had happened last night...what was supposed to continue after he was done with his training, here, every night?

And what was it with all these visions?

Let the weirdness begin.

Morrow led him through the admin office to a back area that had "Major Turnbull, DO" inscribed on a nameplate. Morrow knocked once.

"Enter!" Turnbull's response was gruff and loud, and had actually caused Cherko to jump.

"Sir, Lieutenant Cherko," Morrow said.

"Bring him in."

"I'll come get you when you're done," Morrow said, departing.

"Reporting as—"

"Close the door and have a seat, Lieutenant," Turnbull said.

Cherko sat, mindful of his posture; again glanced to Turnbull's wings.

Turnbull folded his hands before him on his immaculately clean desk. Cherko shifted uncomfortably in the chair.

"By now you've been in-briefed on your new program."

"Yes, sir. But I'm not exactly s—"

"And by 'new program' I think you know what I mean."

Cherko nodded. "Yes, sir."

"From this point on it will simply be referred to as 'The Program.' Understood?"

"Yes, sir."

"I am your only contact on The Program. Not even Colonel Laasko knows of it. You will not discuss this program with anyone unless I specifically introduce you to them. In person or otherwise. Do I continue to make myself clear?"

"Yes, sir."

"Once you've completed your training, I will give you further direction."

Cherko nodded.

"Sir?"

Turnbull paused.

"What's all this about? What will I be used for?"

Turnbull bored into him. "You do not have a need to know for either question. When and if the time comes for you to know any such answers, you will be briefed. You would be well-advised to limit your questions about this program to *none*."

Cherko again shifted uncomfortably and cleared his throat. Again with the no questions. "Yes, sir."

"*This* is your assignment, Lieutenant," Turnbull said, nonchalantly shuffling through paperwork, and not looking up. "This is why you were assigned here. ERO is only a cover for this other assignment."

Turnbull reached for a pen then pushed both the pen and a sheet of paper toward him.

Cherko picked up the paper. Scanned it. Looked to Turnbull.

"*You kidding?*"

"Do I look like we're kidding?"

Cherko looked back down to the paper. Phrases like "in perpetuity," "will never divulge knowledge of the Program," and "grave consequences," resulting in "termination" caused him to pause.

Termination?

Somehow he didn't think "termination" meant just being cut from the program.

Cherko again looked up; picked up the pen.

Swallowed hard.

Looked to the words on the pen: "*Air Force. A great way of life.*"

Though he knew Turnbull was boring a hole through his soul, Cherko didn't want to look back up into those hard eyes again.

What the hell had Masterson gotten him into? Yes, it was spooky, yes, it was extraordinary, but also—

He had been able to influence electronics with his mind.

He was being trained as a psychic spy—or telekinetic satellite operator— he didn't know which, but both greatly appealed to him. He'd never been "anybody" before, certainly not anyone *important*. Just a guy. A navigator washout—and yes, that was exactly how he saw himself—not even good enough to be a *pilot* washout…but, now…*now* he had a chance to make something of himself. Become something important and greater than himself. Someone trained in honest-to-God *superpowers*.

It fascinated him. He had to know more.

He signed.

But he had the oddest feeling of vertigo as he inked the paper. Again something about him in orbit. Looking down to the Earth. It was as if he were having a spontaneous out-of-body experience right on the spot.

Then he handed both the pen and document (he watched both leave his hand in a curiously detached fashion) back to Turnbull, who signed in the space below his signature.

"Best of luck," he said, in a less than believable manner. Without looking up, he added, "Morrow's outside."

Cherko exited the office.

3

Ronnie Morrow swiped his badge and entered the cipher combination. The metal door with the *Use of Deadly Force Authorized* sign on it clicked loudly. Morrow opened the door and escorted Cherko into a narrow enclosure with a heavy curtain drawn across the entire length of the small rectangular room before him. At the far left was a lone desk and chair. All sound felt deadened and muffled, which could only mean that the enclosure was soundproofed. Cherko also noticed the security cameras coldly eyeing from above. Morrow closed the cypher-locked door behind them. It again clicked as it locked. He hit a switch on the wall, and the curtains swiftly parted to reveal the soundproofed glass enclosure that looked out onto the low-lit ERO Operations Floor. Another door was set into the glass wall off on the right.

"This is the Ops floor," Morrow said directing to the room before them. "We have this soundproofed entryway, or 'fishbowl,' as we like to call it, as another layer of security and for guests."

"Fishbowl," Cherko said, "I like that."

"Everybody does," he said absentmindedly as he scanned the consoles and room on the other side of the glass. He then opened the glass door and he and Cherko entered the room.

Were any of these individuals in "The Program"?

All eyes briefly shifted to them before returning to their workstations. Cherko felt like he'd just been strip searched and put away wet, but still stood in the middle of the room in awe. It wasn't much larger than the TOR in North Dakota, maybe even slightly smaller, but he was surrounded by high technology. No Flapper Boards and sixties technology, here. This stuff was clearly state of the art and *sexy*. A handful of consoles lined the wall opposite him, and to his right and in the center, on a slightly raised dais, was another set of consoles most likely for a crew commander, its centerline angled into the corner at Cherko's one o'clock position. Operators sat at some of the consoles and there were two individuals kneeling on the floor underneath another set off to his right, performing what looked like maintenance activity.

"Quite a bit different than what you were used to, I'm sure," Morrow said, smiling. "Welcome to the Ops Center, Lieutenant, your new home."

"Wow…not like my old TOR at all."

Cherko noticed no unit patches on any of the crew members' sleeves, only American flags on each operator's upper-left shoulders where a unit patch would be. Cherko made a move to examine some consoles, when Morrow grabbed him.

"Not so fast, Cowboy. There're some things you first need to know before going any further."

Morrow held up a hand, motioning to the two maintenance guys. Cherko and Morrow waited for them both to close up panels and exit the floor.

"Not even them?" Cherko asked.

"Not even them.

"Okay, first off, you no longer work for the Air Force."

Cherko flinched.

"Oh, you'll still wear the uniform, get the paycheck and all, but you now actually work for an organization called NSA, or the National Security Agency. We're a brand new organization hidden under not only NSA, but another layer of agency, called DEFSMAC, or the Defense Special Missile and Astronautics Center. Both DEFSMAC and NSA are never to be mentioned, whispered, written down, or even *thought* about outside this room."

"Not even out there," Cherko asked, directing back to the hallway and main module outside the fishbowl behind them.

"Nope. In the event of a security breach, you never really know who may be out there; it's only in here, which has extremely limited access, can you be sure—and even then—*question*. You noticed how everyone looked to us as we entered?"

"Yeah."

"Always, *always*, be on guard."

Cherko nodded.

"And, as everyone from the colonel on down has already emphasized, this organization, this location, this *operation* does not exist. You thought PARCS was cool, well you ain't seen nothing—and will continue to see 'nothing,' if you get my drift."

"Got it," Cherko said absentmindedly, as he took in the huge display screens above the couple operators seated at their consoles. The center screen was black, while the two to both sides of the blackened one displayed what looked like star fields. At each console were three screens per operator, each operator's workstation shielded by a vertical separator from the other. The middle screens were high-definition graphics, with the Earth at the center of their displays, sectioned off by country on some, grids by other operators, with what looked like real-time graphics of satellites orbiting the Earth. One of the consoles at one workstation displayed nothing but letters and numbers, while another screen at another workstation looked like an air traffic controller's display. The third at each position was covered by a black cloth cowling. "Sanitized," or covered, no doubt for his benefit—at least until he was in-briefed. There were also all sorts of phones scattered about the consoles, white, black, and red, several keyboards and trackballs, and a variety of push-button control panels. Many of the selections glowed a soft red, while some glowed blue and clear. The low lighting was just enough to highlight all the colored lights and switches.

"DEFSMAC," Morrow continued, "our cover organization under NSA, is a real organization with its own mission, and all I'm telling you, everything—absolutely everything that is said and done in here—is highly classified and compartmentalized. Not everyone in this unit knows about what we do here, or what goes on inside here, and we like to keep it that way.

"Anyway, DEFSMAC was formed on 27 April, 1964, as a result of the Cuban Missile Crisis, to evaluate any and all foreign missile activity and threats. Not unlike your Space Wing at Cavalier, et cetera. But where they differ from the Air Force's standard missile warning units is that DEFSMAC also deals with intel and *technologies*. It's an 'all-source' intelligence agency, using listening posts, early warning satellites, human agents, and even seismic detectors to monitor any and all foreign space and missile events."

"Cool," Cherko said.

"They see all kinds of stuff. All *kinds*." Morrow stared off into space for a moment. "By now you're probably wondering what our organization's actual name is. Our name is actually more sensitive than the others I just mentioned. We're relatively new, and you, despite your tickets—"

"Tickets?"

"Your clearance accesses. Despite your accesses, you don't have the need to know about its origins. Our unit, which is unique—the only one of its kind on the planet—is called 'ERO,' or the Exoatmospheric Reconnaissance Organization.

Once Morrow had said that, an operator hit a switch, and the blank center screen lit up with the unit's vibrant and multicolored emblem displayed. It consisted of two golden satellite "polestars" orbiting the Earth, a glowing moon just visible off to the right. Meteoroids hurtled toward Earth above these two polestars, while off to the left a single star-like object shone against a stunning nebula pattern of space matter. In the center, a silver delta-like object intercepted the meteoroids. At the top were the words *IN TÉNEBRIS.*

Cherko grinned. "Man, that is *the* coolest emblem I've ever seen. What's the Latin mean?"

"'Into the darkness.' We don't wear patches for obvious reasons, but we do like our emblem," Morrow said, nodding absentmindedly and tapping a highly polished combat-booted foot as he stared at the design.

"Okay. Now, our operating location at Falcon was purely opportunistic," Morrow said, breaking away from the ERO coat of arms. "It was never planned to stand up a unit out here, but extra funding and other decisions factored in, and the move was quick and immediate upon ground breaking. I'm told work was done at night until the shell was sealed underground.

"So, what we have here," Morrow continued, as he took Cherko forward, "are the operator consoles. All consoles, as you can see, are sectioned off by blinders. As we talked about compartmentalization, it goes down to individual operator level. Each operator is only concerned with their display. Any events at a specific operator's console are *not* to be viewed by any other operator—anyone else except the Crew Commander. Is that understood?"

"Yes."

"Each operator has their basic Earth Display, as you can see, here, which constantly—24/7—displays real-time data."

"Real time?"

"Yes."

"Interesting."

"We'll get to that in training."

"Gotcha."

"So, we watch things—Jerry," Morrow said to an operator at the center command dais behind them, "could you activate the main screens, bitte?"

A lieutenant selected a switch or two, and there, above them and on the screens to either side of the organizational seal, showed a chunk of rock.

Morrow eyed Cherko.

"We also watch for asteroids, meteoroids, comets, decaying satellites…that kind of thing."

"You gotta be kidding."

"We look inside and outside our orbit. There have been a couple near-misses over the past few years—real ones, *close* ones—chunks of space debris from the asteroid or Van Oort belts—"

"How close?"

Morrow grinned. "Whizzing past the Earth like a grazing bullet, my friend—*way* inside our lunar orbit."

"Holy shi—"

"But that doesn't mean we were in any real danger—but that's how we like it. We just keep an eye on things, is all, and notify the right agencies if we see anything."

"What do we do if we do see something coming our way?"

Cherko noticed a couple console operators briefly turn an ear toward them then return to their screens.

"We just run it on up the chain, Lieutenant, and that's all you need to know. At least as long as you work in here."

Cherko grimaced.

"This display over here," Morrow continued, pointing to the telemetry display of letters and numbers, "is the telemetry display for the specific satellite used in the Earth Display screen I just mentioned. We have a couple of them. These screens make sure they're all A-OK, healthwise. This covered screen," he next pointed to, "will be disclosed upon reaching your need-to-know authorization during training."

"Roger," Cherko acknowledged. "Can I ask a question?"

"Depends."

"Why DEFSMAC? I know what you just said, but, what's really wrong with the Air Force's basic missile warning capabilities?"

"From what I know, and unofficially, the intelligence community didn't want NORAD messing around in technologies it didn't understand, let alone in evaluating raw data. As you'll find out, there's a *lot* of pissing around on each other's organizational fences in this world. Everyone's always trying to one-up everyone else and think they're more important than the next guy. Organizations are so damned compartmentalized that no one really knows what the other is doing, and, yes, not that I know everything, only a handful of people do—way, way above us—but there does happen to occasionally be a duplication of effort. But They Who Has the Big Bucks gets their way, especially cause no one trusts anyone else. And DEFSMAC does deal with a little more than the Air Force's standard missile warning centers."

"All right…"

"But *nobody* does what we do. Nobody. We're it. We're all watching the Earth to make sure no one blows it up, are the final call, and I'm all for as many agencies as it takes to keep that from happening. We all are."

"Can't argue with that," Cherko said.

"One other thing. It's standard operating procedure that from time to time we have…'guests.' Said 'guests' come from other organizations-to-remain-nameless, looking for and giving special tasks to our unit. Whichever operator is chosen by these guests is not to ask any questions, make any small talk, and are to do exactly as directed. All other operators on duty are not to give them the time of day while these 'guests' are on the floor. Which means keeping your nose glued to your own beeswax and workstation. We also call them something else, which is never to be uttered in their presence, though we secretly think they like the term. We call them 'spooks.'

"Got it?"

His face emotionless, Cherko nodded. "Yes."

"Okay, that's the overview. We are *the* premier space watch organization. There is no better, all due respect to PARCS."

Cherko snorted.

"Ready for training?"

"You bet."

4

Clad in sweats and work-out bag slung over his shoulder, Jimmy made his way to the Holiday Health Club. He entered through the main doors and was immediately immersed into the sound of loud rock music blaring over speakers. All his isolation, of being alone and working out at a remote North Dakota unit, and now at an installation that wasn't even completely built yet, faded into the background. The high-energy music got his blood pumping and made him feel *human* again, part of the Human Race.

Cherko approached the front desk.

"Hi," he said to the muscled twenty-year-old on the other side.

"How can I help you, Buddy?" the guy asked, all tanned, ripped, and cocky.

"I'd like to check out your gym," Cherko said, taking in the familiar sights, sounds, and smells. For the eighteen months he'd been in North Dakota, he'd worked out in a thrown-together empty gymnasium in which he was frequently the only one using it. He'd even had to order his own Power Rack. He hadn't worked out among people since he left space training, at Lowey AFB, in Denver, two years ago.

"No problem. Let me get someone to show you around."

Cherko nodded, and turned away. He checked out their protein retail, pictures, and lobby trophies.

"May I help you?" came a female voice.

Cherko turned to land his gaze directly into the familiar deep, dark eyes of Erica Taylor.

"You *work* here?"

Erica smiled a wide, clearly-glad-to-see-him open-mouthed smile.

"Glad to see you took me up on my recommendation."

Cherko smiled nervously, looked away, then back to her.

Again found he couldn't bear to look away from her.

"Nice to see you do as you're told," she added, crossing her arms and shifting her weight from one foot to the other.

"What can I say? I'm a sucker for a pretty face."

"Well, we'll see about that. Come on...lemme show you around."

"I'm sure you will," Cherko said under his breath, which, he found, surprisingly, suddenly came up short...

Cherko and Erica sat across from each other at a table in a Village Inn. It was dark outside their window, and the remains of dinner sat before them.

"So, what do you really want to be when you grow up?" Erica asked, playfully twisting a paper napkin.

Cherko looked out the window past his reflection.

"I'd always really wanted to be an astronaut. I grew up on *Star Trek*, and *Space: 1999*, and all that."

"What about space is so interesting? I mean, don't you think it'd be lonely?"

"Well, it's not like it *happened* for me, but I guess I never thought about that. I just thought about being part of all that high technology and exploration. Adventure. Going where no man—or woman—has gone before, kinda thing. I've just always felt drawn there."

"Drawn *where?*"

"To *space*. I don't know. I always felt like it was my calling. That something was calling me there." He gazed out the window and into the darkness.

Erica looked down to her now tightly twisted napkin. It abruptly came apart in her hands.

"What do you want to be when you grow up?" Cherko asked.

Erica shrugged, looking down to her torn-in-two napkin.

"I've always been fascinated with humans and their wacky behavior."

Cherko smirked. "Oh, uh-huh...."

Erica laughed, looking up.

"Yeah—I'm an *alien*, Lieutenant, sent here to keep an eye on you."

Erica gazed into Cherko's eyes. Cherko met her gaze.

"Really."

His foot found one of Erica's under the table. She didn't move away.

"*Wow*," Erica said, breathlessly, looking away. She swiped at stray strands of hair and cleared her throat.

"What's the matter," Cherko asked, reaching out to her.

Erica was about to say something, when she abruptly paused. Cherko took a more solid hold of her hand. So beautiful, so *elegant*.

"I..."

Embarrassed and realizing what he'd done, Cherko pulled away.

"No, no, don't...don't do that," Erica said softly. She maintained eye contact.

Cherko looked to her, his hand paused partway across the table. He regrasped her hand, and Erica grasped him back....

Chapter Five

1

First Lieutenant Jimmy Cherko stood before a closed door.

"This is where your life is about to forever change, Lieutenant. You can never go back."

Jimmy looked to the man. He felt off…like something wasn't right. Hell, *Jimmy* felt off…

A door.

A common enough looking door. Was the whole situation metaphorical enough for him? Surreal?

Open this door and step out into a new life.

Would he like it?

Wish he'd never opened it?

Change his mind?

The man, the one he currently found himself staring at, a major—his boss (why was he having so much difficulty *thinking*)? Had to be, yeah, that's right. His boss. Major—

"Take a picture, Lieutenant, it'll last longer," the now-grinning man said. "You can still back out—there's still time. But, once you open that door there's no turning back. Make your decision, L-T. I can assure you…it'll be life changing. *Belief* changing.…"

Jimmy looked back to the door.

Did he want his life to change?

Could he handle it?

Grow up and be a man, for Chrissakes.

Jimmy reached for the door and

Seven-year-old Jimmy Cherko stood up on a hill behind his house looking out into the woods before him. It was warm and sunny. He liked the way the sunlight reached down through the leafy trees and hit the moist, dark, north country soil. Heard a woodpecker banging on a tree off somewhere deep in the woods. Breezes rustled tree and brush. The air warm.

Jimmy blinked.

Deer!

If they'd been snakes they would have bitten him, his dad would have said, but there they were, right in front of him. Deer have a way of blending in, his dad also said. Their coats, the terrain. Sometimes you'd never know any were around you until a startled movement. But, right now, a whole herd of them were in the trees before him. He could have reached out and touched them....

Jimmy blinked again.

Carl and Ritchie. *Penny.*

They now stood before him.

Dang it, they'd scared off the deer!

Carl, Ritchie, and Penny.

Jimmy found a sudden confused chill run through him. It was almost—for a second there—as if he didn't remember *having* siblings. He had dreams like that...where he woke up and wasn't sure where he was...or in the dream something was *one* way, then he woke up and found it *another.* It often confused him.

Scared him.

Carl, Ritchie, *and* Penny.

That's what it felt like now.

"So, why are you looking at me like that," Jimmy asked them. "Are we gonna play, or what?"

They leapt at him in unrestrained glee, shouting and laughing and dancing around him, pushing and pulling.

"*C'mon,*" Carl said, "Let's go exploring! It's cool up here! I like this place!"

"Yeah! Hey—what's that thing over there?" Penny asked. She held Ritchie's three-year-old hand and pointed to a round gray metal structure back in the trees.

"I don't know," Carl said, "but let's go look!"

Carl, Ritchie, and Penny turned and headed off toward the structure. As Jimmy followed, he continued looking for the now-spooked deer, no-doubt now grazing elsewhere. Jimmy's dad also used to say how, though you could never see them, bucks would always be not too far away. Watching.

Always watching.

Jimmy followed his siblings, but as he followed them deeper into the strange new world before them, after having moved here last year, he looked off to his right, and saw his mother.

Just standing there.

Looking at him.

Sad.

Was this one of her "sleepwalking" episodes again, only during the day?

And there, behind her...a doe. Looking straight at his mom. Jimmy had to close his eyes and look away to avoid being smacked across the face by a low branch, but he swore the deer nudged his mom from behind. When he looked back the doe was gone.

As Jimmy continued trudging his way through the woods, snapping small branches underfoot, he noticed something else strange about his mother.

It was snowing around her.

Lieutenant Jimmy Cherko sprang fully awake and upright in bed.

Where was he?

He quickly swung his legs around the edge of the bed and stood, groggily rubbing at his eyes. Tried to bring his surroundings into focus.

Where the hell was he?

An Air Force flight cap. On the dresser.

Air Force.

A wave of regret and nostalgia washed over him.

He was no longer in Lake Clear. No longer in the company of his siblings and mother....

He was all grown up and working for the government. At his new assignment.

He sat back down on the bed, head heavy in hands; continued to rub the sleep from his eyes.

Wake up and be a man.

2

Unknown Location, Colorado
6 November 1985
0215 Hours Mountain Time

Cherko sat before the sine-wave training workstation, *psyched.* He had just—*simultaneously*—flattened *five* sine waves?

"Wow!"

"Excellent, Lieutenant," came his instructor's gentle voice. "Your next lesson is to simultaneously flatten various combinations of sine waves. As each box is highlighted, you are to flatten it.

"Begin."

Boxes two and seven illuminated. The tones associated with both filled his head. Cherko focused on them and easily flattened both.

Boxes one, six, and ten illuminated.

Cherko focused on their different tones. He managed to affect ten's wave first, then saw the other two slowly come around.

As Cherko performed his lessons he noticed an odd side affect. It seemed he knew what was coming before his disembodied voice directed him. As he continued with his lesson, he thought *What do you look like?*

Not as you expect.

Cherko pushed away from the console.

Are you really replying to me, or am I making this up?

Your answer is self-evident. Please refocus.

Cherko flattened all three lines.

Your mastery is exceptional.

I really like your voice. Could you continue using it?

"We shall now accelerate," the soft voice said out loud. "Attempt seven."

Seven sine waves highlighted. As Cherko attempted this, his mind felt as if it was being put through a rigorous, though exhilarating, workout. He felt as if new...*channels*...were being opened—*created*—inside him. Or, perhaps not so much *created*, as...

Reawakened?

Suddenly Cherko, on impulse, forced all ten sine waves on his screen to simultaneously flatten.

Then he caused two, four, seven, and nine to move to different frequencies. Played with the *degree* of flattening with all ten waves. Manipulated their phases.

This was child's play.

He stared at the screen in utter disbelief; reached out to the screen and touched it.

He had to be dreaming.

"That will be all for this session," the voice said abruptly.

Cherko's screen went dark, and the chamber's lighting immediately dimmed.

Cherko shot to his feet.

"What? I do something wrong?" he asked, chuckling, laughing, looking about the room. "Hey, c'mon! I'm *sorry*! It just...it just *happened*...."

Silence.

Cherko felt around inside himself. There was something different in there, something...powerful. And it scared him...but at the same time, made him feel...

Special.

He was the first, She/It had told him so. The *first*.

He had unique abilities. Others would follow.

For what?

In a pensive haze, Cherko retrieved his jacket from the seatback of his chair, turned, and shrugged. Entered the elevator.

Powerful and special.

Could be a great shot of confidence—just when he really needed some—or a deadly combination he would be unable to handle and surely regret.

What really was happening to him? What was he being trained for...and, perhaps more importantly—

What was he becoming?

3

ERO Operations Center
12 December 1985
1930 Hours Mountain Time

"Okay, good run," Captain Ronnie Morrow, Cherko's trainer, said, as he exited the break room. "Now we're gonna show you some really cool stuff."

Cherko perked up. He also noticed a "guest" stood behind an operator at the far end of the room. He hadn't been there just moments ago when they'd entered the break room.

"Gonna show me what's behind those black hoods?" Cherko asked.

Morrow nodded. He also noticed the guest. "This is the highest classification of our job. Most of those outside this floor have no idea about this stuff. This is what gives our classification its codeword designation and to which you will now be in-briefed. The only personnel cleared for this part of our mission are the operators, the Director of Operations, the trainers and evaluators. And, now...you."

Morrow brought out a folder with a TOP SECRET/CODEWORD cover sheet on top. "You are not allowed to speak the codeword unless absolutely necessary, and only in properly cleared company and environments, of which this ops floor and its Situation Room are the only cleared areas. I have been told there is one other cleared area back east, but I wasn't authorized to know where. Read this briefing and notify me when you're done."

Morrow directed Cherko to an empty console. As Cherko sat, he noticed the on-duty operators glance toward him. He opened the folder.

Images of a desert filled his head.

Sun, heat, and glare...

Something red.

A ship's prow...*in the desert...*

A *crash.*

No other images followed, so he dug into his briefing.

A ship out in the middle of a desert? Where did he come up with this shit?

After reading the briefing, Cherko replaced the cover sheet and approached Morrow.

"Done?"

"Yup," Cherko said. "Pretty heavy warnings."

"Sign this. It's the form that puts your signature to what you just read. It says if you ever breathe a word of what you're about to see—even if somebody writes a book about it—before you die, you're going away for a long, long time. If you're so lucky."

Yeah, the threats on this form couldn't hold a candle to what he'd signed earlier.

Cherko signed the form.

"Okay. Ready to see the coolest part of the job?"

Cherko smiled. "I just hope it's more than missile warning."

Morrow led him over to their training area. "Have a seat."

Cherko again sat at his console. Morrow removed the black covering. Cherko stared into a black screen.

"I don't see anything," he said.

"Hold your horses," Morrow said, and hit another set of selections on a different part of the console on which Cherko had not yet been trained. Cherko watched as the display apparently *swung over* to an image of the Earth.

A *picture* of it.

Not a graphic representation of the Earth, not an artificial representation, but an actual telemetered, video-fed, real-time black-and-white on-orbit *image.*

"You're kidding," Cherko said. "This real time?"

Morrow nodded. "This is an actual real-time feed from about two-hundred miles up."

"No kidding," Cherko said, pulling himself in closer to the console. He stared wide-eyed into the display. "A real-time on-orbit view of Earth."

"And that's not all," Morrow added. He hit another red-glowing selection switch, which changed the display to show a distant object glinting on the screen.

Cherko stared, speechless.

"Watch this."

Morrow now used the trackball and keyboard. Cherko watched as the display slowly filled in with the image of a satellite, in crisp, mightily zoomed-in fashion.

"This is actually one of our own that we're looking at," Morrow said, casually checking out the satellite, zooming around, up and down, in and out.

"So," Cherko said, still staring at the screen in amazement, "we're spying on our own satellites?"

Morrow chuckled. "It's a little more than that, and you'll be briefed as we train, but, right now…yeah."

"Holy shit."

Cherko looked to the other operators who had now removed all their black cowlings from their displays, and nodded to him. One gave a Thumbs-up. The one with the spook never even looked over, and had already had his cowling removed.

"And with this, you are now officially in the Secret Handshake of Handshakes Club," Morrow said, backing away from the console. "So, now you know our deepest darkest, so let's train you on how it all works, and what it's all about."

Before Morrow could say another word, an alarm sounded, which was quickly stabbed off by the operator with the spook. Morrow quickly focused all his attention on the far console. Though the alarm was silenced, several red lights continued to blink on that operator's workstation. Cherko looked to the clock, which read 0310 Zulu, or 2010 Mountain. Then he looked to the nearest console display, but didn't see anything. As if in a daze, he got up and headed toward the console with the flashing lights. As he got closer, he saw all kinds of motion on various displays. The other operators were adjusting and using their trackballs at their workstations, and Morrow was caught up in their activities. He did not see Cherko, but the operator whom Cherko approached did.

"Captain—we need him out of here!"

Cherko stopped as if slapped awake. He looked to Morrow, just short of terrified. When Cherko looked back to the operator before him, he saw he'd swiveled his line-of-sight real-time video feed away from its target and glared at him.

"Jimmy, you need to come with me—*now*," Morrow said.

Cherko had never heard that tone in his voice before.

"*Now*, Lieutenant."

Cherko backed away from the consoles, looked to the spook who was now looking directly at him. He managed to get one more sidelong glance at another console as he left. He saw something move swiftly across a corner of the screen.

"And do *not* look at any more displays!" Morrow shouted, hurrying Cherko into the adjacent Break Room by getting between him and the console-of-interest. Morrow quickly closed the door.

"*Jimmy*," Morrow said, his tone still thick with intensity, "*don't ever do that again.* Until you are properly briefed and given access to this information, there are still some things you are not yet cleared to see. When I—or anyone else—asks you to leave, you need to do so *promptly* and *smartly*—and without sneaking peeks to displays—*do you understand me?*"

Cherko nodded, nervously, confused. "I'm—I—"

"Sorry doesn't cut it in this world, Jimmy, I can't emphasize that enough." Morrow lowered his voice and came in closer. "I know people who have literally *disappeared* seeing things they weren't meant to see."

Cherko now saw how truly nervous Morrow was.

Could that have been his predecessor's unexpected and abrupt "PCS"? The sudden need to fill the now-vacated billet?

Cherko wiped his forehead. Looked to the closed door behind him.

"Geez, I wish you hadn't done that." Morrow looked back to him. "I'm gonna need you to go into the Situation Room and wait, okay?"

"Am I in big trouble?"

"Enough, but not unsalvageable." He sighed, "You are in training for these operations, but you weren't briefed or trained for what happened in there. I'll get stomped on, since I should've been paying attention to you, but I'll survive. I just need you to make sure you follow direction when told to clear a room. *Got it?*"

"Sorry. I didn't mean to—"

"I know, I know—it'll be all right. Just be honest about what you saw, and why you looked, okay? You'll be polyed again, but just be honest about everything."

"Okay."

"Let me check to see if things've died down, so we can make our way to the Situation Room."

Morrow quickly exited the Break Room for the Ops floor, then just as quickly, ducked his head back in.

"Let's go. Stay between me and the wall, and do *not*—I repeat, *not*—attempt to look anywhere else besides your feet beating it out of the Ops floor. Do I make myself clear? Keep your eyes planted to your feet and the floor."

"Yes, sir."

"Let's go."

Morrow backed up and announced "Trainee on the Floor!," keeping a close eye on Cherko, who did as he was instructed as they headed out. The spook again unflinchingly eyed Cherko the entire time he exited. Once out in the hallway, Morrow directed Cherko to the Situation Room.

"Now, head in there, and I'll be in in a minute."

Morrow disappeared back into the Ops floor.

4

Cherko had been nervously pacing the floor of the Situation Room when a master sergeant and another captain entered the room. No Morrow.

"Have a seat, Lieutenant," the captain said.

Cherko sat.

"We understand you might have seen some things you weren't meant to see," the captain, whose name plate read "Burton," said.

"Apparently."

"Okay, say nothing else until we tell you, okay?"

Cherko nodded.

The sergeant, whose name he couldn't see from where he sat, quietly set a briefcase on the table before him. Opened it. He removed electrodes attached to wires, what looked like a blood pressure cuff, and some long tube-looking thing; flicked some switches.

"All right, Lieutenant, what we need to do is find out exactly what it was you think you saw, why you looked, and as we do this we're going to hook you up to a poly to make sure you're not lying, okay?"

Cherko cleared his throat. "Okay."

"Now, no need to be nervous, you've already been polyed and know the drill. We know this is a stressful situation, so we're gonna make sure we calibrate extra careful."

Burton got up and put the chest tube, fingertip electrodes, and blood pressure cuff on Cherko. As Cherko was outfitted for the poly, he eyed the sergeant making adjustments to the equipment. After a once-over, the captain returned to his side of the table.

"I'm gonna ask you a series of questions, to which you are going to reply a simple 'Yes' or 'No.' There are no multiple choice answers. Understand?"

Cherko nodded.

"Let's begin. Your name is James Francis Cherko?"

"Yes."

Cherko noticed the sergeant jotting something down at the machine as he answered.

"You're a first lieutenant in the United States Air Force?"

"Yes."

Again the sergeant jotted something down. It looked like he was marking the tape as he answered questions.

"You're a woman?"

"No."

"You've been in the military twenty years?"

"No."

"You work at FAFS?"

"Yes."

"You work for ERO?"

"Yes."

"You are currently in training?"

"Yes."

"You have an elevated security clearance and access?"

"Yes."

"You saw something tonight?"

"No—I mean…yes."

This time the sergeant took a little longer marking the poly tape that was now growing and overflowing the suitcase and over the edge of the conference table.

"You like little girls?"

"What?"

"Yes or no, Lieutenant."

"No! What does that—"

"You've given secrets to the Soviets?"

"No!"

"You looked at the display in question tonight to give those secrets to the Soviets?"

"No—"

Cherko shot to his feet. "What the hell's going on here? These questions have no bearing on what happened!"

"Sit down, please, Lieutenant," the captain said calmly, "and just answer the questions."

Cherko looked to his interrogators, who merely looked back as calmly as if they'd asked for a glass of water.

"Sit down, Lieutenant," the captain again requested.

Cherko sat; felt his temperature rise and his palms and underarms sweat. Wiped the growing moisture from his forehead with the back of the hand that had all the electrodes attached to the fingers.

"Please don't do that," the captain said.

The pair attended to their machine, the captain taking a quick glance to the poly, then the connections on the hand just used, before continuing.

"You currently reside at Templeton Park Apartments, #222, Colorado Springs, Colorado?"

"I do—yes."

"You saw nothing tonight?"

Cherko had to think. "No."

"You saw something?"

"Yes."

"You're having sex with Erica Taylor?"

Cherko gave the captain a hard look, which was equally and calmly matched by the captain.

"No."

"You want to have sex with Ms. Taylor?"

"Yes."

"You looked when asked to look away because you're a Soviet spy?"

"No." Cherko bored into the captain, who now just casually looked to his list of questions.

"You are a Soviet spy?"

"No."

"You want to be a Soviet spy?"

"No."

"Do you like your current profession?"

"No."

"You know what it was you saw tonight?"

"No."

"You're lying to us tonight?"

"No."

"You know what it was you saw tonight?"

"No."

"You pick up prostitutes and have anal sex with men and women?"

"No."

"You like sex?"

"Yes."

"You do not intend to sell the secrets that you've been trained in to the Soviets, and you do not know what you saw tonight?"

Cherko scrunched his face as he paused and ran the question over in his head.

"Correct."

The captain shot him a look.

"When you last had sex with an animal, did you like it?"

Again Cherko paused, again glaring at the captain. "No."

The captain and the sergeant fiddled a little more with the poly. The captain jotted more notes, then passed a sheet of paper over to the sergeant. He then looked to his watch and the clock, jotted the time, and closed the file folder before him.

"Thank you, Lieutenant, we'll get back to you."

The captain immediately began disconnecting Cherko from the poly leads, while the sergeant carefully collected all the loose spool-paper and tucked it into the case. The sergeant then switched off the equipment, closed up his machine, and without looking to the captain, got to his feet. Both the captain and the sergeant exited the Situation Room. Cherko remained seated and rubbed his hands together before him. Sweat ran down his armpits and into the sides of his trousers like Niagara Falls. He wiped away rivulets of sweat that continued to sheet off his face, looked to the moisture on his hands, and wiped them on his pants legs.

Jesus fucking Christ.

Morrow met Captain Burton on the Ops floor. The spook stood directly behind him.

"He knows nothing," Burton said. "Send him home. He's had enough for tonight."

Cherko repeatedly hit the steering wheel of his car as he paused at the intersection of Enoch and 94.

Bastards.

You'd have thought he'd handed national security secrets over to the Russians, or something.

Oh, wait, they already asked that.

The lifestyle poly he'd taken up in North Dakota had been embarrassing enough (including that little piss-test and Captain Marchuk who had to actually *watch* his dick as he pissed into that bottle), but he knew that was coming and had nothing to hide. But *this* was a total and utter blindside after he'd thought he'd seen something he wasn't supposed to have seen. Dammit, he knew better!

What the hell had he been thinking?

In a civilian court of law, you were innocent until proven guilty, but, apparently, there was no such thing in the military.

And that highlighted another issue—*he no longer worked for the Air Force?*

He now worked for some agency of which he'd never heard? An agency whose name he couldn't *utter*, not even its *initials?*

Wearing the Air Force uniform, of which he was proud and had labored long and hard to get where he was, yet doing the work of *another* agency.

Sounded like "spy" to him.

A *space* spy.

Cherko took a left onto Highway 94, heading home. Continuing to pounding the steering wheel, he couldn't shake the images from tonight and unleashed an unrestrained torrent of expletives that would surely cast him into something resembling a Purgatory.

But he *had* seen something, goddammit.

He wasn't sure what it was, but it had been swift and small, and it had scurried across that display like a bolt out of the blue.

Cherko took a right onto Curtis Road.

Frick! Wrong turn!

Cherko slowed down.

What the hell, Curtis would get him home, too.

He pushed back down on the accelerator.

Whatever it was he saw or thought he saw, it must have been something important enough to elicit the attention it had. So it must have been some super-secret government project...but it could also very well have been nothing *he* saw, but something else.

All he saw was what he saw.

It could have been a cursor that had moved quickly across the display, a deorbiting or transfer-orbit satellite, even a meteoroid. Could have been anything—heck, even a UFO.

But whatever it was, he'd sure felt as if he'd had his head handed to him on a silver platter...

Lake Clear, New York
11 July 1974

Thirteen-year-old Jimmy Cherko took the hard-plastic action figures with him up into the barn, back behind the house. It was a late overcast summer day. Rain threatened. The barn was large, painted red with white trim, and had been built in the 1880s. It leaned slightly to one side, but remained solid enough. Jimmy hurried up the creaking stairs into the dark loft.

There was but one window, up high on the opposite side of the loft, and a haying doorway opposite, by where he presently stood. The overcast sky darkened the interior of the loft into a creepy, hazy, twilight. Dust particles danced in the wide beam of what sunlight streamed in onto the planked floor before him. His steps across the uneven and loose floor planks also creaked as he made his way to the end of the loft under that window.

There he sat cross-legged, setting up the Gold and Silver Knight action figures.

A little taller than his G.I. Joes, they were medieval knights one of his brothers and he had gotten for Christmas a couple years ago. They came with knightly steeds, and all their accompanying armor, swords, shields, lances, et cetera. He'd had the Gold Knight, while his next youngest brother, Carl, had had the silver one. As with most toys, the knights had faded away into the disuse pile, and while digging around in that pile, Jimmy had found them and had decided to play with them...and try something he just couldn't seem to get out of his head. An urge he'd decided to act out, once and for all.

Jimmy set both knights up in their armor, giving both lances and shields, which he'd previously hidden up here with their horses earlier in the day, and set them about to jousting. Of course, being partial to Gold Knight, the Silver Knight constantly lost. He was just no match for the Might of Gold.

After being roundly defeated by Gold Knight not once, but several times, the two took the fighting to the ground, and by sword. Only twice had Gold Knight been bested, but this last time Gold Knight swept his feet under Silver Knight, dropping him to the medieval barn floorboards. Silver Knight's sword fell from his *Quick-Draw* action grip. Gold Knight quickly got to his feet, grabbed his sword, and prepared to again face off against his opponent.

Silver Knight also got back to his feet, and Gold Knight allowed him the honor of retrieving his dropped weapon.

Honor in combat as well as in peace. That was Gold Knight's way.

The same, unfortunately, couldn't be said of Silver Knight.

The battle continued, Silver Knight's attacks matched blow-for-blow by Gold Knight. The dual went on long into the darkening afternoon. Finally, Gold Knight had had enough. It was time to finish off this cat-and-mouse game.

Silver Knight charged, sword arm upraised. Gold Knight feigned fatigue—but at the last moment, pivoted and swung his sword up and around over his head just in time to slash at the upraised arm.

Jimmy quickly snatched up the double-bit ax he'd also secreted away earlier and with a loud *thump!* lopped off Silver Knight's sword arm.

He then shot to his feet.

Backed away.

Looked to what he'd done to his brother's toy.

The ax momentarily stood upright, stuck into the barn's floorboard planking before it tipped over and clunked onto the floor. On one side of the blade lay one Silver Knight minus three-quarters of its right arm, and on the other side lay the severed arm and sword.

He stared at it.

There was something disturbing about this.

Without touching either, he looked closer at the severing, and saw how there were rings inside the solid plastic of the action figure's arm stump. Just like tree rings.

He settled down onto his knees continuing to examine what he'd done.

No turning back now.

Silver Knight was done for.

Jimmy then shot back to his feet and down the loft's stairs. In the lower section of the barn he rummaged about farm equipment and cans and tool benches. Finding what he wanted, he hightailed it back upstairs. Before heading back to the scene of battle, he went off to his right, to the loft opening, and undid the eyehook latch. Carefully, he peered outside.

Listened for steps up the loft's stairs.

The coast remained clear.

Closing and latching the loft door, he returned to battle, but it was like returning to the scene of a crime.

Jimmy stood above the two downed knights like a circling condor, and set down the paint can and brush. Mesmerized, he looked to the severed arm. He pried open the paint can with the flathead screwdriver from his pocketknife, and grabbed the brush. He painted the severed arm and Silver Knight's stump red, and also added a dash of red down Silver Knight's torso. He set down the brush across the top of the open can.

Jimmy now picked up Gold Knight and brought him to Silver Knight. Gloating over his handy work, Gold Knight watched as Silver Knight moaned in pain; twitched on the ground. Gold Knight was ready to finish him off when Silver Knight—in a surprising act of courage and daring—reached for his sword with his remaining hand and attacked Gold Knight!

Gold Knight was barely able to avoid the killing arc, but it was enough to give Silver Knight a chance to get to his feet. Staggering, Silver Knight feebly charged.

He put up a valiant effort, Silver Knight did, but, in the end, he was simply no match for Gold, as his blood loss accumulated down the side of his body (which Jimmy painted). The scene reminded Jimmy of an old black-and-white LIFE photograph he'd seen in the Saranac Lake Free Library, of a World War II soldier heading toward the reader, his entire left side absolutely drenched in blood.

Gold Knight slashed at Silver Knight's other arm.

Off it, too, was lopped, the hard plastic rattling beside the already severed right arm.

Jimmy painted that, too.

Jimmy didn't know what happened next, but before he knew it, he'd hacked off Silver Knight's legs. And not just totally, but into *pieces*.

It was amazingly easier to do the rest of the job once the first amputation had been committed. He just couldn't stop himself.

He'd started by hacking off only the lower portions of the plastic legs, the calves, and gradually took off succeedingly higher portions of the legs until there was nothing left to amputate. He'd long since stopped painting his handiwork, now lost in the grisly moment with the double-bit ax. He then took off the rest of the arms he'd left behind, hacking the severed pieces in a frenzy of maniacal fascination. Here he'd started with a perfect, full, toy, but had now summarily hacked it to pieces with one of his dad's axes. The carnage lay scattered about at his feet, and into some of the stacked planking against the wall before him.

Then, in his frenzied haze and without thinking, he'd brought the blade down on the neck of Gold Knight.

Jimmy recoiled, the ax raised above him. Tossing the ax into a pile of planking in the shadows behind him, he backed away.

What had he done?

He'd finished off his own champion!

Jimmy fell to his knees before Gold Knight, unable to pull his eyes away. Gold Knight's body lay there, decapitated, the head popped off against stacked boards and slaughtered Silver Knight debris.

Why had he—*what had caused him to mutilate his and his brother's toys?*

Was this something he'd done before?

No.

Was he an evil kid?

No.

Had he enjoyed doing this?

Yes.

Did he want to do it again?

Yes.

Did he want to do it to birds?

No.

Squirrels?

No.

People?

Heck,

(a simple yes or)

no!

Then, why on Earth had he done this? What had caused him to—

He didn't know.

He only knew that it had been an urge he'd felt for some time. Had felt it when looking to his sister, Penny's, Barbie dolls, though he hadn't *done* it. It hadn't been there from the beginning, when Carl and he had opened their beautifully wrapped Christmas presents two years ago, and marveled at how cool they were.

Hadn't been there when they'd had so much fun playing with them the past couple years. Hadn't been there when they actually highly prized them as toys...

But somewhere along the way, the urge had risen...softly at first, quietly...only to have grown to the point where he felt he could no longer put it off, and had to *see*, had to actually *put that powerful urge into action* and see what it would do...what it would look like, how *toys* would look...when mutilated and hacked to pieces.

Decapitated.

Now he knew.

He picked up a body part and examined it. Part of Silver Knight's upper thigh.

Picked up Gold Knight's head.

Both had those plastic "tree rings" inside them. He set them down and got to his feet. Slowly he picked up the ax; hefted it loosely in his grip. He towered above the two mutilated action figures at his feet. His mind was blank, his heart, blank, his soul...*blank.*

No whys nor wherefores, he'd simply done what he'd done. Before he realized it, he'd again swung the ax above him and made frenzied, short work of Gold Knight, as well....

Chapter Six

1

Curtis Road, East of Colorado Springs
12 December 1985
2013 Hours Mountain Time

Fucking *bastards!*

He *had* seen something.

So, what had been the big hairy deal, anyway? He'd already had the program accesses, why the grilling? Heck, he was even in the process of being *trained* in this shit, for crying out loud! Whatever he'd seen, it hadn't been all that much and would learn about shortly. Why not simply debrief him and be done with it? Move on. But *no*....

Cherko's car slowed. He gunned the engine, but it only sputtered. Cherko pulled over onto the shoulder and glanced to the fuel gauge.

Empty!

Bone dry. The indicator was pegged all the way to the left, beyond "E."

"Shit!"

The car knocked a few times before completely shutting down.

"God*damn* it!"

How the hell had he forgotten to fill the tank?

Furious, he looked behind him.

Nothing but darkness. Out in the middle of fricking nowhere.

"Now, what the hell am I supposed to do?"

Cherko looked to the clock. Quarter after ten p.m. He exited his vehicle.

And he had that van to catch that would pick him up in less than two hours.

"Wonderful. Juuust wonderful...."

Walking into the center of the lane, he stood there, hands on hips, burning a hole of pure rage out into the darkness.

He was probably about fifteen miles from his apartment. He just had to start walking, is all. Eventually he'd hit Highway 24, where he could bum a ride.

A light appeared down the road.

A car. From the direction of Falcon.

Cherko walked back over to the shoulder.

Could be a sheriff or deputy highway patrol cruiser, or maybe even someone from the site.

The twin headlights soon made their way to him, and slowed down. Cherko listened to the sound of rubber crunching roadside debris as the vehicle rolled up alongside. The passenger-side window rolled down.

"What seems to be the matter, Lieutenant?"

It was that sergeant from his interrogation. Fucking A.

Cherko cleared his throat. "Car trouble."

The sergeant held his gaze.

"Having a rough time of it tonight."

Cherko briefly looked back to his car.

"Get in."

Cherko nodded and went back to his car, retrieving his bag. He turned on his hazards and locked his vehicle, then went to the sergeant's car. As they left the shoulder, he looked into the rear view and watched his car recede away into the darkness.

And felt an odd, incomprehensible sense of *longing*....

2

Cherko lay in bed, the bedroom's blinds closed.

God, he had a headache.

He shot up to an elbow.

Had he made his other training?

He lay back down.

He had to have, though he seemed somewhat confused at the moment....

And there was...he'd *seen* something, hadn't he—yeah, that's right, he'd seen something at *work*—

He glanced to the clock just before closing his eyes. Almost seven. Everyone was waking up and preparing to go about their caffeinated day, yet here he was in the enviable position of actually sleeping through the normal work day.

Yes, he remembered. He'd seen something at work he wasn't supposed to have seen. Had been interrogated *because* of it.

Yeah, a great night at work.

But, okay, given his oath and debrief to never talk about what had happened, he'd never given an oath to never *think* about what had happened.

What had he seen? What had been on those screens?

There had been something on one of the displays that had set off alarms, something that had been flying around in orbit above Earth. He hadn't gotten a clean look at it, but it must have been something pretty gnarly for him to have been so ruthlessly grilled like so much steak. He'd heard of recent tests involving anti-satellite weaponry.

Or it could have been a—

Cherko shot back upright.

How had they known about Erica?

The phone rang.

What now? Were "they" employing further mind-fuck techniques and going to call him back into work to further dick around with him?

He grabbed the phone.

"Hello?"

"Hi," came the soft female voice. "It's me."

Cherko sighed.

"What's the matter?"

"Oh, I'm fine. Just had a rough night last night."

"I thought I'd heard you rattling around over there. Wasn't sure if I should call."

"I really just had a hard night, is all. I'm okay."

"Can I come over?"

"I'm in bed."

"Can I come over?"

"Sure."

The phone clicked and Cherko rolled out of bed, making his way to the door. He peered out the peephole to see Erica already standing before his door, clad in sweats. Her arms were crossed against the cold, unkempt hair cascading about her shoulders and lightly touched by a soft breeze.

"Hi," she again greeted, as he opened the door. "You okay?" She reached out to his face.

Cherko grinned, nodded, and allowed her in. Erica came to him, kissing him gently on the lips. Then she wrapped her arms around him and Cherko just stood there, exhausted.

"Come on," Erica whispered, "let's get you back into bed."

Erica and Jimmy went into the bedroom, where Jimmy slipped back in between the sheets. Erica snuggled in alongside.

"So…it was pretty bad?" she asked, whispering.

"Nothing happened."

They *knew* about Erica…

What else did they know? What else *could* they know?

Cherko kissed her. Erica said nothing, spooning up behind him. She lightly touched his hair.

How had they known about her?

He'd never told anyone. They'd only been together a little more than a month.

And of course he loved sex. Who didn't? Of course he wanted to be with her—was that a state secret?

Cherko took hold of one of Erica's arms, brought it in tighter, then lifted it to his mouth and kissed it. He paused, then turned around into her. Cherko again kissed her. Erica studiously traced the outline of his face, ending up at his lips. This time Erica planted a long, lingering, open-mouthed kiss.

Cherko's headache quickly dissipated, as Erica slid on top of him, straddling him with her strong, beautiful legs.

To hell with them if they found out about this, too....

3

Lake Clear, New York
25 December 1974

Fourteen-year-old Jimmy Cherko snowshoed through the hard and softwoods of the back forty of their property. Wisps of dancing snow crystals pirouetted across barren and snowpacked landscape. It was late, and he'd had a fun afternoon playing around with his brand new Iverson's snowshoes, exploring the heavily snow-packed woods. The air was crisp and cold, and Jimmy loved being alone. The sound of his crunching about on his shellacked wood and leather snowshoes comforting. But the clouds were getting heavier, and it had again begun to snow. The late afternoon light grew steely gray.

He stopped, listening to the cracking and splitting of timber. The laboring of his breath. Watched his breath puff up about him like frigid ghosts; noticed his breath only came out of one nostril. Breathing in this freezing weather through his nose froze his nose hairs, mildly shocked his lungs. He breathed a little heavier.

Yep, only one nostril.

Weird. He never noticed that before; have to talk to Mom about it.

But, what if he wasn't alone? What if he really was being watched?

The snow came down thicker, the temperature quickly plummeted. What late winter light there was quickly disappeared...

The snow was heavier now, and it lent a distinct hushed sensation to the woods. A calming...coziness. He could even hear it hit the ground and trees all around him.

Cherko came up on a spot he'd come to call "Devil's Den," from the Gettysburg battlefield spot of the same name. It was a huge boulder balanced atop another extrusion of rock, both of which were now heavily covered in snow. Why he called it that was long ago lost to him, since it really didn't look anything like the actual battlefield location. But, it *was* rocky.

He paused.

Again looked up into the heavy, drab, skies. Blinked against the large falling flakes as they lit upon his face. It was absolutely magnificent. Peaceful. He could curl up in its snowy blankets and fall sleep within it.

Cherko looked back from where he'd come. Smiled. Looked to his tracks leading back into the darkening woods. Listened to the cracking and splitting timber. His labored breathing.

Really…what if he *wasn't* alone?

What if he really was being watched by someone?

Some*thing?*

The snowfall was quite heavy; the temperature had dropped to what had to be near zero. What late winter light there was was gone…

Something was wrong!

Though the cold had already penetrated his garments, another chill passed through him.

He looked to his feet. Behind him. Before him.

The only trail was the one he'd made, packed several inches into the snow, yet he'd felt as if he'd already *done* this…already *been* here…already hoofed it up and over at least an acre of land…

But no other tracks.

And it was darker. Later in the day than he felt it should be.

Jimmy stepped up his efforts. Didn't want to get stuck out here in the dark. It wasn't that he didn't know his way around in these woods, he'd explored them plenty, every inch of them, but things not only looked different at night, they also got *colder.* And he didn't want to catch a load of crap from his parents.

Jimmy picked up his pace. There was still plenty of light to make it back in time…

He stopped. Listened to the cracking and splitting of timber. His laboring breath.

What if he wasn't alone?

What if he really was being watched by someone?

Some*thing?*

The heavily falling snow no longer felt comforting, the temperature sharp, biting, and *bone*-cold....

Jimmy again found himself where he'd started. The echoes in the wood around him sounded *different*.

He began to sweat; broke out into an all-out snowshoe sprint.

Something was holding him back! Coming for him!

Frozen branches slapped and stung his face like whipping wire. Tears sprouted from his eyes.

He had to get home!

It was only a short fifteen-minute jaunt, but his legs grew weak, noodley. The cold bitter and biting. He snapped trees branches as he plowed into the darkness...

He stopped. Listened to cracking and splitting timber. Laboring breath.

What if he wasn't alone?

What if he really was being watched by someone?

*Some*thing?

It was dark and freezing. Frozen sweat coated his skin. His toes and fingers numb.

He felt as if the night was closing in around him like some enormously hungry unseen evil entity.

Where was he?

What was happening!

Emotion welled up uncontrollably. Cherko cried, but did the only thing he could do.

He *again* took off in another sprint...

But, no sooner had he taken flight, when he was knocked on his butt after having run full throttle into a tree, a branch tearing into his face. Quickly pulling off a glove, he scrambled for the wound. Thanked God for not having taken an eye. Shoving his hand back into the glove, he got back to his feet. More carefully, he tearfully picked his way through the thickening darkness.

What was happening? *Why couldn't he make it home?*

The sounds in the distant woods were no longer friendly nor comforting. He'd really wished he'd brought a flashlight. It felt very late.

Increasingly exhausted, Jimmy bumped his way to what felt like Devil's Den—again. Openly sobbing, tears froze on puffy and cut cheeks, Jimmy called out to his dad, his mom, hands constantly windmilling and whipping the darkness before him.

Something *was* coming for him!

"Daddy!"

But his bawling only landed him right back where he started…and it was definitely below zero, because of that hard Styrofoam-like sound snow got at that temperature.

Again knocked back onto the ground, Cherko didn't even bother to get back up. He lay there, snot bubbles blowing out his nose as he exploded into huge, soul-searing pleads.

It wasn't his Daddy that found him.

Colorado Springs, CO
13 December 1985
0858 Hours Mountain Time

Cherko sat up alone in the darkness, pulse pounding and sweat pouring off him.

He brought a hand to a long-healed scar on his cheek.

He remembered no such scar…

Snow. Darkness. His *dad?*

Dizzily shaking his head, and emitting a long, drawn-out grunt, he swung out of bed and got to his feet; felt the adrenaline drain from his body.

Good *God*, he was exhausted!

Where was he?

What time was it?

He collapsed back down on the edge of his bed, head in his hands and stared at the clock. Nine a.m.

He still had some time left to catch up on sleep. Why was he so tired?

But, it had all felt so *real.*

He got back to his feet and paced the room. Went out into the kitchen.

The dream was fading fast…something about snow…*snowshoeing?* The Lake Clear house.

Running?

Cherko got a sip of water. Stared out to the empty poolside area from his kitchen window.

He felt like he hadn't been able to get away from something.

He set down the glass. He *really* needed some sleep.

He headed back into the bedroom. The dream…what was it about the Lake Clear house?

But it hadn't been a dream, had it? It had been something more, something *real.* It had been more of

A memory.

Chapter Seven

1

ERO Operations Center
13 December 1985
1315 Hours Mountain Time

Cherko sat at his training console, slowly swiveling and rocking back and forth in his chair.

Ronnie Morrow was late.

He glanced over to the operators and noticed they were different from yesterday. Yesterday's crop must be on crew rest. At least that was a saving grace from his nose-rubbing embarrassment, but he'd thought they still had a couple days before their rotation was up. In any event, this was good. He only had to deal with his embarrassment with Morrow.

Images of that ship's prow again filled his head.

What the hell was a ship doing out in the middle of a desert?

And a car crash. Lights.

Cherko turned away from those in the ops room; and closed his eyes.

Ship's prow...desert. Hot. Sand. Desert. *Dark*.

Cherko found himself entering the ship...dark, it was dark inside. Blisteringly hot. There was some lighting—but it was still dark....

A shadow in a doorway. They speak.

Gone.

Cherko was now in another place...a building. Air-conditioned. Cool. Computers...mainframe. Programmers, coders...talking to them—*he* was talking to them? A coder showed him her screen (you show me yours, I'll show you *mine*)....

The ops door opened, and Cherko opened his eyes and spun around— as did the certified operators.

Morrow.

"Afternoon!" Morrow hailed cheerfully. He set down training material on the console before him, material covered by Top Secret/SCI cover pages. "How we doin today?"

Cherko looked to him.

"As well as can be expected after having had my head gold-plated and handed to me on a silver platter."

Morrow busied about with the paperwork. Cherko eyed him; noticed one of the crew members glance over to them.

"Okay—you ready for some really cool stuff?" Morrow asked.

Cherko stared at him. "What about...you know—the grilling...the poly—"

"Don't know what you're talking about, Jimmy, but let's move on. This is the most interesting part of the job—"

"But, what about last n—"

"Nothing happened last night," Morrow said, still holding the insanely happy smile on his face.

Out of the corner of his eyes, Cherko again noticed the crew casting glances their way.

"*Nothing* happened, Lieutenant. We had some downtime, you were done early...I sent you home."

"But I s—"

Morrow's look turned dark; piercing.

Cherko looked away toward the on-console crew, who pretended to hear nothing.

"Okaaay..." Cherko finally said, looking back to Morrow. His darkness had departed.

"Good! So, let's get to it! Pull off that hood, and let's rock!"

ERO Operations Center
2 February 1986
0210 Hours Mountain Time

Newly (and highly) qualified 31 January as a certified ERO operator, and assigned to grave shift, Jimmy Cherko sat at the workstation he'd been training at for the past three months. All three screens before him were up and operational. His mission for the scheduled support, his fifth for the shift, was to peek in on another domestic spy satellite. It had been having intermittent problems, and Maryland needed answers yesterday.

Completing initial configuration, Cherko swung the on-orbit telescope across deep space toward the Earth...then paused. Glancing to either side of him using only peripheral vision, he briefly slewed the telescope back half a degree. He sat for a moment just staring out into deep space.

Okay, this wasn't an *astronaut* position, nor was it the Starship *Enterprise*, but like his commander at PARCS had promised, okay, it *was* pretty fricking cool. He was swinging around on-orbit equipment and snooping in on officially and unofficially existent satellites orbiting Earth.

Yeah…pretty sexy.

And what else existed out there? Out there in deep space? Other races? Other *worlds*? Aliens? UFOs?

As a kid in sixty-eight, he remembered watching the newly released *2001: A Space Odyssey* at a Lake Placid, New York movie theater. He'd been seven years old. Up to the showing of the movie and after, his family'd periodically eaten at the Lake Placid *Howard Johnson's*, in that back room with the big plate-glass window, at a long table alongside a fireplace. He remembered all the placemats had color pictures from the movie. The big, dark, monolith. The space station. Poole and Bowman, the astronauts. If he hadn't been grabbed by space and astronauts up to that point, he'd certainly been hooked then.

Now, here he was, not quite an astronaut, but yeah, he was "in orbit," all right, and that was pretty damned cool—and he couldn't tell anyone about it.

Redirecting his telescope-control trackball, Cherko swung the video back in toward Earth, and his target satellite. Behind him, Captain Ronnie Morrow, now also his crew commander (he couldn't seem to get away from this guy!), paced, checking in on all the operators.

"How you doing, Cherko?" Morrow asked.

"We have acquisition, sir," Cherko said, continuing to adjust his controls. "Zooming in now."

Morrow nodded and moved on.

Cherko attained target lock and zoomed in. The distant, extremely shiny object quickly came into a more refined and focused view.

This blew Cherko away.

He was moving around a multi-million dollar piece of hardware in space—real time. Not only the subject, but the very *idea* of doing this fascinated him. These things were orbiting about two-hundred miles, more or less, above…say the distance between the far side of Denver and Falcon AFS. Not very far, indeed, when you thought about it, but, wow, literally a world of difference in view *and* concept.…

As Cherko performed his surveillance, an object appeared on-screen, setting off an alarm. It left the atmosphere for an on-orbit trajectory. Tingling with excitement, Cherko quickly swung over to it. His on-screen telemetry identified it as "Experimental," flagged as an "XP" in telemetry.

"Sir," Cherko said, calling Morrow.

Morrow quickly came up behind him. "Keep to your own screens…," he casually reminded the other operators.

"It appears I have a Bravo Romeo," Cherko said in a low voice.

"You know the drill," Morrow said.

The drill.

Cherko had learned that though each of them had some of the highest clearances, accesses, and need-to-know, it didn't mean they had *all-knowing* program knowledge accesses and clearances. He had been trained that yes, there were astronauts. Astronauts the world knew about…and those *not* talked about. Those testing extremely classified craft—also called "platforms"—that not only involved SR-71s and U-2s, but also went way beyond any Blackbird or Dragon Lady platforms and into the realm of hybrid space vehicles. Whispers of one such vehicle was the Aurora. Morrow had neither confirmed nor denied its existence. And the only reason they had been cleared about any such programs had been because they occasionally ventured into their fields-of-coverage—like now. "Bravo Romeo," stood for "Blue Ribbon." The top-of-the-line sightings of ultra-secret, experimental exoatmospheric test vehicles. And they were only allowed this authorization for whatever they viewed *on their own screens*, not anyone else's, so they were to keep their eyes in their own yard.

And, Morrow, had informed him, they also were granted their needs-to-know because the Air Force didn't want any talk of UFOs. Their need-to-know was so that there would be absolutely *no question whatsoever* as to what they were looking at. The Air Force didn't want UFO rumors in the ranks.

Cherko refined the resolution on his target. Whenever acquired they were to say nothing and just track and record. Silent Sentinels. No headings nor coordinates were to be called out. This could happen several times a shift, or go dry for weeks. You were to just sit at your consoles and emotionlessly do your job. You weren't even supposed to think about—to give any further consideration to—whatever you were looking at.

And that was an order.

But when the day was done, the missions, you always wondered…*what had your coworkers seen?*

It seemed very busy up there. As you went about your life, you did so in amazement at all the heavy upper-atmospheric activity that went on above all our unsuspecting heads each and every day…

So…the "drill."

"Bogie acquired and tracked," Cherko quietly said, as he engaged autotracking on the space telescope.

Morrow nodded and casually walked away.

In situations like this, Cherko had been trained that nothing more would ever be said. He would enter his operator-input keyboard command which would terminate system recording on the current system log and began recording a new one, so that the current system's log tapes could be immediately pulled and shipped back east. Where they went was anyone's guess. Not authorized, G.I. New tapes were hung, and operators were even to log nothing in their classified shift logs.

Classified.

Nothing more was to ever be discussed.

Now, wasn't that strange?

Cherko observed the autotracking of what appeared to be the Aurora, as it skirted the fringes of the Earth's atmosphere. Unofficial crew talk was there were pilots in there. People. Real humans just like them, who flew those things. Unofficial astronauts doing a really cool job but unable to tell anyone, including their spouses. Their officer effectiveness reports never contained any information about their super cool work. All they probably had was some generic statements of "data masked," or a bogus assignment listed, yet they continually got the best and quickest promotions.

Such had once been his dream.

He'd thought he'd been destined to be an astronaut, to be shit-hot in training, able to handle anything and everything thrown at him. Cool as a cucumber in all-things life threatening. A regular DoD 007. Work through the pain, get the job done. But his eyesight had thrown him out of pilot training. He'd asked about correcting his vision, and had been categorically informed that that was entirely out of the question. So he'd entered navigator training, attaining a near-perfect academic average…but was prone to flight sickness and unable to perform mental calculations when called upon. He had been, to his credit, able to work through any "pain" and discomfort to close out in-flight checklists during Barf Bag sessions, but that was far from being an in-flight 007.

But up there right now was some pilot who'd been able to get through pilot training, Fighter Lead-in training, survival training, and had flown jets better than anyone else. So good in fact, he'd been handpicked for this highly coveted assignment dealing with testing hypervelocity platforms. Hybrids that could leave the atmosphere at will—go *orbital*. Technology light years beyond whatever was officially advertised.

And inside it was a living, breathing, *pilot*. Maybe two.

Someone or ones of flesh and bone piloting around the absolutely coolest pieces of hardware *ever*.

Cherko's telescope lost track of the bogie after mere seconds. Whoever that pilot was…was at this very moment…having a ball.

As Cherko took back manual control of his on-orbit telescope, he realized there were all kinds of quiet activity going on on the ops floor. Without appearing too obvious, he glanced about him. Morrow went from one workstation to another…and appeared greatly concerned.

He'd love to play poker with this guy some day.

As Morrow hurried past, Cherko cast an unintended glance up to him, and caught a look of surprise on Morrow's face that was quickly erased. Cherko couldn't help but glance over to Michelson and Fender.

"Dammit, Cherko—knock it off!" Morrow threw over his shoulder as he continued past to another console. "You know the rules!"

Yes. Experienced first-hand. Grilling at the hands of Security and its *do-you-like-little-girls* poly. Oh, yes, he knew the rules. And the more he thought about it, the more he began to wonder…*had that been a training scenario set-up to indoctrinate him, or had it been a real-live event?* Apparently messing around with one's head was not only par for the course, here, but encouraged. And it wasn't like he could ask around.

As Cherko performed his visual inspection of the NSA bird on his screens, he heard quiet dialogue going on at the console closest to him.

"...Mach *15*. It just...*disappeared*. I mean it *accelerated*—"

"I think you had an error there, Lieutenant," Morrow said, quietly. "Recalibrate."

As Cherko completed his pass of the reconnaissance vehicle, he received another bogie indication...but this time said nothing.

He pulled back the field of view of his telescope and saw it. There, in the distance behind his target satellite. He glanced at his range and directional indicators.

Relative heading 305.

Speed...Mach 25.

Cherko stared incredulously into his screen. Again enabled autotrack.

Unlike the so-called Aurora he'd just tracked, this bogie did not register with the mainframe's database. It was tagged on-screen as "XID008."

008?

Cherko watched the bogie slam to a complete stop.

It actually stopped on-orbit.

Paused.

Stopped moving.

Then it changed vector—*it changed its frigging course.*

It not only did the equivalent of a change in velocity, or a Delta-V, but it also changed its *inclination*, or Delta-*I*. Maneuvers like that were impossible with current technology—or so he'd been informed from his space training. That was a lot of fuel and capability that he'd been instructed simply did not yet exist for such maneuvers.

In a burst of incredible, unbelievable speed and maneuverability, the object was suddenly right in the face of the telescope—did a complete course reversal without slowing down—then *another* 180-degree course reversal that brought it back up-close-and-personal.

The object again paused—then bolted completely out of view.

All within *seconds.*

Cherko exploded out of his seat and shot backward several fumbled steps.

"*Cherko!*" Morrow shouted.

Cherko stared at his screen, speechless.

"*Lieutenant!* Get back to your position! *Now,*" Morrow shouted. The other crew members looked to him. Morrow rushed to his side; looked frantically to his screen. He depressed selections. Looked between Cherko and his console.

Cherko stared at Morrow.

"Pick up your chair…and get back into position," Morrow commanded. It definitely sounded like a threat. "Michelson—Fender…bogie acquisitions?"

Michelson and Fender looked back to their consoles, then to each other. "Negative bogie, sir," Michelson finally said.

"Negative acq," Fender chimed in.

Morrow turned back to Cherko. "*What the hell's the matter with you?*"

Cherko returned to his console.

"That was no fucking Aurora," Cherko said. "That was *not* ours."

"Lieutenant—*shut the hell up.*"

"Are you *kidding?* There's no way we can do that!"

"Cherko—*don't make me—*"

"You can poly me all you want, sir, but I know what I saw, and what I saw was in no way some experimental Aurora project or anything else we have."

Michelson and Fender looked to each other, then back to their screens. Cherko caught the look of fear on their faces.

Morrow got directly into Cherko's face.

"Do *not* make me pull you from crew. Do you want that, Lieutenant?" Morrow lowered his voice into a thicker, heavily enunciated, whisper. "*Think about what you're doing.*"

Then he glanced to the others. Morrow edged in still closer, his mouth right up against Cherko's ear. He lowered his voice even more, and what he heard in Morrow's voice caught him off guard. For the first time ever, Cherko heard unmistakable fear in Morrow's always confident manner.

"*You do not know what you're dealing with, man,*" he said. "There are organizations involved…organizations you can only *dream* of…people *disappear. Please,* Jimmy…*walk away from this.*"

Cherko backed up. Paused. Jaw set and grinding, he quietly stepped around Morrow, picked up his chair, and set it upright. He sat back down in it and performed his required procedures—but found that someone else had already entered a "new log" command.

The tape had already been pulled.

"I know what I saw."

Morrow came up behind him. He leaned over his left shoulder, and said, "You. Saw. *Nothing.*"

2

Colonel "Buzz" Hanscomb, clad in an astronaut's silver pressurized space suit, cross-checked and verified all system configurations against his checklists. He verified with his similarly clad flight engineer, Major Bill "Skunk," for "Skunkworks," Anderson, that all systems were go for orbit injection of their trans-atmospheric vehicle, or TAV, also known as the X-30. Hanscomb radioed Groom Lake.

"Roger, Star Bright, you're cleared for injection," was Ground Control's response.

"Copy."

Hanscomb flicked up the red-guarded switch protection cap on his fly-by-wire stick to the switch that would activate orbital injection. Anderson and Hanscomb looked to each other.

This was history in the making.

The first time an air-breathing aircraft was kicking its own ass into orbit. It was to be a short ride, like John Glenn's history making effort in the early afternoon of February 20, 1962, but *they* were doing it. The world may never know of it, or would fifty or hundred years from now, long after this program had been declassified, heavily sanitized, and another similarly classified project he couldn't even begin to imagine had taken this program's place...but they were about to secure themselves forever a place in the classified history books.

Hanscomb flicked the switch, and both were slammed back into their seats. Before they knew it, the blue of sky was quickly replaced with the blackness of space. They became two more of the few to see actual on-orbit planet air glow. That view of the thin, fragile film enveloping the Earth known as air, and which was all that separated humanity—*all* of humanity, not just the rich, the poor, nor the evil—from suffocation and total and utter annihilation.

"Ground, we have injection," Hanscomb relayed.

Hanscomb looked outside the cockpit.

It was beautiful, haunting. A religious experience.

And it got much quieter inside the TAV.

It was everything those who'd gone before had tried to convey—and more. More than just hurtling into orbit above Earth at Mach 25, and almost one hundred miles up. More than being housed within a titanium and Inconel structure. Mere flesh-and-blood creatures wrapped up in a laughable concoction of environmental protection material that would go up in a *fitz!* if things went wrong...it was the very concept of what they were doing. Defying the *instructed* laws of gravity. Physics. Conventional aero- and astronautics.

He shook his head and looked over to Anderson. Anderson was already looking to him, grinning through his astronaut faceplate. Gave him a crisp thumbs up. Hanscomb smiled and returned the gesture.

Then both quickly pulled their heads back into the cockpit. There had been chatter going on in their headsets, and they needed to get back to the mission.

"Uh, roger, Ground; better clear all satellites from our flight path," Hanscomb said, dryly.

How easy would it be to increase altitude, to see just how much higher they could go? To turn the nose toward the moon?

Interplanetary space?

Fantasy, yes, but how much closer to fantasy could anyone in their position come? They were closer to fulfilling any fantastical notions than anyone else on the planet right now. After all, when you lived on the edge, just where—and what were—"boundaries"?

Just as he was about to initiate reentry, Hanscomb had a sudden, powerful, fleeting moment of déjà vu—

And everything exploded into a brilliant, white fission of light.

Destruction of the X-30 TAV was instantaneous and absolute.

Chapter Eight

1

100-Mile Low Earth Orbit
4 November 2021
0908 Hours Zulu

Time.

It was ticking away.

He had to get moving!

How much oxygen was left?

How extensive the damage?

He looked to the TDU.

0311 hours.

"This is fucking *insane!*"

Still helpless as a caged animal.

For a moment, there, it had been as if all of Cherko's memories *had* been reality…his reality a *dream*.

But, he was still helplessly trapped within a damaged piece of orbiting hardware flying around the Earth at sixteen revolutions per day, while someone was taking cosmic potshots at him like he were no more than on-orbit skeet.

And those goddamned klaxons!

Cherko forced his head and shoulders violently back and forth within his bizarre, unyielding, restraints, ran restless legs—paused—then launched back into another all-out agitated bout of full-body *angry*.

And what were these damned electrodes attached to his head? Attached leads buried deep within his brain…and that went *where?*

A porthole caught his eye.

Earth.

It passed slowly beneath…peaceful, quiet…a veritable cosmic ballet. But within this life-sustaining capsule were blaring klaxons, flashing lights, and an abso-frigging-lutely *improbable* confinement.

A cold, clammy sweat broke out on his forehead. Beads of it tracked down his face—and, of course into his eyes—around his jaw line, and down his neck.

"*Damn* it!"

Frantically he again thrashed about.

Stopped.

Something felt different. *Changed.*

Cherko flicked his head to rid himself of the sweat running into his eyes.

Movement!

He frenzily scanned the module.

Something no-shit shifted—*moved*—inside here, and it wasn't floating debris!

He blinked, more sweat dripping and stinging into the corners of his eyes.

There, at the opposite end of the module!

He attempted to focus through his clammy sweat. The module danced and shimmered before him.

Not good…this was *not* good.

Cherko willed his blurry vision to focus on the bulkhead behind the shimmering object, and again tried to force coherence into view. This was just like that time, that time—

What time?

What additional analogy was he trying to m—

Maui. Off Maui.

Lanai?

A diving trip.

Yeah…the Cathedrals. His first time out in open water. He'd lost it—thrown up off the back of the boat. Had been told to focus on the horizon…but that hadn't helped, in fact had made things worse. Instead, he found focusing on the *center* of the boat, to his nauseated surprise, had worked.

What a weird fish. Always fighting the norm.

So, now, he focused on the bulkhead, because, after all, he really no longer had any kind of "horizon." He looked back to the shimmering spot on the module deck. Squinted. There was something there through all the haze, noise, vertigo, and smoldering electronics…

A *figure?*…a *kneeling* figure?

Rising up from the floor.

A ghost?

No—a *man!*

A figure in the crew blue flight bag they all wore. An actual person did indeed emerge from the floor!

He wasn't alone—*not alone!* A real, live, additional Human Being inhabited this orbiting tin can with him!

He closed his eyes, trying to stop everything from spinning. It was really beginning to hurt.

Roscoe? Was it Roscoe Pullman?

Wayne?

Whoever it was, of course they couldn't just materialize from the floor...they had to have made their way up through one of the many "snow tunnels." "Tunnels," or passageways that connected the MOL. These passageways reminded Cherko of snow tunnels he'd made and played in as a kid. All those snow banks in upstate New York—not that "up" meant anything here. The MOL was large, and they used these "snow tunnels" to get from one module compartment to another, or to and from all the various service accesses internal and external to this rather large space station.

Excuse me—*spy* station.

Was that right?

Yeah, that was right.

Cherko watched the figure slowly emerge to a standing position.

Man, he had a splitting headache.

His eyes watered and he was having difficulty getting a handle on his vertigo. *Something* was happening—happening *to* him—he was growing weaker, he could feel it. He didn't feel at all good, and he dropped his head back against the bulkhead behind him. When he lifted it back up, the module again swam before him and his eyes went uncontrollably cross-eyed, rolling up into their watery sockets.

When he was able to regain a semblance of control, he looked back to the figure. Watched it calmly float across to a console, hit a couple of selections...and all klaxons ceased. It was like a sudden vacuum sucking out the insides of his head. The idiot lights continued to flash, but their blaring noise had finally been terminated.

Sanity!

Or whatever passed for it up here.

Continuing to fight the vertigo, Cherko watched as the man then drifted across the module toward him and calmly took up a cross-legged position on the bulkhead wall alongside him, perpendicular to his orientation. The man's gaze was direct, unnerving. In the background somewhere, Cherko thought he heard radio chatter, but was still fighting for a genuine sense of mental stability to be too concerned about anything else right now.

"Thank you," Cherko said. He grimaced in pain.

Images flooded his mind.

Roscoe Pullman.

Wayne Garcia.

Rudolf Pedersen.

"You're Rud—"

"What else do you remember?" the still-hazy-view-of-a-figure asked.

"Remember?"

"Remember me?"

"You're Ruuu...Rudolf...Peder-*sen*," he said with a surprising degree of difficulty.

"Do you remember what you were doing before all this?"

"Working. I was—no, I was...was I *sleeping?*"

Cherko looked down to himself, giving a half-assed struggle against his restraints. Felt momentary chest pains.

"What the hell's—"

"*What else?*"

"W-what do you mean, what *else?* C'mon, Rudy, could you please...."

Cherko looked to the time.

How much air was left?

What was the extent of their damage?

Could they expect another attack?

They had an escape craft of some kind—didn't they?

Cherko's breath grew short and shallow. The walls of the module, his immobility, the vastness of space, and that all he ever knew was the most-distant short trip beneath him, all closed in on him.

"I-I—don't understand...don't feel well..."

The man continued to stare. Just stare. An accusing glare. Penetrating. Contemplative.

"Your—"

Eyes were so dark, Cherko couldn't say, but thought.

Had they always been that dark? He'd thought them blue.

"*Think,*" the man said calmly, firmly. "*What else do you recall?*"

"How'd you get here?"

Cherko felt like an errant child under the intense scrutiny of a correcting parent. Felt like he'd done something horribly, horribly, wrong, and had been caught in the forbidden and forgotten act, caught red-handed, hand in the cookie jar, the whole bit. Felt he was about to be punished for a crime of which he had no conscious memory.

But Rudy was right...what *did* he remember?

Something just wasn't right about any of this.

Rudy was right. Rudy was right. Had to remember what was going on, what had gone before. Make sense of his dream, his memories—his reality.

Think, he commanded himself, you're a highly trained astronaut, for God's sake, *think....*

2

Colorado Springs
1 November 2010
0815 Hours Mountain Time

Jimmy stood before the MRI machine at PENRAD Imaging, in the Audubon Medical Campus. He was clad in that tie-behind-your-back garment everyone made fun of in movies and stand-up routines. Hoped no zits or hemorrhoids (if he had any) were visible on his ass end to the technicians hovering about. After his checkout at the emergency room following his little car accident this morning, and his subsequent examination by his primary care doc at Memorial Hospital, an MRI had been promptly scheduled to make sure nothing else was out of whack, yo.

Ha. The joke was on them!

If they only *knew* what went on inside his head, his crazy little noggin, he'd have been committed *years* ago.

"Okay—ready?" the MRI tech, Elizabeth (her nametag read), asked. She was cute. All medical technicians (and dental hygienists) seemed to be, and she was probably barely into her twenties. She looked so alive and vibrant, and had the most beautiful and open smile he'd ever seen. A full mouth with lots of beautiful, white, perfectly formed teeth.

Jimmy nodded. "Guess so. Never been in one of these before. Looks like a torpedo tube."

"You mentioned no history of claustrophobia," Elizabeth said, concerned and quickly re-checking his paperwork.

"Oh, no, it's not a problem; just kidding around. It's who I am, what I do."

Elizabeth smiled. "Okay, please lay down on the table, and we can get started."

Jimmy carefully positioned himself on the beige

(*slab*)

table, making sure Elizabeth saw nothing…embarrassing.

Elizabeth quickly and efficiently placed a caged contraption into place around his head that Jimmy not only found unnerving but entirely disconcerting.

"Comfortable?" Elizabeth asked.

"Yeah, *totally*," Jimmy said.

"Well, you just take a nap, Mr. Cherko," she said, smiling, again flashing her pearly whites, "and before you know it, it'll all be over."

"'All be over' means different things to different peoples."

"Aren't we the comedian.

"Now, Mr. Cherko, you'll hear a lot of mechanical noises around you, thumping, clicking, that kind of thing, but it's just the machine working it technological magic."

"Okay."

"And, please, try not to move."

"Lay there like a corpse with my head in a vise."

Elizabeth laughed. "Well, not exactly, but close enough. Ready?"

Jimmy nodded. Elizabeth again smiled then left the machine for the control panel on the other side of a wall with a large

(*portal*)

window.

Jimmy stared through his head cage into the beige ceiling. He bet the colors to this room were intentionally selected for their calming effect. Most people sent down here were most likely dispatched under more stressful and life threatening circumstances than himself.

But was he—really—any different?

He'd rear-ended a truck and didn't remember doing it.

Had summarily *blacked out*, main.

But nothing untoward had been detected in the ER, nor by his doc.

Hence…Elizabeth and her bright shiny face and killer smile.

So, maybe, he was best not to jump the gun. This damned machine was about to probe into his most intimate of intimates that no open and airy hospital gown could ever conceal from view. If something was growing inside or eating away at him, it was bound to be found out. And now—just this very moment—he wasn't sure if he *wanted* to know.…

"Okay," Electronic Elizabeth said, through the slab's speaker system, "here we go."

Jimmy made a caricature of a face and gave a sarcastically enthusiastic thumb's up.

His slab began to move, and Jimmy felt just a pinch of apprehension.

The slab slowly inserted him into the huge (also beige) human-eating donut. It wasn't thick enough to take in an entire body, but about half of him was easily consumed. And just as his shoulders cleared entry, he noticed increased breathing. *This is silly*, he thought, slowing his breathing. It was nothing like a torpedo tube, and he'd wished he'd never brought it up. It did, however, remind him of a huge donut, one that really was trying to gobble him up.

That's it, run with the donut image, Sick Boy! Funny—laugh, *Sick Boy*, laugh— *at the huge beige donut you're crammed into like so much jelly filling.…*

The slab came to a jarred stop and Cherko took stock of his surroundings. Though he was only in about waist deep and could easily see the room around his feet, and using the angled mirrors in his head cage, he was lucky if he had ten inches of space around him inside this thing.

It *was*, surprisingly, claustrophobic.

"How we doin in there, Mr. Cherko?" came Elizabeth's electronic voice over the speakers. He'd almost forgotten about her.

He'd nodded, realized she probably couldn't see that, then said, "Fine. And, please—call me 'Jimmy.'"

"Now remember, Jimmy, try not to move, and just take it easy. Take a nap," she-who-was-called-Elizabeth said.

Yeah, right.

He was in here because he'd blacked out while driving.

Driving.

Not only were there the obvious concerns, but he'd *blacked out.* Aside from a bender, who blacks out for no apparent reason? Certainly not our lovely assistant, Elizabeth, over there. Or those who built this damned thing, or most of the normal people out there...of which he wasn't sure he could any more count himself among. He wasn't sure about anything, and the beige walls of this frigging donut *were* getting smaller and smaller and closing in on him....

Abrupt and loud mechanical clunking and clicking caused Jimmy to jump.

Quit moving! he chided himself. *Just lie there and play* dead....

Okay, this was ridiculous. He wasn't claustrophobic, and was far from a pessimist. This was just a precautionary examination and everything would turn up roses. Fine.

Juuust *fine.*

So kick back, close your eyes, and enjoy the experience. Take in everything about what was going on, so maybe he could use it in his new manuscript.

Jimmy closed his eyes....

He couldn't move. Couldn't breathe. As rapidly as his lungs were trying their damnedest to make it happen, it just *wasn't.*

He couldn't *see.*

Was restrained.

Something held him down. Pinned him to a table.

A *slab.*

Something was solidly clamped around the length of his body!

Spiders!

Legions of the little bastards were crawling all over him, nasty black spiders with huge, dark eyes...up his legs, his arms, his torso. Into *there*...coming for his nose, his mouth, his *ears*...

No...no!

Jimmy tried to get up, but that wasn't happening.

Where was he? What was going on?

His arms and legs—absolutely immobile.

What—what was that?

Something surrounded him. *Hovered* about him…

Had to get out!

Get *away!*

Leave me alone!

He couldn't talk. Yell. *Scream.*

Couldn't *move!*

Pinned!

Pinned-pinned-*pinned!*

The darkness inside Jimmy blossomed like a beautiful fucking flower.

A black flower.

He had to get out.

Now.

An arm broke free. Then the other.

Spiders!

They clamored along his throat, his jaw, into his mo—

Jimmy lashed out and beat and pummeled and fought that which hovered about him…

"Mr. Cherko! Mr. *Cherko!* It's all right! All right! *Please*, relax…*relax*…"

Voice.

A *voice?*

He blinked. Groggily shook his head.

Whose voice…so full of concern…alarm?

Elizabeth.

It was Elizabeth and her beautiful face, the most beautiful face he'd ever seen.

But where were her teeth? Those gorgeous, model-like, movie-star quality *teeth?*

Elizabeth was crouched before him and had his face firmly cupped (squished) in her hands, his mouth an open, distorted "O." The look of grave concern on her face scared him into full wakefulness. She looked at him as if he were crazy.

"Mr. *Cherko!*"

Jimmy blinked, his cheeks crushed together in Elizabeth's warm, caring hands.

"Mr. Cherko—*Jimmy*—*are you with me? Are you all right?*"

Jimmy numbly looked past her.

"I…"

There were others. In the room. With Elizabeth and him. Several others. Others as in Humans. *Men.* Men in white coats. Hospital *greens.*

Jimmy again closed his eyes. Reopened them.

He was standing—well standing was actually a poor account of things: it was more like he was trying to climb an invisible rock face that came up and out of the middle of the floor. Of a room. A beige room.

He was outside that crazy, insane, Hungry Donut, looking like he was being dipped into the hospital floor by two—no three, he now saw—three dudes in hospital greens. One of his arms was held higher than the other, both his feet dragging along the floor, both knees bent, one an inch or two above the floor, the other higher.

Yes, he did, indeed, look exactly as if he were trying to climb an invisible rock wall.

Were it not for the orderlies—or whatever they were called. And had said orderlies decided to let go of him, he'd have crumpled to the floor in an anything-but-graceful heap.

He thrashed about once more just to corroborate his predicament to his now-conscious mind. The orderlies held fast, shaking him still.

Jimmy caught a glance of the slab he'd been on.

It was still inserted all the way into the Hungry Donut.

How'd he gotten out of that head cage?

Elizabeth got to her feet and cautiously backed away; nodded to the two men restraining him. The men lifted him to his feet and slowly let go, then also backed away. Curiously—Jimmy noticed through his fog—they looked ready to pounce back in at a moment's notice. Looked like they *really* wanted to.

Not without difficulty, Jimmy, initially crouching, stood on his own, hands spread out before him for balance. He looked about the room—the beige room—as if seeing it for the very first time.

Had his ass popped out behind him?

He opened his mouth, which felt as if it'd been closed for an eternity.

"What…what the hell happened?"

3

Cherko made a left as he pulled out of the Audubon Medical Campus. It was snowing outside, big, fat, flakes.

Well, that had been quite the experience, now, n'est-ce pas?

Just a simple MRI he'd been told. Nothing to it, he'd been told; lay on a table, be shoved into a huge-ass magnet, and just nap out. He'd been told.

But an hour and a half later, following some fancy verbal footwork and impromptu sedation, he now also had to "visit" a shrink.

Wonderful.

What the heck was the matter with him? He'd never behaved like this before. He was White Bread Man. No broken bones, no mental illnesses, no near-death experiences—no excitement of any kind on any level. Never. *Nothing* ever happened to him, for Chrissakes, *nothing*. He was the pinnacle of a boring, white bread, existence.

Yet now he was acting psycho. Rear-ending trash trucks and freaking out in MRI machines.

And it had taken three men to handle him.

Three men, he pondered amusedly....

But *still*.

Cherko drove down Fillmore, past quaint and unsuspecting stores and shops. The falling snow was beautiful. Calming. Reached deep into a part of his soul that always brought him back to those naïve days as a kid. The hushed quietness of the woods up behind his home. The sounds of trudging through several feet of it on snowshoes and listening to his only slightly labored breathing.

They hadn't even wanted him driving home by himself and had been just *this* short of all-out committing him on the spot.

Cherko regripped the steering wheel.

Now he had to explain to his wife that not only had he blacked out and rear-ended a truck and freaked out in an MRI machine—wait there's *more!*—he now also had to go see a shrink. She'd still be in Denver (more like on her way back, after hearing about his accident), so he'd just chill out until she came home. Take it easy.

Or work on his novel.

Maybe he'd even throw all caution to the wind and take a walk through Garden of the Gods while it snowed. Clear his head a little and stretch out some sore muscles before he made his way back to his keyboard.

Always...at keyboard.

But, as much as he tried not to worry about what was happening...he actually found it scared the living shit out of him.

Chapter Nine

1

8 December 1985
0715 Hours Mountain Time

"So, what do you feel like doing for your birthday?" Erica asked, draped across Cherko's naked body. She traced a finger along his chest.

"Well, *this* is pretty nice…"

"All day?"

"And why not? I can't imagine another person I'd rather be with—wait, gimme a minute—"

Erica hit him.

"Since my birthday's really tomorrow, and I have to work, why don't we go for a drive today," he said. "Into the mountains. Check out this new territory called Colorado."

"Sounds fun!"

"But, first…"

Cherko pulled Erica's naked form atop him and anchored her with a passionate, open-mouthed kiss. Erica rewrapped herself around him.…

Holding hands, Cherko and Erica drove west along Highway 24. The day, initially blue sky and beautiful in Colorado Springs, had turned overcast and gray through the towns of Woodland Park, Divide, and beyond. Cherko negotiated the vehicle down the steep, windy decline of Wilkerson Pass and into the flat straightaway through South Park. Cherko released Erica's hand and rubbed the back of his neck.

"What's the matter?" Erica asked.

"Think I'm getting another zit."

"Let me see."

"You wanna look at my zits?"

Erica leaned across and looked to where Cherko directed. She felt around the nape of his neck.

"It looks more like a cyst."

"What the hell's a cyst?"

"Oh," she said, settling back into her seat, "it's like an impacted pore or something. Not a huge deal. I've had one or two removed by the doctor."

"*Surgery?*"

"Oh, no," she said, laughing "it's done on an outpatient basis. They just ram this huge needle in there and suck out its puss-laden innards."

"Pleasant."

"It really isn't anything," she said, still laughing loudly at the look on his face. "You should have that looked at."

The two flew past miles of open, empty plains, passing the occasional cattle or herd of pronghorn. Pronghorn...deer of the American Southwest.

Deer.

Deer. Road. Storm.

Mom?

Deer.

"Is that buffalo?" Cherko asked, peering off into the distance.

"Yeah," Erica said. "Ranchers raise buffalo around here. You can actually buy ground buffalo in the store."

"Really. Never had it. But I've always loved how badass they look, out there in the fields. Standing strong against a blizzard, that kind of thing."

"They are kinda neat looking."

"What do people who live out here *do?* It's so desolate. Remote."

"Not sure."

"They must ranch and do whatever's associated with ranching."

"It's too removed from the world for me," Erica said, staring out the window.

"It's kinda like space. Open and vast...empty...but, really, there's all kinds of life forms: ants, bugs, moths. Bacteria. We just can't see them."

"There're bugs and moths in space?" Erica asked, smiling.

"You know what I mean," Cherko said, grinning. "Space is so vast and open, and it's like there's stuff out there, stuff we can't see, and other stuff we can—just like here. There may only be a molecule or two of something for light-years...but even that's *some*thing. Not total emptiness."

"You really are into this 'space' thing, aren't you? Don't you realize that it's probably all romantic and fetching, now, because you're here, down on Earth among Earthlings—*me*—but that were you really up there," she said, bobbing an index finger upward, "you'd be all alone? You'd have none of *this*.

No moths. No wide, open plains. No cars, no buffalo. No apartments. No sex—"

"No sex?"

"*Nooo* sex. Cause I wouldn't be up there. I'd be down here."

"You wouldn't be with me?" Cherko asked, pouting.

"Most likely not. You'd be your bad astronaut self, and I wouldn't be. So how could I be up there with you?"

"Hmm."

Cherko again rubbed his neck.

Thoughts of ERO, satellites, and his training flew through his mind.

Thoughts of…The Project.

What'd it all mean? The Project—his job. Was this what he really wanted? If he couldn't be with those he cared about, what was the point?

And was any of this even *real?*

It all seemed so distant, now, out on these open plains of Colorado, on a cozy morning drive with his new girlfriend.

Had he really been able to mentally mess with computer electronics?

And how did he know he *wasn't being messed with by his trainers?*

What if he wasn't doing *any* of what he thought he was doing, but his trainers were just messing with his head?

But…he had heard those tones—*in his head*—no headphones.

And there had been that voice…that attractive, hot voice with which he communicated…and had been second guessing during his training. Who knew, it was probably more like those sex hotlines, where you *thought* you were talking to some hot chick (not that he'd *used* them, mind you), but in reality….

So, why not test it?

If he could second guess the voice, why not see if he could second guess Erica?

He glanced over to her.

She was still gazing out the window.

She's thinking about sex right this moment.

Right, that was just him mak—

"You know," Erica said, turning to him and reaching out for his hand, "this morning was *really* wonderful." She gave him a lingering look.

"Yeah?"

"I loved waking up to you jumping my bones."

"Did you, now? I thought girls didn't like making whoopee right after waking up."

"That's because they don't sleep with *you*," she said, squeezing his hand, "and they better not—*ever!*"

"What're you saying?" Cherko asked, looking between the road and her. "You want an exclusive relationship? Cause, if you are, better let me know, now, so I can cancel that other date—"

Erica again hit him.

"Ow!"

"That's not funny!" she said, frowning and crossing her arms.

"Kidding! Was just *kidding!*"

"I know," she said, with a pouty smile. Then she reached over toward his legs. "I want you all for *myself!*"

Highway 50, West of Pueblo, Colorado
1400 Hours Mountain Time

Cherko leaned across the hood of the car, staring south. He held a map under his hands against the occasional light gusts of wind. Another small herd of pronghorn grazed directly out before his view. He focused on them. Pronghorn.

Deer.

Road

Storm.

Mother....

His eyes drifted upward towards the clouds. They looked peculiar, swirling. *Felt* out of the ordinary. He looked back down to the fields before him. There seemed to be something that called out to him from down there.

He looked to the map and saw the Great Sand Dunes National Monument was directly south.

Sand Dunes...in *Colorado?*

Cherko looked back up into the sky.

Not only had he mentally flattened sine waves, but he'd also made these points—a bunch of electronic dots—come together in another training session. Several electronic points on a screen, separated by various distances, and he—again, through only the use of his *mind*—had been able to bring them together. Each and every one.

In training for over a month, and he'd been able to do that?

To what end?

But again, was *he* even doing this, or was some hidden government flunky, hiding behind some Oz-like curtain, doing all the electronic manipulation, only making him *think* he was doing it?

Why would the government be training him to do this stuff? Why wouldn't they tell him? They just send a van around to pick him up after work, take him to some clandestine location, then force him into a training program over which he had no say—but at which he seemed to outright excel.

For what purpose?

He'd always wanted some super-sexy job, all right, and apparently that's just what he got. He just didn't know what it was.

You are not authorized an answer....

Be careful what you wish for.

Cherko reached out to the cloud with his mind. What was up there, and what did "cloudness" feel like....

Erica popped up on the other side of the car.

"*Much* better!" she exclaimed, schooching up and wiggling back into her jeans.

Cherko smiled. "Feel better, now, do we?"

"Yup!"

"Couldn't have gone back in Salida, huh?"

"Didn't have to."

"I see," he said, nodding. "I must admit, I've never before been with a *girl* who peed alongside roads."

"I'm unique," she said in a playful lilt. Erica smoothed out her attire, tossed back her hair, then casually hopped back into the car.

"You certainly appear to be."

2

Unknown Location
15 January 1986
0110 Hours Mountain Time

Cherko sat before his screen as still-images flashed up before him on the large glass behind his workstation. As images of everything from flowers and insects to world and cosmic events flashed before him, the sine wave boxes lit up in various degrees of flattening, in rapid-fire combinations, many at a time on his screen. Without warning, the still-images changed to video, and the sine wave boxes mirrored the video images at a blinding rate of speed...all of which Cherko took in easily.

Some were pleasing. Some not so. Images of humans, animals, flowers, and insects. Of a bee pollinating a flower.

Of WWII carpet bombing of Germany.

Of JFK speaking to the American public.

Of a Saturn V launch and subsequent moon shots.

All he took in and assimilated without the faintest idea why.

Then everything went blank.

"Your progress has been most curious," came the soft voice.

Thank you, Cherko mentally replied.

"We had not anticipated your degree of ability, though it was probable. Your degree of mastery is extraordinary.

"During contact," the voice continued, "you will receive information and input it into whatever workstation you are working before. You will do this by the following procedure, which you are to mimic as I voice it."

"Copy that," Cherko said.

"Select the right trackball switch…"

Cherko selected his workstation's trackball switch to the right of the computer monitor.

"…while holding down the right trackball switch, select the F10 key."

Cherko did as instructed. He saw a dialog box appear on-screen with a blank entry field.

"A dialog window appears. In that blank field, you will enter your password. Enter the word 'password,' now. You will be prompted to enter a new one. Use the constraints for passwords from your other responsibility.

"Do this now."

Cherko did as instructed, and came up with a new password.

"You will now get a blank screen on which you will enter all future communications. All entries will be blacked out—even while typing—for obvious security considerations. After each entry, or string, you will enter a forward slash, and at the end of each report you will enter three forward slashes."

"But how will I know what I'm typing if I can't see *what* I'm—"

"Practice."

"Okay…"

"When complete, you will select only F10. When you hit the first F10 and trackball switch, this blank screen remains in the background, so you can seemingly continue on with what you are doing in your official capacity while entering your program data. Do you understand."

"Affirmative."

"That is all."

Cherko sat, casually looking around the room.

"Where am I?"

"You are not—"

Authorized an answer, Cherko finished. *Fine.*

"We are complete."

I'm done?

"Affirmative."

"What do I do now? Do I ever come back?"

"That is no longer necessary. You will practice your data entry at your other responsibility, which we will monitor. You will be contacted when you are ready."

"By whom?"

Silence. All displays went blank, and the lighting dimmed.

Cherko got to his feet; retrieved his jacket. He stepped back from his console and stared at it. Then he turned and entered the elevator for the last time.

3

Cherko lay in bed, staring into the ceiling.

Had he really been attending clandestine training sessions in some unknown location?

Had he really had mental discussions with...*whom*ever?

And had he really influenced electronics through the use of nothing but *thought?*

None of this seemed real in the light of day. Even his ERO job was unreal. The only thing that seemed any kind of real was Erica. She was his only apparent life outside of work. Face it, he went to training at unusual hours, and arrived home tired, exhausted. And all he did outside of work was work out and see Erica.

His life suddenly seemed quite unreal.

He'd come a long way from that upstate New York kid. Reality had come knocking and had come knocking hard. Though his work seemed exciting, it all felt...fuzzy. He did stuff he couldn't tell *anyone.*

But what was the big deal?

He tracked and looked in on satellites? Okay, so he seemed to be able to influence electronics with his mind, which was kind of spooky, yet downright cool, but he could think of all kinds of uses for that.

Scary uses.

What was he becoming?

What was his *real* mission?

And that disembodied voice...he'd considered all kinds of possibilities about that. Could someone really telepathically communicate with him?

Or was it something else?

Not only did the voice sound slightly off, it felt...different.

Alien.

Really alien.

This was just all way too out there to believe. It brought up way too many other issues, like...if he was being trained by an alien, then the government was obviously in on it. The van. Turnbull.

Why?

And not just any "why?," but why would aliens need to work with our government? Weren't they supposed to be so far in advance of us that they shouldn't require our assistance for anything?

It just felt like an alien was goddamned training him!

How do you get past that?

Cherko got out of bed and entered the living room. Looked about his empty apartment.

At one point he'd been a 14-year-old kid with romantic notions of warp speed star travel and green women.

At one point he'd been an average student in high school who'd gotten a Most Improved Student award.

At one point he'd been in college studying physics and having a hard time of it.

And at one point he'd been in the right seat of a T-37, trying to dead reckon a new course as mountains came up *real* fast, his navigator IP whacking him up aside the head. Commanding him to *think*, dammit!

And now…*now* he was standing in the middle of an empty apartment with a new life looming before him like an approaching thunderstorm. One about which he wasn't sure he felt all that comfortable.

4

ERO Operations
5 March 1986
2330 Hours Mountain Time

First Lieutenant Jimmy Cherko entered the ERO ops floor. Major Turnbull was talking to several crew members when he looked up.

"Evening Lieutenant," he said.

"How you doing, sir," Cherko said.

"Need to see you. You can change over when I'm done."

Cherko looked to the gathering of operators preparing for shift change, and nodded. Cherko followed Turnbull off the floor.

The two entered Turnbull's office. Cherko had more images of him standing with others—others not in uniform.

Turnbull locked the door; Cherko took his seat in the usual chair. Turnbull went back behind his desk.

Did Turnbull *know he was being trained by an alien?*

"Everything going well?"

"Yes, sir."

"Typing?"

"Going great, actually. I've done some before, so it's not too bad, though it's been a while."

"Good."

Cherko and Turnbull sat in silence for a moment.

"Sir…do you know much about what I'm to be doing?"

Turnbull leaned forward over the desk. He formed a pensive steeple with his fingers to his lips.

"Lieutenant…we both do as we're told. Nothing more."

Cherko nodded.

"That is all," Turnbull said, sitting back upright.

"That's it?"

"Just wanted to see how you're doing."

That is all. Seems like he was to hear a lot of that.

Cherko got to his feet; left the office.

Returning to the ops floor, Cherko took his briefing, and took over his position on console. Without warning or fanfare, it came.

Prepare for information string.

"What?" Cherko said out loud, immediately looking to his crew members. No one had noticed his outburst; they were all still talking among themselves.

Is this my "contact," Cherko mentally asked.

Prepare.

Cherko casually looked around, hit the right trackball switch on his console panel, then F10. A dialog box, like what he'd been trained on, appeared. He quickly entered his password and it disappeared.

Ready, he sent back.

The communication came unnervingly clear as a bell.

There was no mistaking it for some stray or crazy thoughts. And there were several-second pauses between each information string. When Cherko felt he'd fat-fingered an entry, he asked for and was granted a pause and retransmission. There would be just enough pause for him to backspace over the mistyped entry, and then the data was resent. After each pause he entered a "/" and at the end of the communication, he entered "///". What he typed, but couldn't physically see was:

77900/849657/86115876557/8316/98999

77900/65468438/68488/6841385/5812

77900/5782/425646556/545/54845685584///

Communication terminated.

Is that it? Cherko asked, but there came no reply.

Cherko waited several seconds, and when there was, indeed, no further communication, Cherko closed his invisible window by again hitting F10. He again looked to his crew members, but they were busy with their own duties. Cherko sat back, scratched the back of his neck, and grimaced.

That was it?

This was his huge, new, can't-tell-a-soul mission?

No pictures, no mental video? Just bland old numeric streams? No "How ya doin—how's the weather on Earth"—just prepare and terminate?

As well as he'd done in training, as much as he'd been trained to do this, he'd severely had his doubts that all he was being shown could *possibly* be real, that it was really going to happen.

Yet here he was.

It'd happened exactly as he'd been trained, and he'd performed exactly as he'd been trained. It was real, and there was no denying it. He hadn't made up the material that entered his mind. He hadn't made up the voice he'd heard. There was a decidedly detached and, yes—in more ways than one—*alien* sense to the contact, the communication.

It was a gut feeling.

It was like he was the Go-Between, the translator, between whatever the aliens were doing out there, and what the government was somehow complicit in. But there was no way to yet tell what was going on, because it was all numbers, numbers that just weren't yielding up any of their secrets.

Except that there was one string that recurred.

One string of numbers had been repeated. Seven-seven-nine-something. Zero-zero. Interesting. And when he'd gotten those numbers all three times, he felt something about them. Like they were related to a position. His position.

77900.

Like it was his positional designator.

And there was something else he realized about the communication...unlike his training, this communication felt like a good interior mind-scratch. Like getting your back scratched, only it was his *mind* getting back-scratched.

Chapter Ten

1

Jimmy Cherko, Air Force First Lieutenant, one each, sat low (and in poor posture, his mother would have lovingly chided) on his apartment's couch, casually channel surfing his TV. It was after midnight, and he'd just finished watching a sci-fi movie, the name of which he'd already forgotten. It had been okay. But he hated when movies took the short route to advancing their plots, rather than sticking to more real-life specifics, creating a therefore more realistic and challenging storyline. He should write something. Perhaps based on his life—without getting him into trouble, of course. Something based on his life story....

Yeah, he could do it.

Jimmy hit a channel showing Ted Nugent, rock star, bowhunting deer.

The Nuge.

An unlucky buck hung from a tree branch. Nuge and his buddies were gathered around it, discussing their bagged trophy, and clips from various parts of the show shown earlier flashed up as the end credits rolled.

Deer.

Road.

Mom.

Jimmy's eyes, heavy with sleep, rolled closed.

Deer and his mom. A *storm....*

Town of Harrietstown, New York
7 July 1976
1541 Hours Eastern Time

Fifteen-year-old Jimmy Cherko pumped the pedals of his Scwhinn ten-speed as hard as he could along a deserted stretch of New York's Route 186 between the Lake Clear Airport and Lake Clear Junction. He had a good couple miles to go before he made it home. The growing July storm was starting to manifest itself into something fierce, and he really didn't want to get caught in it—but may not have a choice. It was stupid of him to have ridden his bike into town today and stayed so long; his dad had clearly told him an afternoon thunderstorm was forecast. Yet here he found himself. Independence was one thing, but getting struck by lightning quite another.

Jimmy pumped the pedals and almost lost it, as the bike weaved from unevenly applied weight to the pedals and caught an edge of blacktop. Up on the pedals and leaning low over the handlebars, he glanced behind him before lifting his head back up and looking forward.

Please, God, hold off the rain, he prayed, *please let me get home first!*

Next thing he knew, Jimmy was running headlong *toward* his bike.

A bike which now lay tangled up on the shoulder along Route 186 *before* him...one of its wheels upright in the air and still spinning.

He was on his feet?

Jimmy skidded to a stop, mouth open, hands spread out about him as if for balance. Gasped for breath.

Looked behind him.

Back to his bike.

How...*what the....*

He looked up to the sky.

Deer?

Looking back to his bike, Jimmy found himself standing in the middle of a herd of white-tailed deer.

He blinked. Looked to the still spinning wheel of his Schwinn.

He faced opposite the direction he'd been *traveling.*

Something about the bike seemed so removed, so distant from him just then, and he longed to be back up on it and its spinning wheels, gripping its black-taped handlebars headed home, storm or no...

But he was standing in the middle of a herd of deer. Deer that poured out into and across 186. The empty, deserted road, with a brewing, rumbling thunderstorm above. Jimmy blinked again. Brought a hand to his head.

What had he just been doing?

Why was he standing alongside the road?

He had to get home. Before it rained.

His parents were gonna *kill* him....

He looked to the deer.

Were they all looking at him?

Did deer actually ever look directly *at* people? A whole herd of them? Into your very *soul?*

A smile formed across his face. He reached out. The closest one, standing before him, nuzzled his hand. It tickled, and Jimmy laughed.

A wild, white-tailed, deer was nudging his hand...

Jimmy looked around him. There were about a dozen or so of them, just looking at him, several of their blackened chins working whatever cud they were chewing, ears twitching. One repositioned around him, and he reached out and pet it as it strode past. The deer turned and looked straight into his eyes. The clouds above thickened and swirled, flashes of lightning punctuating thunder that rumbled across the sky like a hungry god. Dust kicked up. He had just had a flash of an image...*of looking down on this stretch of road...at his* bike....

The deer that had ambled past continued to look directly at Jimmy, and he found himself mesmerized by its large, dark eyes. Eyes that seemed oh, so very deep. So deep and dark. Calling him. Beckoning. Jimmy felt moved by those large, powerful eyes. Black, so very black and deep. All knowing.

What did they want him to do?

When?

He'd just been where?

Jimmy felt unsteady. Confused.

Those eyes...*bottomless*. So *knowledgeable*. He felt his whole life gobbled up by them. He couldn't hide. Not anything. Felt like he was under the scrutiny of his—

What about his mother?

Hadn't they just *talked*...hadn't she just told him something?

Jimmy reached out...the doe, the one with the huge, unflinchingly deep, penetrating eyes...eyes that reached deep into his marrow, his spirit...reached out for him, too, its hoof inches from his finger. The space between their touch, no more than an inch if that, felt an entire universe apart, and he felt as if he were flying through all those light-years of empty, not-so-empty space....

The rain held off until just as he came around the bend and down into the hollow of the home stretch of his ride home. The rain came down in powerful rippling *curtains*, and at this point it mattered not if it had just started or had been downpouring for an hour, he was just as soaked as if the latter had occurred. Squinting through the warm and weighty downpour, Jimmy flew through sheets of rain, mere seconds from home. He blew past the State Trooper's house, past the on-again-off-again-bully house, past that cute babe's house, the old Johnson place, their garage, then—*finally*—banked sharply to the left, and flew up the gray, crushed-stone driveway running with water. The red stationwagon and yellow pickup were both parked in the upper driveway. Jimmy dumped his bike alongside the porch and dashed up the steps into the porch's protection.

Mom.

Something about his *mom*....

Jimmy flew down the porch and through the front door. He barreled through the kitchen, where something smelled burned, through the pantry, the back door, and pushed open the screen door with the anticipatory, outstretched hand of a football player punching through an offensive line. The storm pounded the aluminum sheeting of the roof and it sounded like hell and damnation was being visited upon them.

Jimmy found the heavy wooden backdoor open, and hesitated not a second as he again shot out into the torrential downpour.

"*Mom!*" he shouted, his cry feeble against the deafening thunder and blinding lightning. Whipping winds. The rain had become so intense it took him a moment to adjust through the deluge. The parking spot under the Crabapple tree, where his dad parked his State truck was empty, but over by the burn barrel, to the left of the Crabapple tree and along the two cement-block steps that led up to the backyard, he saw her. Her silhouette, frail and waiflike against the summer maelstrom that continued to unfurl its fury. She stood before the barrel, staring down into it. Unmoving. Jimmy ran to her.

"Mom! *Mom!*"

Renée stared down into the empty burn barrel, her mouth open like an afterthought, eyes empty. Stringy, drenched hair hung down about her head.

"*Mom!*" Jimmy again shouted. "*Mom!*" Grabbing her arms, which remained to her sides, he shook her. Renée looked to him like a drugged psycho ward patient.

"Jimmy...*there* you are..."

Jimmy tugged at his mother. "Come *on!*"

Renée came along indifferently; cast a look up into the angry sky, blinking against the watery onslaught. Flinched as chain lightning arced above and the thunder concussioned the area. Jimmy pulled harder.

"Okay..." Renée said, dreamily, and came along.

Once Jimmy had gotten his mother inside, cleaned her up and lay her down in her bed, he quickly set about cleaning up the burned roast and opened all the windows and front and back doors to get rid of the smell. He knew his mother would soon come out of her haze not remembering a thing, and he had to get things right as quickly as he could before Dad got home. Not-so surprisingly, the others had been upstairs napping, and hadn't been aware of a thing.

But if his dad came home too soon, he *would*.

Jimmy quickly worked the hamburgers into patties and threw them into the frying pan, images of looking down upon a stretch of road by the airport again flashed through his mind. As the burgers sizzled in the frying pan, he also recalled something about deer in a road....

His mom groggily poked her head around the pantry corner, a hand to her head, pulling hair out of her eyes and behind an ear.

"Well, what do we have here?" she said, clearing her throat, in a pleasantly surprised voice.

Jimmy shot her a look.

Of course she was fine. This was how it always was.

Jimmy released a pained smile.

"Hi, Mom," he said, as Renée came over and hugged him. "I was just watching these while you went to the bathroom—like you asked."

"Oh," Renée, said, slowly—almost painfully—coming out of her grogginess and again swiping hair away from her eyes. She again momentarily brought a hand to her head, then grabbed an apron hanging on a nearby hook. "I really should put this hair in a—"

Just then Carl, Penny, and Ritchie came bounding and pounding down the stairs and into the kitchen.

"*Hamburgers!*" they all shouted.

"Hey!" Renée said, "what have we here?"

The three children piled in around Renée, hugging her and actively sniffing the air. As if on cue, Jimmy's dad came in through the back door, stomping his feet on the mat just outside the entrance and shaking off his wet Forest Ranger Stetson and gear. Jimmy wearily backed away from the stove and his mother; he collapsed onto a chair at the table.

"French Fries, *too?*" Carl asked.

"Hi, honey!" Renée said, as Everett leaned over and kissed his wife on the cheek. Both were surrounded by their children. Renée peeked into the oven. "Yes, Carl, French Fries, too!"

"*Yea!*" was the combined hoorah.

"It's coming down like cats and dogs out there!" Everett said, as he got out of his rain gear. He looked over to Jimmy. "Jimmy, get your bike out of the driveway."

"Sorry, Dad."

Everett came over and mussed up Jimmy's hair. Smiled at his son.

"You're all wet. Got caught in that storm, didn't ya?"

"Yeah…"

"Maybe next time you'll listen to your Old Man, huh?"

"Yes, Daddy," Jimmy said, smiling guiltily.

Jimmy got up and left the kitchen, leaving behind the sounds of a happy, hungry, and an end-of-day family reunited. He didn't grab a rain jacket as he went outside. He got to the end of the porch, unhesitatingly went down the steps, and picked up his bike. He looked up into the still pouring rain. The lightning and thunder had greatly abated, and the driving, body-pounding sheets had backed off to just a steady and strong precip.

Jimmy muscled the bike up onto the porch, brought it down to the far end of the house, and leaned it against its assigned spot on the porch, beside the other bikes. Then he collapsed into a porch chair.

And just watched it rain.

2

Lake Clear, New York
10 July 1976
0958 Hours Eastern Time

Carl and Jimmy, each clad in Wrangler jeans, Converse sneakers, and ratty T-shirts—Jimmy's a *Juicy-Juice* grape thing and Carl in a plain old white T-shirt—pounded at each other with boxing gloves in the mid-morning July sun. They were out behind their house and around the boulder that presided over the parking area next to the large Crabapple tree. Both backed away, wiped sweat from their brows, and readjusted their gloves, laughing.

"Had enough, Little Brother?" Jimmy taunted.

"Have *you?*" Carl shot back, defiantly.

Jimmy tugged one last time at the white lacing with his teeth, then again took up the fighting stance his dad had shown them. Neither took their eyes off the other as they circled, throwing occasional jabs. They had to sidestep their toy Civil War gear—muskets, blue Kepi caps, yellow plastic neckerchiefs—that they'd left lying against the boulder.

A high-pitched scream punctured the air.

The woods!

It came from the woods up behind the house. From the area up on the hill at the split-log cabin their dad had built for them.

Carl and Jimmy looked to each other.

Penny!

Both broke into a run toward the hilltop cabin, frantically tossing off their gloves along the way. Penny, and Ritchie (the youngest), had been playing up there.

Carl and Jimmy pumped it up the steep, dark-earth slope, grabbing onto trees and brush up the much-practiced route of their ascent. They yelled out to Penny and Ritchey along the way, but Penny just kept *screaming.*

Carl and Jimmy arrived at the cabin to find Penny crying, her little ponytailed head bobbing horribly as her shoulders uncontrollably shuddered. She stood over their made-up table of old and bent silverware, cups, and plates. Gobs of tears flowed out of her red, swollen face.

"*They took him* agaaain!" she wailed. Carl and Jimmy came quickly to her.

"Who took him?" Jimmy asked. Carl shot him a look, then out into the woods. Jimmy followed Carl's gaze.

Had something just moved out there?

"You sure you weren't just playing? Hide-and-seek, or something?" Jimmy asked, trying to soothe his sister.

"We were sitting right *heeere!*" Penny blubbered out between huge sobs and stuttered breathing, *"playing!* Ritchey then said they were coming for him—he could *feel* them."

"Who—" Carl asked.

"Deer," Jimmy said absentmindedly. He felt a knot in his stomach.

They both looked to him.

"Did you see where he—they—went?" Jimmy asked.

Still sobbing, but calming down, she pointed out into the woods.

"Carl—you stay here. I'll be right back."

"No!" Penny cried, grabbing Jimmy.

"Penny—you want us to find him, right?"

Penny was again sobbing. "Yes."

"Well, I have to go look for him."

"But they'll *take* you! Go tell Dad!"

Jimmy paused, trading looks with Carl, who was now also looking scared.

"Jimmy…" Carl said.

"Look," I'll just go out a little ways, okay? I'll shout back every so often. If I get out of view—you two watch from here, okay?"

Both looked to him.

"Just watch from here. If you don't hear from me, you run back down to the house and tell Dad, okay? Run *fast.* He should still be in his office." Jimmy looked around the base of the cabin. He jumped off the front porch and grabbed a large stick. A large, dead, branch, actually. "And I'll take this with me," he said, with a few demonstrative whacks of the stick at a nearby tree. "Okay?"

Both nodded quietly.

"Okay—now be brave," Jimmy said, "keep an eye out if you see anything. I'll be right back."

Jimmy turned; looked to the empty woods before him. He always loved playing in these woods, but now they took on a decidedly sinister edge. He turned back to Carl and Penny. "Shout out if you see *anything*, okay? *I'll be right back.*"

Jimmy reached out and touched Penny on her head. He was surprised at how warm it felt. Surprised at how frail she looked. He looked to Carl.

"Be careful, Jimmy," Carl said. Carl looked nervous.

Jimmy grimaced, hefted his stick, and went into the woods.

His dad had told them that there was really nothing to be afraid of in these woods. There were no poisonous snakes, like rattlers, here, this far north, and there weren't really any mountain lions or bears where they lived— they kept to themselves deeper in. But just the same, he told Jimmy to always be prepared. Carry a pocketknife and know your surroundings. If you had to, mark your passage by nicking a tree or two, stacking some rocks into a "cairn," he'd called it, or any other method to mark your way through the woods. Know where the sun was when you started, and look behind you frequently to get the feel for what things will look like on your return trip. Always let people know where you are. Jimmy tried to live by those words. But now, he wasn't all that sure that there *wasn't* anything to be afraid of up here.

Deer.

It reminded him of that storm the other day. Mom.

What about deer was so strange? Deer'd always roamed these woods. He'd seen them before, but what about them now bugged him?

He remembered how frail and not-all-there Mom had been, just standing out in the rain.

And just now he'd thought he'd seen a deer in the distance as he spoke with Carl and Penny.

As he made his way into the woods, he occasionally knocked his dead branch against trees as he went. Kept looking back to his siblings. As he got farther into the woods, he called back every so often, and Carl shouted back. But so far, nothing. Not even that deer he'd thought he'd seen.

"Ritchey!" he called, "*Ritchey!*"

Nothing.

Jimmy looked at the ground around him, hoping to find something of his. A broken branch or two. A piece of clothing. Something he could grab onto and run with. That's what all the outdoor books said, his Boy Scout manual.

He called out back to Carl and Penny. They returned his shout.

Jimmy then came up to the old water tank. It was dull gray and about eight feet high. Dad had told him it had been used to store water for the family who lived here back in the 1800s, or something. But it was old and rusted out. Couldn't hold water anymore because of the rust holes at its rock-and-cement base. Jimmy again called out Ritchey's name. No response. He tapped his stick against the hollow metal of the tank. Leaned back against it, the hollow reverb of the tank still echoing in his head.

What the hell had happened?

Took him *again...*

Why did that sound familiar, the "took him again" part? It was like it awakened some dark, sleeping memory. About improbable things. Like deer...

Shaking his *hand?*

"Ritchey!" he again called out, still leaning against the tank.

Nothing.

Jimmy pushed off the tank, and continued to tap it with his stick. Coming upon the rusted area, he bent down and looked in—

And dropped his stick and shot away from the tank.

His eyes shot to the direction of the cabin, where Penny and Carl awaited.

He couldn't speak. Couldn't *squeak*.

Ritchey was in there—*and he wasn't alone.*

He tried to yell, to shout, but all were trapped in his throat. It felt like something was holding it *in* him. Not letting it out. He lurched, strained his throat. Screamed empty screams.

Nothing. Nothing came out.

He shot back to the tank and again bent down.

Something was looking back at him through that rusted opening. And behind it, he could see…Ritchey, sitting, *scared*.

Jimmy banged the tank with his hands, and again tried to scream. Useless, it was all useless. Groaning to the sky, he again slammed the tank in anger, and shot away from it.

Ran for Penny and Carl.

He scrambled through the brush, continued to *try* to shout, to yell, but it wasn't until he was about halfway back that he was finally able to.

"Carl! *Penny!*" suddenly emitted from his lips. "I found him—*I found him!*"

Carl and Penny came to him, and together they rushed back through the woods toward the tank.

They found Ritchey sitting on the crumbly stone and cement foundation that encircled the base of the rusted-out tank.

He just sat there, looking out into the woods.

As they came upon him, they all threw their arms about Ritchey, hugging him fiercely. Carl asked Ritchey what had happened, but Ritchey didn't know, and Jimmy wrinkled his brow and made faces as he walked around the tank.

Of course, there were no boy-sized openings. He already knew that.

Only those tiny, little rusted holes. Openings big enough for only a few fingers to escape through.

And the tank was eight feet high.

Jimmy crouched down before it. Gathering his resolve, he leaned down and peered into the opening.

Nothing.

No other—*what?* What was there no other *of* inside there?

Jimmy righted himself and stared at the tank. Then got back to his feet and came over to Ritchey.

"You okay?" he asked.

Ritchey looked up to Jimmy, confused; nodded.

Jimmy put a hand to his shoulder. "Well, come on, then," he said, and the four of them left the tank. But as they made their way back, Jimmy couldn't help but cast backward glances into the woods behind them.

To that tank.

Yes, there really was something to be afraid about in these woods....
He just couldn't remember what it was.

3

Lake Clear, New York
11 July 1976
1717 Hours Eastern Time

Jimmy lay back in the lawn chair, his battered Marine Corps utility cap pushed back on his head. He stared up into the barbecue's smoke as it curled throughout the limbs of the spruce tree above. His dad had built the BBQ fireplace himself several years ago. He used yellow brick for the firebox, then above the brick, up the sides and the rest of the fireplace structure had packed stones, round and otherwise, into cement. It was a cool looking brick, stone, and cement thing, with a heavy iron latticework grill that always bit into his hands when he moved it around. The coolest part about it was the warming tray area part-way up the chimney stack, the year "1969" sculpted into the cement between two horizontal slabs of flat stone. The slabs formed a food storage area. But even cooler than that was the small set of deer antlers above that, cemented into the top of the stone chimney stack.

Deer antlers.

Jimmy stared at them.

"Dad," Jimmy asked, casually redirecting his gaze back up into the billowing smoke from the barbecue, "there's nothing weird in our woods, is there?"

Everett chuckled as he busied about setting up the burgers and dogs on the grill.

"Weird? What you mean?"

"Oh, I don't know."

His dad looked up to him briefly as he rolled up the packaging to the now sizzling meat and tossed it away into the small cardboard box he'd used to bring up all the food in. Kneeling, he leaned a supporting elbow on a knee as he again regarded his son; chuckled and shook his head. "You ask the weirdest questions." He got to his feet. "Well, there're no rattlers. There's always bear, but they avoid human contact unless provoked..."

"There's deer, though, right?"

"Yeah, but I'd hardly call deer 'weird.'"

Jimmy laughed uncomfortably.

"Did you see something?"

Did he see *something?*

The water tank.

Woods. *Lots* of woods.

The rusted-out area at the bottom of the water tank. Him bending over to look into those holes…

What was it about those dang antlers? Jimmy thought, studying them.

"No…didn't see anything. Just asking."

His father continued on with what he was doing, and Jimmy stared back up into the smoke-filled spruce branches; to their tree house that was up in those branches. The hodgepodge of boards and tossed-out wood used to build it. He could see some of the green-painted board used in one of its "walls," the one with a window in it. Watched the smoke dance and play inside the branches, wending its way up ever higher into the sky. His mind drifted…it was 1976…where would he be in twenty years? Thirty? In the year 2000? Why, in 2000—2001, like Arthur C. Clarke's *2001: A Space Odyssey*, he'd be like, *forty*. Wow, that was a long way from now. Would he be an astronaut, like Poole or Bowman? Be in some space station—hopefully not with some insane computer, like HAL, though? Or like Roger Torraway, in Frederik Pohl's *Man Plus*? Exploring interplanetary space? What *would* he be doing?

What would he be doing at fifty?

Sixty?

Eighty?

Would he live that long?

Of course, he would—he'd live forever! Surely, by then, science would have achieved longer life in—what year would that be?

Jimmy scrunched his forehead, trying to work out the numbers. If he was fifteen now, he would be eighty—when?

He counted off in tens, using his fingers. Seventy-six, eighty-six, ninety-six, oh-six. That's thirty years. In 2006, he'd be forty-five.

Wow. What a thought.

So, in forty years from that—in 2046—he'd be eighty-five.

Holy cow!

That was almost too much to imagine! *Eighty-five?*

What would life be like in 2046? Would people be living in space? Would *he?* Would he have a space babe? And they'd go exploring? Well, he'd be old, but maybe he'd still look like, maybe, twenty? And she'd be *hot*.…

What would it be like to be in a space ship? Would it be like being in a submarine, like his dad did in the Navy?

"Dad?"

"Yes, son," his dad said, now kicked back in his own lawn chair, pipe smoking, and his Stetson angled down over closed eyes.

"What was it like in submarines?"

"Well," he said, taking a couple more pensive puffs, "it's kinda like being stuck in a small room. With the doors and windows closed and no way out."

Jimmy mulled over that. "Only under water," he said back to his dad.

Everett chuckled, peeking out from under his Stetson, amused. "Yeah, only under water."

"Was it scary?"

Everett took a couple more puffs.

"A little. At first, and every now and then. But you get past that. You had a job to do, and you just did it. We were all tough guys. Underwater warriors. Not scared a nuthin.'"

Everett again cast a quick, amused glance to his son.

"Wow. I can't image being stuck under water in a small thing like that."

"It was exciting. We were doing brave stuff; going places most people will never go," Everett continued, taking occasional puffs between his words. "It was pretty exciting."

"Why'd you stop doing it?"

"Well…as time goes on you just want to do something different. Like when you're playing with one set of toys and you want to play with a different set?"

"Oh.

"Did you go all over the world? Under the North Pole?"

"We went…everywhere."

"Wow."

Jimmy again looked over to his dad, and lay back like he was. Crossed his ankles like his dad had. Angled his hat over his eyes like his dad, and closed his eyes like his dad.

Everett checked out his son without him seeing him do so. He smiled, again closing his eyes and puffing on his pipe.

"Dad?"

"Yeah?"

"What's the scariest thing you ever did?"

Everett paused for a moment as he puffed. He opened his eyes and pushed back his Stetson, staring up into the blue sky and swirling smoke from the barbecue.

For a moment, he thought—*swore*—he was back on the *Threadfin*, SS410. And they were steaming a direct course for Cuba under 400 feet of water.

October, 1962.

He was a Radioman, Petty Officer, Second Class. Their mission to quarantine Cuba.

Oh, shit, they had thought, every one of the eighty-three officers and enlisted onboard that boat, *what had they gotten themselves into now?*

But, there was something else…something else about that passage…something that sent a shiver down Everett's spine. An ill-defined terror like a nightmare just barely remembered—forgotten. What was it about that voyage that so scared the shit out him—even now.…

Everett got up and grabbed the long, iron poker and knocked around the burning wood in the fireplace. Cleared his throat.

"Well…it was always kinda scary down there, so you just took your mind off what it was you were in and where you were…and just focused on your job."

"And you were a radio operator, right?"

"Yup," Everett said, nodding, grateful that his son didn't press the issue. After adjusting the firewood, he placed the poker back against the side of the barbeque and sat back down. Stared into the fire.

"But probably the scariest thing that ever happened to me was when I was electrocuted in the radio shack on the *Sailfish*."

"What happened?" Jimmy asked, sitting back up.

"Oh…we were doing some work in the radio shack—where all the radio equipment was kept—and, well, something just happened, my feet slipped, and I got shocked—like when you'd stuck that paperclip into that electrical outlet? Only much worse. Knocked me clean on my ass. Knocked me out. I had to be put into a decompression chamber to recover."

"Decompression chamber? What's that?"

"Normally it's used to help divers who get too much of a gas called nitrogen into their blood stream when they dive. If you get too much of it—nitrogen—it can kill you. This chamber helps get it out of you without killing you. Very technical stuff. Anyway, it also helped me recover from my electrocution."

"Wow."

Jimmy paused, mulling things over.

So…in thirty years he'd be forty-five…and in seventy years he'd be eighty-five. It was almost too far to imagine. How old would his dad be in thirty years?

And what would he—little Jimmy Cherko—be doing at forty-five?

Chapter Eleven

1

ERO Operations
1 June 1986
0100 Hours Mountain Time

Cherko had been sitting at his console, performing his on-orbit operations, when the by-now routine and supposedly telepathic communications had made themselves known. He'd just finished transcribing the information strings, when he posed his question.

Why are we doing this?

Because you have been trained to do so.

Why have I been trained to do this, and what is the purpose of what we're doing?

Your answer should be apparent.

You are alien?

From another perspective, perhaps, you *could be considered alien.*

You mean "apparent" in that we're doing this to communicate with you. An alien race.

Silence.

But what are we going to do with all this communication? How are we putting it to use, since I seem to just be transcribing numbers? Why do you need someone like me to do this?

Information string terminated.

He/she/it was gone.

Cherko stabbed F10.

So…he wasn't about to learn much about Project operations.

And wasn't it amazing how easy he was accepting of all this?

He was taking supposed-alien-telepathic communication in stride. Like it was something he did every day.

Which, basically, it was.

Amazing at how the fantastical became…normal.

Who would have believed?

He was sure that was part of the point.

But look at the answers he got…just enough ambiguity so that he had nothing concrete. No straight answers. Was it really alien communication, or was he just being toyed with?

But the upshot of the whole thing was that he had been communicating with something or someone through no visible, physical means. The information presented itself through a wholly nonphysical, mental, medium. Or at least, *he* was addressing its mechanics in this way; he supposed these messages could be beamed into his head from elsewhere by microwaves, or whatever "wave" was capable of penetrating so many feet of concrete and steel and dirt. So maybe the same line of thinking could be applied to the "alien" concept. Maybe it wasn't really all that alien,

(*From another perspective, perhaps*, you *could be considered alien…*)

but the circumstantial facts *appeared* so.

Were *made* to appear so?

The more rational thinkers insisted there was always an answer for everything supposedly unknown. That there only need be the right light shed upon a subject to cast away its ignorant darkness…to peel away any such "mysterious" perception.

Perception.

Things were only eerie and unknown because we were unfamiliar with them. Once brought out into open light and objectively studied, then there was no need for fear, superstition, or conjecture, and said items of interest became as commonplace as a table or the clothes on our backs. Shakespeare had it right, but science *makes* it right.

During their brief conversation Cherko had picked up images. It was not so much like *He/She/It* was being evasive, as it was that *He/She/It* didn't deem the line of questioning as important enough to pursue. That was his true feeling, was what he really picked up. Like all that was needed from the communication was that *it was being performed.*

It just really *felt* as he *perceived* it to be. He couldn't get around that. That what his mind perceived was absolutely not human. Not at any familiar level.

And, just like him, he was sure whatever alien was contacting him certainly had other additional duties to perform. Maybe *He/She/It* was even pissed that *He/She/It* even had to perform such a lowly task with such a "primitive," like himself. Maybe He/She/It had had a bad sidereal day, or even had issues with the task itself. Maybe *He/She/It* thought themselves above such efforts, but that they were somehow necessary for the Project. Like in order to write you had to learn grammar.

And he *had* been told he'd been the first.

So, maybe, it wasn't so much about the information transferred, as he was just part of a protocol, an investigative etiquette of some kind. Nothing more.

The first.

The first for what? Alien communication?

Too unimaginatively limiting. Since—to him—aliens were obviously involved with whatever was going on, any communication with them had to have gone on far and away a *long* time ago. Perhaps that was the big deal behind Roswell, first Big Time (government) contact and all, but by now, no, things had to have progressed way beyond such mundane considerations; he had to be the first for some other form of higher alien interaction, some as-yet unknown method by which their relations were to be put into a more significant application.

But with this string of data he'd entered, he felt something decidedly…unsettling.

2

ERO Operations
17 June 1986
0320 Hours Mountain Time

```
77900/Subject84289346582/68434238/860614/Potentialifo
rRecall77/ResidualPain32/NerveResponseCurve09/BodyNorma
            lization88/03730N10400E///
```

This was Cherko's first communication in which actual words had been involved. And he didn't like what he was getting.

What is this communication? he asked. *Is this an abduction?*

A pause was introduced to the transmission.

Tell me—what are you reporting through me? You're abducting us, aren't you? Abducting humans?

I am not abducting anyone.

But there are those you are in contact with who are. *Why are you doing this?*

You are not authorized an answer. Continue for further information strings.

Before Cherko could press the issue, another string was sent, this time only numbers. Communication termination was immediate once Cherko transcribed the data.

He hit F10. His satellite duties complete for the moment, he got up.

"I'm heading to the john," he announced to the crew commander, and left the ops floor.

Cherko sat in the restroom, head in hands, eyes closed.

Just what the hell was going on—what was he being used for? Just a telepathically activated relay?

A *transcriptionist?*

This was his big job about which he couldn't tell anyone?

Okay, he was apparently communicating with alien intelligence, but about *what* was he communicating? The past several sessions with these guys he'd gotten similar data. Text intermixed with the numbers, but this was the first time where he'd received

Potentiality for Recall.

Residual Pain.

Nerve Response Curves.

Body Normalization.

It sounded like humans were being abducted and tests were being run on them!

Why?

Why the hell would an apparently advanced race have the need to abduct *anyone?*

Jesus Christ, *he was mentally communicating with them,* for crying out loud, and they needed to *physically* abduct humans?

What kind of sense did that make? If they used mental telepathy as a matter of course, wouldn't it also stand to reason that they had other capabilities that no longer required resorting to

(*Residual Pain...*)

abductions and physical—*bodily*—experimentation?

Look to their crafts...flying saucers breaking all the rules of known human physics! He'd never personally seen any—at least not that he knew—but come *on.*

So, now, he was finding, with such advanced technology, alien races were still resorting to primitive snatch-and-grab techniques that involved *pain* responses?

Didn't make sense. Not one lick. Unless—

It wasn't *aliens* doing the abducting.

Or they weren't as advanced as we thought they were.

After all—look at us. On some kind of a proportionate level, we have all this advanced science and engineering, yet look at how we're applying it.

Spying.

War.

Bombs and bullets.

With all our advances you'd think we'd expend more in the way of peace...better fuels and fuel mileages, more food, less poverty, better government, better health care, wipe out disease...*violence.*

But what was getting all the press? All the dollars?

So, on a proportionate, extrapolated level, yeah, humans had all this technology, but its uses were mainly funneled toward the military industrial complex. And if the legends were true, even Atlantis had had similar issues...issues that brought about *its* extinction.

So, what made him think an alien existence would be any different? If aliens *physically* existed, might they also have very similar—not exact, mind you, but an "alien equivalent"—of physical predilections and weaknesses? Greed and power? Maybe to be physical was to be imbued with an inherently physical, ethical, challenge?

But, still—*why communicate all this through him?*

The next time he got one of those messages, he was going to remember the locations, the lat and longs given in the message that trailed after the text. He'd had enough.

He was nobody's tool, alien or otherwise.

* * *

ERO Operations
18 June 1986
0213 Hours Mountain Time

```
77900/Subject9476123904/11120057/870234/PotenialityforR
ecall67/ResidualPain77/NerveResponseCurve45/BodyNormali
                zation65/03901N10435E

     77900/849657/86115876557/8316/98999

      77900/65468438/68488/6841385/5812

    77900/5782/425646556/545/54845685584///
```

As Cherko entered this information, something in his mind "clicked." It was as if his communications had suddenly "stepped up a level." It was like he was now sucking on a mental fire hose that spewed full-bore into the mouth of a hummingbird. There was now more *breadth* to these communications, more depth, and an expansiveness that felt like a wide, open, prairie. Like a whole nother "room" had just opened up in his mind...

Did you do that on purpose?, Cherko was asked.

Something just happened. I'm not sure what.

You ascended to a higher plane of communication.

What does that mean? I feel a bit...overwhelmed.

It is merely another plane, or level of communication. More texture, more data about your communications are made available here.

Was this supposed to happen?

You are the first. Yours is preliminary data.

It's not a problem to communicate at this level?

It is not.

I noticed, as I took down these data strings...I had more imagery, data I find hard to put into words...

Silence.

Why can't you tell me about the abductions? What is the purpose of the Project? Communications are terminated.

Cherko was about to whack his console out of frustration, when he regained his situational sense about him and checked his crew members and commander. Definitely wouldn't be the thing to *do*. So he hit F10, took a deep breath or two to calm down, and tried to bring back the images of the just transmitted communication. Though there were aspects of the images he couldn't seem to mentally translate, there were aspects he could.

A driver.

There had been a *rancher* four-wheelin it across his fields. Looking for stray cattle. It was late. Clear night sky. Headlights before him. Bumpy, jangling, ride.

A light. Off in the distance, up *above* a hill. To his right.

Shadowing him?

Headlights forward, light to the right.

Confusion.

Truck…stopped.

Here Cherko had a myriad of images that blasted confusion and pain…blurs of faces and backgrounds. Examinations…*probing*, on both physical and mental levels.

The rancher came to…in his truck…three miles and several hours later.…

Cherko saw a sign.

He knew this location.

Calhan, Colorado
18 June 1986
0811 Hours Mountain Time

Cherko sat in his car, pulling a short sip from his water bottle and staring out into the field. He took a left onto Calhan Highway, North. This was where he'd seen that rancher. Where he'd been…returned. Somewhere out there.

Why the hell were people being abducted?

Cherko got out of his car and walked to the side of the road, to the barbed-wire fence and "No Trespassing" sign. The early morning breeze felt good. It always felt good to get out after having been cooped up in a windowless environment for eight-and-a-half hours.

But, God, he should have changed out of his uniform. He stood out like a sore thumb.

He went to the trunk of his car and found his binoculars. Pulling them out of their case, he adjusted them to look out over the field.

Nothing.

Lots and lots of *nothing*.

Cattle in the distance.

Then, farther up the field north of him, he found what looked like a lump on the ground. It looked like...

A body.

Cherko brought down the binoculars. A chill ran through him.

A body?

He looked down both directions of the road.

Alone.

He brought his 10x50 binocs back up. He just didn't have the resolution or angle necessary to make out exactly what he was looking at. He brought the binocs back down and looked to the fence before him and its "No Trespassing" sign.

Cherko ducked through the wide spacing of the barbed-wire fence and cautiously hurried toward the lump on the ground, nervously scanning the wide, open, plains. The closer he got to the lump the more evident it became it was a body. But it wasn't human.

A horse. It was a *horse*.

Cherko slowed back down to a hurried and nervous walk and cautiously approached. Constantly swiveled his head. There were no other horses or cattle around it. In fact the livestock he did see were much farther east, up on another slope. As Cherko came up to the carcass, he noticed no smell. None. It was *huge*. As he made his way around the remains he stopped dead in his tracks, dropping the binoculars.

"What the *hell?*"

The neck and head were stripped clean to the bone.

Again nervously scanning the fields, he picked up his binocs; continued examination of whatever-was-left-of the horse. Noticed the depressions his steps made in the dirt and grass around it.

"There's no *smell*..."

He wrinkled his face. Came as close to the carcass as he dared.

All flesh, muscle, and other tissue were totally removed from the frame of the animal's neck and head, leaving only, and nothing but...*bone*. Just as clean as if...

A laser had been used.

There was no blood.

No stink.

No *bugs*.

Cherko looked about the animal. Looked back the way he'd come. He again looked to his own footsteps in the dirt and crushed grass as he approached the carcass.

There were no hoof marks in the dirt *around* the carcass.

How had the horse gotten here if it hadn't walked?

Cherko got another intense round of chills, actually shivered this time, and backed away.

He turned and began hurrying toward his car...and stopped.

A black car was parked behind his vehicle.

He brought up the binoculars. His fingers didn't want to work. Felt thick, clumsy.

The black car pulled out and away from his, driving on up the road in no apparent hurry.

And engine noises were quickly approaching from behind. From the hills where he'd spotted the grazing cattle.

Cherko sprinted for his car.

Chapter Twelve

1

Cherko slammed the apartment door behind him.

Locked it.

Checked back through the peephole, then rushed to the patio door to make sure that not only was it locked, but that its hanging plastic slats were also drawn and flat against the window.

The ride home had been the most paranoid of his life.

What the hell had that mutilated horse been about?

What was that black car about, and why had it stopped behind *his?*

Cherko sat on the couch; stared into the TV and wall unit.

He was an Air Force officer, working in classified satellite operations, but was also—apparently—a covert Air Force *alien* communicator. He *was* mentally communicating with aliens; communicating, among other things, about *abductions.*

Humans were being snatched up by someone or something.

And—he just found out—at the location of one of these abductions was a mutilated horse carcass (no doubt already gone—the area surely sanitized).

No blood.

No bugs.

No flesh or muscle on the head.

And there were no tracks to the carcass by *the once living animal.*

Cherko's phone rang.

Cautiously, he approached it, but let the answering machine pick up. At the beep, he braced himself.

"Hi, honey…it's your mother," came the lolling, familiar voice thick with New Jersey. "I'm out in Las Vegas for a convention—"

Cherko grabbed the handset.

"Mom?"

"Hi, honey! Didn't expect you to be home, or awake, or—"

"Actually I just got in."

"What good timing, then! I just had the urge to call. Felt you needed to talk."

* * *

"You like the new job?"

"It's pretty interesting, yeah."

"So, what'd you say in your letter, you're 'flying satellites'?"

"Yeah."

"You actually sit atop them and ride them like a horse"

(*carcass*....)

she said, laughing that high-spirited laugh of hers.

"No, Mom, it's not like Dr. Strangelove—"

"Why not? It's such a cool image!"

"Because those people would be called *astronauts*, and, as we all know, I'm not one of them."

"I'm sorry, honey—"

"It's okay."

"So…you just, what, how did you put it, hook up to satellites by ground stations and just…follow them around?"

"Yup; pretty much. That's my life…pretty boring."

"You okay? You sound funny."

Cherko paused.

"Mom…you still have, *you know*…"

"Yes."

"A lot?"

"Well, I wouldn't say a lot, not like when you were a child—"

"But it still happens."

Renée sighed. "Yes."

"And you can't find any answer to it—from anyone?"

"Jimmy—what's the matter? What's bothering you?"

"I was driving out east of town today, after work. Out in some rancher's field I found something. Something pretty disgusting."

"What?"

"A dead animal. A horse carcass. Without a head."

"Without a *head?*"

"Well, it actually still had its skull and vertebrae attached…but there was…no *flesh*, Mom, no muscle—or any other tissue."

"I see."

"It was pretty unnerving. And no smell. Absolutely *nothing*. No bugs. No tracks to the carcass except mine."

Renée fell silent for a moment. "What were you doing out in the middle of a rancher's field to begin with?"

"I'd just gone for a drive."

"After work?"

"Sometimes I do that," he lied. "Anyway, I'm kinda surprised at how much it shook me up. I wasn't expecting to see anything like that."

"Guess not."

"So, it got me to thinking…and I've thought about this a lot over the years—"

"You think I'm being abducted."

"Well, don't *you*? I mean, *really*, doesn't that make perfect sense? Missing time, finding yourself all over the place—no memories?"

"Well, yes."

"And I bet you've been having those dreams, again, too, haven't you?"

Renée burst out laughing.

"Mom…it's not really all that funny. I mean, who knows what's happening!"

"No matter what might be happening, I have no memory of it, so how can I really answer your question?"

"But to make *jokes* about it—"

"Really, honey, what else can I do? Hmm?"

"That's just it, I don't know!"

"Well, there you go. All I can do is live my life the best I can, until I find out what *is* going on. What would you do?"

Cherko sighed.

"Exactly. I seem to be able to live a basically happy, normal, life, only thing is every now and then I find myself, well, waking up in strange locations, is all. At least it's not with strange *men!*"

"*Mom…*"

"Sonny, no matter what life deals us, we have to make the best of it. I look at it like this…I could have had cancer or been mangled in a car crash. I don't and I haven't been. I'm apparently healthy, have a good sense of humor, but every now and then…sleepwalk. So far, it hasn't killed me—"

"*Mom…*"

"Well, it hasn't. But you never know. And so far, I've managed to survive. I just have to keep going, live life until some day we either find a cure for whatever ails me or I die. It's that simple."

"I guess.…"

"Whether or not aliens are involved, well, I'm here right now. And if I do forever disappear, you'll know why, then, right?"

"You're so cavalier about all this!"

"What else can I say? I've been to all the doctors, and no one can help."

"What about hypnosis?"

"I've tried that—"

"And?"

"Nothing."

"What do you mean, 'nothing'?"

"I seem to be blocking it, or something. Or there's just nothing *there*. No one can seem to break through to me. I just end up sitting there, quiet."

"Don't you find that odd? I thought hypnosis was supposed to break through all conscious and unconscious barriers."

"Not always. Some people just can't be hypnotized."

"And you just happen to be one of them?"

"What can I say?"

"Well, you could sound a little more concerned…"

"That's not me and you know it."

"I know. Maybe…maybe I'm just tired. I don't know."

"Well, you have been up a long time. Why don't you go to bed and see how you feel when you get up.

"How's Erica?"

Cherko smiled. "Great."

"You two still getting along well?"

"Oh, yeah."

"That's wonderful, honey!"

"It is. She is. I like her a lot."

"Interesting…"

"Mom…"

"A mother can dream, can't she?"

"I s'pose."

"Well, I have to get going, get back to that convention they sent me to."

"Dad come?"

"No—was in the middle of another search."

"Kay. Thanks for calling, Mom."

"What are mothers for?"

"Love you, Mom."

"Love you, too, Sonny."

Cherko was awoken by heavy pounding at his apartment door. It was one o'clock.

A.m. or p.m.?

Jumping out of bed in his shorts and a T-shirt, he rushed to the door. Looked out the peephole.

Men. Two of them.

But he couldn't totally make them out without his contacts or glasses, and them being turned away from the door. Cherko spun around, quickly looking for his glasses.

They wore overcoats—*in June?*

He squinted back through the peephole. One turned back toward him, the wide brim of his hat angled over his face.

Cherko stepped back, staring at the door.

Agents?

That black car.

More pounding on the door.

Cherko unlocked it—

The two men strode in with surprising speed, all but smashing him up against the wall.

"May we come in?" the first one asked, continuing past, while the second ushered Cherko farther inside the apartment, closing the door behind them.

"Can I see some identification?" Cherko asked, nervously and not without some effort.

"Certainly," Talking One said. The other directed Cherko over to his couch and forced him down onto it. He stood beside him.

The men were tall and dark skinned. The talking one's voice was thick with an accent he couldn't identify, his voice deep. There was a definite menacing presence the about both of them.

"What were you doing out in that field this morning?" Talking One asked. Calmly.

"What?"

"That field, Mr. Cherko. What were you doing trespassing on that rancher's property?"

"Nothing—I was just looking at—"

"What?"

"I told you—nothing."

"Looking at nothing. With binoculars?"

Talking One pulled out Cherko's binoculars and smashed them against a corner of wall.

"What—"

Talking One opened his hand and allowed the binoculars to drop to the floor.

Still groggy from sleep, but feeling like he'd just been hit up beside the head, Cherko stared at the man.

"You took an oath, did you not, Lieutenant?"

"Oath?"

"To your country."

"My—"

"It would be very sad for anything to happen to your mother. Your father…wouldn't it, Lieutenant? *Erica?*"

Cherko tried to get to his feet, but Silent One forced him back down, and with quite a bit more power than was even remotely necessary. Cherko worked his shoulders.

Talking One paced the apartment.

"You also might want to be careful about what you tell others."

In one amazingly swift movement, Talking One shot over to the phone and effortlessly tore it from the wall. The phone dinged several times as it bounced and shattered across the floor.

"Hey!" Cherko said, again shooting to his feet.

Talking One spun on him and was in his face before he could blink. Cherko tried to back away, but wasn't fast enough. The dinging of the phone still rang in his head. The aura of absolute and utter menace emanating from the man was crushing, especially inches from his face.

"*You made a promise.* To never, *ever,* speak of your job…and it would be a *reeeal* disappointment if you did. For all involved. A real disappointment, Mr. Cherko. Do we understand each other?"

Cherko stared at the now phoneless wall.

"*Do we?*"

"Y-yes."

"Good. Now…do your job. Don't be so curious," he said leaving Cherko's face, "and everyone gets along."

Silent One left Cherko's side.

"Good day, Mr. Cherko," Talking One said, as both exited the apartment. As they did, Cherko got the curious image of the both of them reverse-oozing out of the place like some nightmarish sci-fi oil slick.

Cherko looked back to his destroyed phone. Then he broke his trance and rushed to the apartment door, flinging it open.

Gone.

He hurried back inside, and fumbling with the patio door mechanism, shot out onto the patio landing.

Gone.

Reentering his apartment, his legs buckled, and he collapsed on the floor next to the couch.

Stuff like this just didn't happen to him.

Couldn't have happened.

2

The drive in to grave shift had been nothing short of nerve-racking. There was no one on the road except for himself—and one lone driver who seemed to keep his distance probably about a mile or so behind. Even when he slowed down, the driver seemed to stay back at about the same distance. Or so he figured, since it was hard to judge distances in the dark. But there was a vehicle that had also seemed to follow him onto Enoch Road, then on to the site itself. After parking, Cherko stayed in his car for a minute or two, to see who it was who'd followed…but saw no one enter the Entry Control

Point before him. A couple cars now pulled in, and his well-devised surveillance plan went out the window.

But not only was there the hang-back driver, but it seemed as if things were out of place in his car. His water bottle, which he always kept up front, was under the back seat. A *Missing Persons* tape of his that he'd been listening to in the cassette player was stuffed down between the seats. He hadn't done that. You'd think if these Men in Black were government, they'd be professional enough to *not* move things...

Unless they did it to mess with him.

Send a message.

And even as he entered through site security, the SPs seemed to eye him a little closer. He could see a silhouette behind that tinted window inside the Entry Control Point. Just standing there.

Then, once inside on the ops floor for shift change, Major Turnbull was there, also eyeballing him.

When shift change ended, Cherko went looking for Turnbull, but he was nowhere to be found, his office vacated and locked.

Cherko sat down at the console and logged on.

Prepare for information string.

Without batting an eye, Cherko tapped the right trackball switch and F10.

His cover job's screens all came up and he checked them all out as he received his communications.

But something wasn't right with his communications, either. They felt...different.

You feel different, Cherko sent at the elevated communication level.

I am a different communicator.

Why?

Are there several of you at your position?

Information was passed, and Cherko noticed this one, though cold and scientific like the other, seemed to also have another element just out of reach. Or was, perhaps, trying to be...hidden?

Unavailable?

Cherko also noticed his data were back to numerical strings, no more text.

Why are these different? Where are the words?

This is the information string to be sent.

You know what I mean, and don't tell me I'm not authorized an answer.

Silence.

More data was passed.

Why will no one tell me what this program is about...how I fit into everything?

Because it has been deemed you are not required to know. Your participation in the program is not contingent upon your knowledge of the data nor the outcome of your actions.

That's the first direct answer I've ever received from you guys. What do you know about the—

Communications are terminated.

horse—

That was the end of that. But he *had* received a direct answer to a question, and that was a start. He'd also had a new communicator...which was way too coincidental. Things were just getting a little too—

"Lieutenant," came the voice from behind.

Cherko spun around in his chair.

Turnbull.

"In my office when you're done."

Cherko entered Turnbull's office.

"Close the door and sit."

Cherko did.

Turnbull folded his hands before him.

"You've been poking your nose into areas you shouldn't be poking your nose."

"Sir?"

"Don't play with me—or this program. This is serious. Gravely serious. It's not television."

"I had no idea, it wasn't my—"

"*I don't care,*" he said, heavily enunciating each word. "When you came onboard you signed paperwork. Part of that paperwork declared you were to keep your nose clean. You have to avoid certain topics, people, places—*events—*"

"But there are people being—"

"*That is not your concern,*" Turnbull snapped.

"What?"

"Your concern is your *job*. Period. It's a dirty world out there, and certain things have to be done by a chosen few. *That* is your only concern. You are only concerned with your part in the big puzzle."

Cherko stared at Turnbull.

"Lieutenant, you may not get it yet, but your life could be at stake here. You saw how serious these people are. *And there is no leaving the program.*"

Turnbull got to his feet, then leaned across his desk. For the first time, Cherko noticed how powerful (and hairy) his forearms were, as they disappeared up and under the rolled-up cuffs of his crew blues.

"You really don't know the extent to which these people can go. There *are* no boundaries with these organizations. You signed paperwork, but believe me, they won't stop there. Believe me when I tell you, you better keep your nose clean, or you might not live to regret it."

Cherko continued to stare at Turnbull.

"Now, go…take a walk and think things out. *Get your head on straight, Lieutenant.* We'll cover for you until you return. *Go.*"

Outside, Cherko walked the perimeter of the rough-textured building, glancing up to the stars. It was a warm, pleasant, June night. He seemed to be asking himself this question a lot, lately, but: *what the hell had he gotten himself into—never leave?*

Cherko walked around to the rear of the building. He left the yellow glow of the construction and street lights for the umbra and anonymity of darkness.

He felt as if he'd joined the mafia, for chrissakes. The ultimate bait and switch. He'd wanted some cool job, thought he'd found one, but quickly discovered that once you entered…you could never leave.

Hotel ERO.

What did that say about career progression, let alone *life?*

How did someone stay with a program forever?

And he never remembered signing up for that.

Not to mention, would he be doing *this* for the rest of his life? What kind of life was that to look forward to?

Cherko leaned against the building and again looked to the night sky. A shooting star arced across the heavens. Those used to be looked upon as a good sign, but it looked like he had nothing good to look forward to any more. He felt a twinge of nostalgia for those lost days of childhood. Those naïve dreams. He was all for growing up, adulthood, but never had he—

Prepare for information string.

What?

Prepare.

But, I'm not at my—

What the hell was he supposed to do?

He scrunched his forehead. Something was wholly different about this communication on every level. He felt an odd mental expansion.

77900/Subject77900/9846128/1682/Recall/0388025N1045246E
///

Communication terminated.

Cherko was able to hold the data string in his head!

This was new.

It was like he could visually *see* each digit before him, like the pages of a book—and wholly retain it. Before, while at his console, it was like he was a voice-activated relay, the numbers entered his head, they were instantly translated through his fingers and entered into the workstation, and he wasn't able to retain them in his memory for any length of time.

This time...he *could*.

And there was a deeper dimension to this communication he couldn't put into words, beyond what he'd felt at his first "expansion."

And the entity sending him the data...he/she/it wasn't even the same one who'd recently changed out his previous contact. This one connected to him in a very deep way he found disconcerting. It was like he felt he/she/it in his *bones*.

Cherko leaned back against the building and again looked to the stars.

77900/Subject77900/9846128/1682/Recall/0388025N1045246E
///

He remembered the string, digit for digit, and it was like each digit had a multi-dimensional *depth* to it. Continuing to stare skyward, he ran the string over and over in his mind. A cold sweat gripped him.

His identifier!

His identifier and the *Subject* preamble were the same!

He pushed away from the building.

Recall.

Subject 77900.

Him?

Since when was he...

Cherko heard a noise and looked to his right.

A light in the sky...coming his way.

Hurrying away from the building, he uneasily made his way through the darkness, and tripped, rapping his elbow against something hard. Cursing, he stumbled about the ground like the typical movie klutz always made to trip during pivotal chase scenes.

The light continued straight for him.

Cherko scrambled for darkness and to put building between him and that light, but everything moved in a frustratingly super slo-mo.

The light was almost atop him when he finally got to his feet. Fear tangled his legs as he tried to run, his feet blocked in invisible concrete shoes. He cornered a dark bend rapping his knuckles on the rough pebble-like exterior, and again nearly tripped as he trudged through piles of what felt like dirt. He stifled his near-tripping by plunging his hands into the pile of cool earth. As he scrambled back into the darkness, he saw and heard the light fly past.

A chopper.

What the hell was a chopper doing out here?

And...*jets?*

Jet aircraft shot overhead—and not very far above at that.

Cherko collapsed against the building, panting, felt a slightly twisted left ankle.

Good Lord.

He paused long enough to catch his breath. He brushed off his crew blue pants then carefully picked his way through the darkness alongside the building to a side door. He stood before it. Looked to the light above the door.

To the soft, calming glow of the yellow light.

So beautiful.

Haunting.

Filled his being.

Cherko smiled.

Smiled into the light...the calming, *haunting* light....

Chapter Thirteen

1

Colorado Springs, CO
4 November, 2010
0330 Hours Mountain Time

Jimmy's eyes popped open.

Somebody was in the room with them.

Sweeping off the blankets, he leapt out of bed, swiped on the bed-side lamp, and almost knocked it off the nightstand in the process. He fumbled after the baseball bat leaning against the wall, then held it out before him.

Scanned the room.

Looked to his bed.

Their bed.

There, laying on her stomach under blankets and bed sheets, her head buried by two fluffy pillows, was Erica.

Jimmy stood near-naked and confused.

Was he more confused at seeing his wife in bed with him or at the intruder in their bedroom?

He continued to hold out the bat before him...shaking and breathing heavily.

Nothing.

There was nothing standing before him in their bedroom.

Licking his lips, he inched forward, cautiously, and checked out the bedroom's small bathroom, faint moon light streaming in from between closed curtains. He turned toward and approached the bedroom door.

Why hadn't Erica awoken? How could she sleep through all this? Was he becoming that commonplace that she no longer was awakened by his nocturnal activity?

Baseball bat up before him like rifle-at-ready, he crept out into the hallway.

He flicked on light switches as he searched their tri-level.

Nothing.

He went through every room, every closet. The crawlspace.

Nothing, nothing, and nothing. Not even a field mouse.

He returned to their bedroom, bedroom nightstand light still on, and bat lowered. Back beside the bed he leaned the bat back up against its station at the wall. Slowly he turned toward the bed. Stared at Erica's still-sleeping body.

Or what he thought was Erica.

Re-grabbing the bat without turning around, he used it to nudge the bundle of blankets and pillows.

She wasn't there.

Again...gone.

Another business trip to Cheyenne? Bozeman?

He lost track. Just another one of those hypnagogic incidents.

He replaced his bat bedside, but this time came to the closed window drapes and pushed them aside. Outside, under the motion-detecting lights, grazed

"Deer."

He left the window and returned to bed. Turned off the light.

"Nothing but fucking deer."

2

Colorado Springs, CO
4 November 2010
1455 Hours Mountain Time

Cherko entered his office after having been in the software development lab for several hours, and thumped his tech order working copy onto his desk. He sat down, tired, and tapped the down-arrow key on his keyboard. Check some e-mail, do his timecard, then head out to see the shrink. Herr Doktor Alda.

Ve have vays....

He was actually kinda looking forward to the visit. Anything having to do with the mind fascinated him. It should be interesting to see what someone else thought of his..."condition."

State of mind.

Whatever.

But nothing was happening. With his computer.

He again tapped the down-arrow key.

Still nothing. His screen remained dark.

What the hell?

Moved the mouse. Again nothing.

"Okay...what's going on here...."

Continuing to tap his keyboard, he peeked under his desk to the machine itself, a black IBM ThinkCentre tower.

No lights.

Not even that little green one that told you the computer was powered on.

Cherko ducked under his desk and hit the ThinkCentre's start button, then sat back up.

Blackness. Still no screen activity. In fact he didn't even hear that boot-up *click-hum-spin-whir*.

"What the hell?"

His computer had been working when he'd left for the lab. Things had been working just fine, then. What'd changed? A virus? Had some updated push from the IT Computer Geeks caused an unintended crash?

Getting down on all fours he went to the back of the computer. Checked and rechecked all connections. Traced all power cords to the surge protector outlet.

And found it.

One cord—the main power cord—was actually about a quarter inch from being pushed all the way into the strip.

Now wasn't that interesting.

Cherko reseated it and instantly heard the subdued whine and whir of the IBM ThinkCentre coming back to life. Backing out from under his desk (and whacking his head on the underside of the keyboard tray), he sat back on his haunches (rubbing his wound).

Now, what would have caused the power cord to inch out of the outlet like that? Might he have kicked it?

Cherko sat in his chair. The screen was already working its way through its NT boot-up sequence. In moments it was ready for his sign-on and password, which he entered. He glanced to the clock. Nearly three; quittin time. And since he had a three-thirty appointment with Alda, he had to leave pretty much right on time today.

He guessed he could have kicked the cord loose just before leaving his desk…the power strip that was all the way back against the wall. The power strip that was out of kicking range.

Maybe.

Maybe not.

No matter, it was up and running, and he had to enter his e-timecard info and punch.

3

It was snowing again, big, honkin flakes, as Cherko made his way up the hill on Austin Bluffs Boulevard, by the university. It seemed it was always snowing the past couple weeks. That was good for the High Country and skiing, but as much as he loved it, it was taking up a lot of his time with all the shoveling and snowblowing. But it did make driving fun. He loved driving in the stuff. Bad weather always gave you something to do other than just sitting there behind the wheel mindlessly droning on from Point A to Point B. You actually had to *do* something—show some actual skill on the road—and he liked that.

Cherko took a left off Austin Bluffs Boulevard and onto Austin Bluffs Parkway. Entering the parking lot, he veered off toward the right, found Alda's building, and parked.

Jimmy entered the small, empty, and actually quite pleasant office of Dr. Walter Alda. He momentarily ducked back out into the hallway, but, still—no one. The building felt empty. Re-entering the office, he immediately went to the walls, checking out Dr. Walter Eugene Alda's plaques and certificates. Graduated from a couple schools he hadn't heard of—except for CU, Boulder. Was also practiced in hypnotherapy. Hm, that'd be interesting to try. Cherko then left the Love-Me wall for the large windows and stared out at Pikes Peak.

The snow was beautiful.

Calming.

After a few moments, he turned back around and found two huge, comfortable Victorian chairs angled toward each other, and took a seat in one.

So, here he sat, awaiting The Great Learned One who was going to solve all his problems and bring him back into the light of day.

Dr. Alda.

The office was small and not at all like what was usually portrayed on TV or read about in books. His had no grand oak or cherry desk, behind which were all manner of psychiatric encyclopedia and compendia, nor upon which were reams of published papers. No, Alda's desk was small and sparse, though he did have filing cabinets and books everywhere. He also had some rather outdated bean-bag chairs, and those bubbly waterfall things that were supposed to calm you. The office didn't feel stuffy nor intimidating. This could be fun.

Three hardback books momentarily got his attention: *Communion, Transformation,* and *Breakthrough.*

Dr. Alda entered the room.

"Mr. Cherko, I presume?" he said, rubbing his hands together.

Alda was tall and slim, wore rimless, wire glasses and sported a graying goatee and well-kept hair. His face was friendly, as was, Cherko gathered, his demeanor.

Cherko rose, hand outstretched in a greeting.

"Yes."

Alda quickly shook his hand. "Dr. Alda. Pleasure to make your acquaintance."

"Good to meet you, too—I hope. You can call me 'Jimmy'"

"Great. Well," Alda said, smiling and gesticulating back to the chair, "have—or return to—your seat. Would you like water or anything? Sorry, no hard liquor; the board frowns upon that sort of thing." Alda took up a seat in the other Victorian. Cherko once again took his. "So," Alda continued, "what can we do for you?"

"Well," Cherko said, crossing his legs and calmly folding his hands in his lap, "I seem to rear-end trash trucks and freak out in MRI machines."

Alda nodded, pinning Cherko to the wall behind him with a penetrating yet sympathetic look.

"Trash trucks, huh."

"Yeah, trash trucks."

"Okay," Alda said, "so, your mom has a history of sleepwalking, and you've also had occasional bouts with it yourself?"

Cherko nodded.

Alda looked down to his notes, stroking his goatee.

"Your mother still sleepwalk?"

"Yes. I just talked with her the other day."

Had he?

He *thought* he had....

Alda looked up to Cherko, his eyes deep, dark, and probing in a way that surprisingly made Cherko's blood run cold. Cherko looked into those eyes; found he couldn't look away. There was something unnervingly familiar in that look, a look that stopped him in mid-thought by a certain...recognition?

"I'd like to try something."

"Okay."

"Free association. Familiar with it?"

Still transfixed by Alda's stare like a stuck bug, and feeling *juuust* as uncomfortable, he said, "You say something, I respond with the first thing that comes to mind, which'll probably turn out to be references to my mother."

"Good," Alda said, smiling. "I'd like you to lay back and kick up your feet on the Ottoman."

Cherko looked to his feet. Yes, there was an Ottoman there. Cherko kicked back; closed his eyes. Thought about the snow outside continuing to fall. Soft, sound-deadening, comforting.

"Now, Jimmy, we're going to clear our mind, and relax…if thoughts enter our mind, we'll simply acknowledge them and gently guide them away.…"

Cherko found the relaxing easy to do. In fact, it was easier to do than expected, and before he knew it, he heard Alda's voice as if it were coming from a very, very great distance.…

4

First Lieutenant Jimmy Cherko opened his eyes.

He was lying down. Looking up into a ceiling.

Something wasn't right. His elbow hurt. His mind…muddled.

Was he home? Had he driven home?

It felt so good to just…lie…there. To not be at work. Calm. Quiet.…

What do you think you—

Jimmy bolted upright.

What do you think you sa—

Something definitely wasn't right. Something…*off—*

A back road. He'd been on a back road…

Curtis Road.

It'd been dark. Was alone. Gas indicator pegged beyond "E."

Nothing but darkness. Out in the middle of nowhere.

Lights.

Down at the distant end of the road. Heading toward him…

You do not know what you're dealing with, Morrow had said. *There are* organizations—

The lights pull up to him.

That sergeant. From his…his…*interrogation*…

No—that wasn't right.

What wasn't right about it?

Cherko swung his legs over and hopped onto the floor. Shook his head; brought up a bloody-knuckled hand.

What the hell? Something…something wasn't right about that. About—

That sergeant's face. Cherko looked at the sergeant's face.

It disappeared.

Just…Cheshired away.

But, he was back on Curtis Road!

What the *hell?*

December 12th, 1985. He'd run out of gas, alright, but—

The sergeant's car was gone.

He still stood in the middle of the road. Alone. It was pitch black. Quiet. He looked back down the road from where that sergeant had come.

Had he?

Lights. There they were. Still there. Heading his way.

But there was something wrong about those lights.

A shiver ran through him. It was cold outside. Late…going on ten-thirty. The hairs on the back of his neck stood on end.

The light had moved, yes it had. But it hadn't followed the *road*, had it; hadn't *stayed* there…

Was this real? Was he really seeing this?

The light had drifted smoothly off the road, out into the fields to the east.

Oh, no. No.

It quietly and smoothly raced across the open, dark fields. Level, like it was on a rail, or something.

What was happening…

The light changed direction. Vectored *toward* him.

No.

This can't be. *Can't be happening….*

The light paused. Was bigger now. Had come closer. Just hovered there, out in the field just beyond him and his dead car.

No, this can't be. Stuff like this doesn't happen to me! Never happens to me!

Was it real?

December swamp gas in the Colorado Highlands?

But how cool! How neat *looking!*

A bluish-white light, he could now see, just hovered out there…like a ship offshore. Waiting.

Waiting for what?

The light again moved. Slower than when it had arrived to that spot. Toward him.

Oh, no.

Cherko's breathing quickened.

What am I going to—

Relax.

Relax? Easier said than—

Cherko's pulse and breathing slowed.

Ok. Did I do that? Did I—

The light was gone.

His car was gone. Curtis Road—*gone.*

He stood in a field.

This wasn't right.

He'd just been on Curtis Road, out of gas—

Something was behind him. He *felt* it. Electricity crawled across the surface of his skin. He was on fire.

Slowly, he turned.

The outline was difficult to make out in the darkness, but it was clearly not his car.

"Oh, my God...."

"*What do you think it was you just saw?*"

Cherko turned a little more to his right.

A figure. Dark...like that other thing...stood just beyond—

Cherko was back, standing...

Where was he standing?

Jimmy had fallen back against, what—a *table?*

What table?

He pushed himself away and looked to it. Blinked. It was suddenly hard...so hard...to think. Jimmy brought a hand back to his head. Looked to his hand.

Healed.

Felt his elbow—no longer tender.

He squeezed his eyes shut and tried to focus.

Someone was coming. Yes.

He turned around and looked up. There was someone...someone in the...*room?*...with him. He blinked, but when he opened his eyes he could have sworn he'd seen someone standing before him, but...but, he now found himself standing back in that field.

Looked behind him.

A dark shape hidden in the dark—*part* of the dark?

We brought you back.

Cherko spun around.

Back where?

Here. To remember.

Remember what? I don't—

As Cherko looked to the figure standing before him, the truth was he *did* remember. This wasn't the first time. No, not by a long shot. From this shadow Cherko felt...familiarity.

Female.

Compassion.

They're coming for you and we are warning you. You are being used.

What do you mean?

They know of your abilities. Been watching you for a long time.

Who?

They will tell you one thing, act another. It is their way. They chose you.

Chose *me?* I *came to* them.

They engineered you to do so. But that is not important. You must be aware of our warning. We will make it so you remain aware of this warning.

How do you—

We must also continue to make the rest of our encounters unknown to you.

Do what? Why—

For your safety. Ours. We cannot give you conscious memory of us for all of our safety. You will remember nothing of our encounter except to be wary of those for whom you work. Wary of all you meet. No one is what they seem. We will continue to watch and monitor you. You gave us permission long ago.

So, I was *just on a*—

I must go.

Wait, not yet—

The figure was gone.

He felt groggy, like his mind had just gone on an extended vacation without him. Fuzzy. He closed his eyes, squeezing them hard. Unsteady, unsteady…mentally tried to reach out into the darkness. When he opened his eyes…

He was surrounded by men and machines.

Choppers, two on the ground, several more (he felt by their thumping concussion in the airspace about him), airborne, circling and hovering. His arms were held outstretched to his sides. He found supremely unsmiling men held him pinned as if in some absurd crucifixion. He was surrounded by other similarly unsmiling men with weapons trained in his direction. Shaking his head again, he came to focus on another standing before him. A man with stars on his uniform. A man who silently nodded at him, chomping a cigar amid a cocky smile.

Cherko inhaled cigar smoke and coughed.

"Sir," Cherko said, clearing his throat, "what's…what's going on, here? Where am I?"

Lieutenant General Hammond snorted.

Chapter Fourteen

1

Lake Clear, NY
12 July 1976
0101 Hours Eastern Time

Everett Cherko lay in bed, eyes closed. Had he slept at all? Dreamed? He couldn't be sure, but it was definitely late. He reached out for Renée.

She was there.

She moved only slightly so, but made one of those sleep sounds that indicated she was definitely in a profound slumber. Thank God.

She was still *in* bed.

He rolled over and looked to her, paused a moment or two, then continued over onto his back and looked up into the ceiling.

Damn that kid, but if he didn't ask the goddamnedest questions.

Jimmy hadn't known what he'd been asking at the barbeque earlier today—*yesterday*, he corrected, looking to the bedside clock hour—but the question had brought him back to 1962. To perhaps the strangest moment of his twelve-year naval career...something he couldn't quite remember, and which continued to haunt him. Something he wished he could ask his skipper about some day, or anyone else who'd been on that boat with him fourteen years ago.

Damn, time was a trip.

Time passed—moved on—but memories, *feelings* didn't. They were still there, fresh as the day they'd first been experienced—

Now wait...hadn't something also happened on another patrol? *Another* boat?

Yes...there had been another time...on another submarine. Another incident that had also scared the crap out of him—

Everett sat upright.

How could he have forgotten—*shit!* Clear as *day!*

A chill ran over him. He cast another look to Renée to make sure he hadn't woken her.

The *Sailfish*, his first sub…something freakish had happened *there*, too—how could he had forgotten? 1957…yeah, '57. He'd made Second Class Petty Officer. They'd been on patrol to the Barents Sea.

A cold sweat sheeted Everett.

Something strange…just like…just like the *Threadfin* in '62.

What the hell?

Why had he never recalled the *Sailfish* incident? Two incidents he couldn't remember, two incidents which caused him to sweat like a cornered criminal.

Everett got out of bed and left the room. Made his way barefoot down the stairs into his ranger office. Without turning on any lights, he walked through the house, into the living room. There he stood before the picture window and opened its curtains; stared out across the darkness into the waters of Lake Clear. Across the road.

What were under those murky waters?

What was under…

2

Barents Sea, 100 NM north of Murmansk, USSR
31 October 1957
0011 Hours Zulu

Sailfish, submersible ship, radar picket 572, U.S. Navy, hung quietly at periscope depth at 10 knots, holding an easterly heading. The Control Room within the *Sailfish* was busy, each man performing their assigned duties as they listened in on Soviet communications. In the radio shack, twenty-one-year-old Radioman Second Class Everett Cherko adjusted his headset and several dials on the receiver panels before him. Tweaked frequencies. He checked his watch. Almost time to terminate patrol and return to warmer climes, no more Rooskies sniffing around for them. There had been intel of increased Soviet activity out here, and other boats had either been elsewhere employed, or in port for extended overhaul. The *Sailfish* had been available and had taken on the assignment.

Executive Officer Lieutenant Ford poked his head into the radio shack.

"You good?"

RM2 Cherko nodded. "Aye, sir."

The XO nodded back, then departed for the Control Room.

Everett pulled off his headphones. Hopefully they'd picked up whatever the spooks'd been looking for. He could begin transcription on their way back.

* * *

The *Sailfish* made its WSW heading into the Norwegian Basin, submerged to 100 feet, 15 knots. Ping Jockey, or Sonarman First Class Billy Bickford, stationed in the forward torpedo room, stared at his scope. Clear of contacts…underwater ridges, mountains, and valleys notwithstanding. Steer clear and they were home free. Back to friendlier waters and even friendlier women.

As boring as this was, it fascinated Bickford that the boat was, essentially, blind. It navigated its way underwater like a bat…and that utterly amazed him.

A loud pinging assaulted his headphones, and the sonar scope displayed not just a blip, but a *huge* one…one that was just…*there*…right alongside their 350-foot-six-inch hull. SO1 Bickford jerked back in his seat. The screen had been clear and empty, and the next moment *something* followed alongside. At shouldering distance.

"Control, Sonar!" Bickford called into the 1MC internal communication system. "Contact—starboard quarter!"

Lieutenant Commander S. R. Hoffman, Captain of the *Sailfish*, looked up from his charts in the Ward Room.

The Diving Officer, Lieutenant (junior grade) Henny, quickly made his way to Bickford's side.

"*Jesus*," Henny muttered. "How in the—"

"No idea sir. One moment the scope was clear, and the next…*there*— just like that!"

"Sonar, this is the Captain," LCDR Hoffman hailed from the Ward Room over the 1MC. "What's contact's range?"

"Fifteen feet, Captain."

Henny then reached over and flipped the gray 1MC toggle switch. "Helmsman, Sonar. Perform an emergency course to port, one-eight-zero degrees."

"Sonar, Helmsman—aye, emergency course to port, one-eight-zero degrees!"

"Let's see what it—" Henny began, but was unable to finish.

Hoffman, Henny, Bickford, and the rest of the men in the *Sailfish* were all struck dumb.

Sonarman Bickford and the helmsman both looked straight ahead, hands dropped into their laps.

Lt (jg) Henny returned to his nav plotting board and stood before it. Stared straight ahead into the bulkhead on the opposite side of the Control Room.

LCDR Hoffman stared down into the charts before him.

Each and every seaman aboard the *Sailfish* developed a blank expression and simply stood or sat or lay wherever they'd found themselves.

RM2 Everett Cherko was transcribing code from their Murmansk diversion when he simply stopped and folded his arms on the table before him. Stared into the receiver panel.

And the *Sailfish* herself came to a dead stop in 100 feet of Arctic Circle water.

All Everett Cherko was thinking about was how calm and relaxed he felt. And that the glass gauges on the receiver panel needed a better cleaning— how had he missed those crevasses where the glass met the gauge rims? He'd need to get at those with a good toothbrushing.

Everett slowly turned his head and looked to his left.

Someone stood in the radio shack entranceway.

A couple someones.

Everett smiled. He was about to say "hello," but felt too relaxed to say anything, really, so just…smiled.

The figures approached.

3

Everett continued staring out at the dark waters of Lake Clear.

Yes, he remembered. Remembered that patrol. Remembered that the *Sailfish* had been diverted to the Barents Sea. Remembered…well, didn't so much as remember as *felt* something else had happened. Something else that seemed to take him to the brink of a deep, dark, abyss…then summarily jilted him. He thought '62 had been bad enough, but now he'd come to find '57 had also turned into a banner year.

Led right into the mouth of madness, then left him hanging.

What was it—what had happened that caused him to bristle whenever he thought back to that—now *those*—patrols? Patrols he could not, for the life of him, complete their memories.…

Chapter Fifteen

1

Colorado Springs, CO
19 June 1986
0700 Hours Mountain Time

Cherko awoke with a start.

Looked to the clock.

Seven a.m.

Looked to the window.

Sunlight. Filtered in through closed mini-blinds.

Looked to his clothes.

He was in uniform and combat boots. Lay atop the sheets and blankets on his bed.

He swung his legs to the side of the

(*table...*)

bed and sat there. Shook his head. Good Lord, he was out of it. Where the hell was he?

Apartments. He was at his apartment.

Immediately nervous, he began blinking to see if he still had his contacts in

Out. They were out.

Getting to his feet he looked to his boots. There was nothing on them whatsoever—no dirt, mud, nothing. In fact they almost looked as if they'd been polished.

He entered the bathroom and leaned over the sink, when a hand fell upon his contact lens case. Opening it he found both contacts inside.

Well, apparently, he'd at least had enough presence of mind to take out his lenses before collapsing into bed.

Cherko continued on into the kitchen, where he grabbed a swig of orange juice from the refrigerator, then sat at the table and ran his hands over his short hair. Tried to recall what the hell had happened after work. Driving home.

Nothing. He remembered not one damned thing.

Colorado Springs, CO
19 June 1986
2325 Hours Mountain Time

A large green plastic bottle of *Mountain Dew* in hand, Cherko had entered the ERO ops floor, received his changeover, and now sat at a console. The smell of coffee was strong. Though he felt fine, he knew something was in the air. He set the *Dew* on the floor by his feet; looked to the support schedule and signed on to his consoles. The glass door behind him opened and closed; he glanced behind him.

Turnbull.

And he had two shady looking characters under escort by a sergeant he didn't really know on the other side of the Fishbowl's glass.

"Cherko," Turnbull said, as he casually approached, "you have guests tonight."

"How long?"

"As long as it takes."

"Great."

"Got a problem with that, Lieutenant?" he said, looking to the other crew members and nodding his curt "Hello."

Cherko meant to say something, when Turnbull cast him a look that said *don't you dare.*

Turnbull turned to Michelson and Fender. "I need both of you to sign off and depart the floor."

Michelson and Fender exchanged looks.

Cherko checked out the two spooks as Michelson and Fender made their support-transfer calls, shut down their workstations, and quietly departed. Turnbull watched them leave, then nodded toward the spooks and their escort. The sergeant escort led them onto the floor. They were not the same spooks from before, but looked just as intimidating.

"I've got them, Sergeant," Turnbull said to Staff Sergeant Bell. Without a word Bell did an about face and left the floor.

"Gentlemen," Turnbull said, leading the two darkly suited individuals to Cherko's console, "this is Lieutenant Cherko."

Cherko got to his feet, all smiles, and extended a hand to the first gentleman.

"Pleased to meet you, sir."

Spook One nodded, but never took his hand. Spook Two didn't even acknowledge him. Cherko lowered his hand.

"These gentlemen will be observing tonight."

Turnbull left the ops floor.

"Would either of you like a chair?" Cherko asked.

Ramrod straight, and hands tucked behind his back, Spook One barely shook his head "No," as both he and Spook Two took up positions directly behind him.

Cherko turned away, raising an eyebrow; he sat back down and proceeded to set up his support. When he was done, he over-the-shoulder informed his guests he was ready to come up on the bird. He heard the two men step up closer behind him.

Great. Now what would he do if "they" contacted him?

These spooks could clearly see his every frigging keystroke, which was no doubt entirely part-and-parcel to why they came on down here in the first place. Not only did they want to see firsthand data, but they also wanted to make damned sure they knew exactly what was going on, exactly what the operator was doing, and exactly who was seeing what no-one-was-ever-supposed-to-see.

His ethereal trainer had never thought of that, had she?

But, more than that, they reminded him of his little incident back at his apartment.

So…if there was a God, *please*, keep whom or whatever contacted him during his supports *away* tonight.…

As Cherko continued support configuration, the spooks shuffled in closer still.

And it was like they didn't breathe.

He should have heard *something*, some sounds of life coming from these two guys, but instead they were both like zombies, hovering behind, just waiting for him to turn around so they could rip off his face, pry open his skull, and devour his gray matter.

Something moved at Cherko's peripheral vision.

Cherko turned to find yet *another* spook…one standing just at the inside of the ops floor, directly in front of the Fish Bowl.

Now, where the hell had he come from?

No one was allowed control room entrance without crew members knowing about it. He looked to the figure, whose face he couldn't see. It was hidden by what looked like a 1940s black Fedora, tilted down over his face.

Like his apartment visitors.

Something wasn't right about this.

There was an unsettling feeling that crawled up his spine about this new one. Spooks in general were scary, but this new one was tall and lanky. In a not-normal way. Extremely skinny. Scarecrowish.

And there was an incredible aura of *stay away* about him.

Cherko shivered and returned to his console. It was just a little too creepy being in the control room with nothing but…*them*. No Air Force. No crew members.

The target satellite on tonight's mission was an optical bird. He was ready for handover from the current mission control in support with the satellite and picked up the blue multi-line phone, or MLP.

"Badger, Falcon, I'm ready for handover."

Cherko activated his resources and passively tracked the satellite without radiating it from the ground station he was now controlling. He awaited end-of-support time from the other controller.

"Passive sent," Badger said.

After mentally ticking off a couple seconds for the network link delay, Cherko banged out his active directive. This caused his ground station's tracking antenna to radiate up to the satellite.

"Active sent," Cherko replied.

"Roger," Badger said.

Cherko watched his telem. His directive had gotten in. He now controlled the satellite.

"We're active on the bird," Cherko said, making a quick scan of telemetry to make sure all was good with the satellite before taking official control and performing his pass.

"We show you active, Falcon."

"Looks good, Badger."

"Have a good one."

"Ditto."

Please, don't *contact me*, he mentally sent…

Cherko sweat. Not a good thing to be doing with two spooks peering over your soul. So, as he ran his state of health, he thought about movies, broccoli, playing in the woods up back at the Lake Clear house, and Erica.

What was she doing right now?

Most likely either watching TV, reading, or sleeping. Or maybe taking a long, luxurious shower or bath, in her dark, candlelit bathroom…thinking about him, as she ran her hands over her—

Okay, that wouldn't do either.

Shifting in his seat, he thought about broccoli.

Broccoli with cheese sauce.

Picking the stuff out of their Lake Clear garden up back.…

Completing his state of health, Cherko flipped those passplan pages face down on console, and proceeded on with the mission.

A UK bird.

According to Capt Morrow and all his training, officially the U.S. and Britain were best buds in the Global Community. But as everyone knew in the Intel world—*and* he was finding out—best buds or not, no one trusted anyone.

Case-in-point, Mr. Spook One, Two, und Three.

The argument was that spying kept friends honest. Well, the fact that an illicit activity was to keep anything honest was quite ironic to Cherko, but he also wasn't naïve. Spying was a necessary evil in the way the world appeared to run, especially in the dark dirty corners of human affairs. Though everyone did it, no one was gonna own up to it, and if caught, there were damned-serious consequences. In other words…sure, go ahead, cheat, we're all cheating…but if you're caught, we're gonna nail ya to the cross. Upside down.

Now, when it came to friendly countries like the U.S., Britain, or Australia, there were extreme efforts in keeping even activities like this friendly, so even if caught among the Best Friends Society, each country's best efforts would be made to keep their activities, even if directed against one of themselves, out of the press. The worst that could be expected, if caught, was some hard wrist-slapping and sternly worded "get the hell out of our goddamned knickers" language. It would all be kept hush-hush.

So, why do it?

It wasn't all about subterfuge. Sometimes it was good to know your neighbors were keeping an eye on your back. Kinda of like a Neighborhood Watch. You watch our back, we'll watch yours.

And everyone knew, in the spacefaring world, that absolutely no one could touch the U.S.'s technological supremacy. No one.

The Soviets were close, but not because of technology. They were good at building robust systems—basic systems—anything that could be easily produced using metal. It wasn't that they were backward, it was just that they were structured differently. It was like building a tougher truck using carbureted engines versus more technologically advanced, electronically-fuel-injected ones. The Russians were masters of the carbureted engine.

And, all altruistic motives aside, everyone also wanted to know what the other really had, and just what they were really doing when they weren't shaking hands. The long and the short of it was, just like with Blackbird overflights of Russia, everyone knew it was happening, but no one could stop it. All they could do was protest and yack loudly, because, frankly, there was no one else on the planet with the technology to touch what the U.S. had and did. End of story.

So Cherko entered the coordinates of his target satellite into the system and watched as his bird swung in on it with its powerful, folded-mirror, telescope. In no time, a small speck appeared on his right-most display screen, to which, Cherko noticed, his two spooks were intently focused. He was about to zoom in, when one of the spooks halted him.

"Swing your visual to the extremes of coverage."

Had one of the Spooks actually just *spoken* to him?

"Yes, sir," Cherko answered, and did so. He swung the telescope back and forth. One direction cast it across the Earth's face, while the other pointed it out into space. He didn't hear anything else out of them, and performed the maneuver again, panning across the satellite.

"Up and down," Spook One added.

Cherko did as instructed. Nothing but a lot of space. What the hell were they looking for?

"Terminate scan," Spook One directed.

Cherko performed a swift combination of keyboard and trackball strokes and brought the unsuspecting target satellite back into brilliant resolution. It always amazed him at the optics involved and what he was looking at. Real time. Maybe he hadn't been here long enough to have the affect yet be deadened to him, but it was something to know he was here, on the eastern plains of Colorado, sneaking peeks at orbiting hardware over other parts of the world. It was like filming a passing car, only this car was a hundred miles up over another continent. In this case...Russia.

His ERO satellite had already been moved—delta-V'd—into better position to view this bird, and the bird they were observing was also tracking across the globe, so they had a limited amount of time. He had to get in and out quickly, and see what the spooks wanted to see. He cast a quick glance behind him, and caught the two pointing and nodding between each other. They both gave him a hard look. Beyond them was the Spook King way in the back, overseeing everything. But he suddenly had the most intense feeling to *not* look, and returned his attention back to his displays.

Well, that had been the most animation he'd seen from any of them so far. So maybe they really were human. Or part thereof. Cherko began to zoom in further.

"No—keep it out. Stay where you're at," came the voice from behind.

Cherko pulled back the resolution. The target UK bird was another spy sat, known as 56900, or at least that's what was listed on his passplan. In his training he'd been told that just because there was a number on his passplan for a satellite didn't necessarily mean that was the actual satellite's vehicle number, especially for friendlies. The less operators knew, the better, and the less to implicate later. Plausible deniability. For enemies, there was no effort to attempt to hide their satellite numbers, so if this was a Soviet vehicle, chances were that the listed number would actually be the listed number from the NORAD spacetrack catalog.

Cherko stared at the satellite. This was boring. What did they expect to—

"*Lieutenant*," came a whisper from behind. Cherko turned his head just a hair toward the voice. "We are going to ask you to do something without question nor comment from you. Nod if you understand."

Cherko nodded, images of two unwanted apartment visitors and a smashed phone filling his head.

"We are going to ask you to close your eyes for a period of time. *Do you understand?*"

Cherko paused, then again nodded, as he eyed his screens and telemetry. *Close his eyes?*

Not only *What the hell?*, but they only had a couple of minutes left in support, and this was one helluvan expensive game they'd be playing…

"When we place a hand to your shoulder—like this," Spook One said, placing a hand to Cherko's shoulder, "you are to think—*as hard as you can*—of one thing and one thing only: *stop*. We will tell you when to terminate. Nod if you understand."

"You want me to *what?*" Cherko said, turning around to protest, but the Spook forcibly and physically repositioned his shoulders forward.

"Nod 'yes'…or 'no,'" Spook One said. "*Time*, Lieutenant."

Cherko nodded, swallowing hard.

Images of his midnight training sessions with that wonderfully disembodied voice rushed back. Okay, now this *was* getting weird. Maybe it was related to all that mind training? As much as he may have believed in the power of the mind, this was getting just a bit too freaky.

"*Close your eyes,*" Spook One whispered up against an ear. He then placed a hand to his shoulder.

Okay; they wanted to pay him to fly satellites with his eyes closed. They were the customer, so fine.

Cherko closed his eyes.

The image on his screen stayed in his head, and he did as asked. Focused all his thoughts on "Stop." As hard as he could. To whatever was going on on that screen.

Stop.

Stop.

STOP.

Cherko felt something (*STOP*) was happening on his screen, but kept his eyes (*STOP*) closed. If something (*STOP*) important enough was happening, the two sets of eyes (*STOP*) from Spook Central, behind him, would definitely let him know.

STOP.

Cherko had the image (*STOP*) of something flying through space (*STOP*). Something small and dark, yet shiny (*STOP*)?

STOP.

STOP.

Wondered how he might look (*STOP*) to the other crew members, if any (*STOP*) happened to look in on him right now…

STOP.

STOP.

His mind created the image (*STOP*) of this object heading for 56900. Cherko forcibly thought *STOP*.

STOP!

Come on, what the hell could they possibly want out of him doing this—

"Open your eyes," Spook One whispered. Coming closer to his ear he then added, "This never happened and we were never here."

Cherko turned around to say something, when he noticed the time.

Late!

He was late!

Where had the time gone? He swore it hadn't been more than a minute or two—at *most.*

Cherko grabbed the MLP; punched in the selection for the next site that was to acquire control.

"Mongoose, Falcon, copy?"

"Ready for handover," Mongoose said, flatly.

He knew he was late, knew they had mere seconds, yet Mongoose played it cool and remained professional. There was no time to chew him out, because, as Mongoose and anyone else knew, if you were late, *everyone* knew, and no one ever escaped the wrath of their chain of command.

And rookies were only late once.

"This is vehicle 56900; stand by for passive." As Cherko spoke over the phone, he rapidly broke down his support. "I'm off the bird. Good support, no problems."

His remaining responses and support breakdown actions were lost in a veritable mental fog.

What the hell had those spooks just had him do?

Cherko closed out the passplan, and wiped his forehead.

What the hell had just happened?

He turned around to address his guests…but—

They'd left. All three of them.

Vanished.

They weren't called spooks for nothin.

Chapter Sixteen

1

ERO Operations
4 July 1986
0238 Hours Mountain Time

Communications terminated.

Cherko hit F10 just as he heard the Fishbowl door behind him open. He'd been nervous the entire time he'd been transcribing his Program information this shift, and kept looking over his shoulder—more so than normal. When he'd first started all this Program work he'd felt special...like he'd been doing some neat covert work, but any more it was taking its toll. In a job that was paranoid to begin with, he'd added another whopping layer of it. But today's shift was worse.

He kept feeling like he was being watched.

Right over his shoulder. He'd see something out the corner of an eye, or feel a definite presence, but when he'd turn to look...nothing.

Of course.

And now, terminating his Program communications, he'd had an even worse feeling.

The door behind him had closed. He spun around.

There they were. Spooks Uno and Dos. Again. And his buddy Turnbull.

For the past month or two he was getting more visits than the other crew members, and he knew something about today was gonna be different. He could feel it. Something about today was really gonna change his life.

Turnbull and the spooks remained in the background as Cherko performed his passplan, but as operations wound down at the two other consoles he heard Turnbull make his way over to them and say, "I need both of you to depart the ops floor after signing off."

Michelson and Fender looked to each other, then glanced to Cherko, who was already looking to them.

Not again.

Cherko continued working his console. Casting occasional glances every now and then toward the spooks. Turnbull watched Michelson and Fender leave before approaching Cherko. The spooks remained back by the Fish Bowl.

In a lowered voice, Turnbull said, "You are to follow each and every directive they give without question. Do I make myself clear?"

Cherko nodded.

Turnbull turned to the two men, and nodded.

"All yours, gentlemen," he said, passing the two as they crossed the control room directly for Cherko.

The two spooks watched Turnbull exit. It was always Spook One that did all the talking, and Cherko well knew by now that he was never to ever ask any questions, so after talking with Turnbull, he returned to his support without a word. These guys just didn't do "hello."

Last month they had him do that kooky mind-game thing where he had closed his eyes and simply *thought*. Focused on an action. Obviously, he felt, it had been related to his special Program training, but since then, it had just been about watching supports like the others. But the only time they cleared out the ops floor was when they had done that little mind game.

Then today.

Cherko continued with his passplan, examining a Soviet satellite in its Molniya orbit, a satellite suspected to be more than just a communications bird. To Cherko at least, for one thing, it didn't *look* like a comm bird. Not enough antenna-like hardware.

Cherko scanned the satellite, logging video to tape, when the input came on a small piece of unusual-looking paper. It was handed to him by Spook One.

You will not turn to look at us, nor question. You will instantly do as directed, at the directed time.

Cherko began to turn around, but caught himself.

You will not turn to look at us, nor question....

Spook One's hand calmly, carefully—and creepily—retrieved the paper.

Cherko cleared his throat and continued with the support. There was nothing of obvious interest here, visually, so he initiated what they called "The Punch." The Punch was a powerful electromagnetic scan of the internal components and workings of a satellite. It was line-of-sight and limited in range, so it was only used on satellites that their birds were close enough to. Entering a series of keyboard commands, Cherko initiated scanning, and what he found was anything but a comm bird. In fact, the system characterization portion of The Punch clearly showed signatures of a laser and EMP-equipped killer satellite.

In a Molniya orbit?

Cherko hated it when he found stuff like this. He was an optimist, and as much as this job was as Lt Colonel Masterson had promised, there were times like these that scared the shit out of him. Here was a weapon against the space treaty currently in orbit and aimed Earthward. Yes, ERO had its own capabilities, but they were not the aggressors. The orbit of this satellite had it passing directly over the poles, and through his intel briefings, Cherko also knew there were U.S. submarine exercises going on down there.

And now he had a visit from Humpty and Dumpty.

On a cleared ops floor.

He didn't have to wait long for additional input, as another slip of weird paper was carefully set down on the console before him.

Disable SGX1109. 02:43:33.

That's all it said. He had sixty seconds.

Spook One retrieved the paper.

Cherko obediently enabled the high-powered microwave pulse package on their satellite, when a hand came to his shoulder and sent a chill through him. Actually caused him to jerk upright in his seat.

"*With your* mind," came the menacing whisper.

Cherko opened his mouth and turned just a speck toward the voice when he remembered—

Nor question.

Instantly *do as directed.*

Remembered their close-his-eyes-and-think-of-"Stop" visit.

It had been Spook *Two* who backed away from him this time, and was giving him the look of death. Spook Two had just spoken to him—the man who never said a word, never even so much as cleared his throat in his presence—had just touched him. Whispered into his ear like a crazed lover.

And behind him he saw that Spook King was again back by the Fish Bowl. Black Fedora tipped forward.

He had less than 40 seconds.

This was the second time they'd asked him to do something through the use of his mind.

Maybe this *was* where he was headed. His next level of operation?

No longer just a transcriptionist—but how did *he* have any kind of mental powers? That bizarre training of his notwithstanding, how had *he* developed any such ability when he apparently couldn't even control his own life? If he could stop things with his mind, why couldn't he control what job he got? Become that astronaut...

Sweat began to leak out his armpits.

If he could mentally communicate with aliens, was the next step to mentally communicate with *satellites?*

Destroy them?

Twenty seconds.

Okay, do as directed. Might as well give it a go. He had, after all, been able to manipulate electronic displays during his training—but would these guys know about that?

If anyone had a need to know about anything, he was sure it were these guys.

Ten seconds.

SGX1109.

Cherko focused on it. He didn't know where "it" was, so he just focused on the designator.

Disable it *how?*

Five…four…three…

Cherko focused on destroying the component. Like changing the sine waves in his training months ago, he just pictured the component blasted and fried. Blackened. Obliterated. *History.*

…one.

02:43:33 hours.

Cherko willed it so.

Cherko looked to his real-time display of the target.

It was still in orbit. Still looked operational.

Looked to The Punch.

Nothing had changed.

Another slip of the weird-looking paper was presented to him.

We were never here.

Then the slip of paper was crumpled up into a ball and held momentarily in-hand before him. Spook Two then opened his hand, dropping it toward the console before him—where it decomposed before his eyes into a smokeless and fine powder before it hit the console.

There was absolutely nothing left of it.

Cherko cast a nervous glance up to the oxygen-stealing Halon fire suppression system above, but obviously nothing was set off.

Cherko sat dumbfounded.

It was time to hand over this mission.

Kicking back into gear he began setting up for handover to Mongoose. He looked behind him, but the spooks were already leaving the ops room (but he—curiously—saw no Spook King). As he got on the phone to initiate handover, Turnbull, Michelson, and Fender returned to the ops floor, Turnbull staring at him from the length of the control room. Cherko looked down to where the strange paper had vaporized, rubbed his hand over the console's surface, but there was nothing left. Not even grains of ash—or whatever should have been left over from whatever had happened to that "paper."

It was like no one had ever been there, and nothing had ever happened.

2

Cherko headed home on Highway 94.

The rest of the shift had had Cherko in a virtual haze. He couldn't really show this state to those on shift, so had to be careful how he'd acted. Had to fake it. Act out "normal."

Spies and covert operatives had to be the best actors ever, and would never get an Academy Award, and he had to be just like them, to learn to compartmentalize. To leave whatever was done at work, at work, and quit gaming it, trying to figure it out, because it would drive him nuts. And because to not do so would have shown that something *had*, indeed, transpired back there, and that would have gone against Program protocol.

Something weird.

We were never here.

Fiz.

People die, Turnbull had said. And those words had stuck with him.

What if…there was a spy within their ranks? Or not so much even a spy, but a crew member with loose lips, spouting off to some girl- or boyfriend in an effort to impress—or maybe not even impress, just offload? To confess, come clean to a civilian that *hey, I do crazy shit with advanced technology orbiting the Earth, and with people and organizations that don't have names, and I don't feel right about it?*

Or say someone talks in their sleep?

Someone in this line of work had to be extremely careful about what they said, and where. *Anyone* could be listening. Lives, could, indeed, be lost based upon a slip of the tongue. Granted these were supposed to be topnotch individuals, but people were people, and in an effort to keep national security secrets both national and secret, compartmentalization and being tight-lipped was of vital importance.

Had stuff like this happened to other crew members, or was he the only one?

At least on his crew he seemed to be the chosen one. The New Guy. That must most certainly have endeared him to his fellow crew members.

But he'd never know.

You just didn't ask questions in this world. You did as you were told and kept your mouth shut. Period.

People die….

And who's to say he had really affected *anything* with his mind? There had been no feedback, no confirmation of outcome. They had simply said use your mind to affect some component, at a specific time, then walked away.

They could have just as easily been totally fucking with him.

Is that something they would do? Did a large government agency expend valuable government resources on flights of fancy?

But he had *changed those sine waves back at his other training.*

Or had he?

Or had he also been fucked with then, too?

How could he ever tell? And just *think* of the possibilities...the *ramifications.*

He'd read Erica's mind on their road trip, hadn't he?

Well, come on, everyone thought about sex. He'd read surveys that said people thought about it some unreal number, like once a second or something.

No; he'd have to try to figure this out another way.

But, really, think about this: would the U.S. Government spend good money to fly two—*three*—goons out from wherever they'd been to this location, to whisper over-the-shoulder bullshit into some lieutenant's ear if there wasn't a reason?

No friggin way.

This was turning into quite the job.

And how did they *know?* How did they know about...his *abilities?* Abilities he himself knew nothing of?

Well, apparently, just like they knew about everything else.

Cherko pulled up to the gate guard at his apartment complex. He smiled and waved at the guard as he was admitted, and drove around the buildings to his unit.

Why fight it, he thought as he found an open slot directly in front of his apartment, which was easy to do when everyone else was leaving for work. Just keep your nose clean, do your job, and always, *always* assume that someone was watching you. That someone knew *everything* about you....

3

The day had been a beautiful, high summer day. He'd worked out, gotten together with Erica after her classes, and made love with her on the floor of her apartment.

Love.

He really felt like he was getting in deep with her. About her. Thought about her all the time. It was so cool to know that someone else—a gorgeous woman somewhere on this planet, in *this* town—also thought about *him.* He always wanted to be around her. *With* her. He found his heart skipped a beat when he saw her for the first time of the day, and seemed to remain elevated when he was around her. Being within any kind of a proximity to her, he couldn't keep his hands off her. Always had to be touching her, whether it was holding her hand, stroking her hair, or kissing various parts of her anatomy. And she never resisted, always responded in kind. They fit perfectly together.

And their passion.

Having sex with Erica was not like the superficial two people just banging away at each other. It was more like becoming one *with* each other. Like one newly created organism in a passionate throe with itself.

God, that sounded stupid.

But that's how he felt. Of course, that took away the separation of her from him that made part of the sex act passionate and erotic, but on another level…it didn't. Added to it.

So, he walked through his apartment with a shit-eating grin on his face as he prepared to leave for work—when the phone rang. He looked to it—considered not answering it—but as he passed by, his hand shot out to it and he put it to his ear.

"Cherko?"

Turnbull.

"Yes, sir?"

"You will not report to work tonight, but will await me outside the ECP. Before entering the ECP. Understand?"

"Sir?"

The phone went dead.

Cherko stood before the Entry Control Point looking up into the night sky. The stars were crisp and bright. The nice thing about working outside a town was the lack of lights to interfere with stargazing. It wasn't long before a jeep pulled up. Cherko looked in. Turnbull's always serious face peered back out at him. He got in.

"Evening," he said.

"Lieutenant," Turnbull said as he pulled away, shifting, "this is Mr. Shroot."

Cherko whipped around, almost pulling a neck muscle.

Another man sat in the back of the Jeep.

"Shroot, Lieutenant Cherko." Turnbull shifted into third.

"Pleased to meet you," Cherko said, extending a hand.

"Pleasure," Shroot responded, shaking Cherko's hand.

Apparently, this guy talked *and* shook hands. Could be a good sign.

"Mr. Shroot will be borrowing you tonight. Your plane leaves at—"

"*Plane?*"

"Here are your orders," Shroot said, handing Cherko his TDY travel papers.

"You've got to be—"

"I assure you," Shroot said, "We do not 'kid.' Our transport awaits at Peterson."

MC-130P, 33,000 feet, Heading 255
6 July 1986
0025 Hours Mountain Time

"So," Cherko shouted out over the drone of the special ops C-130, "you can't tell me *anything?*"

Shroot, arms crossed, chuckled before opening his eyes. "Get used to it. As outgoing as you might be, the less asked, the better. The crew of this aircraft were specifically instructed not to talk to us. You will find that whatever security you've experienced at Falcon…was child's play, compared to where we're going."

Cherko adjusted his headphones and stared to the opposite bulkhead; to the Loadmaster at the far end of the cargo bay, by the aft ramp area.

"So…"

"So, you will be told what to say and when, what to think and when. When to piss and how much. And if into the wind, with pleasure and for how long."

"Wonderful."

"Lieutenant…what we are doing…is for the country, its national security. So that people like your Erica, Renée, and Everett can enjoy the lives they do. We all have our parts, however seemingly insignificant. We're not doing this because we want to…but because we *need* to. Certain activities require the likes of us. We're a necessary evil.

"Now, my advice…don't ask any more questions and enjoy the ride." Shroot repositioned his crossed arms and again closed his eyes.

Undisclosed location, Desert Southwest
6 July 1986
0220 Hours Pacific Time

"*Jesus*, it's hot," Cherko said, as he and Shroot exited the 130, its props still running. Cherko inhaled the smell of JP-4. God, he loved that smell. Shroot said nothing, but directed Cherko toward an awaiting bus to their left. As they cleared the 130's prop wash, Cherko heard a pitch change and turned to see the aircraft spinning around like it couldn't get out of there fast enough.

"Drop and roll," Cherko said to himself.

The awaiting black bus opened its doors as they approached. Shroot and Cherko entered it. The air-conditioning felt great, but Cherko noticed all the windows were blackened out.

Trés familiar.

"Give me your watch," Shroot said, taking a seat.

"What?"

"Your watch. Give it to me."

Cherko handed it over.

"You'll get it back."

After a short ride over a rather unpaved road, the bus took a sharp right and stopped.

"Here we are. Remember what I said. No talking unless asked," Shroot said getting to his feet.

Cherko and Shroot exited the bus and strode the handful of steps to a steel door that Shroot opened. They entered a small, low-lit chamber with cameras aimed directly at them from above. Cameras that tracked their movements. A table was before him, whereupon sat one large, unfriendly looking security guard. Behind him stood another security guard, also large and menacing. Shroot talked with the one at the table and was verified against an access list.

"Please empty the entire contents of your pockets," the guard said. Cherko complied. He dumped his keys, change, wallet, chapstick, contact rewetting solution, handkerchief, and comb into a basket. The basket was then promptly locked away in a compartment in a set of lockers.

"This way, sir," the standing guard said, and directed him toward biometric equipment to his left. The guard wanded him.

Cherko had his picture taken, then stood on a plate in the floor where his weight was measured. He saw a retina and hand scanner, but wasn't directed to use either.

"You have all my other stuff?" he asked the guard, who just burned him a look without a response. Cherko was handed his new restricted-area badge. His picture was in the upper right-hand corner. Along the same edge of the badge, he saw "Temp" printed in large open-block red letters down the side of it. Along the bottom edge he saw "S4."

"Let's go," Shroot said, and they headed to the door behind the two security personnel. "Swipe your badge…you know the drill." Shroot stepped on a metal plate, swiped his badge and bent over the retina scanner, then disappeared behind the door. Cherko did the same. Behind the door was a much smaller foyer-like area, a hand reader beside the next entrance. Shroot placed his right palm at the hand reader then also disappeared behind that door. Cherko followed. There were no green or red lights, and no clicking of a lock releasing or setting. He pulled at the door latch and it simply opened. When he passed through this door, he found himself and Shroot standing inside a huge, narrow corridor that seemed to extend a half a mile or more. There was also the slight hush of what sounded like white noise above them.

Another guard stood before them, armed with some form of a mutant M-16.

"You will now be escorted into another room," Shroot said, "where you will be presented with a blue folder. This folder and its contents never leave that room. You will not leave the room until you have performed the actions described in that folder at the time hack given in the folder. A time display unit is provided in the room. If you need to use a restroom, do it now. You will not leave that room until you have completed the actions detailed in that folder. You have four minutes."

"But, how am I supposed to—"

"Remember our talk."

Cherko clammed up.

"When all actions have been completed, you will exit the room and a guard will escort you to me.

"Do you understand all I have instructed?"

Cherko nodded.

"Verbalize, please."

"Yes, sir—I understand your instructions."

"Good."

Chapter Seventeen

1

Undisclosed location, Desert Southwest
6 July 1986
0240 Hours Pacific Time

The door to "the room" was opened. Cherko stepped through it and it closed behind him.

Locked.

The first thing he saw was the timer, already ticking away. He was already losing time and he just got here. Something about that really unnerved him.

What time was it?

He had no idea, his watch having been taken away from him by Shroot...but there sat this timer, ticking away on an empty desk with the Blue Folder Shroot had also told him about...and some other object of which Shroot had made no mention.

(*complete the actions in the folder*)

(*couldn't leave the room until he did*)

And what was this thing—this tiny vial—standing on end beside the folder?

Cherko leaned in and took a closer look at the vial without touching it. Took his seat. Casting another glance to the ticking timer, he quickly turned his attention to the folder and opened it. Inside, a sheet of paper read:

> You have until the timer reaches 11 to perform all
> actions.

On the next line of typed Courier, was:

> You will now swallow the two pills in the vial. When
> complete, proceed to next direction.

The timer was ticking away from three. It seemed each tick was just over a second in length.

Cherko lifted the gray bottle and examined it. Considered what he was supposed to do with its contents, and scanned the room.

Another surveillance camera was behind him.

Lotsa trust.

Cherko shook the bottle. It didn't feel right...slippery in a odd, hard-to-explain way, but not in a way that would slide from his grasp. In fact it barely even felt like he was touching the damned thing. He brought it in closer. Two small pills were inside.

"No water?"

So what were these supposed to do to him? Turn him into Superman? The Incredible Brain? Cause him to explode?

Terminate him?

He removed the lid, which felt like a hard plastic material of some kind—or glass. Hard to tell. Shaking the bottle, he transferred the two innocuous looking pills into his hand. They were also gray, and smooth, nearly circular ovals. He set the bottle and cap down and got to his feet. Hefted the things in a palm. He approached the door and stood before it.

"I'm quite the captive audience, aren't I?"

Again hefted the pills.

Switched them into his other hand.

Time was a-tickin.

"Here goes nuthin."

Cherko "saluted" his upraised hand and pills toward the camera, then tossed them into his mouth.

They went down easy—actively sliding down his throat, as if he'd taken water with them.

"That felt weird."

He remained before the door a moment longer.

"Well, I don't *feel* like Superman."

Clearing his throat he sat back down.

Cherko had gone to the next sheet of paper in the folder. Things just kept getting weirder and weirder. The next sheet said:

>   Close your eyes. Focus on "Rosebud."

Rosebud?

Wasn't that a sled from *Citizen Kane?*

Cherko looked to the timer. It read 9:64.

Had it sped up?

He was certain it couldn't have been more than a minute or two of actual time passing since he'd been in here.

You have until the timer reaches 11 to perform all actions.

Okay, *Rosebud.* He closed his eyes and focused.

Cherko sat back in his chair, tried to relax—which he found oddly enough, was surprisingly easy to do, even under these circumstances. Maybe the little gray pills had something to do with it.

Rosebud.

Images of Orson Wells filled his mind, as well as other vague black-and-white scenes from *Citizen Kane*, but he quietly set them aside. His instructions didn't say anything about *playing* with the mental images around the term, just to *focus* on the term. As Cherko focused on his task, he felt his body begin to tingle.

Now, something was definitely happening.…

He felt as if he was…merging with…*what?*

Sensed an incredible buildup of power within.

But it was more than that. He felt as if there was

An intelligence.

Activating.

What was activating? Had *he* thought that or—

Cherko suddenly felt dense. Incredibly dense. But not in a heavy way. Felt as if his body was somehow extending out to the ends of the universe…tilting on edge. Rotating.

Growing.

He actually felt tipsy—*like he was psychically drunk?*

Rosebud.

Saw darkness. Felt air, but the air felt funny.

Electrical?

Smelled sand.

His ears began to ring.

Cherko opened his eyes and found himself looking out over a red desert.

2

Brigadier General Harley Becker stood outside in the desert terrain of area S-4, at the Papoose dry lakebed, pacing back and forth while chomping at the bit. He stared at the object before him, currently illuminated in red light and 100 yards away. It was encircled by a top special forces Black Team armed to the teeth.

"C'mon, baby, *do* it," he said, gritting his teeth as he paced.

He nervously glanced to his watch, then spun around to look out into the darkness of the Nevada desert; up into the night sky.

What the hell was really out there?

"Sir!" an assistant called. "*Look!*"

BG Becker spun back around. Figures, the one time he looked away....

His jaw dropped.

The red-illuminated object slowly lifted several feet into the air. It dipped slightly, somewhat unstable.

"Well, I'll be damned," BG Becker said. "It actually fucking *works*."

There were mild hoorays uttered by project personnel, which were quickly muted. Members of the Black Team even backed away a little from the now-hovering object.

Becker's assistant, Dr. Hill came up beside him.

"I told you," he said, turning back to watch the craft.

"And I'd never have believed it had I not seen it with my own eyes."

"We could find no other way, no other way to make it work...it *had* to work, *had* to."

"'Twould appear so, Doctor."

Cherko felt himself floating out of body. It was an extremely pleasant sensation, but he wasn't in that room any longer. He was...*outside*...looking out over a red desert. Everything was red. He spun around in place to check out where he was.

There—people. Pointing toward him.

Man, what a neat *feeling!*

Was he floating?

Rosebud.

Focus on the word.

Cherko rose up. Instantly he was (he felt by something that acted like, but wasn't called, an "altimeter") one-hundred feet into the dark air. He left the redness up here. Reaching out, he felt something out in the darkness was on the way...something was happening...

He looked down, he could still see those people gathered below. Looking up to him. Curious about them, he found himself instantly back down where he'd started, but felt no sense of motion.

Well, *that* was interesting.

Rosebud.

He'd been flown to an undisclosed location, ushered into a tiny little room, told to take some pills, and to focus on a word.

Rosebud.

And now he found himself here. Wherever "here" was.

So…what about the him back in that room?
Rosebud.

BG Becker walked over to Dr. Hill, who was now fiddling with equipment.

"Hard to believe, isn't it Doctor?"

"Well, it depends upon what set of physics one chooses to work with, doesn't it? Under our set, we've only just begun to chart any of this, but apparently under this craft's set, our views are rather Newtonian."

Becker nodded.

"Hyperdimensional physics, General."

The craft shot straight up, out of sight.

"*Shit!*" Becker uttered, taking several steps toward where the craft had just been. Dr. Hill shot a look up into the night.

"*Damn* it, I thought we'd had a script—get those lights back on it!" Becker shouted. Eight-hundred million candle-powered carbon-arc searchlights were instantly swung upward. But within seconds, the craft had instantly returned, startling its security forces. One man was knocked to the ground by nothing more than his own surprise, as the craft and his surprise came within inches of each other. And as the craft instantly reappeared, there had been no ground wash whatsoever. No air disturbance. One moment it was gone, and the next—returned.

BG Becker continued to stare at the craft as it hovered ten feet above the Nevada desert.

"We need this," he said, "we need this *bad.*"

Cherko opened his eyes.

The timer clicked to eleven.

Stopped.

He sat motionless in the chair, hands calmly on his legs.

Well, that was…*incredible.*

Had he actually done what he thought he had?

Had he actually piloted some craft with his mind?

Is this what this had all been about? And why had it been so easy? It's not like he'd ever done anything like this before.…

So, it had never been about transcribing mental alien stenography. Or disabling enemy satellites. Had it always been about *remotely piloting UFOs?*

No shit.

Cherko closed the folder and smoothed his hand over it as it lay before him.

Doesn't this fetch some rather interesting scenarios? If he'd really, in fact, done this…what else was he capable of?

Now, *this* was sexy.

A smile slowly worked its way across his face. He turned and glanced up at the surveillance camera behind him.

The once-again red-illuminated craft settled to the ground. No one moved as they all watched it come to a complete stop. Dr. Hill checked his watch. "Okay!" he declared, "All systems have powered down—let's go, people!"

The transport team moved in to return the craft to its underground storage bay—but before anyone could do anything, incredibly brilliant flood lights appeared out of the night sky and quickly descended to just about ground level, where they hovered.

From out of the dark, appeared men. Scores of them. All clad in black, AK-47s aimed at the individuals gathered around the craft.

The Black Team that had been in place found themselves barrel to barrel with counterparts of themselves in a classic Mexican Standoff. Neither man's cold, steely gazes flinched as they eyed each other, trigger fingers at the ready.

They…were *them.*

Becker fumed.

Overhead, a whisper of blades passed. Becker looked up to see a dark chopper pass overhead and felt the blast of its subdued prop wash. He watched the bird descend just on the other side of the Black Team that now held his group hostage.

Someone was going to pay. Dearly.

Out from the blackness strode a large, lone individual, tall in stature. Becker quietly checked his sidearm and undid the holster flap.

The figure unhesitatingly strode out of the darkness right up to him. He wore no cover, but did wear the dark utility uniform of the Black Team members that held them captive. No name tag, nor any other identifying features, save one.

Stars.

Three of them. The rank of Lieutenant General in subdued stitching.

Becker hissed. "Son of a *bitch.*"

The unknown individual came right up to Becker before stopping. His face was hard, but not as old as Becker would have expected for a man of his rank.

Great; outranked by a younger fast burner.

The LG shook his head with a look of bored disdain. He cast a glance to those around them before he spoke, and when he spoke it was more like he was chastising a wayward subordinate than addressing an honored colleague.

"What the hell you think you're doing, General?"

"Where's your cigar and why haven't you pissed down my legs?" Becker spat back.

"The first one kills, and as for the second—be happy to oblige," Hammond said, reaching for his fly.

"Oh, I think you've already done that."

Hammond eyed Becker for along moment; removed his hands from his fly.

"So, you think you can come into my territory…snatch one of my resources…and use it for yourself?"

"Apparently," Becker said, grinning.

Hammond gave another once-over to the standoff around them. Looked uninterestedly to the craft about which Becker's people were still huddled.

"But I certainly do appear to have you by the balls at the moment, don't I?"

"For now."

Hammond narrowed his gaze.

"*Don't ever—again—fuck with my resources,*" Hammond said. He turned and walked away. "Because, if you do," he called back over the shoulder and chopper noise, "I'll have to take you out! And that'd be a damned shame, General! A *damned* shame!"

Hammond continued back to the chopper.

Cherko sighed and got to his feet, a smile still painted across his face. Well, maybe this was worth the series of life failures and missteps he'd taken to get here. Maybe this was what he was finally meant to do. Wasn't meant to rocket into orbit—at least not as he'd *planned*—but this would certainly serve nicely.

Cherko opened the door…and walked into the barrel of an AK-47.

"Lieutenant James Francis Cherko?" came a voice from somewhere behind that barrel.

"Yes?"

The AK-47 crisply lifted up and pointed away from his face into the ceiling; the stern-faced operative behind it backed smartly away. The hallway was filled with black-faced, black-uniformed men with weaponry, and they parted to allow a tall, powerful-looking man to come forward. A man with three stars on black lapels.

"Lieutenant, we're here to retrieve you," Hammond said.

"Retrieve me?"

"You've been 'misappropriated,' Lieutenant. I'm here to reclaim what's mine."

Cherko saw no name tag on the general's uniform.

"Excuse me, sir, and with all due respect—but who are you?" Cherko felt a wink of familiarity and furrowed his brow. "Have we met?"

"We have detained Mr. Shroot, as he calls himself," Hammond said. He cast a look behind him. Cherko saw Shroot under armed guard and not at all happy about it. "And are to return you to your unit. Come with us, please." The general extended an open hand between them toward the exit.

Before Cherko could ask another question, the general turned and left the doorway. Cherko looked to the men and muzzles before him, then dutifully followed.

3

Unmarked XH-60 Blackhawk, 3,500 feet, Heading 169
6 July 1986
0317 Hours Pacific Time

"Sir," Cherko finally decided, airborne in a black helicopter and heading toward a destination he wasn't all that positive was the right one, in a formation with several other, sleeker, attack choppers. "Can you tell me what's going on?"

Hammond scanned the airspace around them.

"No, Lieutenant, I cannot. At least not until we're on-deck. Secure."

Cherko again looked outside the chopper. He could barely make out the other choppers in formation with them. The quiet thud of the blades made him feel as if he were in a spy movie. Here he was in a chopper, "extracted," it had been called, from an area he now saw was remote desert.

Gee, no stretch of the imagination there.

He'd just been in the most infamous location in the world, a location that officially did not exist. He'd read the books, but in all his imaginings, he'd *never* thought he'd ever be part of something that took him to Area 51. Let alone kidnapped by his own kind. As he was outbriefed by the general, he was told never to discuss what he'd done there, or that there was even a "there" to begin with. Whether or not he'd been kidnapped and to where were to forever remain their dirty little secret.

But perhaps the strangest thing of all was that a frigging general—*a three-star lieutenant general*—had come to get him. *A three-star had come to extract a first lieutenant.*

Had to be a first.

But far from resting on any such laurels that also meant one thing: something about him—about his *abilities and mission*—was important enough to warrant said action, and by a member of said national command staff rank.

This wasn't going to be pretty.

* * *

Indian Springs Air Force Auxiliary Field
6 July 1986
0325 Hours Pacific Time

While their attack escort remained airborne, the Blackhawk Cherko and Hammond were in landed, immediately surrounded by the same type of crack security forces he'd unceremoniously met in that hallway in S-4. He was quickly surrounded by Black Team personnel and rushed away from the chopper, which immediately took off. The attack choppers remained hovering until he was ushered into a dark van. Once inside the van and again surrounded by Black Team personnel in the rear of the van, he heard what sounded like some of the choppers breaking off to go with the Blackhawk, while one or two remained to follow the van to wherever they were headed.

The general looked to Cherko without a word as he settled into the front seat.

"Thank you," Cherko offered.

What else could he say?

He certainly wasn't used to being in the presence of such elevated rank. Hammond turned part way to him and nodded.

The van pulled away from the landing zone and took bumpy roads toward their (to him anyway) unknown destination. It seemed every time he got into one of these things it was never over paved road.

Finally beginning to feel the hour, Cherko closed his eyes to take a nap, but didn't want to keep them closed for too long, given his contacts were still in. He felt his pocket for his wetting solution. Still there.

A bump jarred Cherko awake.

Opening his eyes, he looked out to brighter skies and a nondescript block of a building that looked as if it had been built during WWII.

"We're here, Lieutenant," Hammond said.

The van pulled to a stop and everyone piled out. The way these guys secured an area was powerful to see, the fact they were doing it for *him*—or maybe, more so the general—was humbling, if not *totally* cool. He knew this wasn't a game, was obviously serious business, but he just wasn't used to this kind of treatment, except within the realms of his imagination. He observed how the Black Team interacted with each other: crisp, highly professional, and silent. The phrase existed for a reason: *if looks could kill.* He had no doubt about that.

Spirited into the building within his cocoon of security, himself and the general in the center of it, he wondered how the general felt about extracting a lowly first lieuy.

He feel demeaned?

His stature lessened?

Embarrassed to be paired off with a lieutenant in such important matters, and soon to be—hopefully—explaining himself, again—to a *lieutenant?*

Inside the building the doors were shut. Two personnel remained outside. One of the team members set down a compact box, extended a narrow antenna, and switched it on. A red light slowly blinked. The team member then used a hand-held device as he continued with his comrade-in-arms in checking out the building.

Cherko stood uncomfortably alongside the general, who never looked to him. Thankfully the two Black Team members soon returned, obviously satisfied.

"Area secured, General," one said.

Hammond nodded, and the team members departed outside. Hammond finally turned to him.

"Lieutenant, I'm General Hammond, director of ERO." Surprisingly, he stuck out a hand. Cherko looked to it.

"Pleasure, sir," Cherko said, shaking it.

"Apologies for the dramatics, but I assure you, it was all necessary. What I'm about to tell you does not leave this room, your lips, or your fingertips. That box over there," Hammond said, nodding toward it, "is emitting EMP to deny eavesdropping. But nothing's ever 100% certain. Remember that."

"Yes sir."

Hammond again nodded; came in close to Cherko.

"There are organizations out there that know about you, your abilities. Your involvement in The Program."

"Sir?"

"I understand you are under orders not to acknowledge the Program, so just listen and make up your own mind."

Again, here was a guy of probably thirty-five years' experience and a small universe on his lapels explaining himself to a lowly silver bar.

Though the building had been declared secured, Hammond still looked around nervously; lowered his voice even more.

"Lieutenant…you have been selected and carefully bred to be more than just a satellite operator. There are…elements…out there closely observing…guiding you toward destiny. *Your* destiny."

Cherko didn't know whether it was just that he was tired, or what, but he felt…*odd*. In a dream. He was just a kid from New York, a kid with high-flying aspirations of stars and *Star Trek*. This was the stuff of *fiction*.

But as he listened to the general's words, images flew through his head, and feelings of déjà vu saturated him.

An image of Earth from orbit.

If this was fiction…then it was the truest fiction ever told.…

Chapter Eighteen

1

On July 1, 1947, amid violent thunderstorms that shook the earth, the Army's 509th Bomb Group just outside of Roswell, New Mexico, and White Sands missile range north of Las Cruces, New Mexico, both tracked bizarre radar blips. Blips tore across operator screens at impossible speeds, performed equally impossible changes in direction—sometimes *actually speeding up*—then vanished. Short of known test launches with acquired German V2 rocketry, compliments of Operations Overcast and Paperclip, nothing the U.S. had at the time came close to what was observed.

Highly seasoned radar operators fresh from World War II performed calibrations, recalibrations, and verifications across every component. Surveillance flights unsuccessfully combed the area, and base commanders alerted Washington. Civilians witnessed the anomalous phenomena out on their evening porches.

A bright oval that'd streaked across the sky.

Over the next forty-eight hours, anxious officials tracked additional signatures, while surveillance flights repeatedly came up empty-handed. Whatever was invading the highly restricted military airspace of New Mexico was not lightning.

The government deployed its most experienced crack Counterintelligence Corps, or CIC, operatives into the region, and it wasn't long before they observed disturbing new behavior.

The blips changed shape.

High above all those celebrating Independence Day, one object, after having attained speeds well in excess of three-thousand miles an hour and after having performed multiple hair-pinned maneuvers, abruptly flared up…then all radar screens went clear.

Operators had witnessed a crash.

CIC wasted no time in deploying to the crash site, just outside the town of Corona. Roswell's Sheriff dispatched the fire department, based upon witness accounts of an exploded aircraft.

CIC had arrived on-scene first, posting sentries and stringing floodlights. Before the team was, indeed, a crash—but not like one any of them had ever expected. Plowed into the embankment of a remote arroyo at a forty-five-degree angle, rested a wing-shaped craft, one side jaggedly ripped open. Surrounding the ship lay beings...dark gray-brown, completely hairless, and about four-to-four-and-a-half feet tall...dead and dying. One dying creature's pleas had not been heard *physically* by those who came upon it, but *mentally*. Two had survived. One sat calmly and serenely beside the dying crew, while the other had been caught scrambling up a rise just to the other side of the craft. The unfortunate creature had been quickly brought down by a volley of M-1 rifle fire.

The blur of activity that followed had been quickly and effectively shrouded in mystery and secrecy as everything recovered—including the bodies—had been shipped off to their clandestine locations. Over time, all "alien harvest" material had been intentionally—and unintentionally—distributed across military and civilian research and technology divisions, including the Atomic Energy Commission, RAND, the National Advisory Committee for Aeronautics, even the CIA. A systematic seeding of this advanced technology had begun to infiltrate its way into all things human. An entirely new classification system had been created...an entirely covert *government within a government*.

Majestic-12.

Unimaginable levels of deception, disinformation, and cover-ups sprang up around anything and anyone having to do with Roswell. What people didn't know, they didn't *need* to know. Some insisted on bringing this information out to the public, but, its detractors insisted, to do so would be to blanketly hand it over to the Russians. To let it out would be whole-sale acknowledgment of our own incompetence and deficiency in being all-knowing and all-powerful. And some...some kept it secret merely because that's all they knew...was all they *did*, because, once you got as deep as this was in the Black World, *everything* became classified, and knowledge, after all, *was power*. This new extremism knew no bounds, was beyond human law, and wasn't above making individuals and events *disappear*....

Over the years subgroups and sub-subgroups developed, and things had gotten lost in safes where the only individuals with the knowledge and access to these safes also died, never having relinquished their combinations.

Nothing had been passed on because *no one had had the need-to-know*.

Knowledge *was* power.

Rumors grew, including the possession of one or more live extraterrestrials. Area 51, S-4. Agencies were created under the pretenses of other cover missions to deal with what was called the growing threat of alien intruders. In the sixties and seventies, and through the direct use of some of the alien technology that had been harvested, were created two covert operations, both of which ERO managed on the strictest need-to-know basis:

projects Saint and Blue Gemini. Saint was the surveillance arm through which the CIA tracked and targeted alien craft in orbit with specifically designed reconnaissance satellites, and Blue Gemini was the hunter-killer arm with platforms that swooped down from higher orbits to take out—or capture— these crafts and their occupants.

This was ERO's heritage, its actual mission. What it was all about.

And as Lieutenant General Robert Mitchell Hammond laid all this out for First Lieutenant James Francis Cherko, in that tiny, no-name building that reeked of history and desert rot, Cherko reeled over the possibilities. Everything he'd ever heard, ever read, had all been *true*—and he was now smack-dab in the middle of all of it.

"Why?"

Hammond looked to him.

"What do you mean 'why'? Because they're dangerous. Dangerous and hostile."

"With all due respect, General, but how do you get that? None of what you've told me leads me to believe their intentions are hostile."

"They buzz our installations, our spacecraft and aircraft. *Destroy* our spacecraft and aircraft. None of our pilots have ever come back. *Ever.* They constantly evade us."

"But evading is not—"

Hammond paused as he paced the dusty floor, like someone not used to being questioned—nor considered wrong—but backed off his usual, blistering and soul-crushing reprisal.

"Son," Hammond said wearily, "you'll see. You'll discover their motives. Admittedly we don't know everything, but we do know that they've taken out many, *many* of our airmen when they'd been scrambled to intercept. Destroyed military and surveillance satellites we've sent into orbit. *Astronauts.*"

"You can't be...*Astronauts?*"

Hammond nodded grimly.

"*Challenger* wasn't merely a faulty O-ring. It'd been destroyed through overt extraterrestrial means. *Challenger* was, as are many of our shuttle flights, a cover for another mission, and their particular mission was that of a new generation of alien sentry platform I'm still not at liberty to discuss. It was summarily taken out without so much as a warning. Our clashes with them had been, for the most part, subtle and gentlemanly to this point, but that one action was a clear and powerful message: they meant us harm, and they meant to keep us where they could *control* us."

"I just...I just can't believe this..."

"It *is* war, son. I wish it wasn't, but it is. Though our government is united in its efforts to repel extraterrestrial dominance, we still have our own petty in-fighting, our own bickering, which is what you experienced tonight. Becker and his crew—Shroot—have been unable to fly those damned machines. To figure them out. Their best minds figured it *had* to do with mind control, but they could never make it work—until you. You've been watched for a long time—still will be, I'm afraid, for the rest of your life. And in order to mitigate that, I'm sending you to New Mexico."

"*New Mex—*"

"They'll try to grab you again, and I simply can't have that. They need to find their own damned resources, not keep pilfering mine. I have big plans for you and I'm not about to share.

"You're coming up for promotion soon, aren't you?"

"Yes, sir, next July."

Hammond nodded. "What I have in store for you is far more important than trying to pilot some captured piece of E.T. taxi."

"And what would that be, sir?"

Hammond grinned. "You might have need-to-know of all I've just told you, but as to *that*," he chuckled, "*that* you don't—yet."

2

100-Mile Low Earth Orbit
4 November 2021
0910 Hours Zulu

Cherko hyperventilated as he continued struggling within the unknown metal contraption. The one that enveloped him from ankle to neck.

"There's no need for that," Rudy said, calmly. "Breathe… deeply… slowly—"

"This is *bullshit!* Why can't you just get me the hell out of this thing? There's a war going on out there! There are things I need to be doing!"

"We're safe. It's important to remember. You must remember."

Rudy's voice was soothing and unnervingly calming, but as Cherko looked about the module things felt as if they were fast closing in on him. Compacting in on him at a psychic level he felt accelerating.

He blinked.

Sweat trickled down his face; his armpits. Debris floated before him.

"This is *insane!* You've got to get me out of this damned thing!"

"What else do you remember? What next after that meeting?"

Cherko stopped struggling. Rudy's voice connected with something deep inside.

Yes, that meeting. In Nevada. Right. He'd just been told all this funky shit about—

UFOs.

Yeah. They were real all right, Hammond'd just told him so. And there was this government-within-the-government thing, running the whole show since '47. Silencing people, making them "disappear." He had to wonder...*what would be of such severe importance that this clandestine inner government was willing to kill to keep secret?*

"What happened after that meeting?" Rudy asked.

"I..."

Cherko wrinkled his face. C'mon, pull it out...

Well, soul be damned....

"What do you remember?" Rudy asked, "what do you remember about the path that led you here? How did you get here?"

Cherko rested his head back against the bulkhead, and longingly looked outside the viewport.

"Now, that's the billion-dollar question, ain't it...."

3

Dulce, New Mexico
16 September 1986
0840 Hours Mountain Time

First Lieutenant Cherko ran his Dulce restricted-area badge, scanned his hand, and entered his office. He went directly to one of several safes, spun the combo, flipped the safe's magnetic "Closed" sign to "Open," and removed the report he'd last been reading. He took it to his desk and sat down; opened it to where he'd left off. He'd just come off a Saint/Blue Gemini training support. He was to get console certified, but he wasn't to become just another console jockey. Yes, he'd be certified on-console, but his real work was much more. In his new capacity at Dulce he was tasked with multiple responsibilities: not only was he to keep his hands in on-orbit ops and to further develop his ability at (apparently) controlling alien craft, but he was also to assist LG Hammond in the continued covert and insidious insertion of alien technology into the world.

Any one of these tasks would have been enough to stretch the realms of credibility with anyone, but he was assigned with all three.

And there was also some life-long grooming he was supposed to be thankful for.

But it was the third one that surprisingly caught him the most off-guard.

Inserting alien technology into the world?

Since arriving at Dulce, much of his time had been spent reading. Reading and assimilating reams and reams of highly classified intel. Reports buried in several safes both in his office and Hammond's. Reports Hammond did not want others outside the two of them to ever see. Though these reports repeatedly referred to the Roswell crash, there were other crashes also defined across its pages, as well as a fair amount of information and other technology also coming from another unidentified source only identified as "Alan."

In this new and quite exciting (he had to admit) position he found himself frequently meeting with many outside agencies, even in the few short months he'd been on the job. Many times out of uniform, or in conjunction with some other planned—cover—meeting. He'd met with officials at NSA, NRO, the CIA, and of course, NASA.

AT&T.

Bell.

IBM.

On these trips Cherko and Hammond were always probing these companies for their knowledge on technology…assessing whether or not they could work with them. In addition to seeding ET technology, Hammond was also looking for satellite platforms. Satellites upon which to foist Saint and Blue Gemini surveillance and hunter/killer packages. Since ERO wasn't in the business of actually building satellites, it had to go to those who did…such as the CIA and NRO. ERO only went to government agencies. Not only did it keep it in-house, because they were big enough to do it on their own with their own resources, but also because Hammond felt they were also much more tightly guarded than even a Lockheed or Northrop.

Relentless loyalty to your organization…lack of trust to all others.

So, ERO went to the National Reconnaissance Organization. Got them to build platforms on which to install their black boxes—stuff Hammond never intended on in-briefing anybody.

We lie to them, just like they lie to us.

Cherko flipped another page.

Nobody tells the truth in this business.

To gain their situational trust, Hammond would tell NRO that it was experimental R&D stuff for better spying. Even brought some of NRO's people to totally fictitious labs and facilities to show them *more* lies, and they bought every one—insofar as anyone in this business "buys" anything. NRO had the spy satellite business down to an art, so ERO used them.

No need to reinvent the wheel.

It also added another layer of obfuscation to the whole process, something Hammond was very big on.

He'd told Cherko that if ever there was more room to add more confusion, more layers to the Black Onion, as he called it, by all means *do* it. Can't have enough. The more confusion the better.

And it worked like a charm.

Black Onion, yeah…

And there was one more task Cherko felt Hammond had for him, though he'd never confirmed it and continually danced around it.

On their last trip to NASA, Hammond was wanting something bigger, more ambitious: to put humans in sustained orbit. On an ET spy space station.

Putting up orbital hardware wasn't good enough for Hammond. No, he needed an actual—*physical*—presence up there, and perhaps that was what Hammond had really wanted out of him all along. A pair of boots on-orbit. Cherko stared out across his office and rubbed tired eyes.

He never admitted to it, never said who he had in mind for such an operation, but Cherko was pretty damned sure Hammond was thinking one Lieutenant Jimmy Cherko would make a fine, fine, astronaut spy.

He was sure he'd planned it from the very beginning.

And Cherko wasn't so sure he was against it. After all, it certainly would be a way for him to finally get that astronaut rating. He just wouldn't be able to tell anyone about it. He'd be a secret. A spy astronaut. Go through all the training as the regular ones, but be unable to tell anyone why and for what. That was what his last Houston trip had been all about.

Such was the story of his life, as it seemed to be unfolding, and was the nature of this business. Always hiding in shadows. Always lying and obfuscating. Smoke and mirrors.

But through it all—his on-orbit operations training, his heavy report reading until his eyes bled—something continually nagged at the back of his mind.

This whole battle-against-aliens thing. That aliens were supposed to be hostile.

Something was inherently wrong with the logic, and he didn't understand Hammond's continued defense of it.

What year was it? 1986? And nothing had happened since at *least* 1947?

If extraterrestrials had really wanted to take us out, wouldn't they have done so long ago? Wouldn't whatever we had found out in that desert back in '47—if they'd *really* wanted to off us—wouldn't they had taken us out the very next day? That *morning*?

And why?

For what conceivable purpose would a highly advanced—heck, even a *partially* advanced—race need to rid the universe of the likes of us?

They had control of the skies—*space.*

Just what kind of threat did Humanity pose?

We couldn't even get along with ourselves, for crying out loud.

Was that it?

No, nothing about this made any kind of sense.

Unless Hammond was just feeding him a line of bull. Get what he wanted from him and keep him in line, for some reason Cherko hadn't yet figured out.

Now, *that* made a lot more sense.

Don't trust anybody—Hammond himself had told him so.

He did seem to have this ability that, in the wrong hands, could wreak all kinds of havoc—heck, in the *right* hands—and he wasn't even all that sure just how real an ability it was. He couldn't control cars. Or boats.

Animals.

Or people.

How was he able to control apparently alien technology?

And his apparently telepathic communications had ceased, as well. Ever since he'd been shipped to New Mexico.

It was all highly suspicious.

But the job was fascinating enough. He had to stay the course and try to find out what was really going on, find out more.

Then there was Erica.

Good God, he missed her!

Cherko felt he was constantly under surveillance; even more so in Dulce. At his ERO-furnished apartment he wasn't even *allowed* a phone. Any calls he needed to make—including home or to utilities—he could make from his office.

Of course, he hadn't had any chance to take a vacation, but he seriously doubted he would be just "let go" without someone watching him, tracking his every move.

He was even positive his mail was monitored.

He'd written Erica a letter a week, always expecting to hear back from her, but never—not one response—had he ever received from her since he was pulled out of Colorado.

Yeah, welcome to the Black Onion.

Chapter Nineteen

1

Colorado Springs, CO
8 November 2010
1537 Hours Mountain Time

"Okay," Alda said, shuffling paper around in hand, as Cherko sat quiet in his usual seat. "Since the free association exercise went so well last week, I'd like to try something similar today."

"Okay."

"But first—anything you want to talk about?"

"Oh, I don't know. Ever since my little 'accident,' I guess I've felt kinda, well, out of it. Slightly…'off.' Like what's going on with my life? What's happened to me?"

"What do you mean?"

"I've always tried to live my life in as happy a manner as possible, and for the most part I really am happy, but all these great dreams and goals I had for my life all seem to have bypassed me. I never seemed to get what I really wanted out of life. Was unable to break through and become an astronaut. These are the best years of my life, and I feel things have left me way behind. Somehow I got off track. A *tech writer*? How the heck had I become a *tech writer*? Where the heck had my life so grossly derailed?"

"This had always been a huge goal of yours, becoming an astronaut?"

"I always felt as if I was meant to explore space. Get out there. Spaceships, technology, the Great Unknown."

"Really?"

"It was always a huge goal. That's what I originally set out to do. Went to college to get a physics degree, got it…went after an Air Force navigator's training slot, got that…but then failed actual navigator training, and that's where all the failures began piling up. The really big ones—the important ones."

"How so?"

"I always tell everyone I failed because I couldn't do numbers in my head, and while that's true…I've come to learn that there was another reason that also weighed in heavily."

"And that would be…"

"My inability to deal with the real world."

Alda raised an eyebrow.

"Up to nav training, everything in my life had been theoretical. Academic learning. And it's not that I was some white-skinned waif who never did anything outside and away from books—I was very much into the Greek saying 'a sound mind in a healthy body,' or whatever it was—but, well, when I was in that T-37 cockpit—"

"'T-37'?"

"A subsonic jet trainer, just 'under' the T-38, which was a supersonic jet. But, when I was in there, flying, I had this moment when my IP—instructor pilot—and I were flying a heading, and I couldn't DR—dead reckon—a new one. Basically, before flight you sit down and plan your flights—your headings—but, like everything else, things change—wind direction, speed, sometimes even your objective—and you have to be able to change with them in the air. So, you do what's called 'dead reckoning.' You come up with a new heading in-cockpit. That involves numbers. And you can't always whip out your Whiz Wheel—an in-flight slide-rule-like apparatus for flight calculations. You just have to do the numbers in your head. In today's world I'm sure everything's computerized. Anyway, I couldn't do the numbers in my head, and my IP had to course-correct cause we were coming up on some mountains real fast. The IP had actually whacked me upside the head with the back of his hand. Nothing against my Dad, but it reminded me of him. Or, if you really want to get analytical about things, since that is what we do here, it just made me feel like a kid because of how he treated me. Anyway, that's when I realized I wasn't cut out for this job…that mountains *do* come up fast and that there's really not much room for error. Either you can or you can't come up with the numbers. And I couldn't. It was too real."

"Too real."

"I realized this just wasn't gonna happen. I mean, I had a ninety-eight academic average, but that was the book learning part, it wasn't the out-in-the-world performance that involved lots of numbers. I've never been good with numbers—never—it's always haunted me. As much as I loved to play with them—I actually enjoyed math—I was just never any good at it. No matter how hard I tried."

"I see."

"So, now, I'm this technical writer."

"There's nothing wrong with that—"

"Can't you see the irony? Here I am, in a *technical* field, a field that definitely does require some adeptness with technical material *and* numbers. But it's all on paper—not real, not rocketing into space and applying mathematics and physics to real-time situations. My whole life seems to have taken this weird, metaphysical turn *back* to the theoretical, when all my life I'd been trying to become this man of *action*.

"And all these self-help gurus keep telling you all you have to do is just *wish* hard enough, be optimistic enough—*persist* long enough—and you'll eventually get your desires. Well, damn it, I'm much closer to death than birth, and I ain't seeing the fruit of my so-called optimistic ventures."

Alda nodded thoughtfully, scribbling notes. When he was done, he looked up to Cherko.

"I'd like you to do something for me."

"Sure," Cherko said, again sighing.

"I'd like for you to go over there on my couch," Alda said, and Cherko looked, "and lay down and close your eyes. Relax. I'd like you to think back to your wildly imaginative childhood. Think back to what it was like as that wide-eyed kid with the overactive imagination, where there were no rules, no restrictions."

"Okay."

Cherko went over to the couch. Stretched out on it. Alda followed over to another chair alongside.

"You can take off your shoes if you want."

Cherko left them on.

"Now...relax. There are no rules, no restrictions. Settle in."

Cherko closed his eyes and relaxed, and it felt surprisingly easy to do—and *good*. He loved revisiting his childhood; he'd had a great one and loved thinking about it. Did that a lot. In some ways, he *was* naïve, but he also considered himself somewhat worldly—*but mainly because he'd read about real life from* books.

But he liked that.

In the background of his mind he heard Alda talking to him, heard his words, but it was like he was on his own trip now, a trip that didn't quite feel right...and Alda's words were quickly fading into the distance....

2

White Sand Missile Range
3 August 1987
0125 Hours Mountain Time

Captain Jimmy Cherko sat in the webbed seating of the NC-130H as it nosed down for its landing. He'd grabbed a hop on it out of Houston after his meeting-that-never-officially-happened with a top-level NASA administrator, who-was-never-officially-there. He'd been told to divert to

White Sands instead of heading straight back to Dulce. He was to meet someone at the airstrip who was to further direct him where to go and how to get there....

Cherko exited the 130 and cleared away from the still-spinning props. He was quickly met by a smartly saluting Navy Petty Officer 1st Class who stepped away from a dark SUV. He carried a small pouch and something else.

"Captain Cherko?" the PO1 asked, saluting and shouting above the prop wash.

Cherko returned the salute. "Yes?"

"I'm to give you this," he said handing Cherko the slim parcel.

"What is it?"

"A map. Of the base."

"Okay."

"You're to meet at the location marked on the map no later than 0200, sir."

"Who am I meeting?"

"I do not know, sir. I was just told to give you this. And you might need this," he said, handing over the other object.

"A flashlight?"

"It gets rather dark out there, sir."

Cherko looked out beyond the airstrip. "Right."

"Take the Jeep, sir."

Cherko looked to it. "Thanks."

"And sir—this is very important—but, do not deviate off the roads! Unexploded ordnance!" The PO1 again saluted and left.

Cherko turned on the flashlight, a heavy duty thing that, he found out, carried some massive candle-wattage and nearly blinded him. After having been in the dark in the 130 for the past hour or so, his eyes protested against anything bright and flashy. Blinking and looking away, he looked back to the stiff document in hand. The map was made of that durable chart paper that could withstand the elements. He saw two marked end points connected by a heavy dark line that wove throughout the White Sands Missile Range complex. One end was where he presently stood, and the other way off the paved areas of White Sands Proper, tracing into the out-and-out desert of the actual missile range. Odometer markings were placed at various points along the route. The missile range was essentially total desert interspaced with the occasional launch platform, concrete slabs with leftover electronics and other equipment needed for whatever missions had been set up among the cacti and sand—then deserted.

And lots of sand.

He'd been around some parts of the range for various projects on which he'd worked, since being PCSed from Colorado, but not to where he was directed on this map. And, yes, there was, indeed, a grave concern about not leaving the paved (so they called them) dirt roads. There were all kinds of unexploded ordnance hiding out there.

Cherko headed toward the Jeep.

Colorado.

It seemed more than just a year ago; seemed a lifetime ago. Since he'd been in Dulce, he'd been flying highly sensitive satellites monitoring (he could still hardly believe it) orbital UFO activity, practicing his telepathic UFO control, and seeding alien technology into the world. He'd also been poked and prodded as the government's best minds probed *his* in order to find out why he could control UFOs and not cars or people. And not all UFOs, either. He could only control unmanned (unaliened?) craft, not those under intelligent control. So, it was thought that perhaps UFOs were only controlled by one mind at a time—though it was still not understood why he had this ability and no one else did (or so he was told). To this end, interest in his continued UFO-controlling ability was waning, and his most pressing effort was quickly becoming working this orbiting spy space station project of Hammond's. And he never did find out about any outcomes of his other efforts with Spooks One, Two, and Three.

But Hammond was growing increasingly obsessed with this station idea of his, one populated by *their* kind. Not NASA, not CIA, but covert ERO personnel.

And, he was told, if he played his cards right, he could count himself among the first crew members.

Finally, Hammond had played his cards.

It was all quite sexy. Extremely sensitive operations. Astronaut rating. Can't tell a soul.

Astronaut.

So he continued his frequent trips to Houston, DC, Maryland.

It all was so damned unreal.

All at the expense of leaving behind the woman he loved.

Erica.

He hadn't had any real choice, he'd been told. Told himself. He'd had to leave her, not even for his country, but for the planet. The entire Human *Race.*

Yes, it was worth it, he'd been repeatedly instructed; continually convinced himself.

And he wasn't to ever contact her again. *Ever.* Even with his family he'd extremely measured contact; gave them only his cover story. All his contact with them was monitored. He was in a different place now. For all practical purposes, he had, indeed, fallen off the face of the Earth.

All to *save* the Earth.

And now he'd been given this diversion to some indistinct location on a map. In the dark.

Always in the dark, always unpaved roads.

And it was hard hiding his singular lone belief in alien innocence in this secretive world of distrust and hostility. Something just didn't feel right about it all, and he still couldn't put his finger on it.

He was tired and it was late. He was glad for the AC, but had to continually jolt himself awake when he found himself hypnotized by the two powerful beams of his headlights cutting into the night before him.

Cherko checked his odometer and slowly pulled to a stop; checked the map. He was coming up on the final segment. A left just up ahead.

Cherko got back on the gas and drove until he came to the gnarled wood post that held a sign that came into view of his headlights.

USS White Sands, it said.

A *ship?*

Cherko wrinkled his brow and made the left. There was what looked like a large dark structure down another dirt road that seemed tightly hemmed in by desert scrub. Cherko drove his vehicle through the narrow passage…and pulled to a stop before the illuminated bow of a *ship*.

He shut off the engine and got out of the Jeep. Left the lights on. The door of the Jeep still open, he stared at what was before him. Dumbfounded.

How the hell did a ship get out in the middle of a desert?

Desert Ship.

Cherko reached back in and looked to his map. This was the place. He looked over the map one more time for any more information, found nothing, and tossed it back into the vehicle. Then he pulled out the heavy duty flashlight, and switched it on. Leaving the Jeep's lights on, he closed the door and walked toward his mysterious rendezvous.

3

Holding onto the thick metal rail, Cherko cautiously made his way up the narrow, slightly oscillating gangway that led up to the main deck. He'd seen plenty of movies that showed seamen making their way up these things, but never realized just how wobbly they actually were. It reminded him of that Tacoma bridge oscillation way back, and he wondered how many could safely go up one of these things at once, and if they had to be out of step with each other to not bring it down. Several times, on his way up, he turned back to the Jeep, which still obediently shone its lights into the bow of this land-bound ship.

No shit, he was really walking up the gangway plank *onto* a ship. In the middle of the desert.

But as he made his way onto the top he found that what he thought was an entire ship was actually only part of one…the forward part. The bow section to what had once been a full-size floater (a *skimmer*, his dad would say). He wasn't Navy so didn't know what type of ship he was boarding, but it was impressive enough. As he got to the top of the ramp, he found a light chain drawn across the entryway onto the deck. He paused, flashing his light up and down the length of the structure.

Empty.

"Permission to board!" he hailed into the night. Again, he flashed his light up and down the abbreviated length of the empty ship's deck. Then even shined it up above him, along what must be the bridge.

Nothing.

Grunting, he unclasped the chain and boarded. He fastened the chain back behind him.

Cherko briefly checked out the deck, but saw a hatch in what he assumed to be the side of the bridge structure. He also assumed he was to enter it, and did so.

Cherko directed his light down the hole before him. It was dark down there, but there seemed to be just a hint of light coming from somewhere. One hand on the immaculately painted and polished gray railing, and aiming his light down before him, Cherko descended into the steep, narrow passageway. His steps made a unique "tink" on his way down the metal steps. Sounded exactly like they did in the movies. As he continued to descend, however, it got hotter. He was hoping that whatever he was doing here, whomever he was to meet, they didn't have to stay long. This ship was one massive heatsink.

As he made mid-deck, he found the light. It came from a slightly opened hatchway in the center of the main passageway. He made the landing, always shining his light around him. There were several highly polished wooden doors—oak? Mahogany? He wasn't sure, but everything on this ship was immaculately maintained. Like the saying goes, you could eat off the deck of any Navy ship—or what was left of one. Cherko went to the slightly opened door. It led into what looked to be a briefing, or Ward, room.

The room was sparse, low lit. Paneled in a rich, dark wood. Cherry? Looked like some briefing rooms he'd been in at NASA and NRO. Very official. Lofty. Trophies in many showcases; flags and numerous shots of planes, ships, and National Command Staff military and Executive civilian personnel. It all looked very Navy. Cherko wondered if his dad had ever been in briefing rooms like this. On subs, or the one surface "skimmer" he was on before subs. Of course he had. What was the name of that ship he'd been on—the *Nereus?*

Morning, Captain.

Cherko swung his flashlight around him like a gun as he spun around.

His blood ran cold.

There, standing in the dimly lit hatchway stood none other than Spook King himself.

The tall, lanky, dark figure stood like he'd always found him; clad in its dark longcoat attire and scarecrow thin; shadowy Fedora dipped over its face and arms down to its sides.

It just stood there, like a prop on a set. Just inside the hatchway.

Cherko had an image of this figure standing on some dark, noirish street corner under a streetlight, smoking a partially spent ciggy butt. Of course, the figure would have to move its arms to do that, and he'd never seen it move its arms—or anything else, for that matter.

It was always just *there.*

And just as gone when it wasn't.

Cherko's first reaction was to run, to bolt on out of there—but he also had the contradictory urge to knock off that hat. To peer into the face of the unknown.

"Good morning," Cherko greeted.

We hope you had no trouble finding this location.

"None at all."

The figure still never lifted its head, but he heard its words. Words that seemed to originate within his mind—his *mind.*

"Who are you—what do you people wa—"

But as soon as Cherko'd uttered those words, there, now, stood another figure.

We have something for you.

One moment the Spook King stood before him, and the next—

Another.

Short and slight.

And something wasn't right about this new guy. Something wasn't right...it was hard to *see...*

Cherko's vision swam before him.

He was unable to focus.

Vertigo clawed at his balance and he felt immediately nauseated. He reached out to the conference table. Bright flashes of light went off all around him—or inside his head—he couldn't tell which. He suddenly had one holy mother of a headache.

Did his ears just pop?

His hands sweat and he couldn't breathe.

Anxiety.

Dread.

A deep sense of all-pervading, soul-searing, *dread…*

His breathing constricted, quickened.

The figure's words continued to ring out inside his head like a carnival loudspeaker.

We have something for you!

Little surprise!

For YOU!

Come, one, come all!

See the dogfaced boy…

Cherko rubbed his eyes. Was aware of the texture of his hand against the skin and temples of his head. He swore he felt the bones *inside* his hand…the brain *inside* his cranium. Felt the boney fingers through the warmth of a fleshy palm that didn't feel all that much like his, as he brought (or *thought* he did…) it across his brow. Closed his eyes. Felt the eyes in their orbital sockets. So soft, so vulnerable.

Opened them. They stung—or was that just his *mind?*

Lord, what the hell was happening?

As swiftly as he'd been overtaken by everything…it departed.

The vertigo, the bright flashes of light, the popping. Boney fingers. Headache.

Gone.

He looked up. Squinted.

An odd little figure now tried to fill the doorway, but came far from ever doing so. Would never do so. He could now see it clearly—or as clearly as dark and shadows, low lighting, and a reasoning mind would allow…and wondered if what he saw or *thought* he saw was what he really *wanted* to see.…

The figure was short and slight, but the one characteristic that really, *really* stood out, the one thing that really nailed him and made Cherko prickle all over and feel as if his entire body had been snatched by a giant, icy, body-squashing hand, was the really outsized, out-of-proportion head.

And huge, dark eyes.

Chapter Twenty

1

The first thing that went through Cherko's head as he stared into the deep, dark—*huge*—eyes within that large ungainly and pear-shaped noggin was the old gray water reservoir tank up back behind the Lake Clear house.

Was it still there?

The one his little brother, Ritchey, had been stuck in. Stuck in, he seemed to remember, yet from which he had also—*somehow*—managed to...extricate...himself.

Had he remembered that wrong?

He remembered—gosh, he'd forgotten this—but when he'd first found his brother that day, he'd still been inside that tank. All of his some four-or-five-foot-tall height, or whatever it was kids Ritchey's age then were—within an eight-or-ten-foot tall rusty reservoir tank, and with no way out whatsoever.

No ladder inside.

No branches or debris within it to climb upon.

No openings.

Cherko remembered looking down into those little rust holes. Saw him in there...then...then he was *out*.

Simply *out of the tank*.

The being inside the hatchway entered the room, into what little light there was. The being was probably about the same height Ritchey had been back then.

Greetings, Captain, the alien telepathically sent Cherko.

"Is this...is this for *real?*" Cherko asked.

As prepared as Cherko had always thought he'd been for extraterrestrial contact, it was quite a different matter when actually confronted by it. Was a far, far cry from just *reading* about it, watching them on TV.

Thinking about it.

And realizing the gravity of such contact, that as much as you were sizing up the situation, so was this other intelligence a short space of common Earth air before you.

And just how did these beings *think?*

He was out in the middle of the New Mexican desert, aboard a land-bound ship, in the dead of night, exchanging glances with a being from another *world*.

And far from going stark raving mad up, out, and over the railing of this ship, there was a distinctly unambiguously *calming* effect to the being. A contact that should have been historic—at least to him—proclaimed around the world, but which Cherko knew must have occurred with a handful of other humans long before him. He was simply being admitted into the club. Joining the ranks of the Already Contacted.

Was it carbon based?

How did it translate human thought?

Did it eat?

Should he use the "it" or "he/she" in describing them?

There was a definite feminine quality to this being that went far beyond any so-called human definition of the expression, light-years in ways he simply couldn't grasp, but knew was there in much the same way a blind man knows something is hard, or wet, or soft to the touch.

With just those two words of simple greeting Cherko felt a world—*universes*—of depth, or glimpses of insight into the very soul of this (could he really use the term *individual?*) standing before him.

But there was also an intense note of familiarity that niggled Cherko. Surely he'd never met him/her/it before...but something about this being emanated as though, yes, they *had* met, and if he could just give the two of them a minute or two more thought he'd surely *remember....*

I am the one called "Alan" in your reports. My on-paper description is "Alien Life Form Assistance—Need-to-know," but you may refer to me as "She."

"Okay."

He remembered a line from an old seventies song, something about what would you say to a naked lady (in an elevator)?

Well, what do you say to a naked *alien?*

The two continued to trade looks. "She," as the alien had just instructed him, continued to watch Cherko as he moved about the room.

Cherko was in awe, there was no use sugar-coating it, but he couldn't shake the feeling they'd met before.

"The General says you're hostile," Cherko said, now standing before a trophy cabinet beside a picture of the Secretary of the Navy.

Your general—your leadership—only see what they've been trained to see; expect to see.

"Have we met before?"

We have. I am one of those who contacted you through your "Program," as you call it.

"You're part of the program?"

No.

"You only speak with your mind?"

Does it matter whether or not you physically form your communication through use of an appendage when the essence of communication originates within?

"I suppose not," Cherko said. "Are you male or female?"

Aspects of what I am are largely understood as feminine within your culture.

"God, I have so many questions—I know what you said earlier, but why would others consider you hostile?"

She never looked away from Cherko. It was unnerving to be so intently observed by a being that never blinked. Whose eyes were large and dark enough to engulf one's soul.

There are forces out there that would have us all believe so. Believe so as to further their own causes. Because we no longer choose to work with them, because we do not share their goals nor beliefs. Their fear.

We have something to show you.

2

Cherko and She stood outside the ship's bow, just beyond the Jeep's headlights. Cherko's flashlight angled down into the sand. As they stood in silence, Cherko watched a scorpion approach his feet. He was surprised he felt no fear, and nudged it away with the toe of his Corframs. He trailed it with his flashlight as it scurried off into the dark. When he looked up, he found She watching him.

Suddenly the hairs on the back of Cherko's neck stood on end and the ground around them lit up in a soft bluish glow.

He looked up.

Directly above them hovered a craft the size of a small house. It hung motionless above them, as stable as if it were anchored there in an ethereal brick-and-mortar foundation. Cherko felt a slight ionization—or some kind of electrical or gravitational effect—around them.

He didn't know if he actually blinked or not, but as if he'd opened his eyes...he no longer stood on solid ground, but on a smooth, polished, silver-gray deck. The deck of a ship.

A *space* ship.

"How'd you do that?"

In your terms, it's very much like your Star Trek's *'transporter beams.'*

"You watch *Star Trek?*"

Cherko felt what he could only describe as parental amusement emanate from She.

"Holy crap..."

This is our control center.

Cherko looked around.

Like your Earth vehicles, there are many designs to our ships. Many have been reported in your numerous sightings of our kind. We have one pilot who controls the ship from over there, She said, directing Cherko's attention to another extraterrestrial, one who stood quietly and motionless before a control panel. Its arms were to its sides, facing away from them, but when She directed him to it, it turned to acknowledge them.

"Hello," Cherko said.

The pilot returned to face what had to be the front of the ship, because of the large screen before them. *Hello,* it returned.

The pilot, She continued, *for this design, places their hands into the grooves on the control panel, but for others, it could be placement upon an orb, or nothing at all. All control is done with the mind. Any one of us can pilot our vessels, but—like your cars—it involves training. It is a very focused endeavor.*

She's gaze seemed to burn into him.

Was she probing him?

Within the craft, She continued, *and best saved for another time, are holds, or chambers of various purposes. For the present, however, we are limiting our location to the control center.*

"This is just...unbelievable!" Cherko said. "And it's all so *solid.*" He stamped a foot for effect. "It doesn't feel like we're hovering above the ground at all. Can I look around?"

She nodded.

Cherko walked over to the pilot, who casually regarded him with the same huge, dark, expressionless eyes. Its tiny nasal openings and oral slit.

"This is all so unreal," Cherko said to no one in particular. "You all move at, well, 'normal' speed, not slow motion, as portrayed in our movies. When we interact, there is so much more...an incredibly rich—*psychic*—density to our communications," he said, looking back to She.

Many are frightened by our contact and do not experience what you describe. There is much you will learn and experience.

But now...to borrow one of your expressions...a road trip.

3

"It doesn't even feel like we're moving," Cherko said, standing before a screen that showed a night sky. The pilot stared at it, but Cherko could tell it was more like he was staring beyond it. *Through* it. Becoming one with the act of piloting. He figured he didn't have the descriptor for whatever it was this ET was actually doing.

"Where are we going?" Cherko asked.

We are visiting a family in northern Canada, She said.

"No kidding."

Cherko looked between her and the screen.

"How long will it take us to get there?"

We've already arrived.

"There's absolutely *no* sensation of speed! No feeling of accelerating...slowing down..."

We generate our own gravity. Like being on Earth as it speeds through space—you don't feel it.

"That's all? Independent gravity?"

She nodded.

Of course there is more to it.

During our excursion, I must ask you to not touch nor communicate with anyone in the house unless we bid you to do so. Merely observe. We are looking in on a child with certain organic misalignments, and his mother.

Cherko nodded.

The next thing Cherko knew they were in a living room. It was dark, and he could hear the ventilation system running. Doses of heat were pumped into the room. They really had to be north if the heat was on in August.

She and two other aliens were with him. The aliens turned without a word and Cherko followed. They moved swiftly, fluidly. It was actually kinda creepy. They flew through the dark house unerringly and with surprising speed, which was not as easy for him; for one thing his night vision hadn't yet kicked in. They left the living room for a hallway, then headed up a flight of stairs. Cherko saw one of the aliens carrying something, but he couldn't get a good look at it. It looked like a rod or baton of some kind. He wanted to ask what the thing was but was overcome by a feeling to not ask questions.

Quickly making their way down the short hallway past a nightlight, a cat poked its head out into the hallway and hissed, arching its back, hair bristling. The cat nearly jumped out of its skin getting out of the way, but none of the aliens appeared concerned. Without pause, they entered the bedroom at the end of the hallway.

When Cherko entered the room, the aliens were already grouped around the bed. Before them, and on his side, slept a small child of perhaps four. Cherko had never been any good at figuring out kids'—or women's, for that matter—ages. One of the aliens had already held out the device Cherko couldn't identify, over the child. The child rolled over onto his stomach and Cherko distinctly felt as if that had been made to happen by his guides. The one with the rod-like device then touched the object to the small of the child's back and repeatedly ran it up and down both sides of his spine.

What are you doing? Cherko mentally asked.

We're correcting his condition.

Why?

He is vital to one of your future probabilities. This act itself, what we are doing...is also required.

What do you mean?

She turned to him. *All in good time.*

You do this a lot? Help us out?

We have our methods.

When the one with the rod was done, the group departed the room as they'd entered—quickly and efficiently.

Cherko followed as they again made their way through the home, and unerringly made their way into another bedroom. But here they found what Cherko knew was the mother. She sat bolt upright in bed, blankets bunched about her waist, her hands firmly planted to either side of her into the blankets.

She stared at them.

"No...no, no, *no*...this isn't happening, this isn't *happ*—"

She reached out to the young mother.

Everything is all right. We are here to help. You are safe.

"What is *happening*," the woman continued to wail, eyes wide.

Cherko could feel the fear in her...her concern for her child. She allowed Cherko to come to the woman, and he came out of the shadows and showed himself.

The woman's eyes opened wider. "*Who* are *you?*" she asked. Her voice was thick with terror. "*What do you want?*"

Cherko could see the woman trembling. He looked to his guides, then back to the woman. He now felt more confusion than fear from her.

Continue, She directed.

"I am...a friend," Cherko said. "We're here to help. We've helped your son."

"My son! *What have you done to him!* Where is he!"

The woman tried to get out of bed, but Cherko felt She direct...*something*...toward her and she remained where she was.

"Why are you here?" the woman appealed, now openly crying. "Why *us?* You have no right! *No right!*"

But we do, She said.

Cherko looked to She.

Your child is to live and grow. We've corrected multiple organic misalignments. He will now grow unaffected and will be a strong, healthy son. He will live a long, useful life. You will both be happy.

Cherko watched as the woman suddenly—as if on cue—stopped crying and her face went blank. She stared straight ahead—through them.

You will go back to sleep now, She continued. *Nothing happened here tonight. You will both awake in the morning with no memory of us, this conversation, our actions, nor your son's disorder. You will feel happy and safe. Your lives...safe.*

The group turned as one and departed the woman's bedroom.

* * *

"What happened back there?" Cherko asked She, back on the ship.

We help those in need of our actions.

"Why don't you help everyone who needs such help?"

We have our methods, Captain.

"Where to now?"

We think you will like this.

Cherko watched as the screen changed to another curious image: he appeared to be looking down from on high to what looked like a cloudy *Replogle* display globe. From some off-center angle at the top. He could clearly see fully half of the globe illuminated, the other side dark. Though there were clouds covering large sections of the land masses, and he was at an angle opposite to those continents in the light, he could clearly make out the top of the Russian peninsula stretching toward Alaska. North America was heading into this light.

He was frigging looking at the entire Earth.

From space.

We are sorry we cannot present you with astronaut wings, She sent.

All Cherko could do was stare in amazement.

He was goddamned in space!

Orbiting Earth—well, perhaps not exactly *orbiting,* but certainly hovering. There, below him…was *everything.* For this moment in time and space, he was unique. Outside of the familiar. Outside of bills and mortgages and alarm clocks. Outside of the surly bonds of Earth. Just a sweep of a minute-hand ago they'd been in a desert-bound ship's bow in the American Southwest; another short sweep, and he'd been in the bedroom of a child and its mother in the distant northlands of Canada. Another sweep—

In orbit.

"Won't we be spotted? By radar, surveillance satel—"

No, She said.

"Then what of—"

Cherko felt more translated amusement from She.

You only see what we allow you to see.

"You *mess* with us?"

We prefer to think of it as limiting our exposure.

Cherko looked back to the screen.

But, it's not just us you see so much of.

Cherko looked to She, then back to the screen.

"This is so unreal. It's like…all our bickering, fighting…makes absolutely no sense from up here."

Cherko felt an intense wave of compassion overtake him. Deep, profound, soul-wrapping kindness, concern, and *sympathy.* He looked up and into the large, dark eyes of She and found that this enormous sensation again originated from her.

There was also another feeling Cherko identified, also from She...a brilliant and pure sense of danger.

But as soon as he'd felt that, it was gone. Washed away by the overriding sense of love and caring, as if from—

A mother.

She looked back to the screen.

We monitor your world's condition, She said. *We cannot interfere...it is our "Prime Directive," again, to borrow a familiar phrase from your television programs—*

"It's like you and Gene Roddenberry had something going on," Cherko said, grinning.

We monitor the molecular structure of your atmosphere, your tectonics, your hydraulics, to levels you cannot yet conceptualize. Though there are some in your community already aware of this, it will largely be ignored until it is too late...in your terms, She continued, looking from the screen to Cherko. She held his gaze for a moment, then looked back to the screen, which now displayed the Arctic. It was a little unnerving being stared at by an emotionless extraterrestrial face that was now—and would forever be—more than just some quaint Hallowe'en mask. It was a face so much more full of texture, character, and personality than ever displayed in any sci-fi movie image or book jacket.

Cherko was about to ask what she was talking about, but held his tongue. He'd again felt that he was to hold his questions, because he was to soon be shown what she'd meant.

The Earth image on the screen grew slightly larger in size, and Cherko wasn't sure if that meant they'd come closer or the image was magnified, but he figured it was probably a little of both. Then a second image was superimposed over this one. One that appeared to be an overlay of pixels—billions and *trillions* of them, he surmised—superimposed over the Arctic image. He also saw values associated with each and every pixel. It was unimaginably mind-boggling. They flowed in and out of each other, in the most brilliant, technologically advanced, and spectacular of fashions. As many as there were, as small as they were, he felt he could easily zoom in on each and every one.

Given the current state of your world, and all things considered, your world is heading toward—is already within, actually—a cyclical period of tremendous global climate change. It is not inevitable, but will shortly become so.

"Climate change?"

Global warming.

"What is that, exactly? I've heard of it. Melting ice caps, tropical-like-weather-everywhere kind of thing?"

Without the enthusiastic anticipation you are associating with the image, yes. Though the Earth itself can withstand and rebound from this period within its temporal timeline,

Humanity, as a whole, will be greatly affected. It is not something to be taken lightly in the sense you give it.

"Sorry."

But it is part of your heritage as a race. Not that it should be accepted and ignored; but as a forum of growth and responsibility, a medium *for change. There are forces at work...that are ignoring this for their own self-serving interests, obfuscating its reality, which will bring about your world's collapse and destruction if allowed to continue at present—and forecast—rates.*

"It's not inevitable?"

My dear Captain, nothing is inevitable nor irreparable.

Then that's good, Cherko thought.

No information is good stored and not implemented.

But there was something more. Something *She* wasn't telling him.

Cherko looked back to the screen. Studied it.

So, Humanity was on the fast-track to obliteration from the geological record and extraterrestrials were helping correct damaged children. It all seemed cosmologically comical. Futile. But nothing in nature happens without need, Cherko remembered reading somewhere. We may not know what or why, but everything happens for a reason.

So what was the damned point?

We're all gonna die, but aliens were saving children?

That a captain from the U.S. Air Force was flying around in UFOs and trading environmental philosophies with extraterrestrials?

Or that life, as Humans understood it, was forever changing—and not in a good way?

Chapter Twenty-One

1

There is one more thing we have left to do before we return you, She told Cherko as they descended back toward Earth. *And all of what we have done and shown you must remain undisclosed to your General.*

"Why can't I tell him?"

For all he has seemingly done for you, he is not to be trusted. He, like his leadership, feels we mean humanity harm.

"But we could show him—"

Attempts have already been made, but as much as the General claims he does not fear us—he does—and cannot see past that fear. We greatly regret this.

"So, what am I supposed to do?"

We will make additional information known to you. Information you cannot share with your General. But for now—we have arrived at our final destination.

Cherko was speechless when he saw where they hovered on the control-room screen.

Garden of the Gods.

They were hovering just inside the center garden area to the Garden of the Gods park, back in Colorado Springs, the rocks of the Kissing Camels to their east.

"Why are we here?"

She turned away from Cherko and looked to the screen.

There was a car parked alongside the main road into the park. It's lights were off. Cherko recognized that car.

Erica's.

"You've—*why?*"

Did you not want to see her?

"Yes, but I—"

Go to her. We will return. Will not observe you. We will return when it is time—but you only have until the sun rises.

"I don't know what to say—"

You need say nothing. Go to her.

* * *

Cherko stood beneath the ship, looking up to it.

Now, this would make a really neat picture, he thought as the ship quickly and soundlessly ascended back into the night sky. A UFO hovering within the Garden of the Gods, behind Kissing Camels. Wish Rich Buzzelli had managed to snap off one of *those.*

Cherko looked down the road.

He was back in Colorado Springs. He could hardly believe it. Hardly believe half of all he'd seen and where he'd been tonight.

He looked back into the still-night sky.

Good, Lord, he'd actually been out in orbit around the *Earth!* In *space!*

Who'd ever believe him?

Yet, here he was, ready to see a girl he'd fallen head-over-heels in love with and with whom he hadn't seen for over a year; standing on the main drag through Garden of the Gods, a park he used to run and hike and bike through when he lived here, while an hour or so ago (was that right?) he'd left a jeep parked (and with its lights on, he just remembered!) at the White Sands Missile Range, in southern New Mexico.

In front of a land-bound ship.

Yeah, it was all crazy, but he was living it, baby.

Surrounded by chirping crickets echoing off the dark, pock-marked red rock walls, Cherko walked toward the parked car.

Erica Taylor sat dumbfounded in her vehicle.

What was she doing out here in the middle of the night? What had *possessed* her?

She didn't remember getting into the car—let alone getting dressed—and driving all the way across town to find herself sitting in an empty *park?*

Who knew who was out there in the dark, stalking her?

Yet, instead of starting up her car and leaving…she just sat there.

It wasn't like someone or something was holding her hostage, against her will; she could have started the car and left if she so chose to.…

She just…*didn't.*

Erica rolled down the window an inch or so.

And it was such a lovely night. The sound of chirping crickets soothing. The air warm and quite pleasant. Her doors locked.

No, there was nothing to fear.

She was safe.

She just stared ahead, out her windshield.

All was good with the world.

Safe.

* * *

She didn't know if she first heard her name mentally, inside her head, or if someone had actually called it out. Sometimes—she only *privately* admitted to herself, because this would surely sound insane, but she knew beyond a shadow of a doubt that she *was* sane—but sometimes she actually heard her name called out to her when no one was around. Yes, she was usually meditating or in that in-between sleepy state when that happened, but she *knew* she'd heard her name called out, and it hadn't been her, because, well, she did. *Heard* it.

Erica.

Just like that. Like she heard it now.

Had she dozed off?

Probably. It was after—

She turned to her driver-side window.

A man stood before her.

Amazingly, a part of her noted, she was unafraid.

"*Erica?*"

Erica blinked. Shook her head only slightly, and blinked again.

"*Jimmy?* Jimmy, is that *you?*"

Jimmy backed away from the car. Smiled.

"It's really me."

Erica undid her seatbelt, unlocked the car door, and jumped out of the car, lunging for him. She threw her arms around him and hugged him fiercely. Buried her face into his chest.

"*What are you doing here?* Where—"

Had she gone crazy?

What was she doing throwing herself at an ex-boyfriend who'd up and dumped her without so much as a good-bye?

Erica pushed away from Cherko, who looked to her with a mixture of longing and confusion.

"Where have you been? Why are you here?"

"I—"

"You *left* me, is what you did!" Erica blurted out, and tears burst out from her, surprising her most of all. "*You goddammed left me and never told me why!*"

Erica pounded her upper thighs with tightly clenched fists.

"Erica," Cherko said, trying to come in closer, but Erica thrust out a hand keeping him at arm's length.

"You *bastard!*"

"Please," Jimmy said, in a soft, calm tone, "hear me out—*please?*"

"Why should I? I loved you and you *left* me!"

"I know I can't possibly say anything that could ever make that right. I wish I could, believe me, I desperately want to, but I can't. It was my job. I was pulled away—I had no say—"

"*Liar!*" Erica shouted in a guttural voice just short of Linda Blair's *Exorcist* tones. Sobbing, she turned away; crossed her arms.

"Erica—I love you. I still do. But I have...I have no control over my life."

Erica turned back around.

"*Everyone has control.*"

"*I* don't."

"How. How do you not?"

"I can't tell you. I wish I could, but—"

"Is there someone else? Tell me—is there another woman?"

The question, Erica saw, actually seemed to catch Cherko off-guard.

"No...of course not. It's always and only been *you*. But those I work for—"

"You work for the government—they can't just take you away without a reason—keep you from those you love."

"Yes, they can."

"No, they *can't!*"

Cherko again tried to edge in closer, and this time Erica allowed him. Allowed him to cup his warm hands to either side of her swollen and wet face, and bring his up to hers. He had a weird smell to him, she noticed, not unseemly, but odd—faintly *electrical?*—but, then again, maybe not.

"Right now I don't seem to have any control over my life. I'm trying—but," he said, shaking his head, "it's just not working.

"I wrote, you know. Every week."

Erica searched his face.

"You did not."

"I *did*. They never let them through."

"Who 'they'—the government—*the Air Force?*"

Cherko shrugged. "Whoever controls that sort of thing, I don't know. But I wrote you every week. I still do."

Erica began to cry anew. "I never got them!"

This time she completely broke down and Cherko took her up into his arms. She'd so missed those arms, so strong, so protective, so *him*.

"How can they do this! It's not right! It's *not!*"

"I know," Cherko said, calming her. "I know...."

Erica and Jimmy sat back in the shadows in the center garden area, hidden among the Rocky Mountain juniper and young Ponderosa pine. They sat on a blanket Erica never remembered throwing into her car on the way over here, Jimmy cradled her from behind.

"So...how did you get here?"

"I...flew in. For a brief stay."

"You can't tell me anything about your job?"

"I'm sorry, I wish I could but I can't. I can tell you that I love you, though." Jimmy lowered his lips to her upturned face and gently kissed her.

"I don't know what to say—how to deal with this."

Jimmy remained silent.

"I'll move—I'll move to where you live—I can get any job, continue my degree at another college."

"You'd do that?"

Erica turned around to face him.

"Of course I would. Wouldn't you?"

Cherko nodded, wiping at a tear running out the corner of an eye. "I'd really love that."

For the first time in what felt like a long, long time, Jimmy smiled, and it felt *good*.

"I'll start looking into that as soon as I get home." She turned back around to Cherko. "*God, how I've missed you!*" They again kissed.

"How long are you staying?"

Cherko glanced toward the east.

"I have to leave at sunrise."

"No!"

"I can't help it, Erica." He looked up into the night. "I'm on another's schedule."

"Can't you change it?"

Cherko shook his head, uttering a soft chuckle. "I'm sorry—but I don't have to go just yet," he said, massaging Erica's shoulders. Then he wrapped his arms around her and hugged her fiercely. Erica closed her eyes and sighed deeply.

"*Make love with me*," she whispered without opening her eyes. Cherko kissed her around the base of her soft, tender, neck and ears....

2

Cherko watched Erica as she drove off into the rising sun, which just barely began to kick its morning glow up and over the horizon that wasn't visible from this side of the mesa blocking its view. Cherko looked up to see the ship hovering above.

Right on time.

They were nothing if not punctual.

Again, what a neat shot this would make for another Buzzelli photograph, the early morning rays just beginning to hit the hull of the UFO above him. Hovering in the central area of Garden of the Gods.

He promised Erica he'd be back…but somehow he didn't think he'd ever be able to keep that promise.

Before he'd even completed that thought, he was back aboard the ship, and in the sweep of yet another segment of the second hand, would once again be back in New Mexico.…

The return to his Dulce office had been anything but exciting. After all he'd seen, all he'd experienced, Cherko doubted whether what he was doing was really a help to Humanity at all—or some hidden Hammond agenda.

Maybe it was all simply in service to Hammond himself.

How much of this had Hammond been lying about?

And to what end? The "good fight" against some extraterrestrial domination? Why would he feel that was the truth? Such a battle would be a losing one, were any of it true. He saw their capabilities. There was no way we had anything remotely close to what they had. No way could we ever consider opposing them, let alone consider anything called "winning." It would be like ants fighting against Black Flag—and we didn't even have the numbers to attempt *that*.

No, what it looked like to him was that Hammond was part of some misguided government-within-a-government scheme that was trying to protect humanity from some nonexistent threat for some shady reason.

Why?

For bigger bucks?

More war toy development?

How and why had things gotten so terribly screwed up?

Cherko tossed his satchel and flight cap down onto his desk. He then went to one of his safes and opened it. Pulling out a couple folders, something caught his eye. The tip of a manila envelope was shoved under all the hanging folders. Placing the folders he'd pulled out on his desk, he returned to the safe's drawer, and pulled out handfuls of the remaining folders, pushing the others farther back into the drawer.

There it was.

A sturdy nine-by-twelve envelope.

Cherko pulled it out. It was worn and looked like it had literally been around the world. He turned it over as he returned to his desk.

It was sealed, the metal clasp also engaged through its little paper hole. Tape was sealed over the edge of the flap, with what looked like ball-point pen hashmarks across the tape and running onto the envelope on both sides of the tape.

Cherko sat and placed the envelope on his desk.

He pulled out his pocketknife, opened a blade, and sliced open the package. The enclosure was maybe fifty pages or less of, no, not exactly a report...but what looked like an informal write-up of some kind, perhaps an unofficial memo or Whitepaper?—and there were areas in the document where sections were literally cut out of the paper.

Cut *out*.

Rectangular *holes* that looked as if they'd been cut out with an *X-ACTO* knife. He could see the over-cut slices into the paper around the holes.

What he found turned his world upside down.

Cherko found that in 1932 Bucharest, Henri Marie Coandă, a Romanian aeronautical engineer and inventor, discovered something so revolutionary that it forever changed the face of black-world aeronautical development. He found that if he designed a circular air ship, one that used turbine blades powered by jet engines sucking the air down around and into the airfoil, it created an interesting effect: the airflow around the saucer-shaped airfoil *hugged* the saucer shape through application of surface tension, or Van der Walls forces. The air traveled under the vehicle and—in short—caused by the evacuating effect of the air flow itself, lowered the air pressure above and raised the pressure below, thereby *pushing* the craft up.

He coined the term the *Coandă Effect*, and it became the principle for human-developed flying saucers.

Not UFOs—but *HEUFOs*.

Human-engineered UFOs.

Cherko reread the section.

They had to be kidding.

We'd *developed this stuff on our own?*

Back in *1932?*

The document claimed that the Germans had eventually gotten hold of this engineering principle and had begun their own highly classified development during World War II; development that would have altered the outcome of the war had it not ended so abruptly for the Axis power.

An attack on New York City in bomb-wielding HEUFOs?

Cherko was flabbergasted at the names associated with this and other human flying saucer development.

Himmler, von Braun, Oberth, Dornberger. Schauberger.

Development at Nazi R&D facilities with names like Peenemuende, Kahla, and Skoda. *Underground bases in the Antarctic?* Also associated with the deep black programs were a host of other, lesser-known names: Radu Manicatide, Luigi Romersa, and Andreas Epp.

And these aerospace-disk crafts had attained speeds of well over a thousand miles an hour, with additional claims of sustained and repeatable altitude climbs of up to *forty-thousand feet.*

Successful flights.

Luftwaffe projects called *Feuerball* that were experimental devices designed to mess with Allied radar and electromagnetics, and *Kugelblitz* that were round, symmetrical aircraft.

All during the thirties and forties?

Yeah, "Foo-fighters."

And it just kept getting weirder.

After the war, the U.S. and Russia made a mad-dash to scoop up as much of this technology and the minds behind it as possible. Both scored intellectual coups with brilliant German scientists coming over to each side to continue not only their saucer projects, but to also further both side's space programs.

And to where had these new brains been imported in the U.S.?

The Northwest and Southwest.

And where, Cherko mused, had the initial sightings of so-called UFOs originated?

The states of Washington and New Mexico.

Coincidence?

So what had people *really* been observing?

According to this document...*HEUFOs.*

And the government needed to get control of the situation right quick. Too many people were seeing too many things they ought not to be seeing. Psychological warfare specialists had been called in, and they had put into effect an incredibly effective dual-pronged, self-perpetuating, approach:

1) Get senior military officials to deny everything.

2) Infiltrate the public mindset with extraterrestrial UFOs.

In 1952 Major General John Sanford and retired Major Donald Keyhoe were placed head-to-head. One denied, the other lavished.

The self-perpetuating propaganda machine had been forever set into motion. The public would get so confused it would never be able to figure what part of the dog wagged what.

Cherko flew through the remainder of the document.

It was unbelievable. The government had been, since the 1940s, developing flying saucer technology spirited from the killing fields of World War II Germany, and had been continuing this very same development unabated to the present day. There was simply no telling where all that technology was today. It also wasn't much of a reach to fit Area-51 into the puzzle.

And that went for psychological advancements, as well.

The Germans had performed plenty of experimentation on the human mind, and in many not-so-pleasant ways, not to mention the CIA's own domestic efforts. Psychological warfare had also risen to its own astonishing prominence.

And there was even an author mentioned in these pages that Cherko had never heard of. Whitley Strieber. The document said that at the time of this document's creation, he was pushing a manuscript about his own *alien abduction* experiences. There was also mention of another civilian, Stanton Friedman, who was poking his nose around into the whole Roswell affair.

Civilians were being tracked by our government?

Good God, things were starting to make sense.

Kenneth Arnold had seen saucers *undulating* in the skies over Washington, like skipping across water. That's exactly what he'd said. *Skipping.*

What UFO—*real* not a HEUFO—would "skip" through any atmosphere?

Surely such technology would be far and away more advanced to handle air currents and other terrestrial aerodynamic forces much more gracefully. If what She had told him was correct that they generated their own gravity, it seemed any aerodynamic forces would become entirely moot.

And Hammond *had* told him that a wing-shaped craft had been found in Roswell.

Wing shaped.

Come on, what interplanetary, interstellar, UFO *needed an aerodynamic design?*

The wing form was designed to cut through *air.* Make use of it. UFOs, those piloted by actual aliens—the ones Cherko had been with—had no need for such terrestrial concerns. *They flew through space,* for crying out loud. Any such wing design meant absolutely *nothing.*

No, what all this sounded like was what seemed to be standard government concealment for legitimate national security projects.

HEUFO R&D.

And exactly in a manner in keeping for the protection of such deep secrets as were being developed. The public simply didn't have a need-to-know for everything they were curious about.

That Black Onion again.

He could get behind that.

The author of this document, who's name had been summarily redacted by *X-ACTO,* went on to say that the more far-fetched something was the less likely the population would believe it.

No kidding.

Also throw in intentional muddying of the waters with He-said/She-said (pardon the pun) set-ups with the likes of Sanfords and Keyhoes and you have the perfect self-perpetuating propaganda machine. Self perpetuating and essentially free from any and all Black budget funding.

It was pure genius.

But it was also highly disappointing. What this implied was that Roswell had nothing to do with aliens or extraterrestrial craft, but human-engineered flying saucer development.

If the capability he'd just read about existed in 1932, how far of a leap would it be to say that by 1947—and then again in contemporary time—with U.S. government funding and critical scientific focus that there weren't human-engineered UFOs flying around the unsuspecting skies of the U.S.?

But that still didn't explain his trip with She—and visiting Erica. He'd actually *been* there. To both places. To Canada—and had seen the Earth from twenty-four-thousand-or-more miles out.

Or had he?

If psychological operations had been around for at least as long, how did he know he'd hadn't been drugged or whatever else it was "they" did to people?

He'd read the Project *Blue Book* documents—the real ones—read how people had been abducted and subjected to sometimes horrendous tests involving needles and all manner of degrading experimentation.

Why would aliens—true extraterrestrials—have need of such mechanizations?

It just didn't add up!

No, something else was at work here, something extremely sinister. Hammond was only partially correct, and Cherko didn't know if Hammond was in on it or was merely a voice-activated relay, a puppet for other factions far more powerful. There *was* a war going on, but Cherko still didn't believe it was with extraterrestrials. It was with whatever government-within-a-government was running the whole "UFO" show.

Cherko had always wondered how certain people seemed to escape retribution for "coming out" about anything UFO. After having been a part of some black project (or so they *claimed*). In all the books he'd read, there was always someone who broke their so-called security vows, and they weren't taken out *nor* thrown in jail.

Well, except for one guy he'd read about in all his study. One Captain Edward Ruppelt, U.S. Air Force. He had for several years actually managed the Air Force's project Blue Book, but after having gotten out of the military had severely taken the government to task over their perpetual obfuscation and denial. He seemed to have been a legitimate thorn in their side, and had made many public and not-so-public attacks. Even had a TV show. But on May 6, 1958, in a completely unheralded statement to the National Investigations Committee on Aerial Phenomena, *had summarily* (and curtly, Cherko noted) *recanted his entire stance on UFOs and extraterrestrials.*

Who would do such a thing after a lifetime of effort?

It was highly suspected (though not noted in the reports he'd read) that he'd been "turned," since he'd worked for a government contractor following his time in service.

And to further drive the stake into his heart, he had, at the ripe-old age of thirty-seven, died of a heart attack—his second.

A heart attack.

The first had been three years earlier. A man who had no (okay, *apparent*) history of heart issues and wasn't obese.

But, the report he'd read also went on to say that people didn't just die of heart attacks from obesity and smoking. Stress also played a major role in heart attacks. Lots of stress. It created harmful chemicals that attacked and weakened the heart.

Just as covertly administered compounds also did.

Coincidence?

The first heart attack had been Ruppelt's warning.

It was all speculation. Unless you had been an actual part of the cover-up, an actual black project participant (and in which case if you were, then you truly *were* in a load of trouble), you had no actual standing upon which to base your claims. It was all conjecture. All further fueled the propaganda disinformation machine.

And for that, you were left alone.

The Black Onion.

It all works for the cause. Claims of aliens and claims of denial. The total, utter, confusion of facts. Fact *manipulation*.

Had an extraterrestrial spaceship really crashed in Roswell?

Who knew any longer.

But Hammond *had* mentioned that there had been a wing-shaped craft that had crashed. And that alien bodies had been found. And that there had been crashes at that Foster Ranch, with that debris field, and one farther west in San Agustin.

To apply the logic of what he'd just read, it appeared to Cherko that the debris field had been for real and the flying wing-and-aliens scenario disinformation. To Cherko it would appear that the wing-shaped crash was more than likely a human-engineered UFO, with alien bodies thrown in for fact manipulation. Aliens and their vessels didn't need wings nor vanes, nor any other aerodynamic surfaces. But he also thought that there really might have been alien bodies found at *another* location—knowledge he, Cherko, didn't have, even from all his research. He doubted even alien bodies could have withstood the total annihilation that that debris field strewn across the Foster Ranch had implied.

Cherko backed away from his desk and went out before it. Stood looking to his claustrophobic little office full of papers and safes and binders. Turned back around to his desk. Looked to the document full of rectangular holes cut into it.

Good Lord, what the hell was he supposed to believe?

Had his ride-along with She been real? *Or had all he experienced been psychologically engineered?*

Had his *Program* training all been a massive farce? A script written and played out by some science fiction writer, some new form of electronic equipment beaming data into his head like a maser?

Had he really met with Erica? Had they really made love in Garden of the Gods?

Or had he been drugged, mind-fucked, or whatever else it was psy-ops operatives did nowadays?

Since 1932, who knew where the U.S.—or other governments—were with technology now? Heck, he'd even read top-secret intel about placing a military base *on the moon!* Project Horizon. That could certainly put all this flying saucer technology to good and sustained use. How else would it be so employed?

Certainly not in delivering mundane bombs and bullets.

Let the other "secret" projects deal with that. Projects that were more than likely cover projects for stuff just like *these* HEUFO programs. The more attention elsewhere focused, the better for any classified program. It's all about living in the shadows. And, if for no other reason, just because they *could.*

For the first time since his entry into the Air Force, Jimmy Cherko was truly and completely scared.

He couldn't trust anyone, least of all Hammond.

He had to get out.

3

Erica Taylor returned to her apartment with a renewed sense of hope. Last night had been one of the strangest she'd ever experienced, but she had been reunited with a guy she'd thought to have lost forever. A guy she had fallen in love with at very first sight.

But his story was so hard to believe!

The government had sent him away?

Had kept him *away* from her?

It was almost too much.

Yet there he'd been, tonight, outside her car in the dead of night in Garden of the Gods, while she had no clue why or how she'd gotten there herself.

Bringing her arms in to her chest, she closed her eyes and hugged herself.

And they'd made love beneath the stars.

The smell of his skin, the touch of his lips....

She'd never truly understood the extent to which she'd missed him until he'd come back.

But, his entire life was now one big secret. And, apparently, if she was to believe all he'd told her, he seemed to have little control over it.

Was that something she wanted?

If it meant having Jimmy back—*yes*.

She never wanted to go through that ever again. To be without him. Never wanted to have her heart ripped out ever again. She would endure anything to be with him. He could have the most top secret job anyone ever had, but as long as they were together it would never matter and she would never ask.

So she threw together a strong brew of coffee, stripped, and was making her way into the shower, when a loud rapping at her door startled her.

Throwing on a robe, Erica cautiously came to the door. She visually confirmed that her door, was, indeed, *still* locked, but gave the deadbolt a quick twist anyway. Outside stood an old woman and a child.

"Yes?" Erica asked, warily, peering through the peephole.

"I'm sorry to bother you ma'am," the old lady said, in her creaky, old lady voice, "but could you please let us in? I found this child roaming the parking lot. She's lost. Tired. And I need to call the authorities."

Erica opened the door.

Before her stood the lady and child. The child held a stick in one hand. They both looked to her, and Erica clenched the collars of her robe, holding it tight against her chest.

"Why yes, of course you may," she said, smiling. She squatted down to the child's level, and was about to say something cute, when she suddenly grew extremely uncomfortable and came back to her feet, the smile gone from her face.

She was extremely tired.

Was that coffee ready yet? It smelled like House Blend. Had that been what she'd bought?

"I'm sorry," she said, a hand momentarily to her forehead, "I've had a really long night, didn't get much sleep. Come in. The phone's right over here." She turned and led them to the phone.

They entered without a word.

The lady slowly closed the door behind them.

Erica turned to address them at the phone. She still clenched her robe to her.

Felt incredibly drowsy.

"You look tired," the child said.

"Very tired," the old woman repeated.

"I'm so sorry, it's like it all just hit me."

Erica leaned against the wall. It was so *hard* keeping her eyes open…

"You should go to bed," the lady said.

"To bed," echoed the child.

Erica yawned.

"I should. Yes."

"We'll tuck you in," the child said.

"Okay."

Erica yawned and turned to enter her bedroom.

It was so inviting here, she thought, and began undoing her robe. She didn't remember leaving that light on, she thought to herself as she entered the room. Nor turning down her bed.

"It's very cozy in here," the old lady said. She and the child entered the bedroom behind her.

Erica removed her robe and slid into bed.

The old lady and the child came up along bedside. Stood there, looking to Erica. Erica looked back to them, barely able to keep her eyes open.

"I'm...I'm so sorry," she apologized, "I don't know what's come over me...."

"It's okay," the child said, "we'll let ourselves out."

The lady reached out and soothed Erica's face, closing her eyes. The child extended the rod she had been carrying to Erica's forehead. Gently touched her with it.

She would be all right. Not that it would ever matter, but she would bring her child to term and they would have a wonderful life together.

But she would have no memory of last night, no memory of Jimmy Cherko, and no memory of now, because—to her—none of this had ever happened.

The last thing Erica did remember as she drifted off to sleep, was how thoughtful and kind those two had been in helping her to bed, and that she hoped the child found her parents soon. It was never a good feeling when one was lost.

And, she also thought, what deep, dark, compassionate eyes they had...eyes you could lose your *soul* in....

Chapter Twenty-Two

1

Dulce, New Mexico
14 October 1987
0025 Hours Mountain Time

"Are we again going it alone?" Cherko asked She as their craft immediately departed Earth for altitude. He wore an aircrew member's olive drab flight suit.

Correct.

Cherko nodded.

It had been over two months since their last ride and he'd been antsy. Extremely uncomfortable at work and around Hammond. It was wearing on him having to act like he'd never found that hidden memo. Never read its pages.

And he'd read and reread it. Until it was removed from the safe.

He wanted to get as far away from this job as possible, and wasn't sure how he was going to broach the topic with She and whether or not she could even help...but was sure that she'd already picked up on it, given her telepathic ability. She would bring it up when the time was right, if it needed to be brought up at all.

For now, he just had to sit tight and enjoy the ride, as his dad always used to say.

She looked to Cherko and he looked away, embarrassed.

Okay, Cherko mentally responded back, *I know you can read my mind, but—*

You are now going to experience something extraordinary.

Cherko stood in a section of the ship he'd not been in before. It was a small chamber, low lit. There was a narrow table in the center, maybe six or seven feet in length, and along each wall were what looked like drawers without handles. She and another extraterrestrial attendant stood behind

Cherko as he looked to these drawers and the table. Each drawer was about four to five feet in length. There were twelve of them. Cherko had an anxious feeling about them.

Flashbacks…images of lying on just such a table.

Cherko approached the slab. Touched it. Saw the translucent nature of the table's material. It was like

(*laying on the table…*)

he could look *into* it, the material of the table itself, *through* it…

Cherko turned to She.

I've been here before, haven't I?

You have.

Cherko looked back to the table. It was a silver-gray, and also seemed to have what looked like blue flecking embedded deep within it.

Blue flecks that vibrated? Glowed ever so faintly?

And there was an extreme calmness that radiated from the table. He ran his hand along its edges. As he ran his hand along the table's edge, he looked to the set of drawers to his right. He slowly made his way along the table's edge toward the drawers. When he got to the end of the table, he dropped his hand and continued on to the wall. Stopped inches before it. There were three drawers stacked upon each other, per each wall.

Cherko pushed the top one in. It responded by opening with a near soundless *whoosh*.

Empty.

Though empty, there was a strange material that lined the inside. Cherko reached in and touched it. It yielded to his touch, indenting. "Cool," Cherko said, as he cast a glance back to She and the other extraterrestrial. "It feels weird. Extremely soft…almost like there's nothing there."

Cherko closed the drawer then touched the one beneath it. It, too, sprang open and was also empty. Also lined with that same, soft, strangely yielding material. He splayed open his hand and pushed down into it; held it down. The material formed around his hand. There still wasn't much of a feeling to it and *that* felt weird. Wiggling his hand around in it, there was a softness that was hard to describe, faintly reminiscent of an extremely light gel. He removed his hand and closed that drawer. No residue remained on his hand.

"What is this stuff?"

She just observed and said nothing.

Cherko went across the room to the opposite side of the narrow table. He dropped to a crouching position and opened another drawer. It *whooshed* open.

Cherko jumped back to his feet.

"You've *got* to be kidding."

She and the attendant came up to Cherko.

All is not as it seems. Even your General Hammond does not know this.

Cherko stared into the drawer.

She stared back up at him from inside the drawer.

Or the body of an extraterrestrial that *looked* like She and the other aliens. It's small slit-like mouth was slightly open and its body looked smaller than its almost five-foot stature. It also felt vacant...*empty.*

"Is it—"

It is not dead. But it is, in your terms...empty. Unoccupied.

"Empty?"

All is not as it seems, Captain. Just as you are more than your body...your mind, your spirit...we are also more than what you understand "body" to be. We use these to interact within your world...your corporeal existence. We do not use these from where we come, but to where we go. To our existence, these are the apparel we wear, much like your clothes—but more like your flesh. They resonate with life.

You put these on? Cherko thought.

We do. The translation of our intrinsic structure does not...correspond...to corporeal existence...but our mental and spiritual capacity can interrelate.

So, you're saying that to visit our world you have to wear these?

Yes. To physically interact with you.

Fascinating. What is it made of—it's really alive?

It is, but in a way that far surpasses your current understanding of the concept. All matter is *alive, but your current concepts of the term are misleading and deficient. It is a vastly superior psychological-biological-technological creation. Come.*

She and the attendant led Cherko to the narrow table.

I'm suddenly feeling just a little nervous, Cherko said. *What are you doing—*

She smiled. *Nothing so worrisome. You've been here before. Do you not remember?*

As Cherko was accompanied to the narrow, translucent slab, flashes of imagery again came back...of him being led to a table very much like this one.

By She.

The table lowered and Cherko slid onto it. It didn't feel like a normal table at all, didn't feel hard, uncomfortable. It immediately transitioned back up to its normal configuration, and as soon as he lay back on the table, was immediately...calmed. It was as if a relaxing current or electromagnetic blanket had been wrapped around him...his consciousness.

Was it the deep blue flecking within the table?

He'd closed his eyes.

Relaxed.

He felt *so* relaxed. His racing mind...calmed. His tense, on-the-go body sank into the table like exhausted lead. Felt all worry and stress drain out from him...

(*into the table?*)

Then...then something really weird happened....

2

Hermes 1 Stack
Cape Kennedy, Launch Pad LC-39B
4 May 2021

James Cherko felt the full weight of his life and body press down into the horizontal contour couch of the Multi-Purpose Crew Vehicle, known as "Orion." They'd been lying strapped inside the crew cabin for a little over two hours performing communications checks, leak checks, listening to all launch preparations and constantly updated wind reports piped in through their helmet speakers; performed their own in-cabin pre-flight checklists. Orion was neatly stacked three hundred feet atop the Hermes 1 space launch system, also known as the "stick," awaiting its launch from Kennedy Space Center's launch pad LC-39B.

It was really gonna happen, this time, wasn't it.

They were really gonna pop this weasel.

But there could still be a delay, couldn't there, right on down to T-0, when the computers ignited the boosters and you were going *no matter what.*

Control's countdown and updated wind reports continued past the T-60 seconds mark. The Stick's shaped PBAN, or polybutadiene acrylonitride solid rocket propellant would be ignited, and in less than ten minutes they would all find themselves in orbit. Liftoff was mere seconds away...

But, something didn't quite feel right. He'd felt he'd been here *before...*

Was that right?

And they could still have some kind of glitch that could call the whole thing off. An abort that would activate the escape system and eject the manned capsule from the stick, sending it off on a mini-launch of its own that would land them about a mile down range. Nothing was a done deal until this candle was *lit.*

Cherko's palms sweat. His pulse quickened. All those plane rides that had caused so much airsickness, and he was about to ride the Ultimate Vomit Comet.

"Keep your noggins stable, people," Mission Commander Colonel Bill Dunlow uttered into their helmets.

Cherko watched the countdown clock before him. Thirty seconds.

Thirty seconds!

He looked to the small mirror strapped to the wrist of his orange pressure suit. Angled it around the cabin and out the crew window. Blue sky with a hint of harmless puffy clouds.

This was REALLY, no-shit, finally gonna happen, he could *feel* it. He, James Cherko, sixty years old, was really, *finally*, headed into space with these other astronauts—or *soon to be astronauts*, once clearing the statutory fifty miles, where brilliant blue sky darkened toward ultimate black.

This was it.

...*Five...four...three...two*...one!

T-0.

The PBANs ignited. Cherko momentarily closed his eyes and received the biggest kick in the pants he'd ever experienced.

And the *noise*.

Anything but graceful, the Hermes 1 shuddered and rocked and jerked like all hell had broken loose and lurched free of its two-million-pound contact with dirt and concrete and metal. Spewed 2.3 million pounds of thrust out the ass end of a super-high technology firestick. Once these babies were lit there was no turning them off. Pad hold-down posts detonated and the launch tower's access arms retracted, and Hermes 1 no longer rested on planet Earth. In an instant it was all an incredible inch above the ground as its fiery thrusters spewed hell and damnation out its nozzles. An instant after that, it was a little over a foot above the ground. Several instances later, it was rocketing past the launch support tower and free flying into open air, initiating a roll maneuver to place it into the proper launch trajectory. They were all at the center of all the noise and flash and vibration of the most controlled explosion ever. As the Hermes rolled, Cherko glanced out the cabin windows to watch the launch pad and cape ever so gracefully fall away beneath them. It looked just like every launch video he'd ever seen...except this was *him*, here, *now*, personally experiencing everything firsthand.

The rocket accelerated. Continued to accelerate. Implausibly, it just kept unrelentingly *accelerating*.

Cherko simply had no experiential concept around which to wrap his head. He'd never been a fighter pilot, but had been in a fast car or two over his lifetime. College. A friend's Camaro. They'd taken it for a spin out on I-17, between Flagstaff and Phoenix back in the early eighties. That had been the first time he'd gone faster than seventy-five. Faster than eighty-five. Faster than a hundred miles an hour. As much as it'd scared the pants off him, it'd utterly *exhilarated* him. He'd never felt such raw power, such unbridled speed, hell, such an out-and-out adrenalin rush. Music blasting, scenery blurring past. When his friend had punched it, he'd been slammed back into the seat. As they kept screaming down I-17, he remembered getting nervous about the speed, the feeling of not being in control. He wasn't driving, someone else was. As much as he was his friend and they knew each other, *he* was driving, not *him*, and that had been quite unnerving.

And they'd just kept going *faster*...

But, eventually, his friend had to let up, and they'd slowed to more legal speeds. Kinda.

But now, there was absolutely *no* slowing down.

No legal speed issues.

For the next hundred-and-twenty-eight seconds they would be heading for an altitude of 200,000 feet and an insane speed of Mach 6.1. Until the second stage kicked in. And there would be no slowing down until his mission was over and he was back on Earth.

This new concept of constant acceleration just did not compute.

17,546 miles per hour.

Earth escape velocity.

Cherko and the others shuddered and jerked within their harnesses as if an angry Hermes himself were trying to shake them out of the sky like an evil parent to a misbehaving child. There was no turning back now, and it hit Cherko for the very first time that, yes, they really could very well all perish at any point from now, on. They could all turn into sparkling, fiery bits screaming out of a bright blue sky.

It's not like there hadn't been any precedent for that.

And, in the case of ascent, that was the reason for the escape tower. It would ignite, more explosive bolts would detonate, and Orion would be yanked free from its Hermes stack at a force of well over 10 Gs, the malfunctioning booster would then be safely destroyed over open ocean.

Or such was the plan.

Commander Dunlow read off their altitude.

And through all this Hermes *just kept going....*

It was almost too much to register. As much training as he'd had, Centrifuge and everything else, as much simulator time as they'd had, nothing truly ever prepared you for the real deal. Of being strapped onto a rocket and manhandled into orbit.

Space.

Less than thirty seconds later they punched through the sound barrier. Seven hundred miles per hour. All the vibrations and buffeting that they'd been enduring since liftoff suddenly backed off and things smoothed out. At transonic speeds they were all now in *front* of the noise—or its shockwave. The crew cabin grew starkly quieter. Cherko again glanced out the window.

"Fifty miles, astronauts," Dunlow announced calmly, as they raced through the sound barrier. This made Cherko and another brand-new voyager full-fledged additions to the astronaut corps. Cherko and Pedersen immediately pulled out their Velcro patches with their names and newly minted astronaut wings, and slapped them onto their suits where an empty Velcro-receiving patch had been waiting.

Astronaut.

Finally.

Finally—*and he could never tell a soul.*

Cherko took in the crew cabin. The flight crew beside him and their various monitoring responsibilities, as they rocketed toward their orbital trajectory. Took in the control panels and instrumentation. The feel of the suit encasing him, the gloves.

Flexed his fingers.

Directed his eyes (he didn't move his head, as the Commander had reminded him) toward one of the windows. Blue sky was quickly fading to black.

A sudden reduction in thrust threw everyone forward in their harnesses. The first stage engine had cut off. Cherko emitted a forced grunt as he impacted his restraint harness. Five seconds later they were again thrown back into their couches. The second stage and its liquid oxygen-and-hydrogen engines had kicked in. For the next four-hundred-and-sixty seconds this forced them into an altitude of sixty-three miles, shoving them all back into their contour couches at 3.5 Gs. About thirty seconds later there was another jolt and explosion, and Cherko jumped, feeling a cold sweat—until he saw the readout that indicated jettison of their launch escape tower.

There went their useless-at-this-point safety net.

But something continued to nag at the back of Cherko's mind. He continued to stare out the crew cabin's windows.

Something just wasn't *right*.

All blue sky was now replaced by the pure darkness of space.

After all the unbridled fury of Hermes trying to shake them into human confetti, it had all just...*stopped*. They had "gone through the gate," it was called, and the second stage had shut down. It felt exactly as had been described by others who had gone before: a car wreck.

Ka-*BOOM*, and the exact feeling of being catapulted off the planet.

An internal tumbling sensation.

Cherko felt a sudden fullness in his head from his cardiovascular system having been working overtime to pump blood into a brain during the high-G ride into orbit, but now, suddenly without all those Gs, his face flushed like an embarrassed schoolboy. He reflexively reached for his face, despite having already been briefed on the affect, but of course the helmet prevented any facial contact. Man, itches were gonna be hell.

He was no longer on Earth.

He was a Rocket Man.

They'd reached escape velocity. Officially become an Earth-orbiting satellite. NORAD had a number assigned to them and was dutifully tracking them.

ERO was...

The mission.

Yes, all this excitement was overshadowed by the mission.

What they were all up there for, and it was far from any amusement park thrill ride, nor any national adulation. They had a job to do, a serious one, and one that had a cover story fed to the public. Their real mandate the public would never know. Not even in fifty nor a hundred years, if things extended out that far. Never *ever*.

Cherko gently rolled his head toward the view port and gazed longingly upon the Earth.

It seemed, oh, so much farther away than it could ever have been....

Chapter Twenty-Three

1

100-Mile Low Earth Orbit
21 May 2021
1600 Hours Zulu

Dreams were a funny thing, James Francis Cherko thought, as he stared out the MOL's viewport. When initiated, usually at young, naïve, highly impressionable stages of childhood, they didn't take into account any kind of reality. All that's involved in actually attaining said goals. Cherko's dreams arose during the early sixties and seventies by consuming everything science fiction. Watching *Star Trek* reruns, reading their sixties and seventies paperbacks, and building a ceiling full of spaceship models. He frequently splurged his weekly allowances on books.

Those were days of hard decisions.

No, reality was rarely, if ever, factored in.

And for Jimmy's dreams it was partly because, at his young age and in that era, there really hadn't been much of a reality *to* factor in. No one had really traveled *through* space back then, at least not until the early sixties with Yuri Gargarin's and John Glenn's orbital shots. Even with the 1969 lunar landing, and though the moon was definitely nothing to sneeze at, it wasn't exactly screaming though interstellar space at warp speeds or visiting a city on the edge of forever.

No, sometimes we had to be careful what we wished for.

As an adult…nothing was naïve. Reality tainted and discolored our dreams, dreams we'd labored long and hard to achieve, blinded by our youthful, single-minded determination. Goals that were rosy when generated often became sullied with actualization.

Cherko looked down to Earth.

There was a certain air of surrealism to a guy who couldn't get past navigator training in pursuit of an astronaut rating.

And everything he knew existed *there*.

Humanity loved to wax philosophical about stars and comets and moons. On the one hand being in orbit was a heady, spiritual experience—you don't get much closer to touching the face of God—but get stuck up in a smelly tin can orbiting a little blue planet and see how "romantic" things really were...especially when you couldn't talk to the ones you love *because you didn't officially exist up there.* You weren't officially where you were, *because you were an on-orbit spy.*

Most of Cherko's life had been oriented toward the stars, and most of his adult life had been focused toward space, but now that he was actually *there*, he'd grown homesick. That had never happened before—not when he left home at eighteen, and not when he'd entered the Air Force at twenty-two. But now, everything-and-anything, everyone he ever knew was on that planet below. All his problems, his woes, his loves. *7-Elevens*, TV shows, and pets.

Books.

Cozy beds.

Traffic lights, movie theaters, and *Starbucks.*

Yeah, no *Starbucks.*

People wished upon stars and gazed romantically lunar, *but they just didn't realize what it was they were doing.*

It's so utterly desolate up here.

Lonely.

Nothing.

All wistful desires for space are centered around books and movies *about* space, but even *Star Trek* and *Star Wars* were filmed in studios and virtual reality—all *still on Earth.* At the end of a shoot, it's a "wrap," cameras stop rolling, and reality returned to...sets, ground, and people. Trees. Bugs. What he'd give to see a cloud of black flies. Up here...there's no soundtrack, no rolling credits, no house lights, no huge, expansive estates or their manicured lawns. Up here, all special effects were real. There's no place to return to except straight down.

Earth.

The basis for all human experience.

So what had he finally gotten out of attaining his dream?

Being crammed within a set of strung-together tin cans? Spying on life by being utterly removed from it? Peeping in on satellites, terrestrial targets, even the *official* astronauts and their officially acknowledged space stations and EVAs?

Romantic. *Real* romantic.

So what'd happened to his life, real life, the one he'd lived down there...interacting among people, places, and all-things gravitationally-bound? What had become of his parents, his siblings, his friends, and

Erica.

Geeze, yes, he'd forgotten about her along the way, hadn't he, so fueled had he been by his all-consuming ambition? He'd allowed himself to have been caught up in events of the Black World. The Black Onion. Clandestine operations.

God and Country.

Cherko nudged away from the viewport, drifting down the length of the SIGINT module. Eyed several panels.

It was almost time.

Time to collect more whoop-de-do intel on a country he didn't even care about.

So why the hell was he up here?

Because, plain and simply, it'd been his *dream*.

What he'd wanted out of life since being that starry-eyed kid in Lake Clear, NY. It was now his job. What got him up here. In space. His covert-never-can-tell astronaut rating. He was now one of those elusive, unblinking satellites that some other starry-eyed kid was staring up at from Earth this very minute.

Erica.

Had she also been a dream? Not so much a goal, "dream," but a real, mentally fabricated psychological *delusion?* An illusion created by a homesick mind, not the real flesh-and-blood person he thought he'd loved? The one with the deep, loving eyes and stunning mane of red hair? The one with the most appealing, mesmerizing voice?

Erica.

He had loved her. *Had* been with her. Yes, he remembered that as plain as if it were yesterday and not forty years later. But, he'd been pulled out of Colorado, kidnapped by, essentially, his own kind, then subsequently "rescued" by General Hammond, who was now more than likely long gone and nothing but a distant memory rotting in a grave somewhere. Dust to dust.

On Earth.

Then he'd been sent to New Mexico and his world—everything he'd known—had spun upside down. But he'd—

He'd what? *Returned?* Returned to reclaim her? The love of his life?

Cherko shook his head, snorting. Zero-g wreaked havoc on his sinuses.

Hadn't he returned—*married*—Erica? Hadn't they—

No…wait wait wait…

He hit the control panel before him and squinted hard into its glowing indicators and switches.

He'd made the Air Force a career—attained the rank of colonel.

Hadn't he?

Been a fast-burner. Lost within the skins of the Black Onion, he'd been able to excel like never before.

Then…then how could he have married? It simply didn't fit the timeline.…

Cherko braced himself, wedging two fingertips between modulator/demodulator equipment.

Colonel. Air Force. *ERO.*

Married? Erica? *Civilian?*

How could both be true?

Cherko stared down the length of the module.

Empty.

He was alone in this section of orbiting canister, surrounded by surveillance packages, advanced hardware and software—high technology. Preprocessor and processor modules. Crypto gear. Recorders. O-scopes.

Think.

He was no longer in the military, that much was true, but he still worked for ERO—that much was also true. He looked to his left hand.

No wedding band.

Yet he remembered marrying Erica.

Erica...*what was her last name? Her* maiden *name?*

He grunted.

Erica...*Taylor.* Erica Taylor. Yes!

A...car crash?

Rear-ended a garbage truck?

Bad dreams...dreams about—

Goddammit, they *had* been married....

2

Colorado Springs,
10 December 2010
0320 Hours Mountain Time

Reality always came too soon.

Oh-dark-thirty.

Getting up before the alarm, Cherko quietly left the room and his peacefully sleeping wife and entered the hallway. Having hardwood flooring, he always softly jammed a rolled-up towel into the space between the bottom of the bedroom door and the floor to lessen his morning noise. They'd had carpet across the upstairs, but when Erica had found beautiful hardwood floors hidden beneath thirty-plus-year-old carpet, they'd torn it up. They'd left a short patch on the stairs because of their eleven-year-old Black Lab at the time who'd had bone cancer, and therefore had trouble negotiating slippery surfaces. That had been seven years ago. Since ripping up the carpet, they'd discovered it quite noisy and cold on Erica's beautiful feet in the winter months.

By the low light of the stove's fan hood down in the kitchen, Jimmy made sure Erica's coffee was set up and ready for her when she awoke, then grabbed his tall glass, filled it with ice and home-brewed black tea, and left for his basement writing office. Powering up the printer and laptop, he listened to the haunting wail-bark of the coyotes outside his window. Coyotes that yipped and howled and actually sounded like they were *right there*. He poked aside the curtains and peered outside. Their activity continued, but he saw nothing. He returned to his laptop, entered his password, and brought up his manuscript.

Pausing, he looked to pictures of Erica on his desk.

Erica in that hot little black number.

Erica smiling beautifully in front of their fireplace.

And to possibly the most cutest picture *ever*: an adorable black-and-white of Erica three years old, in some checkered top.

This was his wife, a woman whom he cherished and adored and couldn't believe had married him.

He smiled and took a clanking swig of iced tea.

Time to get back to work.

He pulled out his keyboard, and as soon as his fingers hit the keys, was lost within a world of government spies, Area 51, satellites, and UFOs....

Chapter Twenty-Four

1

100-Mile Low Earth Orbit
21 May 2021
1710 Hours Zulu

Okay, now how in the hell could that be?

Cherko continued to adjust mux/demux components that had been giving attitude the past several days. He input a handful of commands into an attached laptop, one used to monitor input signal conditioning.

How could he have been a technical writer ten years ago, only to now find himself in orbit above the Earth?

He'd been in the Air Force…made a full career of doing covert space ops—only to have gotten out and become a *technical writer?*

The mux/demux rack finally went green. Time to suit up.

Cherko nudged away from the instrument rack and drifted over to another set of panels at the opposite bulkhead; looked to the Time Display Unit.

17:10:54 hours.

Looked to a locker and its own mini-TDU, displaying the same time. A red light was embedded on the locker alongside the TDU. When the time hit 17:11:04 hours, the red indicator switched to green. Hovering before it, Cherko quickly opened the locker and removed the headgear, its visor up. This was "suiting up." Multicolored leads floated about the helmeted contraption as Cherko fit it onto his crew-cut head. It always reminded him of a military pilot's helmet.

Cherko checked that the visor remained in its up and stowed position and went about connecting all the helmet leads into their panel sockets. Once all leads were connected and checked, Cherko lowered his legs from the zero-g floating position and shuffled his feet into the floor stirrups, anchoring in. He adjusted the Velcro straps to his helmet under his chin then activated a panel switch, bringing the unit to life. Cherko heard a muffled *beep* inside the earphones and immediately set about performing end-to-end bit error rate checks with the help of the laptop. Satisfied with the checks, he lowered the holographic visor.

For all practical purposes, he was no longer in the MOL.

As soon as the visor was lowered and in place, Cherko was outside the space station, floating in free space...or so it appeared.

Mildly fumbling about over his equipment as he oriented himself, he grabbed two joy sticks. He then reached over to the laptop and quickly adjusted his visor settings to allow display of a tiny window to the lower right portion of his vision, in his visor's heads-up display. The HUD permitted him to see what was actually—physically—before him, along with the mission's virtual displays. Like a pilot's preflight checks, he twisted and turned the "sticks," as he called them, while viewing HUD indications. Maneuvering, or "flexing" the sticks, he performed quick systems and optics checks, not unlike the preflight operation of aircraft rudders and ailerons. He also gave a quick all-around look at the MOL's optics and flexibility, and the helmet's integration with them. All green. Good-to-Go.

Cherko hit another switch, initiating mission operation.

This gave Cherko a rush like nothing else. Virtually bi-located, all his visual senses were focused outside the MOL as if he were actually on an EVA, while his aural and tactile senses were still inside the station. Immediately Cherko's field of vision went from on-orbit to serious terrestrial micro-zoom, as his holographic visor zoomed him in on a patch of Earth in brilliant clarity and detail. It was as if he'd performed an incredibly quick Earth reentry without the plasma envelope, as the program fed and directed him automated target acquisition data. He held back just a hint of motion

(*home*)

sickness.

The display suddenly fuzzied and began to "snow."

Cherko quickly adjusted with a couple of hurried laptop commands, which momentarily popped up on his visor's visuals. Within seconds, focus returned, and with it the ability to make out landmarks, roads, buildings...*people*. It wasn't just that he could read the proverbial license plates, but he could also tell you how many and what types of insects were plastered all over them. On his holographic visor HUD were several readouts: a Target Acquisition indicator (reading "Acq") that glowed red for no acquisition, Country (Germany), city (Cologne), surface altitude, lat and long, and surface compass heading readings all blinking red dashes. A green "Rec" recording indicator glowed in the upper left.

"Okay," Cherko said quietly to himself, "here we go, in three...two...*one*."

Another muted "beep" went off in his ears, and "Acq" and all the remaining indicators went green and populated with values.

"We have acquisition," Cherko mumbled absentmindedly, flexing his sticks.

He twisted and banked the sticks, adjusting his view. During these missions they were told where to point and when, and were to go in and gather as much intelligence as possible before losing overhead coverage from their air-skimming overflights. Then they were to quickly ship off the data via classified satellite relays that the world thought were commercial satellites, to East Coast intelligence analysts. It was always a secret to them just what they were peeking in on until they actually acquired their objectives. At the moment he was acquiring about mid-way up an office building. At their slant-range optical angle, Cherko had to continually flex his sticks until he could "coerce" as good an image as possible—hence the need for the helmet.

In the early seventies a concept was designed to send a manned laboratory into orbit composed of spies posing as research scientists. The media, of course, had gotten hold of it from leaks that just never went away, and big news was made about how it had gotten too expensive to fund. The program had eventually been abandoned. But, the truth of it was that it *had* actually been funded, and *had* gone operational for many years—hidden within the massive and convoluted bureaucratic layers of government, and at one time or another actually became part of several other budgets, one of which was the International Space Station. Money was funneled, directed, and redirected.

But things always went deeper.

A new classified intel program was under development, one that had gone under various and ever changing names, a program that used and integrated incredibly advanced optical imagery and ground mapping software to fantastically enhance intel beyond anything previously thought possible. Efforts had been underway to marry on-orbit optical, radar, and infrared imagery into a package that could be enhanced by ground-level charting software *that mapped every square centimeter of Earth*. Satellite imagery, modified by this new ground charting software allowed real-time mapping and resolution to permit on-orbit spies to literally *peer into windows and collect real-time* interior *ground-level reconnaissance*.

Cherko continued working his controls.

But what the helmet gave him was far more than just imaging software. It gave him the additional incorporation of a human's discriminating mind. It allowed him to coerce further detail from reconnaissance imagery in ways never before imagined.

He'd been chosen for this mission after extensive testing, brain mapping, and trial and error. When Cherko placed the helmet over his head, and attached the leads, he was literally connected to an artificial intelligence mainframe through which he could teach identification of "fuzzy area" imagery, using his own visual and mental interpretation. He would see an unresolved, indistinct image and "will" it into form.

Was it a head?

Using mental discrimination, optics, radar, infrared data, and interaction with the ground charting software, he would then real-time refine the image with the intention of it *being* a head.

If the object turned out to be a head, then the image was "coerced," but if not, the image would refine into an absurd target, such as a head on a floor lamp. He would see this, and could thereby *re-coerce* the target to make it make sense before final resolution. After this instance was corrected—real time—the system would then *learn* the algorithm and the object, and if further objects were so identified, the system would refine them itself, until it needed further input from Cherko.

Ad infinitum.

Cherko's image coercion and the software's recognition refinement constantly worked off each other.

So, as Cherko homed in on the building before him, he twisted and torqued his "sticks" to bring him in on the side of the building. He always had to work fast. Beat that ticking, ever ticking, always ticking, timeline—the screaming MOL's time-on-station—before their orbits took them beyond their terrestrial targets. As he used this system, it was as if he was floating directly before fiftieth-story windows.

Coming into the side of the building, Cherko flexed his sticks as the system brought him into the particular office window.

But, it was his next action where he really earned his pay.

He flexed *through* the window.

Inside the target.

Things now got tricky.

He saw what looked like a person' sitting at a desk, his back to him, doing what looked like typing at a keyboard. Picking out what looked like a display screen off to the right, Cherko coerced that image. After some flexing, it turned out to, indeed, be a screen, but even better…*words*…on the screen.

Cherko worked his sticks until his wrists ached, but was finally able to make out words on the display. He verified the mission was recording. "Rec" continued to blink green.

Cherko couldn't quite make out the words, but they were probably in another language. He kept his focus, kept steady, now only making fine adjustments with the sticks. Steady hand-eye coordination was essential. He glanced to his visor display of the TDU. Time was running out. Then he saw a word he recognized: *ausgezeichnet.*

German. He'd studied German—

Then lost acquisition.

No matter. They'd been able to get in and acquire the target, and he'd figured out the screen text was German. Just because one was in Germany did not necessarily mean one was *using* German, but in this case, it proved correct. It was not his place to second-guess the mission nor its objectives.

Whatever he collected would help ground-based analysts in further data refinement.

It had definitely been a good run.

2

Cherko drifted from instrument panel to instrument panel. Garcia was in another module working on a backup UHF component that kept tripping malfunction indicators, and Peterson was, according to schedule, in his sleep period.

Cherko floated over to a viewport. The concept of being on-orbit still fascinated him, even though this was…

Was it really his first trip here—or his second?

Third?

He shook his head, sinuses mildly objecting.

Did zero-G affect one's mind? One's memory?

He didn't dare bring up the subject of faulty mental capabilities with his coworkers while in orbit, no sir. Once you got back down to Earth…maybe…in your diary, or with the White Coats, yes…but no, not, and *never* up here. Not much margin for error up here. Who wanted to be held captive with a possible crazy while in orbit? Sometimes what you didn't know really couldn't hurt you.…

But why was he having difficulty remembering things?

He remembered going through their concealed-from-the-public astronaut training with his MOL crew—trained in All-things Astronaut, just not given the face time like the *official* ones. The classes, the WETF, the Weightless Environment Training Facility's twenty-five-foot-deep underwater training tank (he really liked that); endless simulator training runs where every scenario always seemed to have at least *three* catastrophic failures, and, yes, even the T-38 checkrides out over the Gulf. What he called his Barf Bag Runs.

Then there was the shake, rattle, and roll of their Hermes I launch itself. Yes, he remembered that well. Who could ever forget a kick in the butt like that?

Aye, the concept of being where he was and how he'd gotten there continued to blow his mind. This had been his goal as long as he could remember. Years of watching the *Six-Million-dollar Man's Steve Austin, astronaut* had finally become real life's, *Jimmy Cherko…*

Astronaut.

And all of this, every thought, memory, or spoken word just felt oddly incongruous in orbit.

Cherko checked the signal conditioning instrument rack, when the alert came across the secure teletype. It was called a "teletype," a carryover from earlier days, but it was really just another glorified laptop. High technology was run by commercial off-the-self laptops. The message read:

```
Initiate Fast Walker Recon...coordinates to follow...
```

As the coordinates appeared on-screen, something within Cherko...*activated*. He pushed himself over to another set of panels, feet trailing diagonally off behind him. As if working through a haze, he verified the panels were all properly activated and functioning. Then shot back over to his previous station. These messages were of utmost importance and were to be immediately acted upon, no matter what else—including their photo recon coercion missions. He again slid his feet into the stirrups, again slipped on his helmet (helmet lockers were automatically released with these messages), and grabbed the sticks.

"*Rudy?*"

Cherko looked behind him; stared down the length of the empty control module.

No one. Just humming technology and blinking lights.

Lights. Idiot lights.

He returned his attention to his console and knocked down the visor. He could have sworn he'd heard—*felt*—another enter the module.

The coordinates were already entered into the system, its optics already slaved and tracked to the Fast Walker.

Cherko focused in on the target. This was their *real* mission. The terrestrial intel gathering was a legitimate—though cover—operation, but this was why he was really here.

A round craft shot across his field of vision.

Stopped.

Darted back across in the opposite direction.

Display indicators in his visor informed him of a SBIRS missile warning satellite in the vicinity of the sighting.

Cherko flexed his sticks.

In an era of advanced special-effects TV, movies, and books, everything had already been done. Everything already had a history, a lore, and, of course, UFOs were arguably the largest and most prevalent of any lore.

Unidentified Flying Objects.

Either you believed or you didn't, but either way, the government never officially acknowledged *nuthin*. But he knew better. He knew for a fact that elements in the government *did* believe.

UFO Recon was their unofficial, biggest, hairiest, most highly classified mission. Observe, track, record, and, where possible—*interact with*—these craft.

Interact.

That's where he came in. All his Program training. Everything about his life had been oriented toward this one end.

That important mission Hammond had prepared him for all those years ago, on what seemed, now, a planet far, far away.

Just call him Jimmy FastWalker.

Interact.

What that meant was pretty much left up to him, and to which he'd not yet done. No interaction on any of his

(*three?*)

trips here, though he'd attempted contact. And the fact that he was thinking about it, now, was more than faintly absurd. Like an amnesiac memory activated by a forgotten stimulus, and which would have otherwise been left hidden were it not for the incident at hand.

A rather Manchurian Candidate-like response that greatly unnerved him.

When he wasn't called upon to perform this particular mission, he'd never thought about it…never talked about…yet once the message had been received…it set off an unsettling Pavlovian chain reaction.

Then he remembered it.

Then he was all over it.

Then his life was centered around it.

Compartmentalization. The human mind…a strange and wonderful rabbit hole.

Cherko flexed his sticks. Telemetry indicated the craft was—good *God*—the size of a *football stadium*, had changed directions on a dime, and moved at unimaginable speeds for a ship of such apparent mass. Nothing maneuvers at speeds like that…at least nothing we had.

Here goes.

Contact requested, he mentally sent.

Just like he'd been nocturnally trained all those years ago back on those deserted Colorado plains.

As Cherko initiated contact with the object, he felt that again curious sensation he always felt when he did this work up here. *He felt as if the MOL was closing in on him*, like those walls in the trash bin in that *Star Wars* movie into which Luke and friends had been dumped while trying to rescue Princess Leia.

Cherko got a severe case of psychic tunnel vision.

He'd never gotten that below, while working at Falcon or Dulce, but he'd found that once up here—in space—here was a curious, almost frightening psychic claustrophobia he experienced every time he initiated attempted contact. He could keep the fear at bay, sure, but it wasn't easy. Fits of focused paranoia. Feeling *watched*.

Psychically *squeezed*.

Cherko fought the urge to again look behind him. You *never* looked behind you, never, because, if you did...you died. That was horror-movie law.

So Cherko kept continued focus on the task at hand.

Requesting contact, he again nervously sent.

Cherko watched the object terminate its zigzagging movement. Watched it settle. Glanced to the telemetry, which relayed that it still zigzagged after all—except instead of side-to-side, its movement was now forward-and-backward. Explained why it was so hard for him to see what was happening.

It was shooting toward him and retreating.

Requesting contact, he again sent.

Why'd the object do that? Why didn't it just stop? Why was it wob—

The object stopped.

Request con-

Contact confirmed.

3

Colorado Springs, CO
12 December 2010
0111 Hours Mountain Time

Big eyes.

It was raining. Pouring.

Biking...he'd been pumping those Schwinn pedals as hard as he could.

Mom. Had to get to Mom.

Nibbling...they were nibbling at his hand. They were all around him. Bumping into him....

Cherko awoke. Sprang upright and alert in bed. Coyotes yipped and barked outside in the night.

Nibbling at his hand...

Shook his head. Couldn't shake the images.

Why were they looking at him? Did deer really look directly at people—into their eyes?

Jimmy got out of bed; stumbled against the wall.

He had to get to Mom...his mother! *But the storm, the thunderstorm...it was holding him back....*

Jimmy grabbed the bedpost for support. Tried to sort out dream from reality. He could not shake the images. Eyes. *Boring into him.*

He stood before the empty bed. Stared off into the darkness.

Things always looked different at night. In the light of day the bed was inviting, comfortable, but now, at night, he couldn't really tell if Erica was there or not; maybe she was just all the way over on her side of the bed—or if it was really *her* there at all. He turned around and looked to the curtained windows. Light seeped in through the curtains. It was bright out there—there was some kind of really bright light outside. Wrinkling his face, he peered through the curtains.

Moonlight.

Of course.

And deer!

There was a whole herd of them standing out in their backyard under a full moon!

One of the deer lifted its head. Looked directly at him.

Did deer ever...

Another did the same thing.

Then another, and

Jimmy found himself standing outside in the backyard in his bare feet, gym shorts, and a ratty *Diver's Reef* T-shirt. Stared up into the moon. He stood in several inches of snow. It was uncomfortably cold.

But peaceful. It was so peaceful.

What was he doing out here?

He inhaled deeply of the night air.

Staring at him. They were all staring at him!

Nuzzling him.

Deer!

One nibbled at his left hand. He looked to the animal. Brought the hand up before him. Looked between it and the deer. Moonlight glistened off the deer's large dark eyes. Eyes that accused, bored into him. The rest of the herd was over by the gate. The gate that was open and led onto the driveway behind the house....

Had he opened that?

The deer were now all gathered over by the open gate, most actually on the other side of it, milling around under the motion-sensing spotlight in the driveway that was now on, tripped by their presence. The deer turned and casually began to walk away.

Follow them! He had to follow!

Jimmy walked across to them. Thought about the contrast of winter yard to summer yard. How this was at one time a freshly cut summer lawn with that fresh-cut-grass smell and chirping crickets. Inhaled the memory of those summers-past fresh-cut scents.

Loved that smell.

Playing catch with his Dad. Mowing lawns. Swimming in Lake Clear. Backyard BBQs—boy, he could really use a grilled cheeseburger or two right now....

He passed through the gate and padded along the driveway. The deer continued to slowly meander away. They filed into the heavily misted street. Several poured over onto the sidewalk of a neighbor's front yard as they headed into an adjacent field, beyond the mist-shrouded streetlight.

Jimmy stopped.

What was he doing?

He was outside in his shorts, for God's sake! In the *winter!* No shoes, at some ungodly hour, and all while Erica—blissfully unaware—was asleep inside!

Had he locked the door?

Brought keys? A flashlight?

A pump-action shotgun?

The deer had gone off into the brush, he could see their shadowy heads bobbing about in the silvery moonlight. But as afraid—perhaps apprehensive was a better word—as he was, he didn't want to lose them.

Jimmy padded on bare feet along concrete sidewalk. It was *cold.* And it was utterly quiet—not even a tinkling wind chime nor howling coyotes.

Jimmy hit the dirt and gravel pathway that wound its way through the field. No snow here. The texture of the path was curious. All the times he'd walked it he was in sneakers or boots and had never given it much thought. But there were all kinds of pebbles and twigs and dirt underfoot. Frozen firm.

Jimmy looked ahead and saw that the deer were not far in advance of him. They seemed to be taking their time.

But, really, *what in hell was he doing out here?*

One of the deer up ahead stopped and turned. Looked directly to him.

Not that he could really see them, but in his mind's *eye* he saw them...*felt* them...deep, dark, deer eyes. Unblinking. Grabbing his soul like a firm shake to the shoulders.

Jimmy picked up his pace. He was just about there....

He stood in the middle of a field. The field where he used to walk Mac. The long ago gone-to-seed Buffalo grass was now all desiccated and stiff.

He was surrounded by deer...shadowy deer. They milled around him, again with the nibbling, the nudging. Looking to him.

Something was different.

Jimmy made a half-hearted attempt at leaving the circle of wildlife, even though he really didn't want to (but a strange, distant, ever so far-away part of him *did*...). The deer gently nudged back. Nipped at his hands. Something just wasn't right. *Different.*

Different, different, different....

His Mom...he had to get to his mother....

But that had been a lifetime ago. That was not *now*, not *here*. It had been a dream.

Jimmy's pulse quickened; his throat constricted. His legs weakened.

There were coyote and *bear* out here!

Mountain lion!

Was one out there, now, this very minute, pacing the treeline? Deer meat be damned, it wanted something less gamey?

Erica!

And what of her?

She was alone in bed, in a house unlocked and open to all the unspeakable horrors of the night!

Had he just walked all the way here in his bare feet?

Restless, Jimmy couldn't keep his legs from wanting to sprint, to run, run fast, run *far....*

He looked to the deer. They'd all stopped nudging him. All looked to him.

Him.

With their huge, dark eyes. Eyes that were so very large. Penetrating.

It suddenly dawned on him what was different.

A shadow surrounded them.

He looked up.

Chapter Twenty-Five

1

This is all fake.
What's all fake?
This.

Focus...it was hard...hard...to *focus.*
Where was he?
Woods. He was out in the woods?
Didn't make sense. He was just in...he was

Fourteen years old. Free. Free from adult life, adult worry, from work. Free to do as
he pleased. To walk the woods up back if he

Loved winter. Snow. Loved all seasons, but the winter...the low light, snow, creaking and splitting of trees. Being deep in the woods...*loved* that. Winters always turned him inward. *Inward...*

Lake Clear, New York
25 December 1974

Snowshoeing.
Making tracks through virgin snow. Just the sound of the woods, his breath, and the muffled crunching of his snowshoes in snow. Weaving in and out of the trees. Thinking about girls and books and movies. How beautiful it

was out here, in the deep woods of their back forty. Today, he was thinking about girls from school. Girls like Hannah or Linda.

Hannah.

Man, they were *babes*.

He stopped. Before him lay unmarked snow and trees. He watched his breath curl up before him; noticed his breath only came out of one nostril. Jimmy pursed his lips together and angled his breath upward, blowing more vapor up before him.

Turning around, he looked to the lonely path he'd created, stretched out behind him.

No one else.

Just him, his tracks, his breath. The calming, deadening silence of The Moment. There was...how to describe it?...a *furriness* of soul....

He popped his gloved hands together in a mock punch. It was cold, his face cold, but he liked that. Liked it because he was clad in his winter gear, the plaid wool winter pants, heavy down jacket and gloves, *L.L. Bean* boots, and wool hat.

Continued on.

It was late. The sun low and orange through darkening skeletal trees against a blanketed and somber landscape. Howling gusts of frigid wind. He didn't want to go back. Wished this moment would last forever. Alone and on his own. Snowshoeing. The woods, the sunset. The dark steel-gray of the clouds and a dying winter's day.

He smiled.

Crunching in the snow he turned (more like waddled) around.

His tracks.

Still there.

Still his.

Following him.

God, Hannah was *cute*. Her long brown hair. Her smile.

He wished she'd just walk on out of the woods right now...

He shifted uncomfortably, adjusting his pants.

Hannah.

Had to get home.

Warmth. Family. TV. Home...warmly lit up from the inside, smoke coming out of its two chimneys from both the oil furnace and Franklin Stove Dad no doubt already had going for the evening. Mom making dinner, wondering where the heck he was. Carl, Penny, and Ritchie all lying on the floor before the TV, waiting for him to get home so *they* could eat.

Home.

Family.

Man, Hannah…Hannah, Hannah, *Hannah!*

He *loved* her name.

Loved saying it, *thinking* it. Just the two of them. Out here in the woods….

He again adjusted his snowpants.

It was harder—but not impossible—to continue his way through the darkening woods, but he finally came upon Devil's Den. Only a couple more minutes and he'd be home.

Jimmy listened to the now ghostly whisper of wind through the trees, to the woods' cracking and splitting; his open-mouthed and labored breath.

Snow fell thicker now; the temperature had definitely dropped. What late afternoon winter light there had been was

Different. Something *was* different.

Though he felt cold creeping through his garments and even into his snowpants, another chill ran through him.

He looked to his feet (wiggled his toes). Behind him.

It *was* darker. Felt much later than it should be—

"Hi, Jimmy."

Jimmy spun around.

Hannah stood behind a copse of snow-covered branches, in a cute-looking snow suit. Surrounded by deer.

Even Jimmy's thoughts were awestruck.

Hannah came forward, her entourage spilling out around her like liquid meat.

"This was what you wanted, was it not?"

He'd never noticed before just how deep and dark her large, beautiful eyes were. How compassionate and *probing.* Her voice melted away any chill that had seeped into his bones.

"H-hi, Hannah."

"What do you wanna do?" she asked.

The deer milled around the both of them. Jimmy didn't feel right.

"I-I don't know."

"I have an idea," she-who-appeared-to-be-Hannah said, smiling….

2

100-Mile Low Earth Orbit
4 November 2021
0912 Hours Zulu

Cherko floated through the airlocks, inhaling that burnt-metal smell of *space*, and into the farthest-most section of the MOL. It seemed to take far less time than it usually took, and caused him to unexpectedly ram a shoulder into a bulkhead and clip a nearby control panel. That'll bruise. He rubbed it.

What'd he just been doing?

He felt he'd forgotten something. Systems tests: yes, he'd been performing system tests. Preventive maintenance diagnostics had previously indicated intermittent faults in an SDS module. Cherko pushed off the bulkhead and floated up before the panel. He flipped a couple test switches. Sure enough, it was tripping. Top-of-the-line equipment, stuff you'd think would work better than it had been the past couple of days (and what was a "day"—time—anyway? On-orbit station, solar, or sidereal—*psychological?*). Had there been a solar flare he'd missed? An aggressive bout of cosmic ray bit hits?

Of course not, they get warnings.

Cherko glanced out a viewport.

He missed the seasons. Missed rain and snow. Trees. Feeling the sun *through* the trees. Rustling leaves in a breeze.

Heck, breathing unfettered *air*.

Walking. He really missed *walking*.

Floating around was fun, but brought on bone loss and he plain missed contact with firmament. Dirt. *Gravity*.

He missed animals. Cats and dogs. De—

What the hell was he forgetting?

Shutting off power to the panel, Cherko opened it up and slid out the faulty component. He'd isolated the error to an ARU board, LRU 3A45-97. And now, as he pulled the board and examined it, he found a particular contact was not closing its circuit.

"Rudy, this is Cherko, over?" Cherko called into his headset.

No response.

"Rudy?"

Silence.

"Wayne, this is Cherko, over?"

Still no response.

Cherko tapped the board. Dang it, he didn't want to have to travel all the way back across the MOL to retrieve a stinkin part. Where the heck were these guys? Had the short affected all station comm?

Pulling out a red flag from his pocket, he attached it to the still-open panel. Then he took the pulled component with him and began his return-drift to the far side of the MOL. But, just before he left, he paused and took in a moment of reflection. Looked out across the module.

Lights glowed and blinked. Idiot lights. Equipment working (well, most of it did...), humming along in their oh-so-important-life-and-mission-sustaining tasks.

He was in a frigging hollow tube, not unlike those long snow tunnels he and his friends had made as kids, back in New York. Bored and hollowed out long snow banks. Fortified with water to turn them into ice-lined caves....

It felt so empty.

Unreal.

Cherko pushed away from the console and

drifted through the center module.

Empty.

No Wayne, no Rudy.

Cherko continued on through and

entered the command module.

"Wayne, Rudy," he said, without looking up, "our comm circuits are definitely blown—"

Cherko let go of the unit, and pushed past the now-drifting component. Anchoring himself at a makeshift handhold, he scanned the module.

Empty. *Not a frigging soul.*

He looked the way he'd come and started to head back in that direction—and came to a stop.

He'd just come that way, damn it, drifted through several empty modules and there'd been *no* one.

He again surveyed the compartment. The command module. *Really* took it in.

Something was *off.*

He shook his head, closed and opened his eyes.

Had he made it all up?

(*Fake, this is all* fake...)

Gave into a daydream-like daze and unconsciously drifted past them in the other module?

And he seemed to remember the station as being much *longer*—maybe...maybe it was simply his growing familiarity with...

Contact.

What contact?

No contact?

Contact…*confirmed.*

Cherko grunted. A headache, that damned continued sinus ache. He reached out to a battery compartment. Glanced out a viewport.

Something…was…*off*, dammit. Earth…

Where was it…where was Earth?

Cherko pushed off the handhold and shot across to the port.

Something blocked their view!

Contact *confirmed.*

Confirmed!

Cherko stared out the opening. Stared out not to Earth, the glare of the blinding Sun, nor the very depths of interplanetary space itself…

No, what he now stared out into was something that hurt to consider.

Something obstructed his view.

Something was outside.

3

Colorado Springs, CO
8 November 2010
1616 Hours Mountain Time

"So…what do you think it all means, Jimmy?" Alda asked. "The deer…Hannah?"

Cherko sat in the chair, eyes wide. The chair, the office, all strangely unfamiliar, odd. Like he was in a dream.

"Something isn't right…."

"How do you mean?"

"Everything feels…two dimensional. Can't explain it."

"Two dimensional?"

"All storefront, no store. A flat dream. A movie set."

Alda chuckled. "Well, there are some trains of thought that say all of life *is* a dream, Jimmy. Do I seem real?"

Cherko looked to Alda; looked him over; Alda, who held his gaze. Alda, who flensed away his skin, his muscle, his bone with a look. Alda who laid bare his most inner-most self like the entrails of a gutted fish.

"No. No, you don't—what are you writing?"

Jimmy's legs grew restless and began running in place.

"What are you nervous about?"

"I feel like…I'm in two places at once. Or not. Displaced. Like I'm not really here. Not *supposed* to be here…"

"Where do you feel you should be?"

"Feel tingly. Don't know."

Alda nodded, again scribbling.

"I don't remember Hannah—I mean, I *remember* her—just not there…like that. With the deer…at that rock. My home."

"It's not uncommon to mix memories. What does she symbolize to you? The deer—what do they represent to you?"

Cherko looked back to Alda.

"They remind me of…"

"Rudy?"

Cherko stared at a white-tailed deer that now stood in the middle of their orbiting command module. A deer…in all its proud, muscled glory and full-rack-of-antler regalia. The deer stared back at Cherko with its huge, baleful eyes. Twitched its ears. Worked its jaw. It didn't float, it *stood* there.

Cherko didn't know whether he blinked or not, but Rudy now floated before him. No deer.

Confirmed!

"What the hell…"

Cherko looked back to the viewport, but gone was the obstruction that had been outside.

Cherko kneaded his forehead.

"You all right?" Rudy asked, leaning in.

"I, uh…"

"You look as if you've seen a ghost."

Cherko looked up to him; tried to move…couldn't. Felt as if part of his mind wanted to go one way, while another ran off in an entirely different direction. He felt anchored to an amorphous blob in Time.…

"Must've whacked my head when I hit that bulkhead."

Cherko looked behind him, back to the viewport. Earth curved softly away beneath it.

"What'd you see?" Rudy asked, eyes folding around him like a black hole. *"What does it represent to you?"*

Cherko shot to his feet.

"Okay, okay, something's very goddammed *wrong* here. Really, really frigging *wrong*…"

Cherko held a hand to his head as he stumbled across Alda's office. It was hard to move. His feet felt anchored, *leaden.*

"Perhaps you should sit back down, Jimmy."

"I'm not here, am I? Not really. I'm somewhere else. And what's with your eyes?"

Alda's eyes were deep and dark and *hungry*.

"We are where we are. Have a seat, Jimmy. Please."

"I don't want to sit. I'm always sitting. Need to *move*. Need to—"

Cherko stumbled about the office. Knocked books, folders, and papers off tables and stands. Knocked over knick-knacks and one of those calming mini-water-fall things.

"I'm sorry...s-s-sorry—"

Cherko held out his hands before him in an attempt to keep his balance and ward off additional injury, but ended up tumbling over a heavy floor lamp.

Cherko looked to Alda in confusion.

Fear.

Alda was no longer writing things down.

"*What did you do to me?*"

"I did nothing."

"You did! You did *something!* Something's not right!"

"You came to me. Do you not remember?"

"Did I?"

"Have a—"

"*I don't want to sit down.*"

Rudy stared at Cherko.

"I have to *move*...what's happening?"

"What do you think happened?"

"I...I was—no, pulling a board...*talk*—"

Cherko looked to the LRU that drifted before him.

"...next thing...next thing I *saw*...something..."

"What'd you see?"

"Confirmed. Something's...*confirmed*..."

"Yes."

"What's confirmed?"

"What do you want confirmed?"

"This. I want *this* confirmed."

"Isn't this what you wanted?"

"I didn't want *this?*"

"What did you want?"

"I wanted...wanted...is this place smaller? Did we lose a module?"

Rudy said nothing.

"This—here. Our modules," Cherko said, trembling.

"It's the same size it's always been."

"*No...*" Cherko insisted, "it's *not.*" He grabbed the floating part. Held it up before him in both hands like his life depended on it; intently scrutinized it. "Something's *off*, dammit. *Different.* Not the *same.*"

"Where's Wayne?"

"There is no Wayne."

"Where's...wh..."

Cherko put his lips together to form words for his next question, but nothing came out. He exhaled short, quick breaths, as if having just performed some great effort.

"R...rrr...*Rudy.* Rudy. Wherrre's...*RRRudy?*"

The figure smiled.

"There is no Rudy, Jimmy. There never was."

4

100-Mile Low Earth Orbit
4 November 2021
0914 Hours Zulu

"*RUDY!*"

"I'm right here."

"But there is no *you!*" Cherko yelled, restrained in the metallic contraption that crisscrossed the full length of his body. Molded around his feet and all the way up to and around his head in a solid, neat and shiny one-piece covering. "No *you!*"

"No," Rudy said, "there isn't."

Cherko let out another long, drawn out, guttural howl. Shaking side to side against his restraints. Restraints that still blinked and glowed and pinned him in an unknown imprisonment.

"What did I *see?*"

"Why don't you tell me, Jimmy."

"But you're not *you!*"

"Who am I?"

"I don't *know!*"

Cherko continued to violently thrash about within his own little personal prison.

"I don't even know who *I* am!"

"But you do," the figure who looked like Rudy said calmly. He continued to sit cross-legged on the bulkhead perpendicular to him.

"Are you Alda?"

"Oh, no. Alda is me."

Red faced and veins popping in his neck and forehead, Cherko again yelled, "Who *are* you? Who the hell *are* you!"

"You may call me 'Eurphraeus.'"

Cherko stopped thrashing about. Tried to control his heavy and shallow breathing.

"Do you remember me?" Eurphraeus asked.

Cherko blinked, making painfully confused and strained faces. Forced his chin into his chest.

Remember me?

"It...*hurts*..."

You can remember. You can. You will.

Deer...

"What is happening? *What is happening to me!*"

"Hannah?"

"Let's play!"

The snowfall was heavy. It was cold. Dark. Cherko stared at Hannah.

"I know a cool place where we could play! Want to?"

Hannah reached out and touched Jimmy.

The deer closed in around them.

"You tricked me," fourteen-year-old Jimmy said. Jimmy lay on a table in a small, dimly lit chamber. A slab with blue flecking buried within it.

We used an image already in your mind, the figure, a shimmering, vaguely anthropomorphic, ghost-like apparition telepathically sent. There were other—smaller—shadows around this being. Slender creatures with large heads.

We mean no harm. You were freezing. We removed you from the cold. It was time.

"For what?"

Contact.

"What's 'confirmed'?"

In your point-of-view's future. Our future contact was requested and is confirmed.

"What about now?"

The figure smiled.

"Why can't I see you?"

My form is hard to physically manifest. We are highly...removed...from your state of existence. It is easier to manifest into corporeal forms with which you are already familiar. Physically mental forms, if you will.

"Okay."

You like Hannah?

Jimmy blushed.

There's no need for embarrassment. Shall I use that form?

"I'm too embarrassed. I don't mind this, though. It's kind of cool. Like *Star Trek.*"

The form again smiled.

Jimmy...we've been observing you for a very long time.

"You have?"

We've come to you throughout your existence.

"Why?"

To help. Guide. There are many of you out there who we similarly assist.

"Why?"

There are reasons.

"I'm scared."

It's okay to be scared, but we are here to help.

"Why?"

The figure smiled. *We need you to remember...all will become apparent as you recall.*

"What does that mean?"

In time, Jimmy.

"What are you?"

You. We are you.

5

"So, if you're not Alda, you're—"

"Jimmy...*think.* What do deer represent to you? Hannah? Your mother's sleepwalking?"

Cherko stood in the middle of the small office; felt like his head was gonna explode. Had an urge to look up.

"It's important that you bring these memories out. They can't hold you forever. You need to take control."

"My mother? Why do you bring her up?"

"Think back, Jimmy. To the living room that night. You came downstairs, found her huddled on the floor. In the dark. What did you do? *What happened next?*"

"Mom...was very...it was sad. Very..."

Lake Clear, NY
27 October 1972
0445 Hours Eastern Time

Jimmy stared into the ceiling.

He raised up on his elbows and looked about the Lake Clear bedroom. From the rays of a bright moon, he saw his brothers and sister asleep in their beds. He lay his head back down, looked to his clock.

It'd been another dream. A dream so *real*...as if he'd actually been somewhere else. Far, far away. With his friend. His dream friend. His *girl* dream friend—but it wasn't like that. She was in many of his dreams, and they went places, talked. Had fun, like flying through the air like Superboy and Supergirl.

Tonight had been one of those dreams.

They'd had fun together, flying around holding hands. Laughing. Darting around in the light of the full moon, playing with fruit bats.

But something had awoken him.

The room went dark. Jimmy looked to the windows.

A cloud must've covered up the moon.

Jimmy quietly sat up on the edge of his bed. Listened. Again looked to his siblings.

Voices. He heard voices...but couldn't make out what was being said.

He got out of bed and quietly went to the iron ventilation grate in the middle of the floor. He bent over it, placing an ear right down against its black metal. The TV was on. Getting back to his feet, he slipped out of the bedroom.

Jimmy carefully made his way down along the hallway banister, listening to the faint noise that continued to drift up from downstairs. Their Black Lab, MacTavish, lay in his doggy bed at the end of the hallway by the bathroom. Mac had already lifted his head at Jimmy's approach. Jimmy looked to Mac, who quietly snorted and thumped his tail twice on the linoleum as he got closer. Jimmy briefly pet Mac on the head, but continued past to the stairs. Light flickered out into the foyer at the foot of the stairs. Lightly stepping upon the steps, and a steadying hand to the wall, Jimmy made his way down; Mac and his lightly rattling collar got up and followed.

At the base of the stairs, Jimmy turned into the living room. No light was on but for the TV, and he saw no one. Mac stood beside him and yawned; shook his head, again rattling his collar. Then his ears perked up and he angled his head. Jimmy continued farther into the empty and dark living room. Mac went off in his own direction as Jimmy went to the TV. A *Circle Of Fear* episode was on, and he shivered. As much as he loved that show, it really creeped him out. Jimmy again heard Mac shake his head and rattle his collar, but this time a concerned whine escaped his dog.

Jimmy turned to find Mac sniffing and checking out his mother. She sat naked and huddled on the floor between the big stuffed chair and counter-divider, over by the eight track. Mac began cleaning his mom's dirtied shoulder. His mom didn't so much as watch TV as stare through it.

"*Mom!*"

Jimmy rushed to her side. Renée looked up to him, confused, eyes large and glassy. Jimmy wiped smudged dirt and bits of grass from his mom's face, but saw there was plenty more all over her body. Nasty bruising along a length of leg. She trembled.

Averting his mother's nakedness, Jimmy pulled an afghan his grandmother had made from the couch behind him and carefully placed it around her, then wrapped his arms tightly around her. Renée continued to stare ahead emptily.

As Jimmy sat with his mother, his gaze came to the window up and behind her. Reluctantly—almost as if against his will—he pulled away from his mother and went to the window, though he continued to cast a concerned and watchful eye back to her. Moving a reading chair into better position under the window, he got up on the chair and looked outside.

Something was out there. Something he felt *shouldn't* be. Something he felt a burning need to *investigate*....

Jimmy carefully stepped off the chair and calmly made his way out the front door.

Down the porch, and onto the gravel driveway.

The moon was still hidden behind clouds as he walked across the gravel. He came to a stop in the opened parking area alongside the remains of an old 1880s blockhouse. It was then that the moon came out from behind the clouds.

Not ten feet above the remains of the blockhouse's foundation, silently hovered a rock-steady, silver-gray object that glowed in the moonlight. It was about thirty feet in diameter.

Jimmy continued forward until directly underneath it...then, upon re-consideration, backed off several steps. He felt tingly underneath the thing, uncomfortable. The skin of the craft was smooth, cold (there was an envelope of coldness surrounding the craft), and somewhat translucent. There was also a low—queer—sound that came from the ship. Seemed to resonate inside his head and bones.

He suddenly felt tired.

Jimmy looked up into the shimmering gray hull. He reached up...

And found himself surrounded by deer.

Deer that nibbled and poked at him with their little black noses. He reached out to them, but now lay on a table, unable to move. The head that came down to him was not of a deer, but a large and frightening face with huge, abysmal eyes that reflected back Jimmy's soul.

What are you doing to me? he asked, *what have you done to my mother!*

We are examining you. We need her.
You hurt her! Leave us alone!
We did not hurt her. She resists.
She should! You're mean!
We are not mean. She resists because she fears. Do not fear and no harm will come.
Why are you doing this to us? Leave us alone!

Jimmy struggled against an unseen force, but was securely pinned to the table. Something about all this felt very familiar.

I've been here before.
Yes.
Why are you doing this to us!
To ensure Humanity's existence. Ensure its future.

Jimmy felt a prick at the back of his neck…then everything went black.

Chapter Twenty-Six

1

Cherko stared at Eurphraeus—who remained at his crazy position on the bulkhead.

December 1985, Colorado
Curtis Road

Cherko sat there furious. He turned around and looked behind him.
Nothing but darkness. Out in the middle of fricking nowhere.
"Now, what the hell am I supposed to do?"
He had that van to catch in just about two hours.
Cherko exited his vehicle.
"Wonderful. Juuust wonderful...."
A light appeared down the road.
Could be a sheriff or deputy, highway patrol cruiser, or maybe even someone from the site.
The twin headlights slowed down. Cherko heard the tires crunch roadside debris as the vehicle rolled up alongside.
"What seems to be the matter, Lieutenant?"
It was that sergeant from his interrogation. Fuckin A.
Cherko cleared his throat. "Car trouble."
The sergeant held his gaze.
"Having a rough time of it tonight."
Cherko briefly looked back to his car.
"Get in."
Cherko nodded and went back to his car, retrieving his bag. He turned on his hazards and locked his vehicle, then got into the sergeant's car. As they left the shoulder, he looked into the rear-view and watched his car recede away into the darkness.
He felt an odd, incomprehensible sense of *longing*....
But that hadn't been what had happened, had it?

Not at all.

A new memory—the *real* one—surfaced like a re-claimed sunken treasure.

A light *had* appeared down the road and from the direction of Falcon.

Cherko *had* gotten out of the road and gone back to his car.

But neither a sheriff nor deputy, nor Air Force sergeant, had it been.

The light hadn't slowed down…nor pulled up alongside him. No…the light had drifted smoothly off the road and out into the fields to the east, then quietly and smoothly raced across the open, dark fields.

Changed direction.

Vectored *toward* him.

Paused.

Hovered out in the field just beyond him and his dead car.

Cherko then tracked it as it—

Was directly overhead.

He couldn't swallow. Couldn't move.

What was the temperature outside?

Did crickets chirp loudly out here during the summer?

He stared into the underhull of the craft and was immediately brought back to that destroyed blockhouse foundation in Lake Clear.

He felt all tingly. Drowsy. The craft, grayish silver, was also weirdly translucent. It looked as if he could put his hand through—*into*—the hull.

But he didn't really want to.

He also felt an envelope of coldness surrounding the craft. And an electrostatic-like sensation.

He just wanted to stand there…stare up into the night sky. Enjoy the beautiful night air and silence. The waning moon.

It was probably in the mid-thirties.

Cherko went to zip up his jacket, but instead found himself on a table. On a slab of some kind. He wasn't strapped into anything, but couldn't move just the same. Looking off to his right, he saw someone.

Mom?

His mother smiled.

What are you doing here? Cherko mentally asked.

Same as you, it would appear.

Which is?

Don't know. They don't let me know. But I'm used to it by now.

Is that Dad *over there?*

Hello, Son.

What's going on here?

We don't know.

Cherko looked to his other side.

A short, dark, wiry figure stood directly beside him. *She*, that was what he could call her, that was what he picked up from this one. *She* was no more than four feet tall.

How long had—*it?*—she been there?

Her large head, with large, dark-and-deep-as-night eyes looked rather unwieldy upon her nearly nonexistent neck and shoulders.

His first thought was, *well, I guess that's why we have clichés.*

He felt an amused—though patient—curiosity emanate from the being beside him.

Behind She were several others of similar build and appearance, and behind them were taller beings that looked exactly like *humans.* Two of them.

And way back, in the deeper, darker shadowy recesses of whatever this chamber was, was...some *other* form...one he couldn't so much as see, as...*feel.* And this form repelled all attempts at communication and identification.

We mean you no harm, She sent.

Cherko returned his attention to She.

Then why all this? Why can't you tell my mother why you've hunted her her entire life? And my Dad? What's he doing here?

We do not hunt you.

You are no better than our own scientists and explorers...those—under the guise of science—who snatch and grab animals from their own habitat, drug them, tag them, manipulate them, then release them. We're nothing more than catch-and-release fish to you.

But are your scientists not doing this toward a greater purpose?

Are you?

We did not do that to which you attribute us having done.

She turned. Cherko followed her direction to the two figures way in the back of the chamber.

The two figures.

They did everything? Cherko asked.

She turned back to Cherko.

We have no need to poke and prod in so primitive a manner. But we cannot control them. Cannot stop all their actions.

Who are they?

They are from your world. Your government.

I don't understand.

You will. Soon you will discover who they are, and what they have been doing. We will make information available to you.

What is going on here?

Keeping secrets secret. Fear and misinformation. You call it psychological warfare.

Psychological warfare? We're doing this to ourselves?

We have no need to terrorize your race. There are those, however, who do to keep their developments secret...to perpetuate fear among those who've discovered their secrets...misplace the blame.

What are you going to do with them?
Remove them.
What do you mean?
It is not your concern.
I don't understand—my parents—what has this to do with them—me?
You have been engineered. Tracked.
Engineered?
Your lives have never been your own.

"I was *abducted?*"

Eurphraeus nodded.

"Both of us—my mom *and* my dad—*me?* By *you?*"

"That was not me."

"Then—"

"There are others. Others of your own kind who perform abductions. Experimentation. They have been abducting your mother...we removed her from them many times. Have kept them from you. It is you they want."

"Me?"

"Genetic manipulation. Social engineering. We only periodically assess and communicate with you."

"Why? Why all this?"

"Your government has developed its own advanced technology without also developing the necessary advanced principles—you call them 'ethics'— that must also accompany and govern such development. Power. There are reasons."

"Why can't you tell me more?"

"You must remember. What else do you remember?"

"I'm not really sure any more, but—"

"Be sure. Remember how you arrived here."

"On this space station? In this...*thing?*"

"What is the first thing that comes to mind after hearing my words...

"*Now.*"

2

"This...this is crazy," Cherko said, staring out the window at Alda's office. It was snowing.

Cherko looked back Alda.

"So, I'm to believe I've been abducted throughout my life?"

Cherko reached up behind his neck.

"My God—there *is* a bump there!"

Cherko rushed to Alda's desk. Stood before it rubbing the back of his neck.

"Cut this out!"

"Don't be silly, Jimmy. Sit back down, please."

"I'm not being silly. There really is a bump back there—feel it!"

Cherko leaned over Alda's desk, insistent.

"*Feel it!*"

Alda touched it.

"Well?"

"I do not perform surgery."

"What is it?"

"It could be whatever you believe it to be."

"None of this makes sense," Cherko said, backing away while rubbing his neck. "Are you saying...that everything I told you...all my stories...are real? That I'm *not* hallucinating? I really *was* a lieutenant, a captain—the UFOs? Cause that's what *I* believe."

"What do you think it means?"

"Why am I paying you, for Chrissakes? Can't you come up with anything better than that? Anything at all?"

"It is not about me telling you what is or is not going on with you...it is about me helping you better understand yourself...your situation."

"And what is my 'situation,' Herr Doktor?"

"That is for you to define."

"*Dammit!*"

Cherko returned to the windows.

It continued to snow.

3

Cherko had left Alda's office and sat at the stop light on Austin Bluffs Boulevard, waiting to make a left turn. The snow was coming down pretty hard.

He had to have made it all up. He was a writer, had an active (if unmarketable) imagination. How far of a leap was it to say that he'd just made everything up? He was stuck in a dead-end tech writer's job. Was bored with his life. He had plenty of motive to try to find something "special" about himself. Anything...even if *fabricated*.

It's all about what you believe, *right?*

The light turned green and Cherko inserted himself into

A small chamber.

Cherko stood in a small chamber.

What is so hard to believe? came the thought from behind.

Cherko turned.

She stood alone.

You're real.

As much as you.

How do you do this? How do you remove me from my car in the middle of traffic, and what is it—

Unimportant. We need to clarify events.

To me? Why am I so important?

The future of your race depends upon itself. Without it, there is no future.

That doesn't even make—

The "sense" is in the meaning. We have made concessions in coming to your race. We do not agree with all your race is doing. We have tried to redirect efforts, but your government, though many within its ranks feel they mean well, is blind. There is so much more at stake than mere power and technology. So, we take our message to individuals.

What message?

Survival. Redirection. Expansion of consciousness through confirmation of our presence. Your race is focusing far too much on violence and power. Materialism. Immediate gratification. There are those who see the need for redirection, but are...eliminated. Discredited. Interfered with. Simply, those in power want to remain in power. Corruption is taking far too deep a hold. There are so many other paths to take, but those in power are blinded by their own ambition...their own corruption.

Why do you stay?

A greater good. If we can reach some of your race, we can better inform from within the masses, show hope exists.

Individuals.

Yes.

Unfortunately, much has been learned by those in power, and they no longer feel they require our assistance. Those of strong religious beliefs believe us evil. Literature and media have taken hold of and exacerbated fear. Fear is taking hold of minds. This is not by accident.

We are many millennia in advance of your race, and have seen the effects of too much science without conscience. Your technology outpaces your ability to deal with it. Wars do not just start...they are cultivated. Greed...cultivated. Fear...cultivated. A long time ago and once a part of your distant timelines, we behaved not unlike your scientists and explorers...we examined and categorized. But we learned from our mistakes. We attempted to guide your race away from these same mistakes, but they are not open to us.

So, it is not you who are mutilating cattle and snatching and grabbing us?

We have no need for such prosaic behavior.

You brought me here just to explain yourselves?

She studied Cherko, and slightly cocked her bulbous head. *We've brought you nowhere.*

Cherko flew through the green light at Nevada and Austin Bluffs, startled so violently he nearly sideswiped the car next to him.

Cherko spastically merged into the far right lane, then pulled off into a parking lot. He yanked on the brake and gripped the steering wheel.

And once again sweat like Niagara Falls.

Chapter Twenty-Seven

1

Colorado Springs, CO
4 November 2010
1633 Hours Mountain Time

Cherko slid to a stop in the garage, alongside Erica's 2001 Honda.

He wasn't...*right*.

Something was terrible wrong with him, he felt it, and it made him sick to his stomach.

What had just happened?

Cherko hit the garage door switch as he entered the house.

"Erica! *Erica!*"

No answer. But he saw the message light blinking on the answering machine.

The thought *did people still use these things?* entered his mind, but he dismissed it.

Cherko rushed past the message machine, up a short flight of stairs, then hooked a sharp right to enter the third floor of the tri-level...and ran smack into a wall.

"What the—"

He backed up; touched the unexpected barrier.

A wall where stairs should be! *There used to be an upstairs hallway right here!*

Cherko shook his head.

"*Erica!*" he continued calling into the wall. He spun around, again calling her name, and again returned to the wall...

And found a hallway.

One that led to their bedroom and back office.

Without another thought he shot up the stairs, down the hall, and into what should have been Erica's home office.

But no Erica.

He spun around.

It wasn't even her office...but a spare room.

Had the house shrunk while he'd been gone?

Was he losing his mind?

"*Erica!* Where the hell—"

He hurried to their bedroom.

No Erica.

Looked in her closet.

Empty.

Went to his closet.

Clothes.

Spun around to the bed.

There were no pictures of either himself nor Erica. The bedroom was sparse, only basic nightstands, lamps, and a phone. No pictures. No closet full of women's clothing.

No Erica!

Cherko left the room and hurried back down the hallway, down both sets of stairs, past the still blinking answering machine, and out into the garage.

And no 2001 Honda.

Only *his* vehicle.

His legs buckled and he grabbed hold of the railing. Slowly backing out of the garage he reentered the basement living room.

"What…what have I…what's—"

But the words didn't form…*wouldn't* form. Wouldn't leave his brain nor reach his mouth. Forming them—giving his crazy thoughts validity—would mean there was something wrong. Not right. That there was—and most probably never *had* been—any Erica at all.

"*But I remember her…met her at the apartment complex…*"

Cherko closed the door as he continued to slowly back into the living room.

The answering machine's message light continued to blink.

Who used these things anymore?

He did.

He went to the machine and hit play. It beeped twice, then clicked off. No message.

Cherko stabbed "Erase." Stared at the machine.

Erase.

He closed his eyes and rubbed the back of his neck.

That bump was still there.

Was his life being erased?

What had happened at that shrink's office? *What the hell had been done to him?*

Cherko snatched the cordless phone, hit "Talk," and put it to his ear.

Silence.

"Who's there?" he asked. "*Who's out there, goddammit?*"

More silence.

He tossed the phone onto the stand. Looked to his office.

His manuscript. His *story*. He had a manuscript to finish.

Was the story *real?*

That's what the shrink implied.

Were UFOs real?

He'd supposedly just been in one, though he'd been barreling down Austin Bluffs like everyone else. Almost hit another car. Had pulled into the garage alongside his *wife's car*. A car that no longer existed and that had belonged to a woman who also no longer—if ever—existed.

Except for his story.

He entered his office.

That was still there.

His laptop was on.

Cherko sat behind the desk.

What was his manuscript about?

Right. A guy who never quite got what he wanted out of life, but who seemed to have gotten into some very big trouble with the government. A guy who was supposed to be in his *future*.

A guy...who seemed to be *him*.

If any of this was true...even a little patch of it...and he was writing it...could he *change* things? Write how he wanted things to turn out? Hadn't that been what he'd been doing all this time?

It wasn't like he'd been writing about this with the thought—the *intent*—to change the outcome of his life. He'd just been doing what had come naturally...an organic science fiction creation using events from his own life.

Or had it been his life that had been using events from his manuscript?

Cherko began typing....

2

"I'm afraid."

"Of what?" Eurphraeus asked.

"I don't know. There's something about what happens next...I'm not sure I want to find out."

"It has already occurred, has it not?"

"Yes."

"You are who you are, where you are—*now*—correct?"

"Am I?"

"Then what is there to fear? What is done...is *done*. You are where you are—"

"Does this place seem smaller to you?"

"It possesses the same dimensions it has always possessed. It is what it is."

Cherko shivered.

"That race, the one of…*She*…they are in our future?"

"They are."

"Were they really just trying to help?"

"Yes."

"How do you fit into all this?"

"You must first go where you fear to go, James."

"No one calls me that."

"No, no one does."

"I'm feeling rather claustrophobic."

"It will pass."

Cherko looked nervously about the module.

"Something isn't right in here."

"No, something is not."

3

Captain Cherko lay on a narrow slab composed of deep blue flecks within some weirdly translucent material. All worry, all stress immediately evaporated from him. He felt something very much like a magnet running throughout his body, and at a cellular-level. It was extremely prickly, almost painful, like a severely cranked ultrasound machine. Colors assaulted him, shades of colors he'd never known existed, symbols and *numbers*. Good God, he saw it all…

Just before he blacked out.

Cherko stood in a chamber that seemed all too familiar. A table was off to his right, a prone form upon it. An open drawer was at his feet at the base of a nearby wall.

Something just didn't *feeeel* right.

He looked around the dimly lit chamber. Images…so much more *intense*, brighter. He felt…different. Not bad different, just…*different* different.

Not all there.

Light…wispy…*agile*. Had a severe case of feeling quite beside himself. A disquieting sensation of feeling…*unseated*. Loose, as if he wore clothing several sizes too large—

This will pass.

He turned.

That will pass, She again said.

My hands feel—

Cherko froze. His *hands—there were only four digits!*

Cherko brought the hands—*his* hands!—up before him.

Hands that only had four digits and were thin and slender and greenish gray!

What have you done to me!

Cherko advanced on She. Clumsy and dizzy, he almost tripped over the open drawer.

We are in the process of completing your training, Captain.

What training?

As Cherko moved he felt his limbs flop about as if they'd fallen asleep. Cherko—at least he *thought* he was Cherko—bumped up against the wall.

We have incorporated your consciousness into the form we wear. The form we use in exploring your corporeal existence.

Cherko jumped back. As clumsy as he behaved, he was amazed at the agility he now possessed. There was all this speed with hardly any mass.

She continued. *We have been training your mind since before you were born. In utero.*

Cherko looked to his arms, his legs; looked to them as if separated from them...fascinated at the—pardon the pun—*alien* feel to them. Waved them in the air about him, "testing" them. He still felt as if he were trying to control sleep-deadened limbs in apparel two-sizes too large, but was now more fascinated by the experience than afraid. The tingling sensations quickly gave way to feeling and control. He touched his face with the long, slender, four-digit, appendages. Looked to the mesh-like composition of his new skin.

How is this possible?

What we are is far more than corporeal composition, but to travel within your framework requires such a form. A physical form. This is what we use, as you use clothing. Our state of existence is so dissimilar from your own that this form assists us to better interrelate to your state of existence on many levels beyond the obviously physically humanoid appearance.

Where is my body? Cherko asked.

It is in a stasis condition similar to that of sleep, She stood aside and directed a hand to the prone form on the narrow table.

For all practical purposes—to *him*.

Cherko, still somewhat clumsily, approached his body.

It is held under a localized energy field that allows it to exist while your consciousness travels elsewhere.

How do you do this? Cherko asked. He looked to his form. On the table.

Him.

Like a curious dog he cocked his head side to side. It lent a peculiar out-of-body sensation as he looked to his sleeping form. "He" breathed slowly, very slowly, rhythmically, in his olive drab flight suit. The name "Cherko" on his flight suit felt nostalgically distant. He looked to the senior space badge insignia sewn over his left-chest pocket (and unconsciously touched his current left breast area), and his silver-piinged blue flight cap stuffed into his flight-suit pocket at his left calf.

This is me? Cherko asked.

To be precise, it is the form you wore.

Cherko brought his face closer to his sleeping body. His *shell.* Touched the body before him.

This was him…yet not.…

He brought the same hand to his new body.

His mind felt a longing attachment to that prone form before him, but felt a part of the form he was currently inhabiting as well. A bastardized definition of bilocation. His mind still felt the attachment to the him on the slab—the only lifelong intimacy of flesh he'd ever known—but also couldn't deny the experience of standing *outside* himself, in this other…existence.

Gave new meaning to out-of-body experiences.

That is what this really was. A Frankenstein's monster transfer in the oddest of parodies. He looked to the hand that had touched both forms. That four-fingered appliance.

Yes, *appliance.*

The shift in consciousness into your current form is much more than a physical bilocation, She said. *As you are discovering—or rediscovering—it is a far more foundational paradigm shift. It involves, in your terms, a mental, emotional, and psychic shift. A creation of additional neuronal pathways not only in the form you are inhabiting, but also upon your return into your indigenous casing. When you return you will be—as you are now—more than you were when you first departed.*

Cherko looked to She.

I'm not sure I—

You will assimilate as you experience.

Cherko stepped away from the table. Gave himself a really good once over, twisting and examining arms, legs…feeling his head and neck. Though the neck was slender in appearance, it was more than adequate in function. There was little mass to these bodies, but quite enough strength. The oversized feeling of wearing "clothing" too large for him was now all but gone. He began to feel more comfortable in his own…*skin.*

Clichés.

He looked down between his legs.

There is no need for genitalia. Nor will you find a digestive system. Our forms have no need for either.

Then how do they work? *Bodies—as I, we Humans, understand them—require energy sources of some kind, assimilation of energy, its* elimination. *How do they operate if they don't "eat" in some form—*

Part of the difficulty in our two Races communicating is the fact that we communicate in completely different baselines—alphabets, if you will. There are certain things we cannot adequately communicate to your Race, because your Race does not yet possess the necessary *neural structure and development to conceptualize our responses. There is no...“Rosetta Stone”...for which your Race can relate...*translate. *In the most simplest of responses, our forms operate off the energy of life itself, much like your Earth is heated not only from your Sun but through the internal heat of your planet's molten core. Think of our energy as a battery. The life of each of your Race's cells operate on the same level, if you remove the consumable structure of food and water. This appears contradictory, but it is the closest I can come to describing our form's function. Some in your world are approaching this concept, calling it hyperdimensional physics.*

It almost makes sense. Cherko felt what equated to a smile from She.

So, if you are so advanced why do you even need a body?

We do not require *use of corporeal composition, it is an option to our existence and better focuses our consciousness. Consciousness and form—matter—are different forms of the same energy. Taking on the physical “suit” of the body better focuses our consciousness into corporeal existence. We use it to certain advantages previously described, mainly as a cooperative mechanism in which to interface with your Race. But as we use this form, we also use forms you cannot see, due to your specifically focused perceptions.*

You're doing other things in other forms as we speak?

Our interaction necessitates addressing these other forms in order to co-operate. It is like you looking at yourself, but also looking at an x-ray, or thermal view of yourself as well. It's all you, but you only perceive a specific wavelength of view.

Can you—slip, as you call it—other humans into your form like this?

We have guided you through your life in an attempt to expand your growth. It takes careful...instruction...to perform in this manner. It is not something that is entered into lightly, to use your terms. Human composition—its mind, on the whole—is not prepared, nor structured for what we have performed with you. You are...an exception. An engineered consideration. What we have chosen to do is dangerous if not properly, meticulously, performed. It has never been performed on anyone else of your Race. We have done this to you once before, have erased its memory for obvious reasons. This is your second time in this form. You are performing remarkably well, but your mind has been carefully groomed over the course of your lifetime. We have given you increased...attention. We could not do this to just anyone in your line of consciousness. But, when something is done to any of your Race, all of your Race benefit. There are subtle levels of communication performed, new neurological pathways opened and addressed. Shared.

Now...please follow us.

4

The screen—or false—memory to Colonel “Buzz” Hanscomb, as he piloted the X-30 trans-atmospheric vehicle toward orbit injection, was that he and Major Bill, “Skunk,” Anderson were about to execute an experimental sequence of events: piloting an air-breathing aircraft into space. Clad in their silvery pressurized astronaut suits, they cross-checked and verified all system configurations against checklists. Major Anderson, strapped in behind Hanscomb, confirmed all systems were a "go" for orbit injection. Hanscomb radioed Groom Lake.

At least that was what Colonel Hanscomb *remembered*.

What had actually occurred, however, was that Colonel Hanscomb had been alone in that TAV's cockpit.

He'd made that trans-atmospheric trajectory into orbit solo, and had been ready to deliver a payload secreted away in the belly of his hybrid platform. A payload that *contained* Major Bill Anderson, and to which Colonel Hanscomb had had no knowledge. The payload, an unmanned space vehicle, was anything but unmanned. The USV—this USV—was an X-variant. A manned mini-capsule that was moments short of destruction. Faulty engine design would have been the destruction's cause. This USV configuration was designed to insert a human into orbit, specifically, to the ERO manned orbiting laboratory.

"Roger, Star Bright, you're cleared for injection," had been Ground Control's response.

"Copy."

Hanscomb flicked up the red-guarded switch protection cap on his fly-by-wire stick that would have activated orbit injection. Once in orbit, he was to release his payload.

Hanscomb flicked the switch and was slammed back into his seat. Before he knew it, blue sky had been replaced with black space, and Hanscomb was able to see on-orbit air glow.

"Ground, orbit injection confirmed," Hanscomb relayed.

Hanscomb looked outside his suddenly hushed cockpit.

"Control, Star Bright; preparing payload release."

"Roger, Star Bright."

Hanscomb was just about to initiate payload release when all the hairs on the back of his neck stood on end.

Both Buzz and Skunk should have gone up in a brilliant star light, star bright silent flash had not something else also been watching and tracking their progress—and inhibiting their memories.

Cherko-as-alien was led through the ship by She and the attendant. Its curved corridors were narrow and small...perfectly sized for the alien form, a form, Cherko also noticed, that glided surprisingly quick and gracefully. And as he was guided through the ship, he noticed feeling much more at ease within his new form. And he still felt a curious link back to his other body.

Okay, that last thought was just *weird*.

His *real* body. A part of his mind objected, while another part seemed to accept this new form as uniquely "his." It was an unnerving psychic construct.

There is, indeed, a link back to your body, She assured as they walked.

Link?

Each inhabited body is uniquely attuned to the consciousness in which it inhabits. The mind and body both work on each other to focus each other. It is a universal constant, if you will. Each cell possesses a cellular consciousness. There are no "dead" cells. It is an impossibility. When your consciousness inhabits a form, yours or any other, it merges with that consciousness and forever changes it. Matter's consciousness changes the consciousness that inhabits it. It is unavoidable and natural. Like any other event you experience in your Human line of consciousness, you are never the same after any experience. All things change all things, and change is constant. In all multiverses.

Why are you—why all this—me?

Cherko felt an amused avoidance of the question. They came to a door and stopped. She and attendant turned to Cherko.

In this room is yet another experience. You are to remain quiet. Merely observe. Reasons for this encounter may not appear immediately evident, but you must trust us. You will find that one of the abilities of inhabiting our form is its immediate continence. You can direct yourself to perform a function and it is much more easily regulated. We ask that you regulate yourself in this manner.

Understood.

She and attendant approached the door, which opened by a sudden decomposition of sorts, as parts of the door pulled apart to open and they all passed through. Cherko-as-alien looked back to the door as it closed behind them and watched it recompose, as those same parts came back together again.

Inside, Cherko found a darkened room and an immediate sense of relief. There was an incredible sense of calm and relaxation.

And there were forms in this room.

Upright and on narrow tables similar to that which his other form currently resided.

Human forms.

Cherko remained behind She and attendant. What was the attendant's name, Cherko wondered, and was immediately supplied a name that was best represented as "Qxuill."

Cherko followed She and Qxuill into the room, passing the humans lying on the narrow slabs. As Cherko passed them, he looked to them. One stared straight up into the chamber's ceiling, but as Cherko's alien eyes diverted to the other, the one closest to him, a female, he was surprised to see she looked directly at him. Tracked him as he made his way past her.

"Help me...."

Cherko sensed her fear. He extended an alien hand to the woman, and with it, found (since he wasn't supposed to speak) he directed an additional sense of calm to her. A feeling that everything would be all right, and that there was no need to worry. *No need to fear.*

Then he touched her.

He saw the woman close her eyes; felt her settle into an even more tranquil state of mind.

Cherko continued onward with She and Qxuill, who, he also noticed, had observed his actions.

I said nothing, Cherko sent, amused with himself. He sensed a translated feeling of "okay" return from She.

They came upon the other Humans who sat toward the rear of the chamber. They sat on blocks—seats—that extended from the walls themselves. They all appeared slowed...confused. Cherko recognized two men in silver astronaut suits. She and Qxuill stopped before these two. Cherko saw images of the two men flying an experimental aircraft...no, it was more than an *air*craft...it was a *trans*-atmospheric platform.

We trust you are both well, She addressed.

The colonel, "Buzz" Hanscomb, Cherko discovered, got to his feet.

"We are."

The other officer, Major Bill Anderson, remained seated, staring off into space.

We are sorry about your vehicle's destruction, She continued. *Your engine and payload designs were faulty.*

"Payload? What payload?" Hanscomb said. "I was the pilot, I'd know if something was—"

There was a payload installed the previous night?

Hanscomb paused. "Yes...a laser range finder package. But that was an experimental package...to range satellites on-orbit." Hanscomb looked to Cherko. Cherko found he knew all kinds of things about the Colonel. That he had been top of his Elizabethtown, N.Y. high school class, had been in the Civil Air Patrol as a kid. Top of his class at the Air Force Academy. Top ratings as both a pilot and test pilot. Had a huge love for biplanes. Father had flown B-17s in WWII, his grandfather had flown Nieuport 28s in WWI. Twice divorced. Three kids. Flying was his life's blood.

Cherko then directed his attention to Anderson. The Major was a different story. He was a bookworm, a religious man. A Flight Engineer. Flying was a necessary part of his job—which he loved—but he was into the *engineering* end of things, not so much *piloting*. He'd also been at the top of his schooling, including Flight Test school and engineering operations. But he identified more with slide rules and engineering schema than flying. Flying was not his life's blood.

And he was *scared.*

He also loved baseball, an avid Red Sox fan (the Sox...founded in 1901, originally known as the Boston Americans...played the first World Series against the Pittsburgh Pirates in 1903—and won...took the World Series in

1912, 1915, 1916, and 1918…since then—and largely attributed to the "Curse of the Bambino"—have been in one of the longest championship droughts in history…).

Yes, he knew baseball.

It was told to you that it was, She continued to Hanscomb, *But it was actually a test delivery platform to an orbiting spy observatory.*

"A spy space station?"

Yes. An agency of which you have no knowledge.

Cherko picked up on this agency. He was very familiar with it.

Hanscomb looked to Cherko. Cherko felt that Hanscomb sensed a familiarity about him. Cherko knew they didn't know each other, but what Hanscomb was sensing, was, indeed, *Cherko.* The *human* Cherko…the part of him that was human. Hanscomb kept looking between She and Qxuill and Cherko as they conversed.

"Why should I believe you? You're the one holding me prisoner," Hanscomb quipped.

You are not a prisoner. We are holding you because your vessel was destroyed. We could have allowed you both to perish with its destruction.

Hanscomb paused. Looked back to Anderson, who continued to stare at the floor.

"What have you done to him?" Hanscomb asked.

He is having difficulty assimilating where he is and what's happened. He is certain he must have died. There is no other logical solution in his mind. Because of his religious faith, he feels that he must be in some kind of a purgatory because he can't possibly believe all this has happened as it has been experienced.

Hanscomb continued to stare at who he'd thought had been his Flight Engineer. On the *ground.* Cherko could feel Hanscomb's gears turning. The practical Test Pilot weighing all the data and making decisions. Instantaneous, life-changing decisions. That was his life. Risks and decision-making.

"So, if you aren't going to kill us—what's next? I don't suppose you can just send us back, huh?"

Unfortunately we cannot. Among other reasons are that it would bring about obvious and justifiable alarm within your government, since your total destruction was observed and recorded. But we will return you.

"How?"

We will reinsert you into your world…but the price is that you will not remember any of this, because we will insert you before any of this occurred.

"Time travel? For real? I'll get to live my life over again?"

Cherko noted the excitement in Hanscomb's voice. He was ready and willing to live his entire life over again in an instant, even if it meant going back through all he'd just been through.

We have already done that.

Not only did Hanscomb pause in mid thought—so did Cherko.

"*Already* done *that?*" Hanscomb looked between Cherko and Anderson.

She nodded. *That is part of your Flight Engineer's conundrum. Part of him remembers this as much as he denies the experience. In his terms, "it does not compute." He is having great difficulty dealing with it. We allowed the original reinsertion. It was necessary for other reasons.*

"It doesn't make sense—"

It is hard to perfectly convey the true temporal aspects of reality without sounding contradictory in your *terms.*

Here Cherko picked up on one of those reasons She implied.

Him.

This was necessary, in no small part, as an instructional mechanism for *him*, Cherko saw. To see this. Be a part of this. *Learn*. He also picked up on that there were necessary links to both of the flight crew members for their own reasons, the threads of which he felt himself able to follow…but he instead returned to the conversation. This was another very interesting ability…the ability to follow lines of consciousness to their actual *sources*. A veritable mental—psychic—library.

"*You really can travel though time?*" Hanscomb asked.

This time we need to reinsert you both to another continuum. Another probability. We give you your choice as long as it does not impose upon the events that brought you here.

"Choice? Different continuums?"

Anderson looked up.

She, Qxuill, and Cherko observed the flyers.

You can pick an earlier or later future probability, an entirely different life path than you have currently followed. Anything that does not lead to the current time continuum.

"But…how is that possible? You can really *do* that?"

That, in your terms, you have no need-to-know. Please, make your decision, Colonel.

She looked to Anderson.

Major.

Hanscomb turned away and paced the chamber. Anderson looked back down to the floor, then to Hanscomb. Cherko knew Anderson wouldn't pick a flying career. Twice was more than enough for him.

What would Cherko do if he had a chance to re-live life over again, let alone a *third* time? These two had lived their lives testing dangerous, experimental aircraft and "died" doing it. And when given a second chance, *had done the exact same thing over again*. Lived their lives *twice*. It was an incredible testament to their spirit.

And now they were being given that precious gift *again*.

Hanscomb came back to them. There was a fire and surety in his step.

"The future, well, for some strange reason, I've felt I've already lived as far into that as I care to go. And who's to say, at that point, when you drop me off, that I didn't originate back then and just got to visit *now?*

"High technology," Hanscomb continued, "is exciting…but I want to *fly*. Really *fly*. Not the technology flying the craft, but *me*. I want gears and fabric, the feel of the wind in my face. I've lived more lives than any man should be allowed to."

He looked to Anderson, who still stared at the floor.

Major? She asked.

"Baseball," he said, still staring at the floor. He looked up to them. "I want to sell peanuts…and beer. At Fenway Park. I don't ever want to fly again."

She nodded. Without looking to Cherko, She and Qxuill turned and left. Cherko remained a moment longer, looking to Anderson then Hanscomb. Hanscomb looked excited. Paced with a look of epiphany on his face. When he saw Cherko still observing him, he approached.

"I feel as if I know you. You feel…*familiar*…," Hanscomb said. Cherko stared back with his huge, deep, dark eyes.

Then left the room.

Chapter Twenty-Eight

1

How do you plan on doing that? Cherko asked.

She and Qxuill stopped in the hallway and looked to Cherko.

How can you place these guys—or anyone—into another time? How is that possible?

Time is not linear nor immutable. This ship…we travel not only through distance, but through time.

But to…insert the Colonel, for example, into an earlier time. How can that be possible?

She regarded Cherko for a long moment.

There are many things which we can do that may appear impossible. They appear impossible because of your point-of-view's perspective. Your sciences are limited not because of any so-called laws, but because of chosen focuses on certain perspectives at the expense of other entirely valid points of view.

She and Qxuill continued down the hall, Cherko following.

The Colonel said I felt "familiar" to him. What did he mean?

He sensed your Human connection. Within our ships, if subjects

Subjects?

If subjects allow themselves, they can sense more than they have traditionally been accustomed to. The ship—us—we act as catalysts. Of course, if subjects are truly and deeply afraid, then they will experience fear, and on truly unimaginable levels. Simply put, we bring out your darkest and brightest inner predilections.

She stopped.

It is one more reason for our measured contact with your Race. We attempted contact with one of your more well-known personalities, attempted extended and in-depth cooperation with this individual, but he was too immersed in deep-rooted fears—fears the individual tried desperately and unsuccessfully to address and banish—but we could no longer progress and terminated contact. He was not ready. This was someone who was well-aware of his situation, well-spoken, and even willing to work with us, yet the individual still could not get past his fears. Contact by us must be extremely measured and considered. There have been too many perpetuated distortions. It is not something we execute without due consideration—but are willing to explore.

Why do you take such an interest in us?

Why do you take such an interest in your world?

She continued down the hallway several more paces before continuing.

You do not need me to answer your questions. You—your Race—knows its own answers. The problems lie in your Race's continued focus on certain aspects of inquisition at the expense of others. Do not take this to mean the requirement to totally disregard the physical, but there is so much more to be learned from more open perceptions.

2

The trio returned to the control room; the "bridge," as Cherko thought of it.

Much of what we are showing you may not be immediately comprehendible. But it has all been calculated to stimulate your potential. We are not necessarily here to give answers…but to form questions which will lead you to your own answers, She said. *As we have iterated, what is done to any one of you advances your entire Race. It is most unfortunate that there are those who are so afraid of us, but in their fear are also afraid of themselves. In the beginning we thought we could help many who feared us. We quickly found that there are some in your perspective that simply are not ready. Not willing. But there are also elements within your government that perpetuate a culture of fear— intentionally obfuscate. There is little we can do, except to approach those we can—on individual levels—such as with you.*

3

Cherko and She entered another chamber, this one much more darkly lit. They stood in the background as several other aliens surrounded Colonel Hanscomb. Anderson already had been delivered to his Fenway park, which had been an easy delivery. He liked the present and just wanted to be around baseball, so they deposited him in Boston to work at Fenway. Cherko observed what the beings around Hanscomb were doing right now, and had already done with Anderson. There was a mental "reformatting" done within Anderson's mind. Almost and exactly like a computer hard-drive wipe. Cherko picked up that there could never truly be a total rewrite of each individual, but there were certain things these beings could do, similar to erasing a hard drive's index. It went beyond memory, and though he could understand what they were doing as they did it, he found it hard to translate to the human side of his intellect within this being's skin. It seemed they…went out into Time and "pulled in" certain events that would make up

Anderson's new life. Aligned elements as basic as his *cells* to the different time period. Created a new identity and reality *surrounding* him.

Or made him "fit" into this new identity

And they had done all this mentally.

Though it made sense to him as he observed…he could not easily translate it back to his Human self. It really was the highly advanced metaphysical concept to which She had earlier referred. It was as if life was morphed, reworked, or shaped around *Anderson*…or the other way around. Both. Perhaps it was his Human consciousness within this alien form, but whatever it was, it was hard to wrap his head (as large as it was…) around it. What it boiled down to was that Anderson—and now Hanscomb—were both made to fit their new lives. It just didn't quite make sense *how*.

The alien attendants completed reformatting the Colonel. Even in this new body of his, which was, curiously, feeling more and more comfortable, Cherko couldn't understand all that was accomplished—just that it had been. The ship, he also felt, had also arrived at 1919 Earth. That made Cherko feel a little better. Hanscomb wouldn't be inserted into a war. He would be a barnstormer—how cool was that? He'd have *memories* of having flown during the war, but would not have actually been placed within it. Other pilots would remember him. Paperwork would confirm him as having been there. Everything had been taken care of. And Hanscomb, Cherko picked up on, was good with all of it. He just wanted to *fly*.

We have arrived at the coordinates where we will deliver our Colonel, She informed. *We have arrived in the southern end of the state of Illinois. We will leave Colonel Hanscomb with a biplane and necessary memories and capacity for this new life.*

You left him with a biplane? How? Cherko asked.

We created one.

Is it there?

It awaits.

How'd you—

Another ship, much larger than ours, wherein which lies such capability. Come.

Cherko-as-alien stood among the handful of real aliens (as opposed to himself) that grouped about Hanscomb. They stood in the middle of a large field in the dead of a pleasant summer's night. It was hot and humid, he noticed, but neither bothered him. Fireflies busied about and they were surrounded by the stereophonic sound of crickets. Fog danced at their legs and feet. Cherko saw the real aliens still conversing with Hanscomb over by his new Curtiss JN-4D "Jenny."

This is where we shall leave him, She said, still looking to Hanscomb and not Cherko. *He will be left with all the innate information he will need to survive in this continuum. He will fit in exceedingly well.*

Cherko and She watched Hanscomb nod to his alien attendants. Watched as he then made his way toward them, attendants in tow. Hanscomb stopped before She.

"Thank you," Hanscomb said. Cherko felt an intense emotional sincerity radiate from him. "I don't know how you do it, but *thank* you. I'm looking forward to this."

She nodded.

"And I'll really remember nothing of any of it? You?"

Nothing, Colonel.

Hanscomb shook his head. "Don't know how you do it." Hanscomb looked to Cherko-as-alien.

"And you...I wish I knew what it was about you that feels so familiar. But, thank you, too."

Cherko looked to She, then Hanscomb.

I have not done anything, but wish you well.

Then Cherko let slip—or did so intentionally—an image. An image of him flying satellites.

Hanscomb's eyes went wide and his mouth opened—then She touched him, and Hanscomb's gaze went blank.

It was time.

Hanscomb turned away from them and casually headed back toward his new life and plane. Midway there, he stopped and gazed up into the stars. He stayed that way as Cherko and the aliens departed.

4

We want to show you something, She said.

5

Cherko-as-alien looked out the view screen.

We're in Roswell, aren't we?

Yes, She answered.

You're going to show me what really happened?

She said nothing at first.

You've taken us back to that day, haven't you—1947.

We and others like us have always been watching your Race. We've always remained in the background, and for good reason. En masse, your kind has never been ready for who and what we are. Who and what you are. But on this night, something changed.

What?

Observe.

Cherko-as-alien looked to the screen. They were over the New Mexican desert at an altitude of sixty-thousand feet.

Something shot across their view. They tracked it. Locked onto it. Cherko watched as the image was brought into focus on the screen.

A UFO.

But this UFO had *U.S. Army* stamped on it.

Cherko turned to She.

It's true—all I'd read was true?

Your government had developed a primitive version of our craft from its extraction of German scientists after your second world war. Brought them over to your country. Embedded them in total secrecy into the North- and Southwest to continue their work. Unknown to even the most secret of your government agencies, they created ships extremely close to ours in functional capability, but not yet near our current capabilities.

She turned to him.

But that was not long in the making.

At this point in your history, She continued, *they only had rudimentary flight— but it was highly successful. For your scientists, it was an incredible breakthrough. Capabilities only heretofore dreamed. Vertical flight to the edges of the atmosphere, sustained speeds factors in advance of their fastest conventional aircraft—*

We'd created this? Us—humans?

Yes.

They were tested in areas of the country already controlled in secrecy, like your desert Southwest. We'd been observing. That was when we decided to intervene. To make an overt act of our presence known.

She looked back to the screen.

There were several of the U.S. Army flying HEUFOs darting back and forth over the desert. Not all the HEUFOs were circular. Some had aerodynamically shaped surfaces, some fins and vanes.

This is incredible. We developed this? On our own, Cherko repeated, staring at the screen in awe. *And back in the 1940s? It's almost too much to believe.*

We made ourselves known to your scientists on this night. We began by allowing ourselves to be seen from a distance—like now. Hovering just outside their area of operations. We initially allowed them to come to us.

Even as they spoke, Cherko saw one of the Army disks pause in mid flight. Hover. It clearly saw something—

Then we'd fly off, demonstrating our capabilities. We continued like that for a period of time before actively participating in their flight activity.

Cherko-as-alien stood in the bridge. Continued to watch the screen. Right this moment they were doing what She had told them they'd done in *history* books—*but were again doing it real time.*

Not only watching history in the making, *but recreating it.*

Roswell, 1947. The birthplace of all things-UFO. Ground zero.

And all after having deposited one Major Anderson in Fenway Park in present time—the future?—and one Colonel Hanscomb in an Illinois field back in 1919. She and her kind could've just let both perish in their aircraft's destruction—but hadn't.

And now he found himself here. In the cradle of all UFO lore.

Cherko—the him inside this form—shook his head.

Aliens. Spaceships. *Human*-developed spaceships.

He'd never had believed it had he not lived it...seen it with his own eyes—alien or otherwise.

Had it really all started with Roswell? Had that been the Honest-to-God starting point? Had that crash—and what had caused that crash—back on that stormy night in July of 1947 really initiated all this, or had these beings really been around long before? *Way* before. When you looked at the way these beings behaved, as they moved through time like going from one room to the next, really, what was "time," anyway? It was more like a destination, a "coordinate point." If they really could flit through it like he had just witnessed—hell, *experienced*—then there was no "start" to anything. It all just folded in on itself, like that David Gerrold book he'd read way back (and what did *that* now mean?) in his youth, *The Man Who Folded Himself.* A time-traveling guy.

Time really had no meaning. Or it did...but just not in the way we—the Humans with which he was still, vaguely, associated—recognized and used it.

And would you just look at him? He was an alien for Chrissakes! Was wearing this body of a *Gray*. He was now one himself—yet not.

How'd they do all this?

How could one set of physics work for humans and another for aliens? *How did this all work?*

He really hadn't much of a clue, but somehow they had transferred his consciousness not only across bodies, but *species* (that is, if this "appliance" he wore *was* a living, breathing species, and not just some inorganic suit he'd been slipped into).

The implications were staggering.

At first being in this alien form had been like breaking in new gloves, but things fit pretty nicely now. He even felt comfortable in his pseudo-alien mind. And to look back at his own body like he had—*from the outside*—not any mirror or downward-directed gazes, was consciousness expanding. He couldn't explain it, but that alone *did* something to him. Touching this other him with an alien hand that was him *did* something to him.

And couple this with his work in New Mexico. Well, there was a lot to assimilate—providing these beings let him remember any of it.

But, what now?

He really didn't want to go back to that job. All this made his work for the government pitiful. Childish.

The government just didn't know what they were messing with.

Or did they?

He'd always pained over what would cause the government to so zealously guard what they'd found out in that desert back in '47. What was worth them not only threatening people, but out and out making them *disappear*? What could be so damned important that his own kind—Humans—would kill each other to keep something so damned secret? Make Forrestal literally go over the edge? What if—

Before he realized just what he was doing, and like all Human-created stray thoughts, Cherko-as-alien reached out into the consciousness of the alien ship—for just a fraction of a moment in which he wasn't even sure if he was wholly serious about doing what he'd ever so briefly *considered* doing—and wondered if he really could control this ship with his mind. Take it for a spin. Especially this souped-up alien version of it, maybe even take it down into the HEUFO fray and mess around a little...

She and Qxuill, who had been observing Cherko, took no action. There was a loud explosion, a massive and colossal concussion...and all went dark...

6

HEUFOs and UFOs.

Humans. Aliens.

Impact. There had been an *impact*.

Standing in the She ship—*not* standing in the ship.

HEUFO. Aboard a *HEUFO?*

Stood among his own kind—*humans*—aboard the HEUFO. Turned to She, but looked into the eyes of a *human*.

Surprise. Incomprehension.

Quantum entanglement.

Two places at the same time.

Went toward human.

Fear!

Going to crash, human shouted, *going to impact formation!*

Evasive maneuvers—evasive—

Body on fire.

Mind *aflame!*

Pull craft out. Trying to pull ship away—away from humans. Each and every cell within his body, his consciousness—*alien self, or the human side of his alien self?*—torn apart. A trillion-trillion matter-anti-matter reactions...

Unable to think, *control....*

Annihilation.

* * *

Cherko awoke, dazed. The always level control room floor was now on a severe bank, and there was the odor of what he swore was ozone and things electrical. Cherko felt unwieldy. Clumsy again. Like he'd been shaken out of the body, but as he checked himself, he still wore the alien form. Groggily, he pushed up from the canted angle of the ship's deck.

Something was different...*really* different...about the ship. There was—

There was a huge tear in its side!

Cherko got to his feet.

Where were She and Qxuill?

The other members of the crew—*what had happened?*

No.

Oh, no.

What had he done?

A wave of sadness enveloped him.

This can't be!

Cherko rushed to the tear in the ship's hull and peered out into the desert, pitch-black night.

Something wasn't right about this.

Different.

Bodies. There were bodies (*what kind?*) scattered about the bridge...smoke, and destruction...

We're out here, came a calm, telepathic message from She.

Cherko climbed through the gaping tear and landed on the still warm sand of New Mexico desert.

What happened? Cherko asked.

An accident, She sent. *Most of the crew are dead...dying.*

You're dying, aren't you?, Cherko sent.

Our dying is not your dying.

Where are you? Why can't I see you?

We've been separated.

Separated—

A chill ran through Cherko's Human side.

Oh, my God, Cherko sent.

He looked to the ground. To the debris littering the ground, the desert sand. There were fizzling parts, partially burning debris.

More bodies. Two of them.

Where are you? Cherko asked, as he came upon the mangled bodies before him. The bodies that had been thrown out of the craft behind him, through the tear in its side. The side of the craft, to which Cherko looked back to see had

"*Army*" written on it, the "U.S." part torn off. Cherko stopped before the charred and mangled bodies before him.

Human bodies.

West, She sent.

Cherko-as-alien was alone. Alone in 1947, standing among a handful of dead HEUFO operators.

Humans.

It wasn't your fault, She sent. *There was...a glitch, you'd call it. A problem with compatibility, with the ship's consciousness and your own. Yours in the* alien *form. Something went wrong. Ship occupied the same space and time as human ships. Repelled human crafts but they impacted each other.*

Integrated with each other.

Crashed. Your lack of proficiency also caused us to impact another of our *crafts and obliterate it.*

I did this?

It is not your fault, She insisted. *Had already happened in your terms.*

Cherko again felt the wave of sadness.

But—you're all dead. Dying! *I've killed you and your crew! The pilots of our own ships!*

Cherko again looked back into the ship.

And what about my *body!* Me!

They are nearly here.

Cherko looked into the darkness.

He heard them.

But, did he really—or was it more that he *felt* them?

In some manner he sensed their approach. And they were close. The Army. That historical CIC contingent from Roswell.

Oh, my God, Cherko said. *What have I* done?

There is no place to go, She sent. He felt She looking down to Qxuill, who, he felt, had just departed his form. In his mind's eye Cherko saw the history he'd either just created or interfered with.

Recreated?

Saw this ship captured. Poured over. Analyzed. Saw She and her ship captured and her eventual death. Something had definitely gone wrong with their ship and it was down, but way to the west.

And now he was left standing in his alien form before a couple of dead humans—transferred in some out-there quantum-physics-time warp Heisenberg Uncertainty fuck-up into one of the HEUFOs they'd just been observing.

Yes, a helluva glitch, he'd say.

In his mind's eye he saw the entire UFO phenomena play out. Saw it all. All *he* had just created with one uncontrolled, set free, *Human* stray thought....

I'm so sorry, Cherko sent.

Cherko felt She smile.

There is nothing to be sorry about. Since this had already happened in this continuum, it had already occurred. *There is nothing for which to apologize.*

But, why didn't you just tell me…why didn't you—

It was never a matter of informing you about anything…Time is an illusion….

The sounds of jeeps and trucks and other vehicles hurried toward them. Cherko saw headlights popping up and down over hills and zigzagging across uneven terrain.

Coming for them.

In his mind's eye Cherko saw She lay down with her crew.

She!

It is what it is, my friend. I greatly wish I could assist you in your circumstances, She last sent to Cherko.

Cherko hurried around to the backside of the ship behind him, between the ship and up an arroyo's embankment. The area was suddenly invaded by light and noise; vehicles, all directed toward the ship. These vehicles all slammed to dramatic and noisy stops, but kept their headlights trained on the ship.

Shit shit *shit*.

Cherko watched as men departed their vehicles. *Human* men.

What other kind were there?

Many of them were hastily directed into a ring around the perimeter of the crash site. These would be the sentries. Keep what's outside *out*, what's inside *in*…

Another Jeep pulled up, and a man quickly departed the passenger side. He eyed the ship with professional and obvious interest as he approached. All manner of equipment was hastily and efficiently set up.

Floodlights.

Cherko hurried away from the ship.

Where was he to go?

He still had darkness, but it would be chased away in seconds when the floods kicked in and inundated the ship and everything around it. For all his instruction on the fluidity of Time, this was cruel irony, indeed.

"*Are those people?*" Cherko heard someone say. Cherko glanced back and saw the guy who had gotten out of the Jeep peer into the ship, back away in what could only be shock, then poke his head back in. Saw another contingent of men quickly descend upon the corpses surrounding the HEUFO.

I'm so very, very *sorry!* Cherko again sent She and the others.

He turned away and scrambled farther up the embankment.

What the hell was he gonna do? He was in an alien body for Chrissakes, how was he ever going to explain that? He was back in time—lump that onto the shit pile.

And his body—*his real body*—was back on that damned ship!

Jesus, Jesus Christ.

Did aliens send out search parties for their own?

Did they even know of their plight? Did *anyone*?

And just where the hell in blue blazes did he think he was *going?*

"*Hey! Hey* you!"

Cherko knew.

"*Halt!*" the sentry cried. Initially his eyes were as huge, as well, saucers, but when Cherko looked back to him, the man seemed to grab hold of his fear and surprise and did what he'd been so well-trained to do in situations like this.

Brought up his M1 to bear.

Cherko slipped in the loose sand, and started to slide down the embankment. He scrambled for a foothold, but found the feet he possessed not all that well-designed for steep desert embankment maneuvering. There was a loud clacking sound that ricocheted off the arroyo and everything else around him. Just as Cherko then heard a shout of "*No!*," he recognized that clacking sound as the locking and loading of many M1 rifle loads into their well-oiled chambers.

Cherko knew.

There would be no running. Nowhere to go.

Finally able to secure a foothold, Cherko stopped sliding.

Fine timing.

He came to a stop, raised his head, and came to an erect position, just as the rolling volley of M1 rounds slammed into him, tearing into his body and knocking him back against the embankment.

He didn't go down as heavy as the human part of him had expected.

Cherko stared up at the darkness of sky, as he heard another clacking ratcheting of well-oiled gun metal and additional rounds were again chambered into each of the M1s that had just fired.

He'd always wondered what it felt like to be shot.

Cherko rolled his head toward the MP who came upon him, M1 pointed down to his chest…

And died.

Chapter Twenty-Nine

1

Colorado Springs, CO
10 November 2010

"Why am I back here?" Cherko asked Alda.

"Why is anyone ever here, James?" Alda said.

"Thought I was finished with things."

"Why would you say that?"

Cherko paused. "I don't know. Why *would* I? Probably has something to do with my parents, knowing you."

"Let's talk about your parents."

"Of course." Cherko crossed his arms and an ankle just above the opposite leg's knee. He watched Alda scribble on his pad.

"What are you writing?"

Alda smiled briefly, perfunctorily.

"How do you feel about your mother?"

"No Oedipal complexes, here, if that's what you're implying."

"I'm not implying Oedipal Complexes."

"Okay…," Cherko said, uncrossing his leg and arms. His right leg began to run uncontrollably. Alda scribbled notes.

"What are you writing down!"

"Do you feel you had a good childhood? That your mother was good to you? Your father?"

"Aren't those too many questions to ask at once?"

"Fine. Yes, I felt I had a great childhood. My mom and dad were great. My siblings were a pain in the butt, but that's to be expected."

"Is it?"

"Aren't you ever direct about anything?"

"Your mother…you'd mentioned she'd had a mental illness of some kind—"

"*Had I?*"

"Would you care to elaborate? What kind of illness? How'd it affect you?"

"I don't know what was wrong with my mom. I just knew she was…she was always sad. She tried to be happy…a couple times seemed genuinely so…but there always seemed to be some underlying, I don't know—like that Pigpen character from Charlie Brown. The one that always walked around with a cloud of dirt surrounding him? She always had an air of sadness about her. Talking to her later in life, she seemed to have finally come to terms with it—but never seemed to understand just what it was that caused her to be that way. Or tell me about it, anyway."

Alda nodded, writing sporadically throughout Cherko's narration.

"I see."

"*Do you?*"

"Your father—what about him? How had he handled all this? How had he treated you?"

"Dad was fine—great. I never understood how he handled everything. I mean, he was on call twenty-four hours a day with searches, rescues, firefighting, and all, yet he managed to stay with Mom through everything that went on with her as we grew up. Later on, after we all left the roost—"

"After you *all* left the roost?"

"Yes—all of us—after we left…dang it you interrupted me and I forgot what I was going to say—oh, that's weird. I was gonna say they divorced, but that didn't happen. Now, where'd that come from?"

Alda skewered Cherko with his gaze.

"You know, your gaze really does burn."

"Did you notice anything strange about your father?"

"*Strange?*"

"Peculiar. Odd. Out of the ordinary. Did he ever tell you…stories? Mention anything that struck you as abnormal?"

"Now, why in the hell—*why would you come up with a question like that?*"

"It's just a question, James."

"No it isn't. There's no such thing in a place like this. What are you getting at?"

"Same thing as you."

"Really."

"You'd mentioned he'd gotten anxious when you asked him about his submarine days—"

Cherko again crossed his arms. "Did I? When '*did I mention*'? I don't ever remember mentioning—"

"Jimmy…this is not meant to be adversarial."

"Is that a fact?"

Jimmy got to his feet.

"I'm not so sure about that. I don't even know why I'm here! Cause I freaked out in some MRI tube? Why the hell would you be asking all these questions—*anything strange about my father?* C'mon, that has *nothing* to do with me freaking out in a—in a frigging MRI…"

Cherko stopped dead in his tracks.

Tube.

Torpedo tube.

Submarines. *Boats.* Submariners called them *boats*.…

2

Norwegian Basin, 150 NM West of Norway
31 October 1957
0025 Hours Zulu

The *Sailfish* had come to a dead stop at a depth of 100 feet in the Norwegian Basin.

All Everett Cherko thought about was how calm and relaxed he felt here in the radio shack. And what's with that? *Dirt?* There was grime forced deep into the crevasses of the glass gauge receiver rims. How had he missed those? He'd have to go in with a toothbrush and clean those out.

He felt dreamy…like he was in a dream. And it felt *good*…

Everett turned his head.

Someone stood in the entranceway. A couple someones.

Everett felt an urge to bid them "hello," but didn't want to disturb—to lose—the absolute calmness and peacefulness he felt…so he just smiled.

The figures entered the radio shack.

Something about them looked different. They smiled back to him. One waved…or waved something in *front* of him…

Ahoy, sailor, one greeted. Everett nodded in the direction of the greeter.

We need you.

Everett again nodded. *Ok,* he thought. *It's good to be needed. I'm needed here, too.*

Two of the figures—funny, he had a hard time making them out; he must really be tired—touched him, and

Ok, how'd they do that?

Everett stood in a dim chamber, not the radio shack compartment he'd just been occupying—the one with the dirty gauges—no, this was a different one. He didn't recognize it…or did he? Something did seem to feel vaguely, uncomfortably familiar about it…though it didn't look like any of the other compartments aboard the *Sailfish*.

Where am I?

Here, one of the figures answered.

Hey—you didn't move your lips! Everett thought.

We don't have lips, the figure replied. Though the figure didn't laugh, Everett felt what he *swore* was amusement *inside his head.*

Everett gave the figure a good, hard look.

Don't look too hard. You might not like what you see.

Your mouth...no lips...not moving. Oh, no....

There is nothing to fear.

Then why am I afraid? Where am I?

Alongside your vessel.

My submarine? Alongside it? I need to leave—I need to get back to my boat—

There's no hurry. You will shortly be returned. Unharmed.

Why am I here? What are you going to do to me?

We are simply checking up on you.

Why?

Everett felt additional internal amusement.

That is for us to know. You do not have the present requirement to know.

Everett found himself lying on a narrow, warm slab. He suddenly felt quite calm again—just like before these...*figures* (he still couldn't quite make them out)...had come for him. He wanted to roll off the table, to run away, but something inside him asked him *not* to...to be *calm.*

So he stayed. Decided a nap was in order. You could never get enough sleep onboard a boat.

A contraption of some kind, not much larger than a bread box, silently floated over him. As the free-floating *thing* paused directly above his head, a low humming-*like* sound—not quite nor exactly like humming, but close enough—emitted, and Everett lost consciousness....

3

"How would I know this! How would I—"

Eyes wide and terrified, Cherko threw himself before Alda at his desk. His arms supported him as he leaned across the desk and got right into Alda's face. This time it was his gaze that burned laser-hot.

"How in the hell do I know any of this! Dad never told me this—*never—"*

"Hello, Son."

Cherko spun around.

"Dad?"

"You're correct, Son. I never did tell you about any of this. I never told anyone."

"Then how do I—what are *you*—"

"In fact, I pretty much forgot about it. All of it. Except for the fear. I don't remember the events, just the fear."

"Dad?"

Jimmy went to his father. Stood before him as his dad sat on the couch. "How long have you been here?"

"I don't know why I remember it now...not sure—"

Cherko touched his father. His father didn't appear to notice. "*Are you real?*" Jimmy whispered to his dad.

Everett looked up to him. "As real as anything in this room. As real as you."

Cherko looked between his dad and Alda.

"What's going on here?"

"I've been asking you that since you first arrived at my office," Alda said.

Jimmy turned back to his father. "Was that real? Did it really happen?"

Everett nodded. "Apparently. I'd...I guessed I'd—I think the term is 'suppressed'—'repressed?'" Everett looked to Alda; Alda nodded.

"Why now? What was it all about?" Jimmy asked.

Everett shook his head. "I really don't know."

Everett got to his feet. Jimmy backed away, allowing him room to stand. "But as I think about it...there seems to be...*another* time..."

"Another what? Another—"

4

190 NM East of Cape Cod
10 April 1963
0907 Hours Eastern Time

RM1 Everett Cherko sat at his station in the radio shack of the *USS Thresher*, SSN-593, headphones on. He began to wonder if he'd made the right choice. This was his first test-depth sea trial, the first one he'd ever participated in, and though he'd been By-Name requested to serve on the boat by the *Thresher's* very own XO...something didn't feel right. He'd always wanted to get on a nuclear boat, but now, creeping along at two knots, 1800 feet below the surface of the deep blue sea, things just didn't feel right for the first time in his eight-year naval career. This depth was over twice what he'd ever been to aboard the old diesel boats *Sailfish* and *Irex*. This was some serious shit. He swore he could feel the High Yield-80 steel alloys straining against the 80,000 pounds per square inch of water pressure trying to crush them to an ignoble death.

Was that groaning natural?

Was that what nuke subs were supposed to sound like at these ungodly depths?

Something just didn't *feel* right...

Suddenly Everett felt thick, heavy. Very heavy. Like he could feel all his muscles and tendons and bones...all his blood and nerves.

How could he "feel" his body like this? Something had to be wrong with him.

He should go see the Doc.

Surely the Doc'd be able to tell him what's wrong.

Maybe he should take deep breaths...yes, that was it. Deep...*breaths*....

Everett closed his eyes, folded his arms before him on his console and thought of home, Renée, little Jimmy and—

He looked up.

Ahoy, Sailor. You need to come with us.

No! Not again! I'm not—

Everett once more found himself in a dark, familiar chamber not his *Thresher* radio shack. It was a chamber that brought back feelings of fear. Uncertainty and confusion.

Why him? Had he not already given them what they wanted? *Why must they continually harass him!* Keep pulling him out of his life?

We have not pulled you from *life*, came the mental reply that originated from behind. Everett turned. There stood a handful of shadowy figures milling around behind him. He squinted, but could not make out their features. They looked disturbingly short. Not *right*....

We pulled you from your vessel to give you continued *life. We regret to inform you your vessel has gone down. All lives are lost. Internal joints ruptured...an unstoppable chain of events unfolded. Your submarine is gone. There was nothing they could do.*

"*Why'd you just save me? Why not the rest of my crew?*"

Our mission was only about you, not your crew.

"But all those *lives*—put me back with my crew! I'd rather be with them in death than here with you!"

The figure stared at Everett in silence.

This is not about us. It is about you and your continued requirement. You are needed—

"What about all the men onboard—the husbands and fathers? Were they not also needed!"

We must calm you.

Everett felt himself moments from exploding into a livid rage, moments away from launching into the gaggle of spindly figures before him and tearing them limb from limb, but was overcome by an overwhelming...quietness. As hot as his anger had boiled, he was now relaxed, calmed...

We were not there for your vessel nor its crew. We were there for you. It is hard for you to understand, but we need you for purposes not yet realized. Your purpose is not yet completed. For that we needed to take action to ensure your continued viability. Come.

60 NM North of Cuba
24 October 1962
0916 Hours Eastern Time

Everett stood before men of his own design, though his entourage of shadowy figures remained by his side. He stood before a man in a khaki officer's uniform. Looked to his insignia. Commander.

The Old Man. Captain of the boat.

Everett looked to the others around him. They wore patches with a fish in the shape of a submarine brandishing a threaded needle. Across the top of the patch was *USS Threadfin*. Elsewhere on the patch was *SS-410*.

Everett looked to another officer who stood before him. The Diving Officer.

"Permission to come aboard," Everett asked. The D.O. responded with "Permission granted." Everett turned around to find still more men in blue utility dungarees, some with shirts off, their bodies glistening in sweat and grime. Most were clean shaven, but several sported beards, mustaches, and long sideburns. Again, involuntarily he found himself introducing himself to each and every man, one by one.

Everett Cherko, Radioman First Class.

Each acknowledged and introduced themselves in return. As he went about his introductions, he noticed he himself also wore the *Threadfin* patch.

It was like a dream. Just like a dream. Had he always been aboard the *Threadfin?* It was hard to think…so hard to hold a single train of thought….

We are outside of Time and have transferred you to another location and moment, imparted his shadowy companion. *This is for the better. It is better if these transfers occur in private—or at the height of intense activity—to mask questions or concerns at the target location or with its subjects. Through your introduction to each man, each man will now recognize you and "know" you and your position…and you, them. We will also give you your needed familiarity with this vessel before releasing you. All concerns will be mitigated or ignored. You will only remember your place on this vessel, not your place on the previous one. You will not remember any of what came before. Familiarity masks transfers.*

Everett was shown throughout the entire boat, forward and aft, and when all was said and done, was shown to the radio shack, just beneath the sail, or conning tower, which was different from where he'd just come, but not much different from the *Sailfish* or *Irex*. He was back on a diesel boat.

What did that *mean?*

Where had he *been?*

Okay…okay, the memory was coming…he'd…he'd reported to another boat, the *Thresher*. Yes. Actually showed up on the plank…but had been turned away. That was it…turned *away*. There had been no orders cut for him after all. A mistake. His orders had been screwed up. Was reassigned. *Threadfin*. That was his new assignment.

As he sat facing aft in the radio shack, he looked to his group of shadowy figures. To the one with whom he conversed. He still couldn't make out their features, but the one with whom he'd interacted waved good-bye.

Fair winds and following seas, sailor!

Everett waved, blinked…and they were gone.

Chapter Thirty

1

Everett and Jimmy looked to each other.

"Dad...what does this mean?"

"I was kept alive for a purpose," Everett said, "and I feel that purpose was you."

"Me?"

"Yes."

"How does that make you feel," Alda asked.

Jimmy spun around. "Oh, for Chrissakes, would you knock it off!" He turned back to his father.

"Dad, none of this makes sense; these visions—you're being here. *None* of it."

"Think outside the *box* Jimmy," Alda said.

Jimmy regarded Alda for a moment.

"Is that all this is—a box?"

He came back over to Alda.

"So, exactly what kind of a box are we talking about, Alda? A *Rubik's* Cube? Jack-in-the-Box? *Pandora's* box? What kind of vague generalities do you have for me, now, Doc?"

"How about me? I'm the very definition of 'vague generalities,' don't you think?"

Renée Cherko stood in the office doorway. She held interlaced hands down before her.

"*Mom?*"

"Goddammit, what is going on here!"

Jimmy looked to his dad, who only returned a blank stare.

"Alda, what the hell are you doing?"

"Don't blame him, Jimmy," Renée said.

Renée entered the office and sat beside Everett. She cast him a sorrowful look as she sat down on the edge of the couch, her pressed-together hands wedged between squeezed-together knees. Everett made a quick grimace, but said nothing.

"I think it's time we all came to terms with what happened," she said. "Remembered...*really* remembered...exactly what happened."

"You remember? You found something out?" Jimmy asked.

Renée nodded. "I think this place...*helps*."

"This is *crazy!*" Jimmy said. "How could you two be here—*know* about this place—*him?*" Jimmy said, pointing to Alda.

Alda's eyes took on a disturbingly deep, dark stare. Jimmy had to consciously pull his attention away from them. He came back to stand before his mother.

"How is this happening?"

Renée reached out to him.

"Allow me."

2

Renée Cherko dreamed she was pregnant.

Not just once, but many times. Eight to be exact. Eight times between 1960 and 1972. Her husband was a Navy man and usually got shore leave once a year while out on patrol. A submariner. But he had gotten out of the Navy in sixty-five (and after four children), and after a year or two of temporary employment in New Hampshire, got on with the Wanakena, New York, Forest Ranger School. A year and one move later, became a full-fledged Forest Ranger for the State of New York, after a brief stint in Vermont. They'd had four more children between New Hampshire and New York, 1972.

Eight children.

She dreamed this.

But every time she awoke from her dreams, either in the middle of the night or during the light of day, she felt a pronounced, soul-crushing, loss.

She only awoke to four. If she was so lucky.

Where had the others gone?

It would always take her some time before she remembered the reality of it.

She'd lost them.

The doctors had told her she had lost them due to Rh incompatibility; erythroblastosis, to the uninitiated.

But, good God, that's *not* how she remembered it!

She remembered *all* of them—having given birth to each and every one—and that they'd all *survived.* Every one of them! Her dreams had told her so, her memory had told her so, and her *heart* had told her so.

It was only her reality that lied.

So on the nights when she found herself awake between one and four in the morning, she usually got up out of bed and walked the house in the dark. She'd usually start with Jimmy's room, because his was the first one she came upon when she left their bedroom and crossed through the spare room and into the hallway, where Mac slept. She'd take just a short peek—enough to verify that *he* existed and was sound asleep in his bed. Then she'd go down the short banistered hallway to Penny and Ritchie's room, and do the same. Next on to Carl's room, across from Penny and Ritchie.

But usually when she got to their rooms the fear had gripped her and she began second-guessing her senses.

Where they really *there?*

Or was she just seeing lumps of clothing and blankets thrown together to make it *look* like her children were all asleep in their beds?

She would have to fight the urge to go in and shake them, wake them up, and throw off their blankets. For to give in meant she had to admit to some form, however low-level, of insanity—and, of course, there was the chance she could be wrong…and that she just didn't want to know.

But of *course* she had children. Of course. Its proof was right there every morning. Every breakfast, lunch, and dinner. During homework, scraped knees, and sibling rivalries. Bed time.

But there were only four. *Four.*

When she knew she'd had *eight.*

Four—*right?*

After her bed checks she'd then go downstairs. Sometimes Mac would follow her, sometimes not. Sometimes he'd follow, see all was okay, then return to his sentry post back at the top of the stairs. Mac was a good dog.

And sometimes Mac would just sit there in the dark staring at her. She couldn't see his dark, caring eyes, but she knew he was looking directly at her—*staring* at her—because she could see that angular silhouette of his head in the darkness, ears alert.

It always unnerved her.

So she would get up and walk around the house…the kitchen, the pantry, the back porch…or Everett's ranger office. Sometimes, it didn't matter the season, she'd even go outside, on the large front porch that nearly wrapped around the house.

And just sit.

Her and her errant memories. Trying to analyze if she really was any kind of crazy. She knew sometimes dreams could be so real…like you were actually alive and living them like everyday life…she knew this, but even that didn't help.

If she wondered she was crazy…*was* she?

Were those children sleeping—right now, up in those beds—her children?

Were there really four-and-not-eight-children in their home? In their *life?*

Something was wrong, wasn't right, but she could no longer talk to her husband about it, because he—and the rest of the world—thought she was nuts. And she couldn't argue with them. Had no proof.

Her dreams?

Cause she *remembered* it so?

She hadn't a leg to stand on.

But then there were other parts of these somnambulistic periods that absolutely terrified her. Sometimes…

Sometimes, she found herself in the woods.

Yes, at three in the morning.

Sometimes in little more than what she currently had on. Sometimes nothing—*entirely naked*—she would find herself in strange places. Out on Route 30 or 186. Halfway to Saranac Lake. Once she "came to" in the knee-high water of Lake Clear, across the road from their house. Many times just standing out in their front lawn, staring down to the lake, after she'd felt she'd gone as far as St. Regis mountain or the Lake Clear airport, *miles* away.…

Whether or not her memories were false, *what the hell was happening to her?*

She had no answers and it terrified her. Professionals, those called medical or psychological professionals, had no answers. They thought her postpartum. Hormone imbalanced. A sleepwalker. Perhaps even just plain old organically mentally *fucked.* They just didn't know. So they prescribed pharmaceuticals. Therapy. Recommended keeping sharp objects out of her reach. It was a crap shoot.

But still she had the dreams, the intense foreboding and misgivings that something—*something!*—was terribly wrong about their lives. About their children.

About them.

Once she remembered a bright light in the sky over Lake Clear. It was huge. She'd looked it up at the library one day, finding references to Venus, but it was in the wrong part of the sky for that time of the year. Going back the next night, she found no such light.

So, this was the constant nightmare of her life. A constant state of fear and confusion and medication. And when everyone you knew kept telling you you were crazy, you eventually started believing it, maybe even found *comfort* in it.…

3

"It was always easier to go with the flow, not fight the current," Renée said, staring down into the office floor.

Jimmy could say nothing. He stared at his mother, tears welling up inside.

"*Mom...*"

"I fault no one, honey—no one knew what to do with me, and all of them dealt with me—even your father—the best way they knew how. Heck, I didn't even know how to handle me. If I did, I'd have fixed *myself*, don't you see?"

Jimmy sat in his assigned chair.

"This is all so...," Jimmy said, hand to his head. "You never found out? *Never?*

"God, I have a headache."

Renée slowly lifted her head.

"Well, actually...I did."

Jimmy looked up. Everett looked to his wife.

"You found out what was wrong? You found—"

"Answers. That's why I'm here.

"Jimmy, darling, do you remember Christmas Day, 1974?"

Jimmy screwed his brows together.

"Not sure."

"You'd been playing up back with the snowshoes we'd gotten you for Christmas. You'd been late getting home..."

4

Lake Clear, New York
25 December 1974

Jimmy loved snowshoeing!

And now he had his very own! Just the sound of the woods, his breathing, and the muffled crunching of his brand new Iverson's snowshoes in the snow. Weaving in and out of the trees. Thinking about girls and books and movies. By himself—*alone.*

How magnificent it was out here!

He stopped. Before him lay unmarked snow and trees. He watched his breath curl up before him. Jimmy pursed his lips together, angling the lips upward and blew more vapor up before him...

It was late. The sun low and orange through darkening skeletal trees against a blanketed landscape. Gusts of wind howled in the distance. Fleeting snow devils kicked up across the snowscape. He wished this moment would last forever. Snowshoeing through the woods beneath the dark steel-gray of a dying winter's day.

He smiled.

Crunching in the snow, he waddled around.

His tracks still there.

Still his.

Following him.

God, Hannah was *cute*. Her long brown hair. Her smile. He wished she'd just walk on out of the woods right now.

He shifted uncomfortably, adjusting his snow pants.

Hannah…

Warmth. Family. TV. Home…warmly lit up from the inside, the spoils of Christmas everywhere. Smoke curling out two chimneys. Mom making dinner, wondering where the heck he was. Carl, Penny, and Ritchie all lying on the floor before the TV waiting for him to get

Home.

Family.

Man, Hannah…Hannah, *Hannah!*

He *loved* saying her name out loud—*thinking* it. Why, she could just walk on out of the trees, out here in the woods. For him. Just the two of them.

Alone.

He again adjusted his snowpants.…

Devil's Den.

It was only a couple more minutes. Home.

The snow was coming down *hard.*

Was he alone?

The temperature kept dropping. What late afternoon winter light was

Different. Something was *really* different.

The cold creeped through his heavy garments and down into his toes. Another shiver.

It was darker. Felt much later than it should be.

"Hi, Jimmy."

Jimmy nearly tripped over his snowshoe-clad feet as he spun around.

Hannah stood back in a copse of snow-covered pine, fir, and empty beech. Surrounded by deer. She came forward, her entourage spilling forth around her.

"This was what you wanted, was it not?"

He'd never noticed before just how deep and dark her large, beautiful eyes were. How compassionate and *probing.* Her voice melted away all the cold…

"H-hi, Hannah."

"What do you wanna do?" she asked.

The deer milled around the both of them. Jimmy didn't feel right.

"I-I don't know."

"I have an idea."

Chapter Thirty-One

1

Fourteen-year-old Jimmy found it hard to think.

What was that sound?

Where was he?

He opened his eyes (*why were they closed?*).

He stood in their living room. In front of their twinkling Christmas tree.

How had he gotten here? He didn't remember—

Fire…that sound was the crackling of their Franklin stove.

Mom and dad flanked him, also standing…not saying anything. They looked just as confused as he was.

Hannah stood before them. Still surrounded by deer.

Why were deer in their living room?

Hannah spoke to all of them, but spoke without using her mouth.

This is our gift to you.

That was all Hannah said, but all three felt the emotion that permeated her words. The emotion of, *yes, we know…you have been asked to endure much…been through a lot…you have the right—the* need—*to know. So, this is our gift to you.…*

In the living-room doorway stood a group of figures. Short figures. Milling around figures. And with these milling figures emanated an air of excitement…

Anticipation.

Jimmy looked to his parents, and both—especially his mom—stared hard into the group of short, antsy figures in the doorway. Couldn't take their eyes off the doorway. Jimmy looked back to that doorway and got the image of a horse race in his head…all the horses chomping at the bit within their starting gates, ready to be released so they could—

Charge.

The figures charged into the living room.

Jimmy was overcome with the purest sensation of joy and love and…

Reconnection.

Out from the doorway raced Carl and Penny and Ritchie. And behind them *Theresa, Michael, Lisa, and Benjamin.*

Jimmy's brothers and sisters.

Jimmy's mind exploded into a free-wheeling whirlwind of imagery.

Carl, Penny, and Ritchie?

What was going on here?

Theresa, Michael, Lisa, and Benjamin?

The seven, including two-year-old Benjamin, sprinted into the center of Jimmy and Everett and Renée, and Jimmy and Everett and Renée all launched forward to meet them. They met in the center of the living room in a mass of tears, as he inhaled the familiar and emotional scent of each of his siblings, felt their skin, their faces. Collapsed upon themselves and fell to the floor in a writhing, emotional heap. Jimmy's eyes were flooded with tears. He was alongside his mother, who sobbed and shook uncontrollably. His father was similarly overcome, trying to throw his arms around everyone at once.

As Jimmy looked up, tears streaming down his face, he looked to Hannah and the deer.

But Hannah and the deer were no longer Hannah and deer.

We give this to you on your day of days…in an effort to show we care…are not evil. That we appreciate your efforts and understand your circumstances.

After a long while of hugging and loving and crying, the family looked to she-who-was-not-Hannah. She-who-was-not-Hannah directed them to the space above them, in the center of the room. As the Franklin stove crackled and spit and warmed in the background, and the fake-snow-covered Christmas tree blinked and winked, the family looked to a presentation. A presentation that showed the births and life moments in a sort of film, up to the current moment in time, of the children Renée *knew* she'd had, but could not—not ever—*prove*…and would all-too shortly again be forced to forget. All three experienced and became a part of the lives of the seven other children that no longer resided with them in this secluded part of deep woods upstate New York…and it would be this very moment in time, this enormous act of kindness that would stay with them forever, though none would ever understand why.

Renée saw how each time she'd strayed out into the night…into the woods…even tried to take her own life…the deer-that-were-not-deer, Hannah-that-was-not-Hannah had come to her. Rescued her from abruptly terminating her despair and returned her home. Had awoken Jimmy or her husband to come to her aid…

And as the family of ten relived their lives together beneath the hovering hologram, they danced and sang and played and celebrated birthdays and *life.* And the heavily falling snow and cold and real world of outside stayed outside as the Franklin stove crackled and spit, and the Christmas tree winked and blinked.…

2

"We were a friggin human farm team for *extraterrestrials?*"

Jimmy Cherko stood before his parents, flabbergasted. Turned to Alda—who still pinned him with a deep, dark, penetrating gaze.

"But we were well-cared for," Renée said, choking back emotion. "They took as good a care of us as they possibly *could*—"

"*But at what price?*"

Jimmy spun back around.

"Look what they *did* to you! The strain it put on all of us! They kept stealing our family as quickly as we created one!"

Renée remained silent.

"*Dad?*"

"We lived a good life, Son. I have no regrets."

Jimmy noticed his father's voice was thicker.

"They pulled me off a sub I would have gone down on. You would never have known me if it hadn't been for them. I was able to—my purpose to them—was in raising *you*. How can I fault them? How can I fault them in allowing me to raise a son and live a life with my family? I would not have been able to do any of that if—"

"But mom went *crazy*—"

"I'm fine, now," Renée said.

"Now—wherever 'now' is—but when it mattered, you'd gone *crazy.* Tried to kill yourself! I'm not arguing over not having parents and all, but—"

"They watched over me, honey. Made sure I didn't do anything irrational; that you had a *father*. Made sure you were raised with both parents. They could have taken *you*—but didn't."

"Yeah," Jimmy said, looking back to Alda, who merely continued to observe. "But, for my life we gave them the lives of seven others. The rest of our family."

"Honey," Renée said, "those others...Penny and Ritchie...Benjamin, all of them...they all would have died. They all had complications from erythroblastosis. At the time a pretty much fatal blood disease. They were given new life—*elsewhere*—they were not killed nor abused. We saw that that Christmas—don't you remember?"

"I don't know that that makes it any more right."

"Sometimes life throws hard decisions at you, but on your father's salary, my intermittent salary, eight children...*seven of which who would have* died...were instead given *life*. And they did come back every now and then, you were able to play with them up in the woods...were taught and guided by...by *them*...all in exchange. Everyone was able to live and thrive and *learn* from minds and intelligences far superior to ours. And not even as some impersonal, expendable *lab* rats. You felt the emotion. You *played* with them. They didn't have to do any of that. Any of it."

"But why? Why couldn't they have fixed them then *returned* them? For *good?*"

Renée looked back down to her hands. "I'm sorry, I don't have all the answers," she said. Renée looked up. Tears streamed down her face and her voice wavered. "But does it matter? *Really?* Once you all grew up—once *you* did—you moved out anyway. Your siblings would have done the exact same thing come their time, so what was the difference, really? All children grow up and move on. Ours...just did so a little earlier—and with a little help from above."

Jimmy sat back down in the Victorian chair. "I just hope they weren't used in experiments...or—"

"My sense," Renée said, looking to Everett and grabbing hold of one of his hands, "is that they are still alive...have been used in ways to *help* Humanity."

Everett nodded, and said, "I feel they—you included—were all, like your mother says, put to good use in the world."

"Good use. How was I put to good use? Look at me, look at my life."

"You lived a *good* life. Maybe that was your use. To have a good life. To offset the loss of the others."

Jimmy got to his feet and faced Alda.

"So...'this is my life'? What now? Why am I here? To remember? Remember *what?*"

Alda just stared back at him. Jimmy grew uncomfortable. Looked away. Looked to an adjacent wall.

A wall that flickered and shimmered.

"What the hell?"

He came up to the wall; touched it. It felt solid enough, but...

Looked to another section of office. It, too, flickered and wavered.

"What's going on here?"

He looked to the couch—but his parents were gone. Looked to Alda, but he suddenly appeared two-dimensional. Like a cardboard cutout set against a prop background.

Jimmy closed his eyes and rubbed his face. When he opened them, the walls sputtered and flashed...

Numbers.

Trains of ones and zeros ran throughout the paint, the wallpaper, the ceiling.

The air.

Jimmy didn't feel so good. Felt dizzy.

Ran for the door.

Chapter Thirty-Two

1

```
if writing2010 == true {execute;}
else {chkverif lt87; chkverif ero2021}
if lt87 == true {execute lt87;}
if ero2021 == true {execute ero2021;}
```

Cherko slid to a stop in the garage, alongside Erica's 2001 Honda.

He wasn't…right.

Something was terrible wrong with him, he felt it, and it made him sick to his stomach.

What had just happened?

Cherko hit the garage door switch as he entered the house.

"Erica! Erica!"

No answer. But he saw the message light blinking on the answering machine.

The thought did people still use these things? entered his mind, but he dismissed it.

Cherko rushed past the message machine, up a short flight of stairs, then hooked a sharp right to enter the third floor of the tri-level…and ran smack into a wall.

Cherko pushed away from his desk.

What the hell?

He leaned over, peering into the laptop's display, to words he had just written.

Did people still use these things?

Ran smack into a wall…

He frowned. Got to his feet. Sat back down.

Where was he?

The computer was directly in front of him on his desk. And those words…words that were his own, his own creation—

Were they?

Cherko brought his hands to the keyboard.

Laptop? Wait a minute, where was—

Cherko suddenly felt sick, very sick. Something just wasn't right. Breathing fast and shallow, shallow and fast, he…

Looked around his office. What the hell was the matter? He was alone, he was—

But he wasn't. He wasn't even at home.

He looked to the screen.

Laptop? Wait a minute, where was—

Cherko suddenly felt sick, very sick. Something just wasn't right. Breathing fast and shallow, shallow and fast, he...

Looked around his office. What the hell was the matter? He was alone, he was—

But he wasn't. He wasn't even at home.

Cherko again pushed away from his

(*desk?*)

shooting to his feet. He spun around, lightheaded. Braced himself against the wall with his hands up before him; his face inches from—

Cherko spun back around to his desk.

Have to slow down my breathing!

He looked into the screen.

Cherko again pushed away from his

(*desk?*)

shooting to his feet. He spun around, lightheaded. Braced himself against the wall with his hands up before him; his face inches from—

"Oh, no...no, no, *no*...this can't be happening..."

Trembling and sweating, he looked up.

He was no longer at home, but in...what?...a *vault?* A classified computer lab like at *work?*

"Something's wrong...something's very wrong, here," Cherko closed his eyes.

Focus. Have to focus.

Cherko sat back down, gripped the elbow rests of his chair. His stomach was much worse, his vision swam crazily before him. He wiped clammy sweat from his brow, his cheeks.

He was *doused* in the stuff.

His chest felt like something powerful had reached around it and was squeezing the life out of him.

Cherko opened his eyes to find his hands flying across a bulky keyboard. He had no control over what his hands were doing, but the words, they just kept *coming....*

Cherko leaned closer into the screen. The words, they were so familiar, so *right*. They seemed so much a part of him. Who he was. Each character, so perfectly kerned, fonted, and arranged.

Alive.

Felt words coursing through his veins...words animated and exploding with an energetic importance that felt like the very breath of *life....*

Cherko closed his eyes and let the words come.

The words coursed through him, filled his being with vitality…became his heart, his core, his spirit. Without these words…he was nothing. A shell. A blank screen. A—

Cherko opened his eyes.

Screamed.

Before him was a face, a face in a soundproofed and electronically isolated vault within a vault. A face not his own. A face that bore directly into his soul and knew every inch of who and what he was.

There were no secrets.

Yes, he was a shell. A blank screen. A schema. He was…

A program in the process of being coded.

2

100-Mile Low Earth Orbit
4 November 2021
0915 Hours Zulu

"*I am* not *a piece of* code!" Cherko cried, struggling, sweating, and hyperventilating within his confinement that now entirely encapsulated him from head to toe in one solid piece of pseudo-metal-composite material he was still unable to identify. Hundreds of pulsating, multicolored, fiber optic-like leads ran from his head behind him into a panel somewhere.

"This is *insane!* There's no way! I'm a *man*, not some mindless hacker-inspired *program!*" James Cherko shouted to Eurphraeus.

No longer was he in an orbiting space station, spy or otherwise, but now more of a metal coffin. An electronic coffin. A tiny compartment that rapidly closed in on him…

"It is what it is," Eurphraeus said.

"It makes no *sense!* First you show me dying in a spaceship crash in 1947, then you show me as nothing more than *ones and zeros?* "Am I *dead?* Is this all in my frigging head?"

"You are not dead. You exist."

"But…the memories—the manuscript! *Here.*"

"Look around you. What do you see," Eurphraeus asked.

Cherko, eyes fearful and wide, took in the command module—or what there was of it. It was a shrinking *box.*

Was *continuing* to shrink.

It was barely ten-by-ten, and shrinking by the moment without the faintest whisper of sound.

Cherko's head hurt. He looked to Eurphraeus. "No…*no-no-no!*"

Eurphraeus was no longer.

"*Eurphraeus!*"

The module contracted. Shortened. With each twitch of an eye the module continually—maddeningly—reduced in size. Cherko thrashed about.

It shrunk still more.

Cherko could no longer breathe. Maddeningly hyperventilated.

The walls of the station collapsed in on him until all he could see was…

Circuitry.

Software.

Electrons.

Cherko was no longer constrained within the strange metal constriction that had crisscrossed, then entirely enveloped, his body.

He free-floated in space…

In orbit above a fragile, eggshell-blue planet.

He changed his perspective with a thought and looked out in the opposite direction, toward that of deepest black space.

Stars.

Panicking, he reached out for something to grab onto—

But was in freefall.

A controlled, on-orbit freefall, where his stomach tried to launch up and out his mouth…except he had no stomach—no *mouth*.

And, of course, there was nothing upon which to grab hold.

Eurphraeus!, Cherko called out into the cold, starry blackness, *What's happened? WHAT'S HAPPENING TO ME!*

Cherko 360'd, but it was all the same.

Alone. Totally alone.

Except for the cerulean planet turning beneath him.

He had no arms nor legs with which to "flail." No support structures, no space station, no *body*, because…

He was *the orbiting platform.*

I don't understand! Cherko again cried, *I don't want to die!*

James, life is not dependent upon corporeal expression. Never has been, Eurphraeus sent. *Your world, your existence, however, has focused upon that.*

My body—what happened to my body—where is it?

It no longer matters.

It does to me!

Search your memories—

I'm tired of memories! Tired of searching! I want my body back—my life!

You have a personality…you have Thought. Consciousness. From where did those originate? Where did they go upon the loss of your own physical platform? They remain with you, do they not?

Cherko…computed.

How did I get here! What…what's happening to me!

Before Cherko finished the thought/calculation, he remembered what had happened. It finally made sense. All of it.

Cherko saw his death. Yes, he had, indeed, been shot. Shot and killed in Roswell, in a post-thunderstorm-ridden arroyo in 1947.

There *had* been a crash. A *UFO* crash. He'd been *in* it.

His whole life had been involved in tracking and, he'd come to find out, *seeding extraterrestrial technologies.*

That was the huge government secret: *he* was the huge, fucking secret.

In 1987 he had been assigned to Dulce, New Mexico to work an operation involving extraterrestrials. During his last exchange with his E.T. contacts he had been taken aboard one of their ships and shown things…how to transfer his consciousness into the form *they* wore while visiting their planet.

But there had been an accident. A crash. *Two* crashes.

A human-engineered UFO, a HEUFO, developed by his very own U.S. government…all occupants of the craft had been killed upon impact. All *humans.* Something he had done had gone terribly wrong.

And behind this craft—the one marked with "U.S. Army" on its torn side—had been something else. Something *not* human.

Him.

But, in another location far to the west and beyond the Foster Ranch debris field, had been another crash. One not much talked about. She and Qxuill and the other occupants of the vehicle he had been in had been dead or dying. Had also been found. And much to his irony, Cherko—the human *body* of Cherko—had also survived the crash, but only barely.

He'd been separated from his body and had been stuck not on some other planet with an alien race, no…the irony of it was that he had been stranded on his very own planet, in a different time, *and as an alien himself.*

What was he supposed to have done?

Events had taken on their own momentum.

Cherko had been gunned down by extremely nervous trigger fingers. Nothing more than a mistake. A purely human one. A major case of mistaken identity.

Until someone found his body—*his human one*, that is—inside the real UFO. Not a debris field, not a HEUFO, but a real live extraterrestrial space ship. Found by some passers-by, then summarily surrounded by yet another contingent of government operatives. Army Counterintelligence. One man in particular. And on this human carcass, on this body that was Cherko, or perhaps more to the point what Cherko had *worn* for twenty-six years…had been his wallet, within which were his military and civilian IDs.

With late 1980 dates.

That was what all the ruthless secrecy had been about all those years. The stark, unforgiving intimidation and outright murder to keep secrets *secret.*

It had been bad enough that elements within the U.S. Government had created their own super-advanced flying machine and kept it from their own kind, from those who were led to believe that they had held the supposedly most classified clearances to date, but then to discover that they were also being toyed with by an *extraterrestrial* race, one they could not ever hope to better even with their super-advanced technology…

And it had also been bad enough that they had found actual extraterrestrial bodies at that crash scene, bad enough that they had actually *captured* a live alien life form…*but to have found a human body* amongst that alien wreckage, held in stasis inside an *alien ship…alive…*bearing documents of a future military member of the very same U.S. Government that was now in possession of this crash site ship and its occupants…*that* was simply far too much for most 1947 minds.

Besides all the obvious and logical questions that arose, the Army now had to deal with not only an alien craft and bodies—but a very human one, as well. One that had been heavily damaged in the crash. One that, though it had been encompassed within an unknown alien technology, had been damaged beyond the current state of Earthly technology by whatever had caused the crash and landed it in less-than-perfect condition onto the desert floor.

Good God, what had been going on up in those skies above New Mexico?

The UFO—at that time still largely unexplored—had been removed from its crash site and hastily spirited off to various locations, wherein which it eventually ended up at Edwards AFB. Area S-4.

The best minds on the planet poured over the damaged ship, but none had found the human remains, because they had been removed before it had even left New Mexico. While the ship had been temporarily housed in a hangar on the Army's 509th Bomb Group airfield enroute to its other location, She, the only surviving crew member of that ship had cut a deal with the CIC operative about the crash. She had told the truth, that what the Government had was for real. That the human remains *were* from the future, and because of a catastrophic onboard ship error, the craft had ended up in 1947 as they had found it. That it had been an error on their part that Captain Cherko, USAF, 1987, had been injured.

Was he still alive?, CIC asked.

The mind of Captain Cherko was, She informed, but his body was quickly dying and mangled beyond any meaningful repair. Then She volunteered the following:

We can save him. We can save him until your race gains the necessary technology to receive him back. Time is an illusion, means nothing to us…and now, to him. It's more advantageous for him in many ways…aids in his development in ways only he can now appreciate, She said. *We will do this, and I will offer myself for your study.*

The agreement had been struck.

Cherko's body had been removed from the ship by another set of aliens who had indeed come in search for him, but men in dark suits had swiftly and deftly descended upon each crash-and-debris site and removed *everything,* and together with the best minds of the day, began formation of the Black Onion.

The culture of secrecy and disinformation had begun.

There had been no crash.

No aliens.

No nothing. *Ever.*

And "they" threatened and killed to keep it that way.

She cooperated as long as she could, because, she, too, had been dying as a result of that crash, but not in a way humans thought. And the aliens had taken Cherko and preserved the only part of him worth saving: his *mind*…by way of his brain. The interface for the mind and the body. The seat of human consciousness, the only thing with an ounce of life left to it.

The brain, Cherko now saw, was an extremely complex interface between the physical and nonphysical, the body and soul. Cherko was kept secret in remote locations where not the U.S. Government—nor any other earthly government—could reach him. But as worldly technologies continued to advance and grow, human surveillance and detection methods also progressed, and it became increasingly difficult to keep him hidden. It wasn't so much that humans would find what was left of Cherko, but it was the surrounding extraterrestrial support structure they would find that was keeping Cherko alive and led to other areas best kept hidden. The hidden structures, chambers, equipment, and technology used to contain him not of this world.

It has often been said that the best place to hide anything is directly under the seeker's own nose. That was exactly where Cherko had been secured.

Placed in Earth orbit.

His brain—steeped in and protected by alien technology—had been placed on an extraterrestrial platform, a satellite, impervious to detection by Earthly technology, in a high-end polar orbit. There he was to be kept until Earth had evolved enough to deal with his condition, they were told. Writers, whose very lives and families had been threatened and were left in the dark as to exactly what they were doing, and why, were secretly brought in by the government to fabricate a make-believe fantasy life for him. A secret life that had then been coded into an artificial intelligence program. And the alien race had reached agreements with certain human contacts to help expedite said technological developments through the measured and controlled seeding of alien technology.

Again, the paradoxical irony of Cherko's Dulce position.

Later, the measured and well-thought-out seeding of mis-information about what exactly had crashed was meticulously leaked into public awareness.

UFOs were the perfect cover.

Took the heat off highly classified government projects. Fact and fiction were blended together.

There had been no government HEUFO.

But there *had* been a UFO.

Yes.

With extraterrestrial casualties.

One side would deny everything, while the other decried *conspiracy!*

But things had not turned out exactly as She had expected. After She (as far as the Government knew) had expired in government custody, those in charge had gotten greedy. Begun using the alien technology for self-serving ends, because, in all reality, everything can be reverse engineered if given enough time and resources. Intent.

And because the powers in control had never been able to locate that future Air Force officer found in that 1947 crash.

But Cherko had not been left idle in his condition, either. His mental capacities had been developed and refined by his E.T. handlers. Once Cherko had become accustomed to his situation, he had worked with the extraterrestrials that had given him his continued life.

Absolute power corrupts absolutely is not an empty epithet, and there was a reason, Cherko discovered, that alien contact had not been further advanced. The Human condition has its challenges, those who run the events and affairs of their Race were not about to yield to any non-Human authority.

Enter one young, fast burning general, Robert Mitchell Hammond, who became privy to the on-orbit payload that was Jimmy Cherko.

Hammond had his orbital test bed. His on-orbit *platform*.

And Hammond had kept it all to himself. But…even generals die…and with Hammond's death, went the knowledge of Jimmy Cherko's existence.

There are reasons why there are wars and poverty on a planet with plenty. Reasons why individuals suffer. Having anything handed to a Race that needs to solve its own issues first does not advance that Race. A Race seeking external answers to its own issues does not advance that Race.

And there are reasons why there are renewed pushes for space exploration, math and sciences, studies into the nature of time and space. A rise in the interest of metaphysics. The publicly expressed cover stories are always reasonable enough. They have to be. But for each reasonable proclamation there are always, *always* the untold, ulterior and covert *driving* motives….

Chapter Thirty-Three

I see, Cherko said, *I finally…see.*

Cherko sped through his polar orbit.

Why the sadness? Eurphraeus asked.

Earth is dead. They finally did it. Killed themselves off.

Cherko had seen as satellites and other technologies attacked…destroyed…retaliated…

Long-dormant payloads activated…warheads launched…

Populations…entire societies…*gone.…*

The path your historical timeline perspective followed indeed destroyed themselves. Had your perspective's Race chosen to change their path, they would not have visited this scenario. As contradictory as this sounds, there are other timelines in which this perspective did not occur.

But I lived there, in that one.

Yes.

Cherko sped over the surface of the Earth. Reached out with his mind. Explored. The atmosphere had been poisoned, boiled off—gone. Obliterated by a technologically advanced, highly reactive bio-chemical reaction that had seared the atmosphere of everything and anything.

He explored what had once been mountains and streams and oceans and forests. All that had once brought him so much joy and awe…now silent. There were no longer buzzing insects and annoying houseflies, no fresh-cut aromatic grass, and no leaf-rustling trees. No longer the scent of pine and earthy humus. The sound of chirping birdlife. Or the golden, early morning rays of the sun warming sea and soil. The sound of breakers against a sandy beach. Or playful dolphins in oceans.

No Mom nor Dad. Carl, Penny, nor Ritchie.

All had been stripped by the intense drive of the few who had managed the logical conclusion to their violence and hatred: total planetary annihilation.

That was what they wanted and that was exactly what they got.

As if by a gigantic hand that had taken a planet-sized sheet of sandpaper and rubbed the Earth clean, the planet had been stripped to bare rock and sand. Not even an atmosphere. No different than Mercury or Venus. With the gaining of knowledge from advanced alien seed-technology and plain old-fashioned Human Ingenuity, with the massive amount of effort expended toward creating better bombs and technology to wage wars, to spy, to perpetuate violence with the unbridled creativity of the human mind to create and discover new ways to do *anything*, including ferreting out the most secret of secrets to other governments, the end result had finally been achieved. Those hell-bent on destroying all life had finally succeeded, because Humanity as a whole had *allowed* it.

There can be no peace if there are only plans for war.

How long? How long has it been?

Eurphraeus smiled.

Instead of Eurphraeus's voice, Cherko's head was filled with images. Powerful images. Experienced—

War.

War that involved the many orbiting platforms. Satellites. A conflict that flew instantly out of control as soon as it had ignited, as malevolent technology was not only directed against Earth, but itself. The alien satellite upon which Cherko had been hidden had been hit. The satellite itself had not been damaged, but he had been. His consciousness. His consciousness had been directly integrated into the extraterrestrial bio-technology, and the recovery mode had done something to him. Something his keepers had not counted on. Cherko saw that his keepers had to bring him out carefully…allow him to…reboot…on his own. Work through his own "program errors." An extremely delicate and intricate effort that had to be allowed its own progress in order to save his consciousness. The system, the programs that had sustained him had not been damaged, but the recovery mode had kicked off a vicious cycle of events that had been interfered with by Cherko himself.

Deep, long-buried, and primordial aspects of Cherko's consciousness had interfered with program recovery. Though he had come to terms with his situation long ago, with this space war something entirely unexpected happened. Something the creators of his platform had, again, not counted upon.

This was the first time the creators of his platform had ever done anything like this with Humanity. These aliens were so far into Humanity's future that they had forgotten certain constants to the makeup of human consciousness. When consciousness was removed from a human body, it *changed* things. Changed a human's perception of itself. The perceived need for a body…the role of the mind, the *soul*. It was nothing short of dramatic, essentially *cataclysmic* consequences.

Death that was not death.

Each organism is uniquely designed to inhabit the form in which it inhabits, uniquely designed for the consciousness within which it inhabits, the *Time* within which it is placed. Once removed from its own specifically designed "platform," dramatic changes occur. Changes that can be for the better, but for the most part, as had often been observed in the Human Race, not been. There are deep emotional ties that bind humans and their timelines. Certain instances, such as the separation of mind from body, reach throughout all continuums, and affect different—and related—events across Time itself.

Just such an emotional correspondence had reached back into Cherko's Roswell trip, and had, paradoxically, *caused* the crash.

He saw how scientists in his time were just beginning to discover the nature of simultaneous time and inter-related events when they discovered quantum entanglement...that separated atoms—those not in contiguous contact—reacted to the exact same event that the other experienced from a great distance....

Hyperdimensional physics.

Cherko saw that deep within his consciousness an elemental part of him had cried out in fear. A fear that had taken over his thinking consciousness, had grown and festered thanks to this impromptu system recovery. A fear, a common thread that ran throughout all of Humanity and that had driven much of Humanity's actions. This is what they had not foreseen.

Fear had become a glitch in the program.

As system recovery continued, these fearful elements continued to interrupt and corrupt, calling for continued recovery attempts. Tripping and re-tripping itself. Created an "infinite loop." System, file, and access contentions, not only with the highly advanced bio-technological system sustaining Cherko, but in Cherko *himself*. His mind. Physical neuronal and dendritic damage. Damage that had to be corrected through regrowth. The only remaining physical aspect to Cherko, his "platform"—and it still exerted an influence.

How, his reasoning mind considered, could he still be physical yet not inhabit a body?

How could he be up in orbit and not be physical?

How could he be part of a spacecraft—*or computer programs?*

How could many a millennia pass, and he still be him?

What of his *soul?*

Cherko saw that his consciousness and these quandaries continued to surface after collateral damage to the extraterrestrial satellite, and that they'd continued to interfere with the satellite creators' programming. To have attempted to directly correct these issues could have done irreparable and grave damage to the conscious fabric that was James Francis Cherko, and the extraterrestrials did not want that. Since Time is but a corporeal illusion, the satellite's creators had decided to allow Cherko his own "time" to correct himself, to resolve his issues in his own way, and come to conscious memory—conscious correction—of his situation on his own. They looked in on him, made sure all was on track, but allowed him, pardon the pun, his *space.*

Cherko again looked down longingly toward the planet that his Race and he had once called home. Memories of all he had known continued to fill his head like a rabid feeding frenzy.

What a waste. All that effort, all those lives—all that living*—gone. Because of a few bad individuals. Because of some meaningless hatred.*

Nothing is ever wasted and nothing is meaningless, Eurphraeus said. *What is in one is in all. Those deeply buried issues within the Human Condition had to be worked out for the Human Condition, in its* entirety, *to grow.*

Eurphraeus continued to send images.

Cherko saw that there were untold probabilities for any existence…and just as the one timeline continuum he experienced existed, so did others where the more violent human tendencies and its surrounding issues did *not*.

So, did any of what I experienced—what I thought I'd experienced—actually happen? Or had I made it all up? Had I really—

Cherko was instantly back to July 1947. Roswell. He really had influenced the course of history with his presence there. He really had been "killed" in that remote arroyo. But the fears created from his far-future on-orbit malfunction had also created another him, a psychic and mental construct within Cherko himself—a ghost in the machine, as it were—just as real as any flesh and blood body, one that followed a 2010 timeline. It had been Cherko's imaginative effort to deal with those created and surfaced fears of failure and desire, and corrupted programming and consciousness. Facts from his actual *lived* life continually tried to break through his glitch-frozen fearful consciousness.

He'd created a him who could take control and create whatever he wanted. It had been the perfect fix: create a new life, reprogram it…

Live it.

Did you really need a body if you really lived your life in your mind?

So, what now? And why me? Why am I so important to have been singled out by you?

Eurphraeus smiled.

Cherko saw that there were other Races out in the universe, and these other intelligences were not as divorced from human reality as thought. Many were future instances of *human* consciousnesses, future probabilities untold millennia into *their* various futures. Some set so far into the distant and murky future, so radically departed and removed from their original human ancestry as to be, for all practical purposes, an *entirely new race.*

This is of what She and Qxuill were.

She and Qxuill may have been many, many millennia in advance of Cherko's timeline, but he also saw that they were nowhere near Eurphraeus's even more distant and removed timeline. And Cherko saw that there were different *versions* of extraterrestrials depending upon the probable versions of timelines visited. Cherko saw that an even closer version than She-and-Qxuill's historical timeline had gotten involved with Cherko's at-the-time present-day government. But that elements on both sides of his experienced timeline, present-day and future, had still been too enwrapped within "scientific" principles to see the outcomes of what they were doing. Greed had interfered on both ends, the continued need for power, whether through extraterrestrial science and the historical engineering of the race for their own ends, or Humanity's power and future engineering of the race for *their* ends. Throw in a couple wars and international conflicts, and you have the logical conclusion.

I am an entity that is so vastly removed from the physical realm, Eurphraeus sent, *that it is extremely difficult for me to form any corporeal expression in your existence.*

You were never on a UFO? Never abducted me?

To borrow a familiar term, my platform has never been physical, though distantly ancient memories *originated from your timeframe that are directly tied to what I am. Those who abducted you were from your future probabilities. You are an extraordinarily distant ancestor of* my *consciousness.*

The images came to him as Eurphraeus communicated that last thought.

Erica.

A son.

Cherko and she had created…a *son.*

You and I are of the same lineage, Eurphraeus sent.

The overwhelming feeling of familiarity. The attention and guidance throughout his entire life by alien visitors. It all finally made sense. He wasn't just some random life form upon which an extraterrestrial race had capriciously decided to bestow its benevolence. No, there was a much more direct tie. A tie that could place everything in much improved, more highly focused perspective.

The children were the parents.

There was nothing random about any contact.

Nothing statistical or otherwise. This was personal.

This was *family.*

Cherko saw…Erica give birth to their son. A boy who'd grown up to be like the father he'd never known. Had also been guided and overseen in a manner not unlike his own Earthly life by alien visitors who'd removed all knowledge of him from Erica's mind. Aliens who'd made it their business to make sure both Erica and her son *were left alone.*

Hidden from prying government eyes and manipulation.

Left alone to live their lives organically. To live life together as *they* wanted. Lives masked from government interference as his had *not* been.

And the irony of it was that this boy had been his father's son: had become an astronaut in his own right. Had spawned his own progeny and lineage that had forged out into the deepest, darkest reaches of space until *they,* too, had become but distant memories themselves.…

You and I are of the same lineage, Eurphraeus had said. And he now saw that. Saw it in all its brilliant, mind-bending, clarity.

Cherko experienced consciousnesses and probabilities that existed between himself and Eurphraeus. Felt as if his consciousness were a star on the verge of not only a nova, but a gargantuan supernova.

Each person, he saw, each earthly personality that ever existed had their own Eurphraeus or She or Qxuill. Saw the many future "aliens" visiting their ancestries.

All of the universe was related.

Everything—every star, molecule, idea, or life form—was tied to everything else.

In the timeline Cherko had lived, it was obvious Humanity had gotten out of control. Had focused far too much on the physical. In having barreled down the path of violence and greed and fear it had gone far beyond where it had ever been meant to go. Should ever have tread.

There were some within the government, an extremely rarified few, who had glimpsed this understanding and learned from it, and some who though had glimpsed this knowledge, had still chosen the path of greed and power. Distorted the efforts of She and her kind for their own ends. Some truly felt Humanity could not handle the extraterrestrial truth; that all of Humanity's sociological structure would collapse...bring about the end of the world.

But it had not.

What *had* brought about the end of life was humanity's own self-perpetuating preoccupation with fear.

Yet Humanity had been where it had needed to be.

Humanity had finally taking off its training wheels. Finally directly faced its own fears.

Humanity had to realize no external *anything* was ever going to save it from itself. Humanity had to learn to live with itself, to answer its own questions, solve its own quandaries.

Peacefully.

Even for advanced beings it is not technologies, nor the corporeal that are important to mankind, but the mind...the *soul*.

So, what of me? Where do I go on from here, if there's no longer any place for me down there?

Mom. Dad. Carl, Penny, and Ritchie.

Theresa, Michael, Lisa, and Benjamin.

Erica.

All gone.

Your decision, Eurphraeus answered. *You are in-between continuums.*

Cherko saw his answer. Yes, Earth, as he'd known it, had been wiped clean. Was ready to begin anew. In this new beginning—this new reboot—Humanity was but a dim memory, as were Atlantis or Mu.

Humanity had worn out its welcome.

A new direction was needed. One that would come and be used in a way human consciousness had never before been used. In peaceful endeavors.

Endeavors that would interact and mutually benefit from other "Beyond-Earth" direct contact and cultures—those that have never been corporeal. Artifacts, Cherko saw, from his timeline, would be unearthed, just like Atlantis or the pyramids. Life would go on, as it always did. But even all of what he was seeing was but a sampling of the countless probabilities…each of which would follow their own focus and logical conclusions.

Cherko also saw that since he was no longer constrained by the physical he could reexamine his life—take a break, as it were—or move on into other realms. He could even experience other probable existences of his previous human continuums, many of which were decidedly more friendly.

I no longer need my brain?, Cherko asked. *Geez, I sound like the Scarecrow. Won't I die if I…if I leave it?*

The brain, Eurphraeus continued, *is an interface for consciousness's entry into corporeal expression. Because of your current condition you have superseded that obligation.*

I can just…leave?

You can.

All reality, Eurphraeus said, *is but a change in focus. For me to exhibit myself to you as I do now, in nonphysical discussion, is but a shift in focus. There are no great intergalactic distances involved in space travel or in finding those such as myself. It is all an illusion. As is Time. To contact other intelligences is no different than changing channels on a television or radio. However, in your reality, many have had the settings on the same station for so long they have become stuck. Once unstuck, as you now are, automatically enables other capabilities. Simply put, you are free to roam.*

And all it takes…is a shift in focus?

Cherko again looked out upon the Earth.

A once beautiful, blue planet, it now lay dead and lifeless. There had been so much beauty in that world, those lives—births to deaths, families to strangers—all gone.

Erica and his son.

All had chosen to focus upon sadness and disharmony to some extent during their lives. Humanity had chosen to explore the darker side to existence.

It was time for a change.

A chance to explore all that was *good*. A world where there was no need for rape, greed, or murder. They simply weren't programmed into human consciousness. Perhaps the endless reaches of space were more meant to remind humanity of the vast unknowns within each individual. Were merely a direct construct of that analogy in *physical* existence…

Everything affects *everything*.

No thought, deed, or action ever went untouched by any other thought, deed, or action.

Quantum Entanglement.

I would like to see more, Cherko sent. *I want to learn…to move on.*

It will not be without its challenges.

What is?

Cherko found himself free from his still orbiting alien platform. Free from a concept of "self."

He gazed upon the Earth and smiled.

On a tiny chunk of dirt and rock illuminated by a nearby star, forces converged and heaved and breathed. Tectonic plates shifted and ground. Cataclysmic fire spewed forth from within deep planetary fissures. Comets slammed into its churning surface...

And then came the rains.

Air...sweet and so long gone...*returned.*

Something stirred.

Pushed its way upward with untold restless ferocity borne of incalculably primeval legend...forced its way up through untold millennia of rock and dirt and chaos. Broke the surface in a powerful explosion complete with memory of all that had come before. Civilizations come and gone.

Bright blue skies.

Nourishing rains.

Snow and cold, sun and warmth.

Birds, bugs, deer, and fish.

And this time it would not be denied.

A flower.

* * * * * * * *

About the Author

F. P. (Frank) Dorchak began writing at the age of six. He writes gritty, realistic paranormal fiction that delves into the realms of the supernatural, the unexplained, and the metaphysical to explore who we are and why we exist. Frank is published in the U.S., Canada, and the Czech Republic with short stories, non-fiction articles, two novels, *Sleepwalkers*, and *The Uninvited*, and the story "Tail Gunner," in *The You Belong Collection – Writings And Illustrations By Longmont Area Residents* regional anthology.

http://www.fpdorchak.com

F. P. Dorchak books and short-stories:

Sleepwalkers (**http://www.fpdorchak.com/Sleepwalkers.html**)

The Uninvited (**http://www.fpdorchak.com/The-Uninvited.html**)

"Tail Gunner" page 78, *The You Belong Collection – Writings and Illustrations By Longmont Area Residents* regional anthology
(**http://www.fpdorchak.com/LiteraryCredits.html**, #19)

Research Reading

ABOVE BLACK, OneTeam Publishing, 1997, 2006, by Dan Sherman, ISBN 0-9660978-0-7

ALIEN AGENDA, HarperCollins*Publishers*, 1997, by Jim Marrs, ISBN 0-06-109686-5

BODY OF SECRETS, Anchor Books, 2002, by James Bamford, ISBN 0-385-49908-6

BREAKTHROUGH, HarperCollins*Publishers*, 1995, by Whitley Strieber, ISBN 0-06-017653-9

COMMUNION, Beech Tree Books, 1987, by Whitley Strieber, ISBN 0-688-07086-8

CRASH AT CORONA, Paraview Special Editions, 2004, by Don Berliner and Stanton Friedman, ISBN 1-931044-89-9

DARK MISSION: THE SECRET HISTORY OF NASA, BY Richard C. Hoagland and Mike Bara, Feral House, ISBN 978-1-932595-26-0

DEEP BLACK, Berkley Books, 1988, by William Burrows, ISBN 0-425-10879-1

DREAMLAND, Villard, 1998, by Phil Patton, ISBN 0-375-75385-0

LEAP OF FAITH, Harper Torch, 2002, by Gordon Cooper, ISBN 0-06-109877-9

ROSWELL: INCONVENIENT FACTS AND THE WILL TO BELIEVE, Prometheus Books, 2001, Carl T. Pflock, ISBN 1-57392-894-1

RULE BY SECRECY, Perennial, 2001, by Jim Marrs, ISBN 978-0-06-093184-1

SKY WALKING, Collins/Smithsonian Books, 2006, Tom Jones, ISBN 978-0-06-088436-9

THAT CRAZY LADY DOWN THE ROAD, Earth Star Publications, 2005, by Judy Messoline, ISBN 0-944851-14-2

THE DAY AFTER ROSWELL, Pocket Books, 1997, by Colonel Philip J. Corso (Ret.) and William J. Birnes, ISBN 0-671-01756-X

THE RIGHT STUFF, Bantam Books/Farrar, Straus, & Giroux, 1979/2001, Tom Wolfe, ISBN 0-553-38135-0

THE ROSWELL LEGACY, New Page Books, 2009, Jesse and Linda Marcel, Jr., ISBN 978-1-60163-026-1

The works of Seth, Jane Roberts, and Rob Butts

The Zeta Reticuli Incident (and Commentary), AstroMedia Corporation, 1976, Terence Dickinson

TOP SECRET, The Dictionary of Espionage and Intelligence, Citadel Press, 2005, by Bob Burton, ISBN 0-8065-2650-5

TOP SECRET/MAJIC, Marlowe & Company, 2005, by Stanton T. Friedman. MSc, ISBN 1-56924-342-5

TRANSFORMATION, Avon Books, 1988, by Whitley Strieber, ISBN 0-380-70535-4

UFOs AND THE NATIONAL SECURITY STATE, Hampton Roads Publishing Company, 2002, by Richard M. Dolan, ISBN 1-57174-317-0